ON MARIAN PLACE

Terry Hickland

Charland  Publishing

Dedication

I would like to dedicate this book to my late father-in-law, Alexander Bell, a great man whom, sadly, I never got to meet. He had a fine collection of books; one in particular - a biography of Ian Fleming - inspired me to put pen to paper. (Who said dead men can't talk?). I do hope that you will have the same pleasure reading this story as I have had in writing it.

CHAPTER ONE

Detlef Schmitt arranged his workplace into some kind of order before making his way to the station chief's office, where a familiar voice invited him in. Angela Wenzel sat back in her chair and took a good look at the detective who had recently arrived at counter intelligence headquarters. The pair had grown up in the town of Fallersleben, Angela being ten years older. When she had last seen Detlef, he was a scrawny, pimple-faced youth. Now, he was a tall, tanned, athletic-looking individual. Angela had heard that her former neighbour was now a duty officer in Hannover and was therefore surprised when she saw his name on the list of Pullach's new recruits.

"Hello, stranger! Long time no see," she said, getting up to greet him. "My, how you've changed!"

"You were the last person I expected to bump into!" he exclaimed as they embraced one another. "Should I call you ma'am?"

"Angela will do fine. We don't stand on ceremony too much here. I'm glad to have you on board, Detlef, and I really mean that; your service record is exemplary."

"Thank you. My father always told me to never do things by half measures."

"He was a good man, Detlef."

"Yes, he was."

"In case you have not had a chance to check your inbox today, this is a memo I e-mailed to those involved in the G8 summit, which is taking place from the 6th to the 9th of June," she announced, passing him a copy.

Schmitt began to read the document. It appeared that many of Pullach's employees were participating in the event, one way or another.

"I know that you are trying to find your feet here," she continued, "but I have selected you to head up a team, working as close protection officers to the Japanese Prime Minister, Hirohisa Tsushima, for the duration of the summit. Jürgen von Harz and ten additional members of staff will form your unit."

"That's only a few days away, Angela; it leaves me little time for preparation. I really feel it would be better if I stayed behind, to familiarise myself with current operations," he protested.

Ignoring Schmitt's objection, Wenzel handed the detective his itinerary.

"Bonn wants 1994 to be memorable, for all the right reasons. Your officers will be replacing personnel who were due to carry out the task but have been sent overseas on a mission, at the last minute. Draw down whatever your requirements are for the operation from the stores. Now, let's go and I'll introduce you to the rest of the guys."

****

"Ladies and gentlemen, we will be landing at Templin in fifteen minutes. Please stow all loose items in the overhead lockers and fasten your seatbelts," requested the captain of the German Air Force Bombardier jet as it made its final approach.

A few minutes later, the tyres of the undercarriage gave a small chirp, struggling to achieve the momentum imposed on them as they touched the runway. The jet began to reduce speed before it taxied off to the right, coming to a halt at a bombproof hanger. The former Cold

War military airbase, which lay ten kilometres south of Templin, just north of the village of Groß Dölln, had been constructed by the Soviets during their occupation between 1952 and 1954. Both the airfield and the hotel were surrounded by dense vegetation, consisting mainly of spruce and fir trees, which provided total seclusion.

The flight carried close protection officers and other support staff for the G8 summit. When the cabin doors were opened, the passengers released their seatbelts and began to exit the plane. As they made their way down the steps, they were met with a light, easterly wind, and a fine drizzle.

"Would you secure the car, Jürgen?" asked Schmitt, interrupting von Harz who, trying to ignore his boss, was thanking the female flight attendant in an attempt to curry favour.

Seeing that von Harz was flouting his authority, Detlef spoke again.

"When you're quite finished with your overworked chat-up lines, Jürgen, ensure there are no issues with the vehicle and that it is in serviceable condition. Then, go and stow our gear; I need to make the operations' briefing."

"I'll get on to it, at once," von Harz replied, more than a little uncomfortable with the obvious put-down.

After the briefing, Schmitt walked out of the hanger and crossed to where von Harz was waiting in their assigned bulletproof vehicle.

"Anybody we know?" enquired von Harz as the pair left the airbase, setting out on their journey to the Hotel Bergensee.

"No; there were a lot of new faces. A commander named Gisler gave the briefing, with another guy from the Special Operations division filling in the blanks," replied Schmitt.

"Was there anything of interest or just the normal stuff?" von Harz asked, as the car neared the airport security gates.

"It's all in the manual; be sure to read it from cover to cover during your free time this evening."

Arriving at the exit to the airbase they were met by members of the G8 security taskforce, their firearms hanging in front of them by a shoulder strap. As his colleagues looked on, one officer examined the detectives' warrant cards. Having verified their identification, he waved them through the cordon to continue their journey.

The vehicle made its way through the maze of road junctions as they left the aerodrome complex behind them before coming to Prenzlauer Straße. Von Harz approached the junction and stopped, waiting until a police patrol car had passed by before turning right onto an expanse of empty road.

Pulling down their visors to shield their eyes from the sun that had just broken through the clouds, the detectives stared, without direction, as the car propelled them effortlessly past the unending forest wilderness. It was easy to see why this remote location had been chosen for the G8 summit. With a little time to kill, they began to discuss the career paths their friends had chosen following their national service in the German Bundeswehr. Schmitt had not seen von Harz since their unit broke up.

"Have you heard from Carl Janzyke recently? Only for your intervention, that sack of shit Stein would have ruined his life," declared von Harz.

"Don't make me out to be the hero; we all played a part in taking him down," replied Schmitt. "It's been a while since I last spoke with Carl. Fortunately, he was able put the whole sordid incident behind him and is finishing his legal studies. He'll probably follow his father into the court system."

"What became of our former pervert drill sergeant?"

"Frankly, I have no idea; I've never given him a second's thought. The last I saw of Claus Stein, he was being led out to a waiting prison van."

"I must say I never envisaged that you'd walk through our door!" admitted von Harz before abruptly standing on the brake pedal. He swerved and narrowly avoided hitting a wild boar that had unexpectedly run out from the forest.

"Christ, Jürgen, keep your bloody eyes on the road!" Schmitt demanded, grabbing on to the dashboard. "What do you mean by that? Are you going to have difficulties working with me? Perhaps you still blame me for what happened at camp?"

Jürgen was a prickly character. The way Detlef remembered it, he had always had a problem with authority. He recalled the fact that von Harz also liked to party heavily and had once been put on a disciplinary charge having returned after curfew, intoxicated. He had blamed Schmitt for reporting him but it was a Bundeswehr guard who had spotted him sneaking back into the camp and summoned the MPs.

"I have no issues with you at all, buddy. As far as I'm concerned, it's a totally clean slate. I didn't mean it to come out the way it did, it's just that…. I thought you were set on a career with the regular police?"

Schmitt did not provide an instant response.

"I wanted to do something different, that's all. More to the point, how are things with you?" he replied, changing the subject.

"The usual. I got myself a small apartment in town; it's nothing much."

"Are you involved with anyone?"

"No, not at the moment. Work seems to bring complications to my relationships, though I wouldn't mind trying my luck with Claudia Reinhold."

He turned towards Schmitt, trying to gauge his mood.

"I can't see you being her type," he replied, looking straight ahead. "The woman is destined for a brilliant career, if she plays her cards right. As I said earlier, keep your eyes on the road, Jürgen; I would like to arrive in one piece."

Von Harz fell into a sullen silence, justifiably embarrassed for nearly causing an accident.

Their car approached the entrance to the hotel and they were, once again, stopped at the outer cordon where two dog handlers stood with their German shepherds. One of the guards checked their papers as the other officer, using a mirror, searched under the vehicle for explosives. As soon as the detectives' identities were confirmed, the two tonnes of Ingolstadt armour charged along the sweeping drive to the hotel's main building.

"This would be a nice place for a holiday," remarked von Harz, as he slowed to let Schmitt out of the vehicle.

"Yes; there would be excellent hunting in these parts."

"Served on a plate will do me. I've no time for all that stalking around in the cold, getting wet," countered von Harz as Schmitt removed his seatbelt.

"Actually, it's an acquired art."

"Whatever…. I'll park the car in the motor compound and bring our kit up to the room," said von Harz, giving up on their forced conversation.

****

Schmitt walked in through the main entrance of the hotel and was greeted by an open log fire, shrouded in fine white marble, with a boar's head hanging above it. Having asked a member of staff at the reception desk for directions, he made his way to a room at the rear of the building.

"Good morning. I am Detective Chief Inspector Schmitt, here as the personal protection officer for the Japanese Prime Minister. My colleague, Detective von Harz, will be here shortly, along with the rest of our team," he announced, presenting his identification to the supervisor.

"Welcome, Herr Schmitt, we've been expecting you," replied the man, returning the warrant card. "Everything is on schedule. We are currently checking the hotel for any questionable items that we feel could pose a hazard to the conference and those attending it. There will also be systematic scans of the delegates' rooms every day, for anything out of the ordinary. All members of domestic staff in the hotel have been given grade two clearance for their designated work areas but we are taking nothing for granted; they will all be monitored very closely."

"Thanks for the update."

"Don't mention it. Call me if there is anything your crew needs and I'll have it brought over from operational HQ, Templin."

Schmitt made his way back to reception where von Harz was waiting.

"I have secured the vehicle in the motor pool and put the kit bags in our room," he reported.

"Right then," said Schmitt, "let's go and see how the other half lives, starting with the Japanese Prime Minister's suite."

****

Stepping out of the elevator, the two officers walked a short distance along the corridor before entering the luxurious apartment. They examined the main living area and the adjacent bedroom. As they peered around the bathroom door, a dog handler was conducting a physical search for explosive devices, with the help of his faithful Labrador.

"I'll be finished in a few minutes, gentlemen," said the man, as the dog sniffed along the bath panel.

"Take your time," replied Schmitt.

"Don't these guys sleep on the floor?" asked von Harz, viewing the sumptuous, king-size bed.

"No; in days gone by, they used to sit on the floor to eat or to socialise," answered Schmitt.

A rather morose police technician nodded curtly as he entered the room to scan it for concealed forms of electronic, eavesdropping surveillance equipment.

"What cave did he crawl out of?" whispered von Harz.

"We can't all have your sunny disposition, Jürgen," Schmitt retorted.

The technician completed the scan of an area near the bed and walked on; it was then that Detlef noticed the stunning, ornate writing desk.

"I don't believe my eyes," he murmured quietly.

"Have you found something suspicious, Detlef?" asked Jürgen as the technician glanced over at the two detectives.

"I'm not sure.... take a look at this!"

"What, that old table?"

"If I am correct, it's much more than that; it may be a missing Jean-Henri Riesener reproduction bureau. Queen Marie Antoinette commissioned the original and around one hundred replicas were made, though many were lost during the war," explained Schmitt, running his fingers over the fine, veneer inlays.

"It's just a table," grunted von Harz.

"Possibly.... Anyway, I'll have to leave it for now. Let's go get some food and check the schedule for the next few days. This place will be hectic, of that we can be certain!"

CHAPTER TWO

The following morning, the two detectives were already waiting in the makeshift reception area at Templin airport when the Japanese delegation arrived. Schmitt made the introductions.

"Prime Minister Tsushima, welcome. I am Detective Chief Inspector Detlef Schmitt and my colleague is Detective Jürgen von Harz."

"I am pleased to meet you both," Tsushima replied. "This is Miss Asami," he added, introducing his private secretary.

The detectives shook the dignitaries' hands and, formalities over, led them out to the parking bay. The sky was overcast, with a breeze that gently swayed the tall fir trees as the A6, flanked by two escort cars, cruised along the deserted road to the hotel. Tsushima commented on the outstanding scenery to his secretary, who nodded in agreement.

"Herr Schmitt, how beautiful your country is. To find peace and solitude one must come here, I think!" he exclaimed. "I have never seen such an expanse of forest. You are blessed by many lakes in this region, no?"

"Thank you for your kind compliments, sir," said Schmitt, using the vehicle's additional interior mirror to scan the road behind them for any possible threats as von Harz drove. "Sometimes our lives are too busy to notice the beauty that surrounds us in our own land."

"Yes, you are quite right," replied Tsushima as their vehicle pulled up outside the hotel.

****

The rest of the week passed in a blur, apart from a few, out of the ordinary, incidents. Late one evening, Prime Minister Tsushima decided to go for a jog. This put the team on high alert as it was close to midnight and the inky blackness of the forest could conceal many dangers, such as an assassin. The death of a Japanese dignitary was not something that Bundes Chancellor Herzfeld wished to have beamed around the world.

On another occasion, a laptop overheated and caught fire in the French Prime Minister's room, triggering the fire alarm system, with all guests being evacuated until the blaze was brought under control by hotel staff.

With the summit drawing to a close, the delegates gathered to have the obligatory G8 photos taken in the sunken garden at the rear of the hotel; this offered them the opportunity to exchange contact details and say their goodbyes. Afterwards, Schmitt and von Harz drove Tsushima straight to Templin as he had several pressing engagements in Berlin and Paris.

On their return to the hotel, von Harz made one last examination of the Japanese Prime Minister's suite before signing the room over to the hotel staff at reception.

"Everything's clear, boss," he announced as Schmitt entered, having just come from a debriefing session.

Ignoring the detective's update, Schmitt gazed across the room.

"Just give me a moment," he requested.

"Not that old relic again!" jibed his partner.

Schmitt settled into an oxblood leather wingback chair, hands folded behind his head. He carefully studied the exquisite veneer inlays and the two, familiar, tulip-shaped handles mounted on the single drawer. After a short period of contemplation, he then rose and walked over to the bureau, crawling underneath it to examine it more closely. The detective noticed an old, tarnished manufacturer's label, with both a discernible address and serial number which he wrote down.

"Are you ready to go yet, Detlef? I feel the need to have a cold beer and, if possible, meet the same gorgeous air hostess who was on the flight to Templin….in that particular order!" joked von Harz.

"You're really beginning to aggravate me, Jürgen; shut the door!" demanded Schmitt as he took out his mobile phone and hit the quick dial.

"Hi, dear, how are you? Where's Erhard?" he asked, when his partner, Amélie, eventually answered the call.

"I'm fine, and Erhard is asleep at long last, thank goodness! How was the conference? Did something happen?"

"No, no, it went smoothly, for the most part. We're just tying up a few loose ends here before heading back to the airport. I'm ringing you about something completely different. I am sitting here, in one of the hotel's luxury suites, admiring one of your favourite examples of antique furniture."

"What is it?"

"A Riesener!"

"No! Honestly?"

"Yes, the real thing. I need you to remind me how to gain access to the secret compartment."

Amélie explained the procedure and wished him a safe journey home. Placing the phone in his jacket pocket, Schmitt slowly began to remove the drawer before carefully laying it on the bed. He knelt and scrutinised the construction of the old writing desk, ensuring its authenticity.

"Come on, Detlef; we're supposed to hand the room back undamaged. The flight's waiting," urged von Harz, who was eager to be out of the hotel and on his way home.

"If I'm right, this might be a lost slice of history!" exclaimed Schmitt, excitement growing within him.

The detective proceeded to unscrew both handles and cautiously slid the front panel of the drawer one centimetre to the left, where it came to rest. Following a little hesitation due to its age, he eased the right-hand side panel forward and removed it, as Riesener had designed it to do. This revealed a small void under the base of the drawer.

"Amélie seems to know her way around furniture," observed Jürgen, finally taking an interest in the unfolding events.

"She ought to; she has a master's degree in fine arts and antiquities. She once showed me where to locate the panel on a similar piece, in an antique store she managed near Munster," replied Schmitt.

He lifted the drawer to eye level and looked into the void. Using the tips of his fingers, he gently extracted an old, dusty manila folder which had been hidden away inside the compartment. He placed it on the bed and warned von Harz not to touch it, asking him to find some type of surgical gloves. While his colleague was away, Schmitt studied the folder. On the front, was the image of an eagle holding a wreath, inside of which a swastika was visible. Below the emblem was written, *Property of the Reichsbank*.

Schmitt sat on the bed, stunned. As a boy, he had read many adventure books describing secret passageways in castles and finding buried treasure, but this surpassed all those childish, adrenalin-filled tales. What was inside that file and where was von Harz? He always took his sweet time. No doubt, he was chatting up some unsuspecting chambermaid. *Knowing my luck, it will be empty or there will be an IOU placed inside as a practical joke*, thought Schmitt. He grabbed a bottle of water from the mini bar. Everyone else had helped themselves so one more wouldn't matter, he decided, as he took off the lid and quenched his thirst.

Von Harz returned from the hotel kitchen with a handful of surgical gloves. Schmitt put on a pair and began to examine the folder's contents. The documents were in exceptionally good condition, with no mould or water damage; some of them had been stamped by the Reich Chancellery and dated January 1945. There were also lists of names, rail transport orders, a blueprint for a bunker and a requisition order for gold and foreign currencies. Schmitt lifted the drawing to study it more closely, noting that it had come from the planning and design department of Albert Speer's office. He returned the documents to the file.

"Are these for real, Detlef?" von Harz enquired.

"I don't know, but they have certainly been here for quite some time, given the amount of dust. They're intriguing, to say the least. Jürgen, fetch me a clean, plastic bag; I'm taking them back to Pullach," Schmitt declared.

"Are you sure about this?" queried von Harz.

"Just do as I ask," snapped his boss, irritable from lack of sleep.

Detlef had already made his mind up as to his next move. He re-assembled the writing table while he waited for his colleague to come back. When von Harz returned, Schmitt carefully placed the folder in the new, sterile bag and the pair left the room, taking the lift down to the ground floor.

Schmitt approached the receptionist.

"Hi, I need to speak with the manager," he declared.

"Of course, sir. One moment, please. Might I take your name?" enquired the girl as she placed the call.

"Detective Chief Inspector Schmitt."

Almost instantaneously, the Polish manager appeared at the reception desk.

"Good afternoon, Detective, I am Herr Kowalski. How may I be of help?" he asked.

Kowalski was a tall, effeminate individual, dark-complexioned, with a wavy mop of black hair, brown eyes and thick, gold-rimmed glasses. He was wearing a cheap, ill-fitting, navy-pinstriped suit and bore the manner of a person who was used to making people feel good, people who didn't mind the cost if they were well catered for. Herr Kowalski, thought Schmitt, would run a mile at the first sign of a disgruntled customer.

"Would you follow me, please, Herr Kowalski?" Schmitt requested.

"Is there a problem?" quizzed the manager. "We can sort it out here, no fuss."

Schmitt repeated his request.

"If you would just follow me, please."

"But, Detective…."

"Please…. follow me, sir," he insisted, his slightly raised voice startling the young receptionist.

When they arrived back at the executive suite, Schmitt began questioning the manager as to the history of the bureau and how long it had been in the hotel's possession.

"Well, now…. I really couldn't answer that; it's just a part of the fixtures and fittings. As a group, we have many hotels and resorts, with personal furnishers who oversee the decor of the buildings," he replied, rather limply.

There was a moment of awkward silence. Kowalski looked at the inspector. Schmitt's face betrayed nothing but the hotel manager had enough sense to know that the detective was in a foul mood. Kowalski edged slowly towards the door and thumbed its handle tentatively. He so wished to be back in his office, leaving the young temp at reception to deal with this person.

Schmitt knew that he was being fobbed off.

"Sorry, I don't quite follow you. Do you know the provenance of this piece?"

"No…. Granted, it is a bit out of the ordinary compared to our other furnishings. But this room is one of our finest so it was decided to place it here."

Schmitt was all but losing his patience with Kowalski.

"Either you tell me where this writing desk came from or I will charge you with obstructing a police officer in the course of his duty!" he threatened.

The hotel manager was quite ashen faced.

"Now, just hold on, there is no need for that attitude! I have only been in this job for a year and the bureau was here long before I arrived. Detective, this conversation is going around in circles. Please, allow me to fetch the caretaker. He has been living in the area for at least forty years. If anyone can help you, he can."

"Finally. Now you are making sense, Herr Kowalski. Go, fetch him….and be quick about it; I don't have all day to wait on you!" shouted Schmitt down the corridor as the man made a hasty exit.

Kowalski tripped on the lace of one of his fake crocodile shoes in his panic to reach the elevator, feverishly punching the buttons to speed the opening of the doors.

"Shit, Detlef, you're going to give the poor sod a heart attack," chuckled von Harz, watching as the manager eventually disappeared into the lift.

"Bloody yuppies! Why couldn't that jumped-up porter just give me the relevant information at the start, instead of all the amateur dramatics? These service sector prats take bullshit to a new level the more promotion they get," Schmitt complained as he sat down on the bed and sipped from the bottle of water, impatiently waiting for the manager to return with the hotel caretaker.

Fifteen minutes later, there was a knock on the open door.

"Detective Schmitt…. I would like to introduce…. Herr Bösen," the hotel manager wheezed, somewhat out of breath.

"It's Detective Chief Inspector, Herr Kowalski, if you don't mind. You may leave us for the moment," retorted Schmitt, annoyed at the manager for getting his title wrong in addition to wasting his time.

Herr Bösen was in his late sixties, of average height, with grey hair, an Amish-type beard and silver-rimmed, oval glasses. His protruding belly was being supported by the bib of worn dungarees that had been patched on numerous occasions. They were covered in paint and grass stains, as were his Moses-type sandals.

Once the formal introductions were over, Bösen walked across the room and sat down in one of the most ostentatious chairs, without invitation.

"What do you want to know, Detective?" he asked.

"Tell me a bit about this place," Schmitt requested.

Bösen began to describe the history of the building in a slow, droll manner.

"Well, the site that the hotel sits on today was originally the hunting lodge for Field Marshall Hermann Göring's gamekeeper. It was built in 1934.... or was it 1935? I don't know who constructed the original dwelling but the new owners built additional wings on either side of the old place. Göring's main residence, Carinhall, was just over the lake, in amongst those trees."

The gardener pointed out of the window, across the large expanse of water, to a forest near the water's edge.

"You mean this is the actual area where Göring lived?" asked von Harz.

"You didn't know, Detective? Yes, Göring purchased the land over there and built a magnificent house on it."

"Where did you live, Herr Bösen?" Schmitt enquired.

"Just down the road, in the village of Templin, with my parents and sister. According to my father, the lodge had many visitors. I think that Italian guy, Mussolini, may have called in at some time or another when he was passing.... I can't be certain. My memory's not what it used to be, Herr Schmitt. Father said that there were always plenty of SS officers staying at the lodge during Göring's famous hunting trips. They tipped him generously for carving up their trophy kills which they would then take home with them. As you know, after the war the Russians occupied half the country and they used the building for the party hierarchy's weekend getaways. Many of the East German elite, such as Erich Honecker, would have stayed here."

"How long ago was that?" asked Schmitt.

"Up until the 1980s, when the diplomats from Moscow moved in and gave the building a facelift. It was used for ministerial gatherings and international assemblies, inviting dignitaries from Cuba and other communist countries to attend state functions," explained Bösen.

"Herr Bösen, what can you tell me about this bureau?" enquired Schmitt.

"You will have to forgive me, I don't know much about fine furniture; I stick with the flat pack stuff. It's easier to replace if the dog takes a liking to it, if you know what I mean!" replied the caretaker.

Von Harz could not contain himself and started laughing as he apologised to the old man for his sudden outburst, telling him that he had brightened up what had been a very dull week.

Does the recruitment policy in this hotel pride itself on employing incompetence? Schmitt asked himself, at the same time eyeing von Harz who had turned away, struggling to curb any further fits of laughter. Taking a deep breath, he continued with the questioning.

"Once again, Herr Bösen, do you know where this bureau originated from and how the hotel came by it?"

"Well, it's always been here at one time or another," replied the man.

"Could you be a bit more concise when you say, *'one time or another'*?"

"I believe it came from Carinhall.... Did you know that Göring named it after his first wife, Carin Fock? She was originally from Sweden where, incidentally, she also died. Göring was absolutely grief-stricken and later had her re-interred at the big house, with Hitler attending the service."

"No, I didn't know any of that," replied Schmitt, shaking his head.

"Anyway, Göring furnished the house and the lodge with the mementos he got when Germany invaded Europe. The military landscape changed around April 1945 as the Russian war machine advanced from the east like a large combine harvester, cutting down swathes of German battalions. The Russians' ultimate goal was to capture Berlin, the heart of the German Empire. Having read the latest despatches from the ever-nearing war front, Göring decided to remove the contents from both properties, transferring them to the Berchtesgaden, in the south of the country. He gave the order to the Wehrmacht or the Luftwaffe engineers, I'm not sure which, to blow up Carinhall rather than let the Bolsheviks have it. The demolition team set about the task and made short work of it, reducing the house to rubble," explained the old man.

"An interesting account, Herr Bösen, but you still haven't answered my question," Schmitt reminded him.

Parched from his story telling, the caretaker suddenly decided to break off his narrative and gave a sly grin as he rose from the chair. Making the most of being relieved of his normal duties, he helped himself to a mineral water and some schnapps from the mini bar. Sitting down again, the old man pocketed the schnapps and surveyed the grandeur around him whilst taking a few, noisy gulps from the bottle of water.

Suitably refreshed, he carried on.

"I wasn't old enough to witness what actually happened, you understand? But I do remember my father telling me of the Russians going from house to house and searching them rigorously. They found all manner of items that were looted from Göring's home during the evacuation. Bottom line is, after reunification the Federal German Government sold the property to a group of private investors. These guys ploughed one hell of a lot of Deutsche Marks into completely redesigning the building. The architects felt that the grounds immediately to the rear of building were too dangerous to excavate, due to the risk of unexploded munitions. So, the building contractor brought in a survey company to check the surrounding property, using ground radar.... I think that's the right name?"

"Yes, you're quite right, Herr Bösen. They would have needed a detailed survey to be carried out, for safety reasons," Schmitt replied.

"During the tests," continued the gardener, "the equipment uncovered unexpected anomalies in the ground. There was a larger than normal cellar area, in the region where the extensions were to be built. After going into the existing cellar, the rendering was stripped off, revealing a false wall. The builders dismantled it, brick by brick, and unearthed various items from behind it."

The two detectives sat on the edge of the bed, mesmerised by the tale.

"Do you know what was in the annex?" asked von Harz.

"Annex?" queried the caretaker.

"The room," prompted Schmitt.

"Ah.... right.... I couldn't follow you, young man. Chairs and some ornaments, I don't know exactly what there was. I had been working nearby, attending to the lawn, and there was a bit of a commotion when the builders opened the wall. Nosy as I am - my wife says I take after my mother! - I went to see what was going on and arrived just as they were removing the table. It was dusted down and, after some debate, the decision was made to put it away until the renovations were completed."

"But why was it put into the blocked-up cellar in the first place?" quizzed Schmitt.

"The Russians were coming and the people in the east were fleeing to the west. Those who didn't get out were literally abandoned during the German army's great retreat. Given what our countrymen allegedly did to the Russian people, would anyone really have known what the future would be after everything died down? Someone had the sense to put their little stash away. As the Russians would say, '*бросок костей*'."

"Sorry, what was that you just said?" queried Schmitt.

"It means they rolled the dice and took their chances in concealing their spoils, hoping no one would discover them," replied Bösen.

"Then, four years ago, the Russians relinquished their occupation of the east," commented von Harz.

"Thank you for this remarkable story, Herr Bösen; you have been most helpful. We won't detain you any further," said Schmitt.

CHAPTER THREE

"If I may ask, sir, what has sparked your interest in this old table?" enquired the caretaker, mopping his brow with a stained handkerchief, bemused by all the questioning. He had always thought it was a hideous creation, fit only for kindling.

"I can't go into that right now," replied Schmitt, "but, once again, let me take this opportunity to thank you for helping us with our enquiries. If we need any further information, I will not hesitate to contact you."

The old man stood up, his chest filled with pride. Having helped the police unravel some of the history of both the writing desk and the building, Herr Bösen couldn't wait to go home and tell the wife about his day! She would be pleased for her husband as nothing much happened in their humdrum lives at their age, except for the occasional lucky sweep during a game of skat at the weekends in their local pub. That eyesore was something his snob of a sister-in-law, who was married to a doctor, would gladly have in their museum of a home, thought Bösen as he waited for the elevator to arrive.

"What now?" asked von Harz.

"Damn it, Jürgen, I'm going to seize the bureau!" answered his boss. "The hotel owners will have to produce a bill of sale if they want it back."

"Are you sure we can legally do that? You just can't walk in, take their property and tell them to go to KaDeWe for a replacement," argued the detective, not knowing whether Schmitt was serious or not.

"I'm very sure! I have good grounds to believe that this piece was looted during the war by Göring's art thieves. I know, for a fact, that there were only one hundred ever made. If this is an authentic reproduction, it could be worth around DM100, 000! I've taken a note of the serial number and the manufacturer's address; if they are still in business, perhaps the true owner can be traced."

"Well, it's your decision. I don't want any part in this."

"Go and make yourself useful, then. Take a statement from old Green Fingers, while it's all still fresh in his mind."

When von Harz had left, Schmitt deliberated for a moment. Was he stepping outside of his powers? He picked up the phone by the bed and dialled reception.

"Hi, this is Detective Inspector Schmitt again. Is Herr Kowalski available?"

There was a moment's silence and then a ringtone before the phone was answered.

"Kowalski, Detective Chief Inspector. I do hope Herr Bösen was of assistance to you. I trust you have enjoyed your stay and that you will pay us a return visit under more informal circumstances. Well, if that is all, may I wish you a safe journey home," said the hotel manager, hoping that a bit of his famous spin would get this dreadful man out of his hotel and back to wherever he belonged.

"Herr Kowalski, would you meet with me in the Prime Minister's suite once more, please?"

Schmitt heard the manager exhale in apprehension.

"Is something wrong? Was the caretaker unable to help?"

"I need to speak with you, in person, regarding another issue."

Kowalski complied with Schmitt's request and was in the room within minutes.

"Thank you for coming, Herr Kowalski."

"I wasn't aware that I had a choice. Is there a problem, Herr Schmitt?"

"I must inform you that I believe this writing bureau to be stolen property. As such, under Section 261 of the German Federal Criminal Code covering the possession of illegal assets and the proceeds of crime, it will be confiscated until its true ownership can be authenticated."

Kowalski glowered at Schmitt before replying.

"Enough is enough, sir; you have got to be joking!" he yelled, turning to leave the room in disgust.

"I can assure you that it is no joking matter, said Schmitt, standing his ground. "Based on the information provided by your caretaker, which I have no reason to doubt, this article of furniture had been stored in a bricked-up cellar for nearly sixty years. Concealed inside were these documents," he explained, holding up the clear plastic bag containing the manila envelope. "Given the nature of its contents, I have just cause to remove it for further investigation. My colleague is taking a sworn statement from the caretaker, as we speak. You will also be required to make a formal statement, Herr Kowalski."

The manager grew pale on hearing the news.

"The item was part of the fixtures and fittings when the building was purchased, Herr Schmitt. Our management will have the bill of sale for the property."

"Don't try and be smart with me, Herr Kowalski. Have you never heard the saying, *'caveat emptor: let the buyer beware'*?"

"I will need a receipt for everything, Herr Schmitt. What are those documents anyway and when will the bureau be returned?"

asked Kowalski, trying to regain some control of the situation.

"The documents seem to be from around the time of the Second World War; they will need to be analysed to ascertain what they relate to. As to the bureau and its contents, of course I will give you a receipt. However, I must advise you that it will not be returned until we receive the relevant paperwork proving ownership of the piece. Other than that, I will keep you informed of any developments. Now…. would you be so good as to have your porters bring the desk down to the loading bay. My own people will take over from there. At this point, it is state's evidence, in connection with an alleged robbery," replied Schmitt.

"You…. expect us….to move it as well? This is insult to injury! Fine…. I'll see to it at once but please, say nothing to the press about this," Kowalski pleaded, having just had the hotel's first state conference shattered into a thousand pieces by this untimely misfortune.

****

The detectives returned the armoured car to the air logistics department at Templin airport. There, it would be loaded onto a military transport plane for onward shipment to its next destination. Having stowed their hand luggage, Schmitt and von Harz fastened their seatbelts. The Bombardier jet, with its engines at full throttle, sped down the runway, taking off into the evening sky as the G8 conference ended for another year.

****

"Did you miss us?" asked Amélie the following morning as her partner - having slept a little longer than usual - came into the kitchen.

"Of course, I did!" he replied.

Detlef hugged and kissed her before lifting his son, Erhard, out of the high chair and cuddling him.

"I still can't believe you actually uncovered a Jean-Henri Riesener bureau!" said Amélie as she set the table for breakfast, having bought the ingredients from the local delicatessen on Stuntzstraße that morning while her partner was asleep.

Over breakfast, Detlef described the events that had occurred at the G8 conference, detailing the bureau's chequered history and the papers contained in its secret compartment. His find was now secured in the evidence storage area at Pullach.

Amélie gave him an affectionate dig in the ribs.

"I made you what you are today by educating you on the virtues of antique furniture. Then you go and stumble across not only a missing Riesener but hidden documents as well!" she pouted, in a feigned, indignant look.

"I was only doing my job!" protested her partner, putting his hands up, pretending to have been hurt by her jibe.

The couple had been together for almost three years and had a four-month-old child. Amélie was becoming bored at home and had been exploring the possibility of returning to work on a part-time basis but had yet to find suitable daycare. She felt that getting out of the house would benefit not only her but Erhard as well, by providing them both with more social interaction.

"I've found a nice little kindergarten just off Werner Platz, two minutes' walk to the tram from the U-Bahn. They have a place coming up soon," she explained, as Detlef went into the nursery to change the baby's soiled diaper.

"How much do they charge?" he shouted, holding Erhard whilst trying to open the wipes.

"Are you putting a price on our son?" teased Amélie.

She finished making a ham and cheese brötchen, poured herself a cup of Jacobs's coffee and sat down, dreaming of what she would do with her free time once Erhard was settled.

****

"You look pretty relaxed for a man in your position, Detlef; the job must be agreeing with you!" exclaimed Wenzel on meeting Schmitt in the corridor.

"I'm getting there, Angela."

"Have you seen the latest reports coming out of Bosnia?" she asked as she steered him into an empty conference room.

"Yes. I watched it on the evening news last night."

Detlef wondered how anyone could fail to be moved by the wretched scenes of floods of refugees, trying to escape what could only be described as ethnic cleansing.

His boss opened a brown manila file and handed him a two-page, government Hansard.

"That transcript comes from the top. The Foreign Office is concerned that the Bosnian-Serb Government is funding the war by any means possible. Intelligence from NATO suggests they are receiving assistance through their contacts in the Serbian Mafia. We believe they are using Germany, amongst other countries, to try and bankroll the conflict."

"That is not good news."

"Agreed; primary sources of income include drugs, alcohol, tobacco, counterfeit goods, luxury cars and people trafficking; whatever sells. It appears that the proceeds are supporting the purchase of armaments on the black market. The UN arms embargo has all but cut off their legitimate sources, although Russia is still trying to slip whatever they can across the border. American intelligence agencies are monitoring the warring factions and we are receiving situation updates hourly, via satellite."

"What exactly will our input be in all this? Black Ops, land based insertion and infiltration?"

"This has come directly from the Justice Department: these people are to be put out of business with all of the force at our disposal. If it requires us to continue the investigation in a foreign jurisdiction, I have authorisation to do it. We don't have time on our side. Once the process begins of asking other countries for their co-operation or processing arrest warrants, the individuals we are seeking may well have fled that country. We need to take those involved in racketeering out of the equation. Employ whatever measures you see fit; forgiveness can always be sought later."

"If it's an undercover operation on foreign soil, I take it there are no blurred lines in that anyone is fair game, including German nationals?"

"Correct. Anyone found to be involved in illegal activities against our nation will meet the same fury, regardless of who they are. Both the Government and I will be very displeased if we see stories hitting the headlines of German citizens aiding and abetting these thugs. There is wholesale slaughter being carried out, just because law-abiding people are expressing their entitlement to self-determination. Your team is to take on these people, with immediate effect. Move all your staff to C floor and let me know, by close of play today, what additional resources you're likely to need. Whatever you do, please don't implement any clandestine operations without passing them by me first. Keep me posted, Detlef; if the shit hits the fan, I want to know when to duck. Is that understood?"

"Yes, Angela. I'll keep everyone on a tight rein," he replied, electing not to mention the small matter of his seizure of hotel property for the time being.

Schmitt went to brief his staff and to organise the move to the upper floor. When the transfer was complete, he relayed the chief's instructions to his team. Everyone involved in the case was directed to keep all intelligence information flowing as one-way traffic into Pullach, for their eyes only. As the investigation was in its embryonic stage, Wenzel did not want anyone trying to make a name for themselves by leaking sensitive information and scuppering the whole project in the process.

The priority was to urgently update intelligence on the ex-Stasi and former Eastern bloc security officers who had worked for Pullach. Many of their past double agents had either become involved in illegal activities or had gone to work for Russian intelligence after the collapse of the Soviet Union. Some of these individuals were believed to be involved in the sale of drugs, smuggled alcohol and tobacco. A few were also suspected of dealing in ex-Soviet military armaments that were in plentiful supply. The unit would try to bring on board only those who could be trusted to assist them.

****

Unaware of the strangers in the area, the good people of Dachau were going about their customary business. An operation had been planned before the G8 conference and the team waited anxiously for the suspect to return to Germany.

"Yes, yes, have visual of Victor 1, now moving onto PonkratzStraße. Heading towards the junction.... stand by.... Target turning left onto LuffriedStraße. Has stopped.... looking in shop window.... Suspect has turned around; seems a bit edgy. Showing interest in saloon car with dark tinted windows; may be spooked and preparing to double back. All go.... Victor 1 proceeding in the direction of the shopping centre."

"Will be with you in five, over," said the tall figure, dressed in tracksuit bottoms and hooded top with a Bayern FC scarf around his face.

"Understood, 47," replied the controller.

The radio went silent. Everyone was on tenterhooks as the Volkswagen van sat motionless, along with the other vehicles parked in the street. To the bystander, it was just another delivery van. Minutes seemed like an hour until the radio burst into life again. Von Harz, who had been tailing the suspect, recommenced his commentary as the sting neared its conclusion.

"Stand by.... stand by.... Five, four, three, two, one - in you go, Vuković, you bastard!" screamed the detective.

The individual being followed was grabbed by the shoulders and von Harz bundled him inside the van as the side door slid open.

"Drive, drive, drive," urged Schmitt, slamming the door closed as the vehicle pulled away from the kerb and merged into the München traffic.

Vuković had been casually strolling through the town with his personal hi-fi earphones in his ears. He had no idea that he was being followed through the maze of streets. Earlier, he had left the apartment of one of his drug dealers in the Dachau area of München and began walking towards the S-Bahn, back into town. He had stopped briefly to buy a packet of Camel cigarettes from an automat fixed to the wall of a bakery. The seasoned criminal preferred to use the S-Bahn when visiting his clients to inform them where the drugs pick-up would be when they had paid for the deal. There was also less chance of being stopped on the train and it was easier to give the police the slip.

Vuković was oblivious as he drew near the windowless van until the moment he was dragged inside. His face slammed into the rubber mats covering the floor as a knee was driven into the small of his back. He groaned in pain and tried to break free before his hands were restrained with cable ties and a hood was placed over his head to protect the identities of those in the vehicle.

As they pulled away into oncoming traffic, other drivers angrily sounded their horns while bringing their vehicles to an abrupt stop in order to avoid a collision. The van sped through Dachau, to an abandoned factory complex in Heßstraße where it entered an old warehouse, disturbing roosting pigeons. It came to a screeching halt at the far end of the building.

"Who is this? Where are you taking me?" mumbled Vuković as his head was pressed to the floor.

"Dragon, why have you been avoiding me?" asked von Harz in Serbian, his mother's native language.

Hauling the small-time criminal to a sitting position, he began to frisk him for contraband, finding a minuscule amount of cocaine, along with nine hundred Deutsche Marks, a lighter and the packet of Camel cigarettes.

"Who the fuck is this?" asked Vuković, trying to breathe through the confines of the hood.

Von Harz gave him a slap on the head.

"I ask the questions, you smelly little prick; I do hope you haven't soiled yourself again. You know who I am, alright. Where did you get all this money?"

"Jürgen, oh right. A guy owed me, okay!" answered the dealer.

"Don't okay me, you shithead! Where the hell have you been hiding?" demanded the detective as he drove his boot into the captive's groin for his insolence.

The pimp, come drug dealer, winced. After a few moments, Vuković managed to catch his breath and began to explain, in a rasping voice, the reason he had not been in contact with his handler.

"I had to go back home for my father's funeral and to tidy up any outstanding matters concerning his estate for my mother."

Unsympathetic, von Harz merely increased the pressure with his boot.

"I'm sorry to hear about that.... not!" he taunted.

"What do you want, man?" demanded the pimp, struggling to get out of the detective's vice-like grip.

"What I asked for, two weeks ago. I want to know who is bringing in the coke and how they're getting it through the borders. I don't want to hear about your family life back home, or lack of it," sneered von Harz, as he gave Vuković another slap across the head.

The crew were unable to see the anger on the criminal's covered face, caused by the taunts about his dead father.

"There is no need to speak of my family like that, Jürgen. I've been asking around but no one's talking."

Von Harz felt that he was being given the runaround. As far as he was concerned, the drug dealer had, without warning, gone missing, the result of which was this covert operation.

"I allowed you some leeway in your illegal dealings as long as you kept me informed of any Serb Mafia activity. Where are the people you are currently doing business with: are they here or in Zagreb?"

"Both! I have spoken with someone new; I know him only as Dragomir. He's Bulgarian, I think. He told me that he would be in touch soon."

"Describe him to me."

"I met him at night. He was tall, dark skin, black hair.... like all bloody eastern Europeans," muttered Vuković.

Von Harz punched him in the stomach, exasperated by both the lack of information and being messed around. The drug dealer cried out in pain, squirming to try and protect himself as his hands were still restrained behind his back.

"You will get more of that if you don't co-operate. Now.... how will he contact you? Have you a number? An address?" von Harz demanded to know.

"He.... will.... send a text message for me to meet with him. That's all I can tell you," moaned the Serb.

The team already knew, through another reliable informant, that a major Serb crime figure had been in München with his minders. Once again, there was no name or a face for the individual. Who the character was meeting or where he went was unknown. He had given the members of the local police narcotics team the slip. The Serb had arrived, unannounced, one night, issuing a decree to his crime syndicate partners that any outstanding debts owed by them were to be paid immediately or they would be met with summary punishment.

Euro intelligence operatives had reported that a shady Swiss arms dealer had taken an internal flight from Berlin to München, staying at the Continental Hotel for two days before flying to Lagos, in Nigeria. Private limousines, hired through the hotel, had tracking and eavesdropping devices fitted to them. Muller, Reinhold and eight other detectives monitored the dealer's calls and movements, shadowing his travels throughout the city but there had been no rendezvous with the elusive Serb.

"I think this meeting has already taken place, pants pisser," said von Harz, throwing Vuković to the floor yet again.

"I've told you all I know!"

"Fine…. Has there been talk of someone making enquiries to purchase new or used military equipment, possibly ex-Soviet? Think very carefully of your answer, Vuković."

"No, I definitely haven't heard of anyone looking to make a deal of that kind. It wouldn't interest me anyway. I'm mainstream; I get my bit of action through street deals and the tricks my ladies turn with the johns. What you're asking about is way out of my league. For fuck's sake, I got a D in every subject at school!"

"You're holding back about this, I know it."

The prisoner curled up to protect himself, fearing another assault. Von Harz grabbed him by the throat.

"Please, Jürgen, I don't know anything," he said hoarsely.

"I swear, if you're messing me about, Vuković, I'll continue this conversation with you outside your flat. You and I will have a nice barbecue, deck chairs and all the trimmings for all your clients to see. We might even get a few scores ourselves while we're at your gaff," threatened von Harz.

"Listen, Jürgen, I'm being straight up with you, man. I've had to crack a few heads myself to get the money in since I got back. Give me a break!"

Von Harz let Vuković stew while the vehicle exited the warehouse and headed for München city centre. As the van pulled up to the kerb in a back street near the Hauptbahnhof, the side door slid open.

"Get out, you weasel!" ordered von Harz, as he cut the hand restraints before pulling the hood from the criminal's head and shoving him out into the bright, afternoon sunshine. The vehicle raced away, fading into the lunchtime traffic.

Detlef had been silent throughout the interrogation, allowing Jürgen a free hand, given his language skills. He did not wholeheartedly agree with von Harz's method of questioning but some of the pond scum they dealt with responded more positively to a bit of rough. Now, he listened attentively while his colleague provided an account of the information extracted from Vuković.

"Why are the drug barons tightening their credit terms so abruptly with the large and middle tier dealers, Jürgen? Normally, these organisations always have enough capital to make wholesale purchases."

"Perhaps the Serbian godfathers have taken a hit on their normal smuggling route or have had their drugs seized by other law enforcement agencies who have kept quiet about the knock," von Harz suggested.

"Rival drug cartels have been known to hijack consignments and redirect them to Asia," added Schmitt.

Detlef considered his best course of action. A few, well-planned raids carried out on other informants' businesses might produce more results. The Serbian Mafia could well be thinking of extending their marketplace and such expansion would require large amounts of funding. He would get the team to liaise with local robbery detectives and the narcotics squad, having them monitor their caseloads to see if there was any connection between the drug bosses' meeting and an increase in crime levels. Schmitt was determined to stamp his authority at Pullach by bringing the Serbs' illegal dealings to an end, by whatever means necessary.

CHAPTER FOUR

The inquiry team was in the conference room at Pullach, brainstorming new leads on the Serbian case. Wenzel, who had been out of the country for a few days, briefly put her head round the door.

"Detlef, please see me in my office, immediately."

Schmitt woke with a jolt, having dozed off in his seat as Lang provided an update on the financial aspects of the investigation; Erhard had kept him up all night. As he entered the room, the chief gestured at him to close the door.

"What the hell happened at Schorfheide?" she demanded.

Wenzel had just taken a call from the owner of the hotel, who had complained of an abuse of process regarding the confiscation of the table and its contents.

"Angela, during the operation I came across an antique bureau in the Japanese Prime Minister's room, which I believe to be one of the many artefacts plundered by the Wehrmacht during the war. I'm convinced that the piece is stolen property, given the nature of the documents that were concealed inside it as they appear to originate from the Reichsbank."

"Why didn't you tell me that you had confiscated this bureau?"

"I was waiting for the right moment."

"That's a cop-out, if ever I heard one! You know the protocol; I should have been informed at the start."

"I apologise," said Schmitt, looking down at the floor.

"You can't just walk in and seize something. You should have left it there and sought a warrant."

"Perhaps, in hindsight, I should have."

"Hindsight, my eye! You're fishing on a limb, Detlef, using the broad statute of the law; it may be time barred. Because I have known you for so long, I will only let this pass if you can demonstrate who the rightful owner is. If it turns out the hotel has a legal claim to the table and its contents…. well, I will decide later what further action is required about your conduct."

"I will be able to confirm who the lawful owner is, Angela. There were only one hundred pieces made. I have the manufacturer's details and the bureau's serial number."

"Are the papers genuine?"

"Our laboratories will be able to determine that."

"Investigate the case in your own time!" Wenzel snapped. "You may use the facilities here at Pullach but let's not side-track the staff from their other duties. In the meantime, I will keep the hotel management and their solicitors at bay. Don't ever let anything like this happen again. You have a great career in front of you; try not to let your ego balls it up, Detlef!"

"I won't, Angela, I assure you of that. I'm genuinely sorry for putting you in this position," replied Schmitt, feeling his cheeks beginning to burn.

Detlef left the office, annoyed that Wenzel had even brought the subject up. How things had changed between them since they grew up together in Fallersleben, all those years ago.

****

Later that day, having read his team's operational reports on the various cases they were dealing with, he entered the lift and went down to the laboratory with the manila folder found in the Schorfheide hotel room. He wanted to get the view of the forensics expert, Dr Heidi Konigsberg.

"Have you been avoiding me, Detlef?" she asked, with a flirtatious toss of her hair.

"I know I'm good but I can't be in two places at once just to keep you all happy!" he replied. "Heidi, when you have a moment, would you check out these old documents I found during the G8 conference?"

"I'll do it now," she replied, buttoning up her lab coat and putting on a pair of surgical gloves. "Is this everything that was contained in the folder?" asked Konigsberg as she slowly took out the contents and laid them on a sterile sheet of paper to avoid contamination.

"Yes, it is. For a start, we have five pages of names, addresses and dates of birth. Something that I find most intriguing is this blueprint, titled *'Eichhörnchen Nest'*. It relates to a reinforced room or bunker with one entrance or exit, measuring twelve by three by twenty-four metres. The other documents pertain to various overseas' bank accounts. This form is a transport authorisation from the Reichsbank to the Reichsbahn, requesting the shipment of one tonne of mixed gold coins and bullion, along with thirty million Reichsmarks. There seem to be additional British, French and American currencies thrown in. Altogether, it totals approximately three quarters of a billion Deutsche Marks in today's money. The instructions were that the consignment was to be taken from the Reichsbank in Berlin to München Hauptbahnhof by train, for onward delivery by road to the Eichhörnchen Nest bunker. The order, dated January 1945, appears to have been executed by SS Captain Frank

Gotthard, the Reich Chancellery finance administrator," explained Schmitt.

"Are these documents for real?" asked the forensic officer as she tried to comprehend the history behind them.

"I have asked myself the same question a number of times, Heidi. Would you be able to test them using carbon dating, to determine their age?"

"It's worth a try. I might also carry out a few new procedures for fingerprint analysis. The documents were probably last handled in 1945, although anybody who held them may well have passed away by now."

"You never know, it could be the start of a mystic renaissance!"

"Ok, enough; I get the gist of it. I'll look at it later, when things quieten down a little. By the way, what's the protocol when such documents are found? Is there a war records department we need to notify?"

Detlef hesitated for a moment. He recounted the events in Schorfheide and the dressing down he had received from Wenzel.

"Please….do it in your spare time, Heidi. Angela is a bit sensitive regarding the subject. I would much appreciate it if you keep this under the radar. If anyone asks, you haven't seen anything."

"No problem, Detlef. You can count on my discretion."

"Thanks, Heidi. I owe you big time!"

"I'll remember you said that!"

Schmitt chuckled and turned to leave, his mood beginning to lift.

****

"Good afternoon, all. Things are undeniably grim in Bosnia. One would need a heart of stone not to shed a tear for those unfortunate, displaced people," declared Chief Wenzel as she addressed the case conference after lunch.

Schmitt noticed that she seemed rather drained. Frau Wenzel's position was not an easy one; she had to fight her corner very hard in the male-dominated industry of counter espionage. She was looking worn and bleary-eyed, perhaps through lack of sleep. *Join the club!* he thought as he pictured his son.

She handed out a series of documents whilst briefing the team on new information received from Interpol and foreign intelligence agencies.

"Have we found out where the money and arms are coming from, people? It's not just Germany the Serbs are targeting. The world knows the Bosnian economy is on its knees. There's next to no gross domestic product, the place has been shelled to kingdom come and nothing's getting made or sold, so how are they continuing to fund the war? Their military machine seems to have no shortage of arms' suppliers. Intel suggests their weapons' arsenal is being replaced on a regular basis. Bosnia is not, by any stretch of the imagination, a big country, so how are these covert deliveries being missed?" asked the chief.

One at a time, the members of the team provided recent information updates and gave their analysis of the overall situation concerning the illegal shipment of armaments to the Serbian militia. Intelligence indicated that Israel, Russia and Ukraine were supplying weaponries via middlemen.

"People, I want you to look at any bulk purchasing of fuel; the warring faction vehicles can't run on fresh air. Investigate suspicious deals taking place on the German market and find out who the end users are. There are reports which indicate that fuel may be used as currency for arms," explained Wenzel.

During the conference, a member of staff informed Schmitt he had a call, which he took at his desk in the other room.

"Schmitt here," said the detective.

The line was momentarily silent as the call was being transferred. Schmitt flicked casually through the latest Swiss intelligence report on the Serbian Mafia's activity in south Germany and northern Switzerland, which had been placed on his desk during the meeting. After a few seconds, the transfer was completed and the caller identified himself as Officer Claus Hübel of the German Customs and Excise.

"Herr Hübel, how can I help you?" asked Schmitt.

"Thank you for taking my call, Herr Schmitt; I was finally directed to this department. An incident has occurred during a case of staff holiday relief cover which may be of interest to you."

"Please, call me Detlef. Could you explain?"

"Well, one of our officers uncovered what he believes to be a major alcohol smuggling scam along the German border."

Detlef put down the report he was half reading, straightened himself up in the chair and began to listen intently.

"A customs officer, providing holiday relief, had been on duty at the Austrian-German, SubenStraße border crossing, in Hortkirchen, late one evening. A MAN F2000 tractor unit, pulling a bonded tri-axle trailer loaded with 23 000 Deutsche Marks' worth of alcohol arrived at the checkpoint. Nothing appeared to be untoward; all the customs' seals were intact. The paperwork was duly stamped and the consignment passed on its way. The following week, the officer was sent to work at another Austrian-German border crossing, this time at SchördingerStraße, again filling in for an employee who was on holiday. A vehicle from the same logistics company arrived at the crossing, carrying a similar consignment. The officer does not know what alerted him, perhaps just intuition. He began to rigorously examine the documentation. The consignment notes produced by the driver were identical to the paperwork he had processed at the SubenStraße crossing point, right down to the docket number that was used to clear a similar shipment the previous week."

"What was the outcome?" asked Schmitt.

"The officer, a little unsure if he had made a mistake, passed no comment and the vehicle continued on with its load. He made a note of the incident, pending further enquiries."

"Who owned the vehicles?"

"Kaolin Gütertransport AG of Deggendorf."

"One of our own firms trying to avoid paying duty?"

"Well, sort of, that's why I'm ringing you. The haulage operation is owned by a parent company, Bacutrans; its base is in Bosnia," replied Hübel.

Due to the on-going military conflict, incidents involving Bosnia were being red-flagged by a lot of German government departments because of pressure from the E.U. and NATO.

"Detlef, I know you guys have the resources to really look into this case. I think there might be more to these incidents than meets the eye. Given that the Bosnian Government has all but collapsed, we will get no meaningful co-operation from them. I have directed our main VAT office to send over the relevant records concerning the transport company in question to my office. If you want, I can forward anything of significance on to you."

"Yes, I would appreciate that, Claus. Please send your findings over, marked for my attention. Thanks for the call."

Schmitt returned to the case conference where he informed Chief Wenzel and the team of his conversation with Officer Hübel. After the meeting, he went over to the communications room where audio analysts were busy intercepting and reviewing electronic dialogue by means of satellite, wiretapping and eavesdropping software. The data consisted of local and international phone, text, fax and email communications. The enormous processing capacity of the computer systems could identify key intelligence wordings. This included dialogue where an individual used certain words which intelligence officers viewed as suspicious. Once triggered, the program would flag up a particular word or phrase to one of the many officers on duty, who began monitoring the chitchat more closely.

Detective Claudia Reinhold managed the electronic surveillance section at Pullach.

"Anything interesting, Claudia?" enquired Schmitt as she monitored phone traffic from a specific phone line through her headset.

"As you know, Detlef, when Vuković was picked up in Dachau, four weeks ago, we switched his phone with one I had modified. It is fitted with one of our latest, in-house, sophisticated tracking and eavesdropping software systems," Reinhold replied.

"Is it working?"

"Don't be silly! The phone's performing well. The program allows us to switch Vuković's handset on remotely, without his knowledge. Now we're able to listen in on his conversations, as and when we want. The screen of the phone remains blank, not that the dimwit would notice, given the amount of cocaine he samples. No, you don't need to worry, the device is doing just what it says on the tin, Detlef."

"I'm never worried when you're on the case; it's when you're not officially sanctioned to carry out your mischief that I begin to fret!" joked Schmitt. "What's our little cokehead been up to then?"

"Talking crap, as usual! Men's conversations, mostly, such as how he's getting his best lays ever from the new girls he taken delivery of…. that kind of thing."

Schmitt grimaced.

"Who's his latest conquest?"

"He has been forced to bed one of his new girls. Such toil! His regular tart won't let him bang her unless she gets free candy. The thing is, Vuković is really in love with her and gives her what she wants. She's found a really good meal ticket and is reeling him in nicely but the fool can't see it. We have also fixed her phone; a local police patrol gave her a shake down in the street and swapped it. Judging by the conversations she has with her friends back in Hungary, she'll either sell him out or eventually get a kiss on the head from a Glock for being greedy, in view of the amount of money she has been thieving from him and sending home."

"Well, you lie with dogs, you rise with fleas. So, he's not turning any high-grade information?"

"No. Vuković's more interested in getting those owing him money to pay up to keep his tart happy and himself alive. Allowing his bitch to rule the roost is bad news. It's causing some discontent among his other street girls, though, as occupational hazards go, she would need to be stoned to let Vuković into her pants; he's repulsive!"

"Is there anything else of importance, Claudia?"

"The name of an east German ex-Stasi sergeant has been mentioned twice by Vuković when he rang someone by the name of Dragomir Dragovic."

"What is the ex-Stasi's name and who is this Dragovic?"

"The Stasi guy is an Erich Niemeyer; I'm currently waiting for an information update on his file. From what I've read so far, he's a nasty piece of work, by all accounts. I'm also waiting for further intelligence on Dragovic."

Schmitt stopped at the door and thought for a moment, regarding what had been said. He had come across the Stasi sergeant's name before but couldn't quite remember where or when. He thanked Reinhold for the information and left to go to the canteen.

As he walked along the corridor, he suddenly remembered the circumstances under which he had encountered Niemeyer. Some years ago, when Schmitt had been a beat officer in Hannover, he had noticed a vehicle - with East German licence plates - blocking a loading bay. Niemeyer, who was on his way back to the car with his wife, produced his driver's licence from his wallet when requested to do so by Schmitt, who subsequently issued him with a parking fine. The man had become aggressive and was close to being arrested before his wife eventually intervened, accepting the parking ticket on her husband's behalf.

Schmitt had checked with the border agency some time later, only to discover that the couple had hurriedly left West Germany, using the Helmstedt border crossing. Their car had been spotted a few days earlier; first, near a military installation in Dortmund and later, parked close to a Government minister's home. A report was drawn up on the incidents. The couple were suspected to have been on a spying mission for a Russian intelligence agency, evaluating the strength of the allied military forces stationed in Germany. That was the last Schmitt had ever heard of the Stasi agent, until now.

CHAPTER FIVE

Schmitt's team had stepped up their electronic surveillance on anyone associated with the Serbian Mafia syndicate.

"Vuković has been calling this number a lot; we've traced it to Yugoslavia," said von Harz, pointing to the telephone number in the file he had been reading. "Someone named Knezevic, who keeps asking when he will be getting the shipment he's owed."

"What is he owed? Is it alcohol, tobacco or some other type of contraband that they're talking about?" queried Schmitt.

"The gist of the conversation seems to be that a consignment should be arriving shortly. Perhaps it is a reference to the arrival of new girls for his knocking shops?"

"Keep me informed of any developments, Jürgen. I'd best be getting home."

****

The next morning, Schmitt had the investigative team assemble in the conference room. Chief Wenzel opened the proceedings.

"People, where are we with the alcohol duty scam?"

"Our enquiries point to the fact that it seems to have been going on for over six months, from the time Bacutrans took control of the company from its German owners. It's too early to say if any Revenue officials are involved," replied Schmitt.

"Have you some idea of the volumes being smuggled by the company?" Wenzel asked.

"There are two consignments a week that we know about. The

involvement of a reputable German haulier has given some respectability to the operation. The vehicles are all clean and well-maintained. Furthermore, the management team has won numerous awards for their logistical innovations."

"Is someone chancing their arm with false paperwork or is it more organised, Detlef?"

"We have considered various scenarios," said Schmitt. "One; if the transit forms are forgeries, they are of high quality. Two; the fraud could have been carried out using stolen, bonded documentation although none has been reported missing. Or three; someone from inside the department is ensuring the scam is successful, either through collusion or incompetence."

"Liaise with your contact, Detlef. Find out as much as you can on the scale of the operation. Is there any other form of contraband being smuggled over the border that we aren't aware of? People, expand your investigations. Look for other possibilities and come back to me when you have something concrete to contribute. I will then arrange a meeting with the judge from the finance ministry to see how we should proceed with the case," ordered Wenzel.

As the meeting closed, Schmitt and his team returned to the office, prepared to delve a little deeper into the activities of the new owners of Kaolin Gütertransport AG.

"Good afternoon, Herr Hübel, Detective Chief Inspector Schmitt here. How are things with you?" he asked, having called the customs officer for an update on the alcohol smuggling case.

"We are considering suspending two of the border guards but, at this present time, we have nothing tangible on the supervisor whom we suspect of facilitating the scam. What has your investigation uncovered, Detlef?"

"It's early days yet, Claus. I'm working on a proposal to carry out a joint-agency raid on the haulage company's various premises, that is, with your department's assistance, of course. Why target the two guards, though? Did one of them not alert you to a possible crime?"

"His reporting of the incident might be a case of sour grapes. He could have been cut out of the deal."

"That's a possibility. I hadn't considered that."

"Can you say what action, if any, your department may take, Detlef?"

"My team intends to monitor the bonded vehicles of Kaolin Gütertransport as they are crossing the border. We want to identify if there is a sustained pattern to their smuggling activities for a few weeks, before making a move. As part of the operation, we intend to apprehend the staff members you suspect as being complicit, at both the border crossing and at the main processing office, as the vehicles are being cleared. I will require a copy of your report to support our planning strategy."

"I will run this past my superiors, Detlef, but I don't foresee any problems arising with the structure of it. I'll get the report to you as soon as possible."

****

A few days later, Schmitt was waiting with Chief Wenzel, his in-depth report on the smuggling case in his hand, ready to be presented to one of the judges from the finance courts. The streams of evidence against the transport company were damning. The investigative team had gone over all the bonded goods' documents from the last six months.

Given the large amounts of tax being evaded, Schmitt decided to strike the haulier's main office, their outlying warehouses and the border customs' clearing area.

As arranged with Officer Hübel, the suspected officials linked to the case were left on their normal duties to avoid suspicion. The task force at Pullach were told to be on standby for a multi-agency sting operation. As part of their intelligence strategy, an additional distribution warehouse had been detected in the Moosburg area.

The premises had been uncovered accidently, by officers covertly following one of the transport company's vehicles that had deviated from its normal route. Having checked with the land registry offices, it was found that the nondescript property belonged to Kaolin Gütertransport. It had been purchased two years earlier, to be developed as a freight groupage centre. The plan was shelved after a parts distribution contract the company had tendered for with a major car manufacturer did not materialise. The local planning authority had not granted permission for the building to be used as an operating centre.

The officers parked up a short distance away from the premises. Using field glasses, they observed that, once at the warehouse, the company vehicle was quickly unloaded as an assortment of light goods vehicles came and went. It was suspected that the consignment was being broken down into smaller units to be distributed throughout the country, possibly to pubs, clubs and illegal cash and carry outlets.

"Judge Janzyke will see you now," said the secretary, leading Schmitt and Wenzel into the judge's chambers before closing the door.

"Good day, Herr Janzyke, thanks for taking the time to see us. I would like to introduce Herr Schmitt," said Wenzel, before being interrupted.

"Please, Angela, I don't need an introduction to this young man. Detlef, how are you keeping?" asked the judge warmly as he came over to greet him.

"I'm very well, thank you, Judge," Schmitt replied.

"Forgive me, Angela. This officer did me and my family a great service some years ago. I will always be in his debt," explained Janzyke.

Frau Wenzel was taken aback. The judge was a very private man and was not given to mixing with low ranking police officers. Wenzel made a point to look closer into Schmitt's personnel file when she found time.

The group retired to the lounge area of the judge's office, discussing a range of cases before coming to the main one.

"Paweł, we have a very serious issue concerning the smuggling of large quantities of alcohol by a Serbian-owned, German haulage company," Wenzel announced; she outlined the case of the suspected illegal funding of the Bosnian conflict, describing, in detail, the amount of evidence the task force had uncovered so far and the level of complicity.

"I think, at the very least, the management at Customs and Excise have a lot of questions to answer, Angela. Exactly how was this breach allowed to happen? The border guard! Yes, I can understand this, perhaps. But a senior official? No. I will request a full inquiry into the lapse of process," replied Janzyke, having digested the testimony.

Judge Janzyke got up from the sofa, walked over to his desk and sat down. Taking out a multi-layer form, he began writing out the various warrants to enter and search the properties of Kaolin Gütertransport AG. The conditions of the warrants included gaining entrance to the properties, the confiscation of documents and contraband likely to be used as evidence, and making arrests where appropriate.

Before the contingent left the judge's chambers, Janzyke asked Schmitt to remain.

"I can't thank you enough for what you did back then, Detlef. Anyone else would have turned and walked away. Karl's life would have been ruined. You didn't walk away though and for that my wife and I will forever be in your debt."

"Sir, I did what was right. You and your family owe me nothing. How is Karl? I hope he is keeping well."

"He's doing fine, studying hard for his bar exam, Detlef. I will send him your regards."

As the two men shook hands, the judge gave Schmitt his personal business card.

"You know you can phone me, day or night, if you ever need help, Detlef," Janzyke called out, as the detective went to catch up with Wenzel.

****

There was a buzz in the conference room as Schmitt opened the meeting three days after the warrants were obtained.

"People, in one hour's time we are going to raid the head office and warehouses of Kaolin Gütertransport AG, Deggendorf, along with another warehouse at Moosburg. You all know what to do as we've gone over this several times. I want you to hit your designated areas as soon as you're out of the vehicles. No one leaves the premises; all communication with the outside world is to be shut down. Search everyone and confiscate their phones or pagers. I don't want any part of the operation to leak out. Go over that building with a fine-tooth comb. Anything that appears suspect is to be removed. If in doubt, ask me. Are there any questions?"

Schmitt looked around the room.

The team shook their heads. They had rehearsed the operation twice already with other multi-agency task force members. The meeting lasted twenty minutes before the staff went to prepare their kit along with other equipment, including body armour required for the operation.

The joint task force struck their assigned targets at 5.30 pm, just as the company's shifts were changing. Additional local police support, along with staff members from Pullach, entered the premises of Kaolin Gütertransport. State immigration police, along with Revenue and Social Security officials assisted in the operation. Their first task was to lock down all sites, including the warehouse in Moosburg that was used to store smuggled alcohol.

"Can I help you?" asked the night manager as the team rushed the building.

Schmitt produced his warrant card.

"My name is Detective Chief Inspector Schmitt. I have a court order to search these premises."

"On what grounds, Detective? We've done nothing wrong," he argued.

Schmitt ignored the man's protests.

"I have reason to believe that Kaolin Gütertransport AG has been defrauding the Government of alcohol duty. The investigative team will examine all company records and check the legal status of your employees. We have the right to seize items that may assist us with our inquiries from these and any other premises belonging to, or registered in the name of your company," declared Schmitt.

The manager made no reply and, shrugging his shoulders, went with the rest of the staff to the conference room to be processed. The company switchboard was closed and the employees' personal mobile phones were tagged and put into evidence bags for forensic examination later. This would keep the operation low-key until all the relevant agencies had completely secured their targets.

"Detlef, have you got a moment?" asked Reinhold, as Schmitt walked into one of the many offices being examined.

"What is it?"

"These invoices indicate that large amounts of Fullers Earth are being bought and transported by the company. It is used as a fertiliser by farmers but can also be used by criminal enterprises to filter rebated diesel. This could be evidence of fuel smuggling," she explained.

"Possibly."

"They seem to have been transporting large consignments into Italy. Once there, the trailers have been unhitched, for onward delivery by a third party."

"Gather any relevant documents, Claudia," Schmitt instructed his colleague before leaving to check on the progress of the other teams.

As he was entering the operation's hub, there was a commotion occurring in the reception area of Kaolin Gütertransport.

"Take your hands off me!" protested an individual who was

being led by uniformed police into the office that had been designated for processing files.

"What's going on?" demanded Schmitt.

"Sir, this gentleman saw the police cordon and tried to flee after abandoning his lorry in the street. On examination of his vehicle, we found ten pallets on board, containing disposable nappies. Upon closer inspection, we discovered cartons of illegal tobacco concealed inside the casing," stated the officer.

"Take him away. Lock him up until I have time to deal with him!" barked the detective.

"No way! You're not locking me up," protested the driver. "I'm just trying to earn a living! That prick of a manager was paying me cash in hand to make sure the extra pallets got delivered."

"Officers, remove this man, we'll process him later," commanded Schmitt. "Alpha 8."

"Go ahead."

"Muller, go over the inventory in the Moosburg warehouse and check for any suspicious consignments," ordered Schmitt. "We've just intercepted a large amount of contraband tobacco in a shipment of disposable nappies."

The joint-agency teams worked together as one, throughout the night and on, into the early hours, with officers sifting through reams of paperwork and computer data before eventually removing them as evidence for further examination at Pullach.

****

The next day, the team met in the conference room. Following the previous night's activities, they had been given a few hours off to sleep and freshen up. Frau Wenzel chaired the meeting. The members of the unit reported on what had been uncovered. This included some antique rugs, illegal tobacco, suspected laundered fuel, and illicit alcohol. The discoveries confirmed the widespread evasion of alcohol, fuel and tobacco duty. In addition, a total of thirty Turkish-made Ghost TR01 compact semi-automatic pistols were found by Muller's team in the warehouse at Moosburg. They had been concealed in bales of glass wool insulation. However, the detectives were unable to find any ammunition.

Social Services had run identity checks on all the logistics company's employees and found that half of them were in the country illegally. Documents recovered indicated that a lot of the staff were paid in cash. Six of the men had outstanding international arrest warrants for murder, armed robbery, people smuggling and drug-related offences. Having been arrested, they were taken to a hastily arranged court hearing before being remanded in custody until a formal trial date could be set.

Schmitt contacted Interpol to acquaint them with the recent arrests. He requested that they inform the relevant countries, should they wish to make an official demand for extradition of any of the suspects following the completion of sentences handed down by a German court.

CHAPTER SIX

Local detectives were tasked with questioning the workforce of Kaolin Gütertransport; the employees were being processed in several police stations. A clerical assistant entered the conference room in Pullach as Schmitt's team analysed the data gathered from the overnight raid.

"Detlef, sorry to interrupt, there's a phone call for you."

Schmitt took the call in his office. After around eight minutes, he replaced the receiver and exhaled loudly before returning to the meeting.

"People, that has just ratcheted the case up another notch," he announced. "The call I received came from Officer Hübel, of Customs and Excise. He informed me that border guard, Ernst Einhard, has been found, shot dead, in his apartment."

Officer Einhard had been arrested for fraud and was suspended - on paid leave - following the completion of a preliminary, internal investigation. Angela and the others looked on, stunned, as the disturbing news was relayed to them.

"The residents heard someone hammering on the victim's door, followed by shouting, then silence. Police were alerted when a neighbour went to investigate the disturbance and found the front door ajar. On entering the apartment, Einhard was found slumped in an armchair, with a gunshot wound to the head. There was no sign of a struggle and residents heard no gunfire. SOCO are currently processing the scene."

"My God.... that's horrendous! Does Hübel think there is a connection to the case?" asked a shocked Wenzel.

"That's not all, Angela. Customs supervisor, Manfred Friedel, has been found dead, in his car, in a supermarket car park, having also been shot in the head. The owner of the store phoned the police after a member of staff, who was collecting litter, noticed a car with its windows broken, at the far end of the car park. The employee decided that it warranted further inspection and seeing the red spray on the windows he, at first, thought it was an act of vandalism. That was until he looked through what was left of the front passenger side window. Friedel was slumped over the steering wheel. From what Hübel says, early indications seem to suggest that both men were killed between ten and eleven o'clock last night. We will know more when SOCO complete their investigations of the two crime scenes."

"Detlef, Jürgen, grab yourselves a coffee and get to the locations of the shootings as quickly as you can; they may provide valuable information as to who carried out these killings," ordered Wenzel, hurriedly ending the meeting.

As they drove through München's midday traffic, von Harz asked the question that had been nagging him since hearing the news.

"Do you think these were professional hits, Detlef?"

"There's more to this case than the evasion of excise duty, Jürgen. It seems they have been gun running as well and now two of the suspects have been shot within an hour of one another. Someone wanted them silenced before we got to them."

When they reached BarerStraße, Schmitt parked the S2 up on a grass verge. The area was already congested with police vehicles and media vans.

"Bloody vultures!" yelled von Harz as he got out of their car.

"Watch what you say around the media, Jürgen!" warned Schmitt. "There is enough bad press at the moment, without these guys hearing that sort of language."

"Sorry, Detlef, it won't happen again, but two people have just been murdered and they swamp the area to sell airtime!"

The pair made their way up the urine-stained flight of stairs to Einhard's apartment and put on protective clothing before going in. The scenes of crime officers were already busily processing the site.

"Ah.... Stefan!" said Schmitt, grabbing his friend's gloved hand and shaking it vigorously.

The two officers had both attended Police College in Munster. Stefan Weber, who was five years Schmitt's senior, oversaw the forensic side of this investigation.

"Do you try to make my life difficult on purpose, Detlef?" asked Weber as he took the - now contaminated - glove off, replacing it with a sterile one.

"What have we here, Stefan?" he replied with a cheeky grin.

"A resident in the apartment below heard somebody banging on the victim's door. There was a great deal of shouting and then silence. We've managed to get the slug out of the chair; no shell casing, a very clean and professional hit. As you can see, the place is in pristine condition," said the forensic officer, sarcastically.

The apartment was, indeed, unkempt, smelling of a mixture of sweat, nicotine and dirty laundry. Part of the grimy, floral-patterned seat that the deceased had been found in was now saturated with blood.

Schmitt sent von Harz out to question the neighbours and tried to keep out of the way of the officers processing the crime area whilst he walked through the flat. Given its dishevelled state, it was hard to tell that the place had been thoroughly searched. It took a trained eye to spot it, but Schmitt and Weber had noticed the slight disturbance of the deceased's personal items. Schmitt took Weber to one side.

"Stefan."

"Yes, Detlef, I also noticed that a subtle search has been made here; the shooter was obviously looking for something."

"Could you get me a copy of the report as soon as possible? This is now part of a very large, on-going investigation."

"I'll do my best, though we've got a lot on our plate at the minute."

Weber lowered the protective mask from his mouth.

"You do know about the other one at the shopping centre?"

"That's my next port of call. Again, it's part of the same case. There is much at stake here so I would really appreciate both reports as soon as you can get them to me. Amélie is going to divorce me before we are married, given the amount of time I've spent on this investigation!"

"How is the lovely lady, Detlef?" asked Weber, feigning interest. "It's been a while since I called round to see her," he added, raising his eyebrows to the right in a joking manner. "A ravishing beauty like that? I'm sure you must have her locked away when you're at work!"

"You behave yourself, you old rogue!" cackled Schmitt. "I have to run; don't work too hard, Stefan!"

Weber shook his head, turned and went back into the apartment.

Von Harz was waiting for Schmitt at the car.

"What did you find out from the residents, Jürgen?" questioned

Schmitt as they got into the Audi and left the crime scene.

"Nothing much. Most of the neighbours were indoors for the night. Some of them heard the door being pounded and raised voices before everything went quiet. The only positive sighting was from an old man who had been out, walking his dog."

"And...?" pressed Schmitt. He was becoming slightly irritated as he tried to concentrate on the conversation and drive at the same time. The temporary roadworks he was manoeuvring the car through weren't helping his mood.

"As I said, the old guy was walking the dog. He came to a pedestrian crossing and pressed the button. The light turned green and the buzzer sounded to cross the road. As the old boy was mid-way across, he noticed or, more to the point, heard, a dark-coloured BMW approaching. It was being driven erratically and failed to stop, nearly running both him and his dog over."

"Did he get the registration?" asked Schmitt as their vehicle headed onto the southbound dual carriageway.

"Cataracts," answered von Harz.

Detlef banged his head off the steering wheel in frustration as they slowed at yet another set of temporary traffic lights.

"You're telling me that the old duffer was practically wiped out at the crossing but his sight is so affected by cataracts that he couldn't identify the registration of the vehicle that almost sent him to his Maker? Did no one else witness the event?"

"No one; it was getting dark. You may not have noticed but the street lighting is very poor around there. There seems to be a lot of vandalism."

They drove on in silence, through never-ending heavy traffic, caused by ongoing road re-surfacing in the area. The Audi came to an off ramp before proceeding on to another carriageway that took them to the supermarket off WolfratshauserStraße.

The detectives were stopped at the entrance by a uniformed officer who directed them across the site to an area that had been cordoned off with crime scene tape.

"Who's in charge here?" asked Schmitt as they got out of the car.

"I am Detective Bucholz, gentlemen. May I help you?" enquired the small, portly officer, stamping his feet to improve his poor circulation.

"Hi, my name is Detective Chief Inspector Schmitt, counter intelligence. My colleague is Detective von Harz. Can you update us as to what happened here?"

The two officers displayed their badges and Bucholz checked their identification before outlining what he knew, so far, of the killing.

"We have a Caucasian male who was found dead in his vehicle over there. He died as the result of a single gunshot wound to the head. An identity check has confirmed him to be Manfred Friedel, formerly of AlteBergStraße; he was in his early forties."

"Were there any witnesses?" asked Schmitt.

"No, but I have had a brief chance to examine the store's surveillance tapes. CCTV recorded a red Opel Kadett arriving at around 10.15 pm. It was driven to the south of the lot, parked up and the lights were turned off. The vehicle never moved again. There seems to have been a small, unidentifiable burst of light, to the west of the car park, adjacent to the dual carriageway, at around 11.10 pm."

"Have you found anything there that would have caused it?

Perhaps it was a camera flash?" suggested Schmitt.

"That could be a possibility. We did find a fresh set of car tyre tracks on the grass verge and my officers immediately cordoned them off."

"What has that to do with this incident? Countless motorists inadvertently mount the verge from time to time."

"That is true, but someone reported a hit and run incident to the local police station last night. A large, blue truck clipped a dark grey BMW car that was parked on the side of the carriageway adjacent to the car park. Two minutes later, the car sped off and has not been found."

"What about the truck?" queried von Harz.

"It was a Johnny Foreigner, with a Polska sticker on the number plate. Local units are still trying to trace it," said Bucholz. "The driver may have been asleep at the wheel or could have had a momentary lapse of concentration which caused the collision."

"You'll never get the driver!" barked Schmitt. "Those people won't want to be involved. Don't waste any manpower on it; just put out a general alert and see what it brings."

"We shall be contacting the member of the public who reported the incident to see if they have any further information on the occupant of the BMW, which had been reported stolen from the Ramersdorf area. One more thing; there were no spent casings found anywhere but we did locate what seems to be a bullet, although when forensics get here they won't be able to touch it until we get a court order," Bucholz said, pointing towards the police tape on a nearby tree.

"Why not? This case has top priority," Schmitt declared.

"It's protected woodland, sir. The tree huggers will probably go nuts as we need to cut the tree down to retrieve the slug," explained Bucholz.

"You mean to say; this case is going to be held back over a damn tree?" argued Schmitt.

"Don't blame me!" said Bucholz, holding his hands up in defence.

"Forgive me, you are doing a great job here, Herr Bucholz. See what else you can find out and please keep me informed," said Schmitt, shaking the man's hand.

Schmitt and von Harz ducked under the cordoning tape to begin their examination of the vehicle and the surrounding area. The officers surveyed the car before walking round to the passenger window.

"Opened like a melon!" exclaimed von Harz as he caught a glimpse of the dead body, slouched forward in the seat.

"I can see that," said Schmitt, peering inside the vehicle. "Whoever carried out the hit made it from five hundred metres, clean through both windows, before lodging into that big oak tree."

"All from the side of a main carriageway? The shooter risked being intercepted by the traffic police for illegal parking. Whoever they are, they're good!" exhaled von Harz, looking across the car park towards the busy carriageway.

"I agree; the killer was very skilled. Possibly ex-military? They had a window of around ten minutes or less to complete the hit before a passing patrol would arrive to investigate either the illegal parking or the hit and run report. I think something like a Mauser or some other high powered rifle has been passing wind," suggested Schmitt as he performed a three sixty view of the car park.

The apartment blocks adjacent to the carriageway caught his

attention. Perhaps the BMW car had no connection? The hit could have been very easily carried out from any one of the ground floor apartments, given the trajectory's angle. Detlef considered this for a moment before approaching Bucholz again.

"Herr Bucholz, could I trouble you once more?"

"Yes, of course, sir."

"Could you have your men carry out door-to-door inquiries at those ground floor flats adjacent to the carriageway? See if there was any suspicious activity or unfamiliar individuals in the vicinity. Check the identities of the tenants. The shot could have originated from any one of their apartments."

"Right away, sir, I'll call in extra manpower," replied Bucholz.

The intelligence officers continued with their investigation of the area.

"The poor guy's date evidently kept their secret tryst," noted von Harz, absorbing all the grisly details.

"Having lured him here in the first place. Someone knew exactly where to position the vehicle. That person may well have a military background, since the location was chosen to isolate the target and minimise the risk of taking casualties whilst providing a fast exit route. Get Reinhold to check the deceased's phone records and look for any other CCTV footage of his arrival here, as well as that of a potential killer," ordered Schmitt. "Well, what are you waiting for?" he growled. "Move it!"

Von Harz immediately scurried off to call back to base and relay the message to Claudia. Then, crossing the carriageway, he began visiting nearby stores to see if they had caught the incident on their surveillance tapes.

Detlef put on a pair of latex gloves before gently opening the passenger door of the car. Reaching over, he removed the mobile phone from the victim's inside breast pocket. Having examined its recent call history, he returned it and, taking one last look, walked away from the scene. He had seen enough death for one day.

****

The Serbian Mafia was currently involved in exploiting anything that would make a profit, from stolen luxury cars - destined for the Middle East - to prostitution, small time neighbourhood extortion, money lending and drug dealing. It was the Government's ambition to put these groups out of business, as quickly as possible. Schmitt's challenging task was to guide his team through the many layers of the investigation to reach the main players and try to seize their illegal assets.

Intelligence received by field operatives suggested that the godfathers were investing their ill-gotten gains into legitimate companies, property and share trading. They were selling low-cost merchandise at inflated prices or receiving payment for bogus, non-delivered orders. The team was now targeting suspect bureaux de change that were believed to be laundering illegally-earned money.

Kaolin Gütertransport AG had been a German-owned, general haulage company, founded in 1956 in the town of Deggendorf by two brothers, Heinz and Gunter Werner. Initially, the company distributed goods for the American armed forces. Later, it began to transport building materials, an important service as Germany started to rebuild its economy after the war. While the country prospered, the company diversified into other areas of freight, including farm supplies, bonded cargo and fuel. The brothers retired in the early eighties, leaving the business to their two sons who had been working alongside their parents for many years, learning the skills of the everyday transport operation.

After the collapse of the Berlin Wall in 1990, more and more pressure was put upon the company, because of former Eastern bloc transport companies vying for a slice of their work. The younger generation of management had known only prosperous times, unlike their fathers who had faced many recessionary periods when money was scarce.

In 1992, the company had over one hundred vehicles delivering throughout Germany and abroad. The logistics operation experienced more downs than ups. The brothers were approached by a German middleman representing Bacutrans, a Serbian-owned transport company based on the outskirts of Zagreb. The concern was interested in developing an operational transport hub in the west. The two men had been losing the determination to carry on with the business, spending more time on the golf range than focusing on the firm's financial standing. The Serbian operation eventually made them a substantial offer for the company and its licenced operating centres.

The current freight order books stood at twenty-five per cent below pre-takeover of the company from their fathers. With staff morale at an all-time low, the partners eventually sold the operation as a going concern, to Bacutrans. The purchase enabled Bacutrans to exploit their lower, eastern European labour and running costs, providing continuous traffic, both inbound and outbound. Part of the current top tier management in Kaolin Gütertransport AG was replaced by a Bacutrans management team from their head office in Zagreb.

****

A week later, the two crime scene reports had arrived from SOCO. Schmitt gave them a cursory glance before summoning everyone to the conference room.

"Heinz, please brief us on the case to date," Schmitt requested.

"Right. Customs officer, Markus Fischer, informed his superiors of a suspected fraud taking place at several border crossings. After a brief internal investigation, three customs officials, including Fischer, were monitored by the human resources department and fresh background checks were carried out. Currently, only two individuals have been implicated in the crime. First, we have Ernst Einhard, a border guard. He had a gambling addiction, to the extent that it affected his home life and, as a result, his wife ultimately left him. Up until the time of his death, they remained estranged, with Einhard's days revolving around work, the bookmaker's and his local pub. He had three thousand marks, yet unaccounted for, in the bank and an outstanding two thousand marks' bookie's tab. There was no sign of any life insurance policies or property. Einhard's task, we think, was to turn a blind eye to the counterfeit freight and alcohol smuggling operation, in return for which he would receive backhanders. We can only assume he assisted the crime syndicate to feed his betting habit. He was found, shot in the head, in his apartment. A 9mm calibre slug was removed from the body. No shell casings were found at the scene and no one witnessed anything. The evidence points to a professional hit. We can only speculate, as to the reason for his murder."

Muller paused for a quick gulp of coffee and then continued.

"Manfred Friedel was a senior accounts' supervisor based in SeligenthalerStraße customs office who had passed regular personnel vetting. He was found, shot dead, in his car in a supermarket car park, time of death approximately 11.00pm. We are certain he was killed by a .62 calibre sniper's rifle; the slug was recovered from a protected oak tree. The tree was felled and a section removed, which caused quite an outrage within the local community as the forest is a natural heritage site. Once again, we can only speculate that he was lured to a meeting and murdered. We are still analysing his mobile phone records for further leads.

A confirmed bachelor, Friedel lived alone, in a small apartment on AlteBergStraße in the Landshut district. He enjoyed the company of call girls and was a frequent visitor to the red-light districts of München. He holidayed in Marbella, Spain, purchasing his flight tickets through a travel agent in Austria and paying for them with cash. A search of his flat revealed a receipt for a safe deposit box, registered in the name of his partially-sighted mother. Following a court order, the box was examined. It contained fifty thousand Deutsche Marks and deeds to a time share apartment, also registered in his mother's name and using her home address. Frau Friedel has been questioned. She is genuinely distraught by both her son's untimely death and the fact that he had so much money hidden away, in her name. The mother has never left Germany in her life so we can dismiss her as having had any involvement in the case."

"Thank you, Heinz," said Schmitt. "I want you all to make enquiries with land registry, banks and lending institutions; bounce the names of anyone involved in these investigations with them. See if there have been any knock-down, real estate sales recently, or large cash withdrawals. Start hitting the foreign exchange shops. We need more answers and fast, people. We'll meet again next week. Get moving!"

With that, Schmitt brought the meeting to a close. He still had nothing concrete to give Wenzel for the ministers of the German parliament in Bonn.

****

A few days later, Detlef arrived for work before his staff, after yet another sleepless weekend because of Erhard. His son had developed a rattling cough, due to a chest infection that was proving hard to clear. He fixed himself an extra strong coffee and unwrapped the jagdwurst-filled brötchen he had bought from the bakery in Stuntzstraße. Now armed for the task in hand, he went to the evidence store where he began to sort through the confiscated files from Kaolin Gütertransport. After some time, he stood back and surveyed the remaining mountain of boxes stacked in the corner of the room. It was beginning to seem more and more unlikely that he would find anything of benefit to the investigation.

Detlef decided to give up. His guys were the experts in the field of finance, let them earn their wages, he reasoned. As he was leaving, a carton marked *Goods Refusal Notice* caught his eye. Opening it, he examined a handful of the forms and statements from customers who had refused consignments, requiring credit notes to be raised. Apart from the normal receipts for freight damaged in transit, one document - dated four months prior to the Pullach investigation - stood out from the others. It was a notice from the Department of Health, informing the company that an inspection would take place at their registered operating centre. The review was in relation to a breach of food safety regulations. Two separate consignments of milk, totalling forty thousand litres, had been delivered to a dairy for processing. The shipments had been refused due to exceptionally high levels of hydrochloride found in samples taken. The haulage company responded, stating that there had been a mix up with the solvents used to clean the tankers at the end of the working day.

Hydrochloride was the base ingredient used to produce cocaine; had Knezevic been referring to a major cocaine shipment when speaking with drug dealer Vuković? Spot checks had been stepped up at all German border crossings but current intelligence was that only a couple of small-time drugs couriers had been apprehended to date.

"Good morning, Detlef, you're an early bird today!" exclaimed von Harz, throwing his coat over some nearby boxes of files. He sat down on a plastic storage case and began eating a salami sandwich.

"Morning, Jürgen. I think I might have solved the puzzle of the consignment that was requested by the guy in Yugoslavia. I believe there is cocaine coming into the country in bulk shipments," Schmitt declared.

He handed his colleague the documents he had discovered and began to explain his suspicions that large quantities of the drug were being smuggled into Germany through milk consignments transported by Kaolin Gütertransport.

"That's an ingenious way of bringing them into the country," observed von Harz.

"I'll get a couple of officers to shadow the dairy vehicles. Let's see what they uncover," said Schmitt.

CHAPTER SEVEN

On her way to another appointment, Frau Wenzel had stopped by Judge Janzyke's chambers to apprise him of recent events. She described how Schmitt's team had unearthed multiple financial irregularities at the registered headquarters of Kaolin Gütertransport AG. The money trail seemed to end at a bank on Marian Platz in München. Angela also presented a detailed report on the murder of the two customs officials.

"Okay, Angela, I think it's now time to act. I will issue you with the warrants required to examine the company's financial accounts at the Munchener Assistance Bank. I fully agree that your officers should look at other overseas' trading records, in order not to attract unwarranted attention which may compromise the main investigation," cautioned Janzyke as he walked back to his desk to sign the necessary papers.

****

That Friday, at four o'clock in the afternoon, the unit from Pullach was at the bank, ready to carry out an audit.

"Wait here, guys, while I talk to the manager," said Detlef to his team in the crew bus. Stepping out of the vehicle, he walked towards the main entrance of the bank.

"Good day, I am Detective Chief Inspector Schmitt. May I speak with the manager?" asked Detlef, presenting his warrant card to the receptionist at the front desk; reaching for the telephone she dialled a number which was answered at the other end.

Some minutes later, a well-dressed man walked over from the elevator. He was a tall person, of light build, with a feminine appearance and long, slender fingers. He gave Schmitt the impression that he may, perhaps, have been a pianist. His clothes were expensive, of a fine Italian cut and styling, which were fitting for a person who enjoyed the trappings of his position.

"Good afternoon, Herr Schmitt, I believe you wish to see me? My name is Eugen Köhler, manager of the Munchener Assistance Bank Group," he said, shaking Schmitt's hand.

"Herr Köhler, I am here on official business. Is there somewhere we can talk in private?" enquired the inspector.

Using the elevator, Schmitt was taken up to the eighth floor, arriving at a well-appointed, bright, airy office with modern furnishings and sizeable windows that offered a panoramic view of the city. Schmitt noticed a large portrait adorning one of the walls. It was of an elderly, but handsome, man, with striking blue eyes, dressed in a graduation outfit. There was also a slightly smaller picture of a large family gathering.

The manager strolled over to his desk, offering Schmitt a seat opposite him.

"How may I be of assistance, Detective?" he enquired.

"Herr Köhler, I have a warrant, issued by the finance courts, pursuant to Section 261 of the Criminal Code covering money laundering; this includes the disguising or false accounting of illegal assets. My detectives will be carrying out a routine audit on accounts held within your bank, namely those with overseas trading transactions," explained Schmitt.

Köhler studied the warrant for a few minutes before replying.

"I'm sorry, there must be some mistake, Herr Schmitt. There have been no irregularities or crimes reported so I am at a loss as to why your department has decided to visit us."

"My team will be making an immediate start with the examination of your bank's records."

Köhler sank back in his chair, his face drawn, trying to take in what he had just heard. He quickly tried to gain control of the situation.

"Herr Schmitt, this bank has been in existence since the early nineteen hundreds. We are a well-respected lending institution, closely monitored by the financial regulatory authority and we have never had any reason to be audited. Whatever information you require can be sourced by my personnel," he countered, in a dismissive tone, as he called his secretary to come in.

Detlef took several long, deep breaths before he spoke again.

"Herr Köhler, cancel the secretary. We can do this the hard way or the easy way. I can walk my uniformed staff straight through the front door of your bank. Alternatively, with your co-operation, they will discreetly use the rear entrance of the premises. An audit will be carried out, without assistance from your employees. We will start now and, depending on how long it takes, we should be out of here by, let's say…. Sunday night at the latest."

Schmitt casually looked around the office while Köhler came to a decision.

The manager stared at his desk for a moment, trying to think of a solution that would stall the detective.

"Herr Schmitt, I must make a call to our CEO."

"Of course, you must, but put it on loudspeaker, please."

Köhler lifted the handset and dialled the number; the call went through immediately.

"Father, I have a Detective Chief Inspector Schmitt from German counter intelligence here. I have been ordered to have the call placed on loudspeaker. He has a warrant from the finance courts, granting him permission to carry out an inspection of overseas accounts held within our bank."

"Eugen," replied the man, in a soft, but aggressive voice, "tell this person and his people to get out of my bank! They have no authority to be there. Let the solicitors...."

Schmitt brusquely interrupted the exchange between the CEO and his son.

"Good day, Herr Köhler, my name is Detective Chief Inspector Schmitt. As I have already explained to your son, under Section 261 of the Criminal Code covering money laundering and the concealment of illegal assets, I am instructed by the Federal finance courts to conduct an audit on accounts held within your bank. The matter is not up for discussion. My people will move in within the next ten minutes. We will be examining random companies and any documentation that merits further investigation with, or without, your approval. Should you or any member of your staff refuse my people access to your records, I will not hesitate in charging you or them with obstruction. Do I make myself clear?"

There was an uneasy silence before Herr Köhler senior, ignoring the detective's question, spoke to his son once again.

"Eugen, please assist Herr Schmitt, whatever his requirements are. Have the relevant employee stay with each officer until the audit is complete. Please call with me when they have left. When you have a moment, speak with the janitor. Ask him what the problem is with the air conditioning and how long it will take to fix. Good day, Herr Schmitt," said the bank owner, abruptly ending the conversation.

During the tense exchange, Schmitt had got up from the chair and walked over to the window, idly looking out over the vista. The manager nervously returned the handset to the cradle, having been ignominiously dismissed. Schmitt could see by Köhler's manner that he was visibly shaken and seemed to be in fear of his father.

"Herr Köhler, is there a problem with the building's utilities that will hinder our investigation?" asked the detective whilst viewing the city.

"No….no…. we are to upgrade our ducting system next week," replied the manager, to change the subject.

"Good, that's cleared that matter up. With no further delays, you are to make available both the electronic and paper files of every customer. This will enable us to be as swift as possible with our inquiry and we will be out of your hair in no time. Tell your workforce to enjoy their weekend; we won't need chaperoning…. Just as a matter of interest, Herr Köhler, how come you have such a delightful garden in this jungle of high rise buildings?" asked Schmitt as he admired the small plot at the rear of the bank.

The beautifully manicured lawn was laid out in a pear shape, bordered with flowers and foliage. Three ornate, wooden benches provided a rest area. At the far end of the garden stood a tall maple tree and, adjacent to it, a Japanese-style pagoda with a swinging seat.

"Oh…. well…. I have never really given it much thought, Detective. It's my father's little oasis," explained Köhler, now feeling calmer. "He works here two days a week, keeping a close watch on the group's activities. Summer or winter, he can be found sitting under the maple tree. It provides him with *"a clear perspective on life",* as he would put it. I have asked him, on many occasions, to use the land to build on. It could provide the bank with more, much-needed workspace, but alas, any discussion on the subject has always been dismissed. Father is adamant that our employees should use it for recreational purposes, to escape the pressures of their jobs. I think it was an admirable and thoughtful action on his behalf."

Still with his back to Köhler, Schmitt made no reply and continued to take in the view of the München skyline before suddenly leaving to brief his officers. He had endured the bank official for long enough.

****

The team of investigators parked the van in the staff car park and unloaded their equipment. Most of the weekend was spent going through any financial records linked to their inquiries. The records were in both paper and electronic format, dating back to 1971.The hard copy information was stored on mezzanine shelving and the electronic data on a large, central server in an annex off to the left of the main vault room. The detectives also noted the vast number of safe deposit boxes, fixed to three of the four walls of the bank's treasury.

Schmitt called the audit to an end around seven o'clock on Sunday evening. The officers loaded the van with the computer printouts of financial records that had been examined and, as the caretaker began locking up behind them, Detlef quizzed the man regarding the repairs to be made to the bank's air conditioning system.

"I'm very sorry, sir, I haven't a clue what Herr Köhler is taking about. The system's working fine," the janitor replied.

Schmitt shook his head and climbed into the crew bus. The team wearily headed back to the office at Pullach.

****

Eugen Kohler, as instructed, stopped by the family home on Monday evening, after leaving the bank. He was welcomed in by the butler before being led through to his father's study. Eugen mustered as much courage as possible before walking in.

"Good evening, Papa. How are you?" asked the son as he tried to keep the momentum going; otherwise, he would fall apart. "As you requested, I spoke with Tomas regarding the audit and he has assured me that it is a routine enquiry. They are carried out, from time to time, on banks with international clientele. He promised to make a few more phone calls to ascertain why we have been singled out. The police were quite thorough with the audit and have taken copies of documents away. I know you wanted our employees to remain with the investigators at all times but…."

The nervous twitching began as the young man laboured in his delivery.

"It…. it was impossible. I…. I…. don't know what records they took as Herr Schmitt instructed me to send all members of staff home," stuttered Eugen.

Curt Köhler sat bolt upright on hearing the news. The veins in his temples were now bulging at the thought of the bank's control being undermined by outsiders.

Eugen knew what was coming next. He hoped his mother was not at home. Perhaps she was in town, shopping. He had not seen the white Karmann Ghia in the driveway as he parked his Porsche Carrera.

"Are you some form of imbecile?" roared his father. "No

documents should have been removed from my bank unless you knew their contents! Now, neither you nor I have a clue what these people have taken. Damn it, Eugen, I brought you up to behave better than some local council worker that couldn't care less, as long as he's paid on a Friday evening!" he bellowed, continuing the verbal onslaught.

Eugen was now shifting from one foot to the other as he stood in front of the elderly man. He was wringing his hands behind his back, as had happened since his childhood when he had done something to displease his father.

"But, Papa!" he argued. "They had a warrant, signed by Judge Janzyke of the Finance Court. It authorised them to seize any documents they wished. I…."

"Shut up, moron! You were clearly told to have staff with them always, weren't you? At least we would have had an idea of what they took, you bloody fool. Now we don't know if it is routine or if they are checking out one of our customers who has been up to no good and that could be any one of them, given their backgrounds! Do you ever use that brain of yours?"

Curt Köhler's face was crimson with rage as he slammed his fist down on the table, disturbing the nearby paperwork.

"That's enough, Curt!" interrupted Frieda Köhler, hurrying into the room to defend her child. Her hasty entrance caused the study door to strike the oak-panelled wall. "In case you have forgotten, that is our son you are talking to, not one of your servants. What on earth is going on?" she enquired as she reached out to hold Eugen's trembling hand whilst removing her scarf.

"Get out, woman, and leave this to me! I have warned you before not to interfere in matters relating to work. This is none of your damn business!" yelled Köhler.

Her husband rose from his desk and walked across the room. He held open the door to the study, an indication that his wife should leave immediately.

Frieda momentarily stood her ground.

"It is my business where my children are concerned. Eugen is your son; don't ever forget that he's the only one you have now. Treat him with the respect he deserves!" shouted Frieda into her husband's face, in as strong a voice as she could call forth before fleeing from the study in tears.

When Eugen's mother had left them, the door to the study was closed firmly behind her before Köhler walked over to the young man and whispered into his ear.

"Have you been dabbling in something you shouldn't have, boy? Don't lie to me; I'm going in to work tomorrow and I'll soon find out if you have been!"

The man pondered for a moment as he walked back to his desk and sat down. Why, after all these years, had they decided to audit the bank now? That thought deeply vexed Köhler.

"No I have not," replied his son, "and I take exception to that allegation! And why must you treat Mother so harshly?"

His father fixed him with a steely glare.

"Your mother should know better than to interfere in affairs that don't concern her. Damn it, this is a complete outrage!" he barked. "Civil servants coming into my bank to tell me what they are going to do? Speak to me later, if you uncover anything that may shed some light as to what these people are up to."

Eugen's voice was barely audible.

"Father, please understand, I could do no more. Detective Schmitt would not take no for an answer during the implementation of the audit."

"No one is going to interfere with my group," replied the old man, in a menacing tone. "One more thing, Eugen. I hope, for your sake, that you have not been up to any shady dealings which have compromised either me or my bank. Now, get out of my sight and close the door behind you; I want some peace and quiet."

Seated at his desk once more, he continued to process the correspondence he had been interrupted from completing earlier.

As he closed the door to his father's study, Eugen heard his mother softly weeping in the lounge. He went and sat with her for half an hour before he left, making his way back to his penthouse apartment in the west of the city.

When his partner, Ralph Lutemeyer, returned home, he found Eugen in the bedroom, sobbing hysterically into a pillow. Once his father carried out his own audit, Eugen knew that it would all be over. Father would surely uncover what he had done.

"What's the matter?" questioned Ralph, cradling his partner in his arms.

"I should never have let you talk me into this, Ralph!"

"Into what? What's happened?"

Köhler recounted the events of the previous weekend. Ralph had been away on business, working as a security consultant.

"It will be fine," Lutemeyer reassured him.

"Fine? How can you say that? I begged you to either reduce or stop bringing the cash into the bank. I wasn't happy with the arrangement in the first place. It would only take something to happen outside for an arrogant pig of a detective like Schmitt to arrive at our door, demanding we open our books."

"Who?" asked Lutemeyer, trying to comprehend what had been said. "What did he look like.... this detective?"

"Tall, blond hair, blue eyes and perfect teeth," replied Köhler.

"Where was he from?"

"I'm not sure.... North Germany, perhaps. He was well spoken."

Lutemeyer thought for a moment, then asked, "Counter intelligence, did you say?"

"Yes," replied his partner, dabbing the tears from his eyes. "Why do you ask?"

"No reason, just curious that's all," replied a very interested Lutemeyer. "Listen, forget about all this; let's eat out tonight and catch a show. Worry when there is something to worry about."

Lutemeyer placed a jacket around Eugen's shoulders and steered him in the direction of the door.

CHAPTER EIGHT

Some weeks later, Schmitt informed his team that Officer Hübel had sent him a copy of the Customs and Excise internal investigation file. Having read the report, Schmitt's initial assessment was that, on the surface, Officer Friedel seemed to be a conscientious member of staff.

"Friedel was seen by his colleagues as industrious but rather dull. The man was hardly a spendthrift; he rented a tiny apartment, owned a ten-year-old Opel Kadett and had led his co-workers to believe that he spent his holidays in Tyrol. This, we now know, is not the case. Friedel was a frequent visitor to his time-share villa in Marbella, his flights to Spain departing from Innsbruck, Austria. It appears that he had also been enjoying the services of Eastern Bloc call girls who are controlled by a Croat, by the name of Dubravko Huzjak. Over the years, Huzjak has been linked to many crimes but has only served one prison term, for a road rage incident."

"Could I just stop you there, Detlef?" interrupted Muller. "Jürgen, wasn't your grass in touch with this guy regarding some sort of delivery?"

"No," Jürgen answered, "the name we've got is Goran Knezevic. There is still a lot of phone chatter but we've been unable to gather any further information concerning the suspect."

"Carry on, Detlef!" instructed Wenzel who had just walked in to the room; she seemed to be out of breath.

"Customs Officer Markus Fischer, who first reported the smuggling scam, has been totally vindicated; he played no part in this crime. Fischer is a dependable employee and a family man with a modest lifestyle. He holidays in Italy with his wife and two children in their caravan. He has two thousand marks in the bank, a life insurance policy and a three-year loan on a four-year-old Audi 80. That's the current position of the case," concluded Schmitt.

"Has anyone any further information or a viewpoint they wish to express?" queried Wenzel.

"May I?" asked Lang in a rhetorical manner.

Wenzel signalled for him to begin.

"We are currently trawling through the financial reports of Kaolin Gütertransport which make for interesting reading. Their operational profits are very high; the rates charged for both delivery and storage are unbelievable. Freight traffic has increased by seventy per cent but there appears to have been no increase in fleet size. On paper, the company seems to have taken on a lot of subcontractors, although we have not yet established if the vehicles are fictional as they are foreign registered. Consequently, it will take time to analyse the information. The business has also seen a significant rise in fuel costs, and invoices indicate that they have doubled their distribution of petroleum products to independent retailers," explained Lang.

"Peter, take whatever resources you need and check it out. No company turns itself around in such a short period of time doing things by the book, in this current climate. Detlef, what's your opinion on the whole operation to date?" asked Wenzel.

Making himself more comfortable in the chair, Schmitt outlined his analysis of the case so far.

"There is more to this than just tax evasion, Angela. Professional hits don't come cheap. Why would someone put out a contract to have

86

a pair of corrupt officials whacked? Something else is being covered up."

Schmitt emptied the last of a packet of roasted cashews into his hand.

"Whatever it is that's going on," announced Wenzel, "get to the bottom of it, people. There are two dead Government officials on our patch, killed in suspicious circumstances, and we have been left holding the parcel. The prosecutor wants answers urgently. This meeting is over."

Detlef remained behind for a while after the others had left the room. Every time he thought they were making progress, something knocked the whole investigation back. It reminded him of the old set of Russian Matryoshka dolls that Amélie had bought for Erhard at the Saturday flea market two weeks earlier; open one doll and another appears.

****

"Angela, the finance minister is on line one," said the receptionist as Wenzel entered her office.

"Thanks. Put him through, please," replied Wenzel. "Good morning, Commissar Wenzel, Bundeskriminalamt, speaking. How may I assist you, Minister?"

"Good morning, Frau Wenzel. Herr Kampfle here, calling from Palais Schaumburg, Bonn. I believe your department is currently involved in an audit of the Munchener Assistance Bank on Marian Platz?"

"I am not at liberty to discuss individual cases, Herr Kampfle."

"Yes.... I fully understand and I would not dream of asking leading questions, Frau Wenzel. Is there any particular reason why this bank was chosen?"

"None whatsoever, Minister. I am sure you are aware of the revised anti-terrorist and money laundering directive?"

"Of course, I am!" answered the finance minister tersely.

"Well then, you must be familiar with the process. It states that all banks involved in international trade are subject to inspection without prior notice."

"I would like to know how many other banks have been inspected."

"With the greatest of respect, I refuse to answer that question. You and I are public servants and, as such, we must be impartial. This office is autonomous. The investigations we carry out are confidential; we are accountable only to the offices of the Department of Justice. I will not have our integrity tarnished, or compromised, through outside interference."

"I don't very much care for your tone, Frau Wenzel," replied the minister, annoyed at the lack of co-operation.

"May I enquire as to the significance of this, or any other inspection we may be involved in, to your department?"

"I merely wanted to confirm if the inspection was ongoing as there is some concern that the reputation of the bank could easily be damaged, through ill-founded rumours. Thank you for your time, Commissar Wenzel. I would appreciate it if you could keep me posted on your department's progress."

"As I have already stated, our enquiries are confidential, Minister Kampfle. Good afternoon," replied Angela, putting an end to the conversation.

Wenzel hung up the phone and immediately placed another call.

She heard the phone ring five times before being answered.

"Janzyke."

"Hi, Paweł, thanks for taking my call."

"How can I help you, Angela?"

"I've just had an interesting phone call from Bonn."

"Oh, really? And are they promoting you? Do you want a reference, Angela?" teased the judge.

"Don't be silly, Paweł! It seems that our current auditing of the Munchener Assistance Bank records has come to the attention of the Bundes finance minister."

Wenzel rewound the Grundig recording device on her desk to allow Janzyke to hear her altercation with Kampfle.

"What has the case got to do with him? It's absolutely none of his business!"

"I don't know. He was very interested to learn what the department was doing and what stage the review was at. He is well acquainted with current EU laws; we are obliged to target any bank in Germany that has international trade connections. I'm not happy about this, Paweł. I was not appointed to this position to divulge confidential information to meddlesome ministers. What concerns me most though is why he inquired about the case in the first place."

The phone went silent as the judge gave the matter some thought.

"I can't answer that at the moment but, in the meantime, I'll have one of my researchers look into our friend's dealings to see if we can determine a reason for his sudden interest in the investigation. It's a bit strange, to say the least, for a man in his position to interfere in the affairs of another Government department. Keep me informed of any further developments, Angela."

"Thanks for your input, Paweł. I'll be in touch."

****

"So, you finally decided to come home then?" teased Amélie as Schmitt arrived back following a weekend security meeting in Berlin. "Your son has been missing you!"

"And I've missed you both; it's a pity they didn't hold the briefing at Pullach."

"Never mind, you're here now. I thought we could all go to the open-air market for the week's shopping? Perhaps have a look around some of the stores?"

"Must we?"

Detlef just wanted to hit the sack. He felt drained and was annoyed that Wenzel had sent him to Berlin in the first place.

"There are other things in life besides your work!"

"I know, love. Sorry, I'm a little ratty."

"We need a few items for the apartment and I would really like your opinion. I hate having to make all the decisions but you're never here long enough to help out."

"I appreciate that I haven't been around as much as you would have liked, dear," said Detlef as he walked over and put his arms around her; he held her tightly, smelling the pleasant scent of her freshly washed hair. "Let me have a bit of a rest and a shower and I'll be a new man."

"I don't want a new man, I just want you."

She kissed him tenderly, the pressure on her beginning to subside.

"I'll go and look in on the little guy first."

These last few weeks, Amélie had seemed different, distant

perhaps. As he leaned over his sleeping child's cot, Detlef wondered if the move to München had been too much for her. She had wholeheartedly supported him when he applied for the post but, with the arrival of Erhard, their lives had been turned upside down.

After a few hours' sleep, Detlef took his family into town for the afternoon. It was a bit of a break from the everyday hustle and bustle of their busy lives. Erhard was in his pushchair, sporting denim dungaree shorts - which revealed two chubby little knees - and a matching sunhat, set at a jaunty angle.

The family used the subway; Schmitt watched the tunnel walls speed by, the carriages gently rocking from side to side. He gazed affectionately at his son who, in turn, was gazing at the little mobile attached to the stroller's hood. Amélie squeezed Detlef's hand just as the train came to a halt at their stop. They caught a tram to Isartplatz and, from there, they walked to a department store that a neighbour had recommended.

Amélie looked through the various displays for a large set of cutlery and place mats that she needed when entertaining guests. A sales assistant found the perfect set and informed Amélie that although it was temporarily out of stock, a delivery was due shortly. The couple decided to pay for the goods in advance and collect them when they arrived.

As they boarded the tram to go home, Detlef gave his partner a wry smile.

"Who's picking up the order then?" he asked.

"You know what side your bread is buttered, mister!" replied Amélie, pecking him on the cheek.

****

Curt Köhler had been working in his office at the bank on Marian Platz when there was a disturbance outside the door.

"Tomas…. please…. you mustn't go in!" pleaded Eugen as the finance minister forced his way past him. Eugen Köhler had been very busy since the police raid, trying to stay one step ahead of his father as he attempted to cover up the large deposits that he had been personally clearing through the bank for Kaolin Gütertransport.

"It's all right, Eugen, you can leave now. Please, sit down, Tomas, I've been expecting you," said the bank's CEO.

"Why haven't you returned any of my calls, Curt? I've left numerous messages with your secretary. My position in Government has enabled me to act as – how would one put it? – your guardian angel. Now, because of contacting Commissar Wenzel on your behalf, I have been summoned to a meeting with Judge Janzyke at the finance courts next week," fumed the irate minister.

Herr Kampfle had not been getting much sleep lately. He was the person Curt had been referring to when he had asked his son to speak with the janitor during the police audit. Due to a long-standing agreement, Kampfle had been obliged to make the call to Pullach.

"I am more than aware of that, Tomas," said Köhler blankly, drawing on the cigar he had just lit.

"You know? How do you know? The matter is supposed to be confidential!"

"The duty editor of our leading morning paper, the Bavaria Echo, called me. His current affairs department has received information which draws attention to the hypocrisy shown by a certain finance minister in his own tax dealings. He wanted to know if we should run it as a front-page story," Köhler replied frostily as he watched the blood drain from the minister's face. Tomas would never be the man his father was; he was just the result of an ill-advised workplace affair.

"I'm not here to play charades, Curt. Run what, exactly?" asked the minister guardedly.

"Run a story highlighting the fact that you have been a greedy, stupid prick. It appears you have been avoiding your tax obligations, my friend. You thought that by using a UK-registered shell company no one would ever discover your murky little secret, didn't you, Tomas? Did you honestly think that little offshore account would keep you immune from the Federal tax authority here?" challenged Köhler, snapping closed a file he had been reading.

"Where did you get that information from? Let me see those papers! Are you trying to blackmail me?"

"Coercion is not my style, Tomas. I was gifted the dossier, let's leave it at that."

"Curt, your son's questionable management has probably got us into this mess; don't try and place the blame at my door! Perhaps this situation would not have occurred if you had taken care of the boy, rather than spending your time in the company of whores."

"Tomas.... Tomas, old friend, my private life is of no concern of yours! You were supposed to carry on where your dear father left off, protecting my group from prying eyes. To date, you have failed miserably! I will advise the editor to hold off exposing your pathetic attempt at tax evasion for now. Be assured though, you had better bring the investigation of my bank to an end pretty damn quick or the story will take on a life of its own. From a financial perspective, I won't have some other daily taking a march on my newspapers by breaking the story first."

Unbeknown to him, Judge Janzyke had given authorisation for the information on Minister Kampfle to be leaked to a journalist from Köhler's newsgroup, the unsuspecting reporter eager for a front-page exposé.

****

The morning case conference began at eight o'clock sharp. Schmitt was chairing the meeting as Wenzel was away on business. Detlef had been working through reports and documentation regarding the investigation the previous week. He had put the information in a sequenced order, hoping that perhaps the team might see something he had not.

"There seems to have been more money lodged than first anticipated," he announced. "Kaolin Gütertransport has been sending out exorbitant invoices for logistics services and they are being paid by bogus companies. Who buys three thousand alloy wheels for their trucks but doesn't use them, instead selling them at an inflated price? Claudia, what have you got?"

"The raid on the logistics headquarters has been receiving a lot of chatter on the phones we have been monitoring," replied Reinhold. "They are pleased that the company has been allowed to return to normal, for the sake of the law-abiding staff. However, they are really pissed off with Judge Janzyke that their financial assets have been blocked at the Munchener Assistance Bank."

"Their accounts are frozen and rightly so. Do they think they can have their cake and eat it?" interjected Detlef.

"There has been no talk about the shooter," continued Reinhold. "It could have been on a need to know basis."

"Okay, concentrate on the milk operation for the moment,"

ordered Schmitt as he began to bring the meeting to a close. "One more thing; intelligence indicates that four of Kaolin Gütertransport's milk delivery vehicles are currently in for routine maintenance with their local dealer. I have arranged for our people to take part in a bit of breaking and entering tonight. They will fit electronic tracking devices and, by tomorrow morning, we should have live satellite data coming through of the vehicles' movements. Crack on, everyone; we need to bring something big to the table."

Schmitt went back to work at his desk where he began analysing new information that had come in. After a few hours, he finally called it a day and left to go home. As he was driving, his mobile phone rang.

"Hi, sweetie," said Amélie as she peeled potatoes for dinner, whilst holding the phone to her ear. "The new cutlery and place mats have just arrived so I need you to call into the store in town to collect them. If you remember, we have already paid for the order."

Schmitt looked at the carphone, laughing.

"You mean I've paid for them and now I have to collect them as well!" he quipped.

"You're a star, honey!"

The call was ended and Debussy's *Clair de Lune* resumed playing on the car stereo.

Schmitt soon arrived at the Baaderstraße multistorey car park in the city centre. Low on fuel, he filled the car with petrol before parking in the only available space on the top floor. He hurriedly made his way towards the store on Isartplatz. The shop assistant was more than helpful with the order; so, strong were her advances that, had Schmitt been inclined, a date could have been arranged.

Having collected Amélie's order, Schmitt climbed up the

concrete staircase and exited the fire door to where his Quattro coupé was parked. Looking for the keys, he briefly glimpsed a figure behind him before he felt a sharp pain piercing his left arm. The place mats fell to the ground.

The adrenalin began to kick in. Schmitt quickly spun around as the assailant came at him again with what looked like a ten-centimetre blade. He managed to block the succession of lunges, using the box of cutlery. Hitting out, Schmitt struck his aggressor on the temple, causing him to momentarily lose his balance; he quickly recovered before continuing with the assault. Schmitt repeatedly hit the man in the face until he began to sway. Then, slipping on the scattered place mats, he lost his footing and fell back, towards the steel parapet. As a result of his weight bearing down on it, the rusty guardrail gave way and the attacker dropped his knife, unsuccessfully making a last-ditch effort to save himself before plummeting off the building.

Exhausted, Schmitt collapsed against one of the car park's support columns. When he looked up, an elderly couple were kneeling beside him.

"Are you okay, son?" enquired the man. Having witnessed the assault, he and his wife had hurried to assist the officer in whatever way they could.

"Please stay where you are. We have phoned the police," said the lady as she gently held on to Schmitt, pressing her handkerchief to his wound to stop the bleeding which had already left a small trail in the car park.

Schmitt was in shock. What had just happened? One minute he was walking to the car, the next he was fighting off some madman wielding a knife. He tried to gather his thoughts as he lay, propped against the concrete beam, the old lady now stemming the flow of blood with her scarf. What puzzled Detlef was that the attacker had said nothing. He didn't ask for money or the keys to the car, he just carried on with the frenzied onslaught.

The police arrived on the scene five minutes later, accompanied by an ambulance crew. The medical team treated the detective at the scene before transporting him to hospital. The police officers took statements from the couple and from Schmitt as to what had occurred. Whilst the crime scene officers processed the area, they also took Amélie's tableware as evidence.

The person who attacked Schmitt had died instantly, the moment he fell through the roof of a delivery truck that was unloading behind the car park. Fragments of the vehicle's bodywork had punctured his heart. Further enquires identified him as Ivan Zivkovic, a Yugoslavian national living illegally in Germany, in a council flat complex southeast of München. The deceased had been charged in his native land with the attempted murder of a prostitute and her mother. The charges were later withdrawn, due to suspected witness intimidation, after the mother had inexplicably retracted her statement.

****

"Take a seat, Detlef," said Wenzel, having signalled for the detective to come in as he passed by her office. "How are you feeling? You were very lucky; the blade just missed a main artery by a couple of millimetres, from what I've heard!"

"I think I felt it somewhat, Angela," he replied jokingly, although still in some pain; the wound had required ten stitches, forcing Schmitt to take a few days' sick leave. "I'm fine now, thanks."

Opening a file on her desk, the chief began to update him on the incident in the car park.

"Initial police enquiries have suggested that the attack was a case of opportunistic robbery with a fatal twist. They believe the assailant was most likely looking for a car and money. Due to Zivkovic being a foreign national, his poor language skills may have exacerbated the situation."

"But that's just the point, Angela; he did not speak at all!"

Wenzel gave Schmitt's comment some consideration before continuing.

"A mobile phone, fifteen hundred Deutsche Marks, two grams of herbal cannabis and various SIM cards were found on the body. Since the preliminary enquiry, Muller has been checking the deceased's phone records. A lot of the numbers match those uncovered during the ongoing Bosnian investigation. He is still processing the current and deleted text messages on the assailant's phone."

"Do you think there is a connection, then?"

"It's a possibility, Detlef. However, given the number of immigrants in the city, it could have been just a random mugging, someone looking that little bit extra for their next fix. Zivkovic may well have been off his head, as he appeared to be a cannabis user. I'm waiting on the toxicology report, as we speak."

"Okay, Angela, thanks for bringing me up to date. I'm a bit pushed for time as Eugen Köhler is waiting downstairs with his brief. I'd better get a move on."

****

Eugen Köhler had been formally summoned to Pullach, to be interviewed by Schmitt and Peter Lang, who was in charge of the financial crime unit. Having studied the bank's own accounts for Kaolin Gütertransport, it was found that money was coming in from different companies, both at home and abroad.

"Herr Köhler, Herr Schäfer, thank you both for coming here today," said Schmitt. "Herr Schäfer, as your client's legal representative, I have to inform you that Herr Köhler is not under caution, yet, but may be arrested at any time."

"My client," the solicitor replied, "is here to assist the authorities in clearing up any misunderstandings they may have regarding accounting irregularities. Shall we proceed, gentlemen?"

The interview was a long, drawn-out affair, lasting six hours, with one break for client-solicitor discussion. Despite the overwhelming evidence, Köhler remained uncommunicative. He could not explain why he had failed to inform the tax authorities of the vast amounts of money being deposited into the bank. However, he did acknowledge that what he had done was in contravention of EU legislation regarding money laundering.

Köhler understood the gravity of the situation. His signature and fingerprints were present on each and every document and cash lodgement he had illegally processed. He was at a loss as to how he was going to get out of this predicament.

Eugen loved his partner so much; it was a love that consumed his every waking moment. He had never felt that way about anyone before. Yes, he had had a few brief relationships but none like this; this was real. The very threat of Ralph leaving him didn't bear thinking about. He fervently hoped that Schäfer would come up with something to get him off the hook. Meanwhile, the best he could do was to stonewall the two detectives.

"Herr Köhler, we have studied the video footage of the lodgements being made. It's the same person making the deposits each time. Who is he?" queried Lang.

"No comment," answered the banker.

"Be assured, we will identify him; with your assistance, that could be sooner rather than later."

"No comment."

"Herr Schäfer," interrupted Schmitt, exasperated by the lack of progress, "given the fact that we find your client guilty as charged, he's not doing himself any favours at the moment. There are no fingerprints, other than his, on the lodgement slips. If Herr Köhler gives us the identity of the courier, we can lessen the charges to aiding and abetting. Otherwise, he is going down for it all."

In a hushed tone, the solicitor discussed the detective's ultimatum with his client.

"Herr Schmitt," announced the lawyer, "I have advised Eugen that it is in his best interests to co-operate but, alas, he feels that he has nothing further to add to this matter."

Detlef had had enough; there were other matters requiring his attention. A prison stint might make the banker more compliant, he thought.

"Herr Köhler.... please stand up," ordered Schmitt as he abruptly kicked back the chair on which he had been sitting and got to his feet. "Eugen Leopold Köhler, you are hereby charged with assisting others to launder the proceeds of crime through your financial institution. In addition, you failed to notify the tax authorities of cash deposits in excess of ten thousand Deutsche Marks that you processed. You are also being charged with perverting the course of justice by wilful obstruction of our investigation, in view of your lack of co-operation during questioning."

"Herr Schmitt, this is utterly absurd!" Köhler argued.

"Eugen Köhler," said Schmitt, "you do not have to say anything. However, it may harm your defence if you do not mention, when questioned, something which you later rely on in court. Anything you do say may be given in evidence. Do you understand?"

Ashen faced, the prisoner just nodded.

"Herr Schäfer," demanded Schmitt, "please ask your client, for the record, to verbally acknowledge the charges I have laid before him."

The solicitor nudged Köhler.

"Yes, Detective, I indeed understand the ludicrous charges placed before me, which I totally refute!"

"Herr Köhler, please put your hands behind your back," ordered Lang, placing him in handcuffs.

"You will be immediately transported to Stadelheim Prison where you will be kept on remand until bail has been posted. Peter, go ahead and take him away. Have a pleasant journey, Herr Köhler," the detective added scornfully.

"Herr Schmitt, I wish to apply for bail, on behalf of my client."

"Take it up with the judge at Herr Köhler's arraignment."

"Herr Schäfer, be sure to get the earliest court date available. Spending a few nights in prison won't be the end of the world, once these baseless accusations are dismissed," Köhler insisted as he was led out of the interview suite.

CHAPTER NINE

"He was a talented operative and, more than that, a very old friend, Ralph," said Dubravko Huzjak, owner of the Bon-Bon Club - a seedy nightspot off München's MarsStraße - as the sound of *Zombie* by the Cranberries filtered through the speakers of the nearby dance floor.

"Dubravko, you promised me he would be sorted! I carried out my jobs as you asked, the deliveries, tying up all the loose ends. I met my end of the bargain. You assured me you would have him dealt with, yet he's still carrying out the investigation," stated Lutemeyer contemptuously.

When his head cleared, Ralph raised himself off the floor to a sitting position; Huzjak had had enough of the German's insolence and headbutted him before he could react. Blood streamed down his face. He touched his nose gently. As he thought, the cartilage was shattered. A little dazed, Lutemeyer felt the slight vibration of the firing mechanisms as Huzjak pressed the cold muzzle of the Polish-made PW wz.33 pistol against his temple.

The ill feeling between the pair had been building for a considerable period. Lutemeyer's rapid rise within the Serbian crime syndicate had galled many long-serving lieutenants and his arrogant behaviour had generated extreme disapproval within the organisation.

They had first met in Stadelheim prison, while Lutemeyer was serving time for sexual assault. Huzjak was coming to the end of a three-year term for causing grievous bodily harm to a motorist by using a baseball bat during a road rage incident. He had warmed to his fellow inmate and had begun to use him for various tasks during the last six months of his sentence.

Upon his release, Lutemeyer had been recruited by his old cellmate and was soon used on numerous jobs, including acting as a getaway driver during bank raids. He also worked as a general courier for drug and money transactions. He particularly relished being given the order to carry out punishment beatings. His victims were tortured, sometimes having their ankles broken, if they tried to swindle the crime bosses or carry out freelance drug dealing in the area. Repeat offenders were simply bundled into a car or van and taken across the border to a remote spot - normally a dense forest - to be shot and buried.

The bar owner, already on his hunkers, grabbed him by the hair and lifted his head.

"You listen to me, you German piece of shit! Keep your fucking personal issues out of this. You're a big boy now. If you have an axe to grind, deal with it yourself, that is, if you want to keep your job here. What you failed to inform us was that the guy you wanted rubbed out was special ops trained. That omission has cost Ivan his life and I will now have to replace him. Finding someone I can trust won't be easy.... not unless.... do you want the job?"

The ex-con gingerly shook his head, as the pistol was still firmly pressed to his temple.

"No.... thought so.... now get the fuck out of my bar!" demanded Huzjak, releasing his grip on the man's hair. Using his thumb, he un-cocked the firing hammer of the pistol. Having replaced the safety catch, he tucked it into the belt in the small of his back and tossed Lutemeyer a bar towel to stop the bleeding.

"Remember, we need that money back! Concentrate your efforts on Köhler. You do whatever it takes; go talk to him in prison if you must. Just get those bloody funds transferred!" barked the Serb as he walked behind the bar and poured himself a large glass of Asbach brandy.

Ralph staggered to his feet, unsteadily making his way out of the club and into the bright sunlight of MarsStraße. He walked some distance to where his car was parked on TillyStraße. Once inside, he found a bottle of water and proceeded to clean his face of blood whilst considering his next move.

Holding the water bottle against the bridge of his nose to reduce the swelling, Lutemeyer recalled that first meeting with Eugen Köhler. Huzjak had ordered him to enter into a relationship with the banker, to coerce him to launder the vast amounts of money that had accumulated through the Serbian Mafia's criminal activities. Eugen had unexpectedly received a ticket in the mail for an all-expenses paid break in Phuket. The accompanying letter, from a reputable travel agent, informed him that he was the lucky winner of a spurious prize draw. Winning a trip to Thailand came as a complete surprise, no doubt, but he had willingly - albeit naïvely - accepted his 'prize' anyway, much to Lutemeyer's delight.

Ralph had stayed at a nearby hotel, shadowing his prey the entire time. Late one evening, Köhler had been drinking in a notorious gay bar when an Afro-American male began coming onto him. The man was exceedingly drunk and would not take no for an answer. Rather than let the situation get out of control, Lutemeyer stepped in and asked the individual not to be bothering his partner. A fight broke out, with Lutemeyer dropping the American to the floor. The police were called and both parties refused to press charges; it was put down as a catfight. The pair spent the rest of the holiday together before returning to Germany, where Ralph was invited to move in with Eugen and their relationship developed.

During a little pillow talk session, Eugen broke down and described to his lover how he had been humiliated on a night out. He had gone for a meal with friends before visiting a few clubs. Around one in the morning, he had found himself alone, at the Bon-Bon. Seated at the bar, he was nursing a Bushmills single malt when he was joined by a young man who sat down next to him and struck up a conversation. Eugen bought a few rounds and was soon the worse for wear. The next he knew, a taxi was ordered, taking the pair to a rundown hotel on BayersStraße, where he paid the night manager for a room. Sometime later, their door was kicked in and the flash of a camera partially blinded Eugen as he struggled to pull the bedding over his exposed flesh. The intruder tore the blankets away from the naked couple and continued to photograph them in the bed before hurrying out.

Ralph later found out that Huzjak had taken a call from the manager of the Bon-Bon Club. Eugen Köhler was subsequently pressured into paying the club a substantial sum of money to make the issue of having sex with an underage male go away. His wallet had been stolen during the set-up and a background check was carried out through a corrupt police contact, confirming he was who he claimed to be. Having discovered that Köhler was in the banking business, Huzjak saw an opportunity and instructed Lutemeyer to befriend him.

****

While Schmitt had been on sick leave, the forensic science officer, Heidi Konigsberg, had also been off with a sprained wrist, the result of a fall. The contents of the manila folder brought back from Schorfheide had remained unprocessed, in a filing cabinet at the laboratory, until her return.

"Hi, Detlef, have you got a moment?" Konigsberg asked as she popped her head round the door of his office.

Locking up behind him as a matter of protocol, he accompanied her to the lab in order that they could go over the results of the tests she had carried out.

"That knife attack must have been awful," sympathized the technician as she took a folder from her filing cabinet.

"Yes, it was; I'm lucky to be here to tell the tale. Anyway, enough about me, Heidi, what have you found out?"

"Well…. let me see," said Konigsberg, leafing through the folder to the relevant page. "The carbon test has confirmed that the paper is circa 1940s. It was manufactured by a company called Loeschhorn on Schadowstraße, Dusseldorf, which seems to have carried out a lot of work for the Wehrmacht. Additional chemical analysis of both the paper and ink finds them to have been used around 1941-44. I've done nothing regarding the identities in the list of names found in the folder. I'll let you sort that one out on your nights in, babysitting!"

"Please, don't remind me!" yawned Schmitt. His eyes were reminiscent of an English bloodhound, saggy and bloodshot from lack of sleep due to his young son.

Konigsberg continued with her report.

"There were three sets of fingerprints on the documents. I ran yours and von Harz's through the system to exclude them from the test."

"Given their age, I would imagine the people who handled them to be long dead, Heidi."

"I thought you might say that. Nonetheless, I did get a hit off our own computer system."

Schmitt looked up from the copy of the report he was reading.

"You are joking? A set of sixty-year-old papers and someone's fingers are still active? What were they charged with: coming back from the dead?"

"Sorry to disappoint you, Detlef; the charge was driving while under the influence of alcohol. In June 1992, police in Hannover stopped a black, 300s Mercedes car which had been weaving along the towpath adjacent to the canal in the middle of the night. They found the driver to be twice over the drink drive limit. He was half clothed and with a prostitute who was allegedly resting her tired head on his lap!" replied Konigsberg, flirting a little now.

The detective thought for a moment before eventually asking the question.

"Who was the driver.... anyone important?"

"The guy is one Herr Curt Köhler of München," Konigsberg answered with self-confidence in her voice. "He is the CEO of a large group of companies both here and abroad which includes a bank on Marian Platz where, incidentally, I do my banking."

Detlef did not reply at first. Was he hearing right; Eugen Köhler's father's fingerprints were present on sixty-year-old papers?

"Are you sure, Heidi? That makes no sense! The odds are too great for a coincidence like this to occur. It sounds like a dodgy movie plot!" argued Schmitt. "Köhler's son is already linked to money laundering for the Serbs. Now you're telling me that his father's fingerprints seem to be all over old, forgotten paperwork?"

"Well, that's not the best bit," said Konigsberg as she interrupted Schmitt's train of thought. "Having taken the contents from the old folder, I carefully emptied all of the remaining matter, including any dust particles, onto a sterile sheet. In the miniature debris field, I found an eyelash. Oh.... you should look surprised!" said Konigsberg as Schmitt felt chided, kicking himself for failing to examine the inside of the envelope more thoroughly. "Men," she continued .... "they can't control their facial expressions as well as women.... poor, dear Detlef! Anyway, I ran it through the DNA analyser and the test results have come back. It has been confirmed as belonging to Curt Köhler!"

"Is the DNA report definitive?" asked Schmitt, his excitement growing.

DNA testing was the newest and biggest advancement in the police forensics arsenal in linking someone to a crime. The forensic lab had been using it extensively, having gone for training in England.

"I can tell you're impressed, Detlef!" crowed Konigsberg. "There were various other, unidentifiable, DNA profiles found on the documents. At least three other people have handled these papers. They are either dead or not yet on our records. The only person I could positively identify was Köhler. The fact that we had his blood sample on file was a big plus. But, if we forget his previous criminal conviction for the moment, the reality of the matter is that the paperwork seems to have originated in the Reichsbank during the 1940s and Köhler did indeed handle it."

"Heidi, pinch me, please; I need to know this isn't a dream! What you're saying is that this person, if these tests are correct, and I know they are, may have sat at the hub of Hitler's war office finance machine and is living and breathing amongst us?"

"It can't get any better if it is him. But he would need a damn good explanation as to why his DNA is all over the documents. The other papers you found are also within the same timeframe, 1943-44. The bunker has me stumped though, Detlef. I first looked through the war ministry's database, which drew a blank. There were no records of the building ever existing. I then studied atlases, encyclopaedias and reference books. I found no mention anywhere of a place called the Eichhörnchen Nest, not even as a Waffen-SS special ops programme or Volkssturm weapons bunker."

Schmitt handed the lab technician a cup of water he had got from the dispenser. After taking a drink from his own cup, he voiced his thoughts on the point in question.

"I'm beginning to think it was just another one of Himmler's hair-brained projects. The blueprint could relate to anything, anywhere. It could be in the frozen wastelands of Siberia, for all we know!"

"What do you mean?"

"Just think how many blueprints Albert Speer's office produced for Hitler every time the allies bombed a factory or military installation. We could be chasing this structure, that is, if it was even built, for years to come and be no closer to the truth. Thanks for all you have done anyway, Heidi. I'm going to examine Herr Köhler's war records at the archives office in Berlin."

With this parting comment, Schmitt left the lab, taking with him copies of the Schorfheide documents and Konigsberg's report. Feeling hungry, he was about to head for the canteen when he remembered he had an urgent call to make. Schmitt returned to his office.

****

"Firma Hansmann, Grosse Tischlers," said the soft voice on the phone.

"Hi, is that Hansmann Carpentry of Dortmund?"

"Yes, Herr Hansmann senior here. How can I help you?" replied the elderly man, who was the third-generation proprietor of the business.

"I don't know if you can," said Schmitt. "I am Detective Chief Inspector Schmitt of German Counter Intelligence in München. If I were to give you a serial number, would it be possible to trace a piece of furniture your company handled and to tell who the product was sold to?"

"I can't say for certain, young man. Let me have the number and I'll see what I can do."

"The number I have is ST009723, year 1923."

"You're not asking much, are you, sir?" teased the manager. "This may take some time, given the number you have quoted. Are you sure it is correct?"

"Yes, I took it from your company's own label."

"The serial number you have given me is too old to be on our computer system. I will have to retrieve the ledger covering the numerical codes from the store. Please allow me a few minutes to source it, Herr Schmitt."

"There is no hurry, Herr Hansmann."

Detlef heard the creak of a chair as the man rose and padded off down the corridor. Not long after, the sound of quickened footsteps signalled the owner's return. A heavy item was placed on the counter and Schmitt listened as the man's old and worn fingers gently leafed through the dog-eared pages of the ledger until they found what he was looking for.

"You are in luck, sir. We still have the ledger, no thanks to the British Tommy and their RAF Lancasters! Yes, here we are. My.... do you have the bureau there beside you?" asked the old man excitedly as he read the contents of the invoice.

"No, but I have seen it and it is in excellent condition, given what it has been through," answered Schmitt.

"My.... my. Right.... okay. The information I have in front of me is for a Jean Henri Riesener reproduction writing bureau, made by my grandfather, Günter. It seems to have been sold to Monsieur Dovid Solomon, of 2 Rue Beaujon, Paris. It was delivered to him on the third of March 1923."

Schmitt wrote the details down on a blank piece of paper in the file belonging to the piece of furniture.

"Could I be so bold as to ask if the bureau is for sale?" pleaded Hansmann tentatively. "I would be very eager to purchase it, for sentimental reasons, Detective."

"I completely understand your attachment, Herr Hansmann, but I am afraid that the bureau is currently part of an enquiry in which I am involved," replied Schmitt. "I will attempt to trace the rightful owner first. Could we perhaps leave the matter at that, for the time being? Again, thank you very much for your assistance."

"At least I know one bureau has survived," said the manager. "It is the first to have surfaced in all these years, out of the nine which were made here in our carpentry shop. I should be thanking you for making an old man very happy!"

Before the call ended, Herr Hansmann asked Schmitt to keep him informed should the piece come to auction. Detlef made no promises but agreed to pass his details on to the bureau's owners, if they were traced.

****

"That's as much as I know for now, Angela," said Schmitt, over lunch in the canteen, as he concluded detailing the call he had just made.

"When do you think you will have information regarding the actual owner? The hotel proprietors were on the phone again last week, as if I haven't enough on my plate!"

"Angela, I assure you I'm working on it as quickly as I can. The minute I get a positive lead, I'll let you know."

Wenzel changed the subject as they walked back from the dining area, in the direction of her office.

"The results of the forensic tests carried out on the Reichsbank papers seem to have come up trumps, Detlef."

"Heidi has worked her magic; the findings are more than I could have hoped for, given their age."

"So, this old codger may either have been a wheeler dealer or an office cleaner in the Wehrmacht? Strange that, after all this time, an old folder that turned up in the north of Berlin, leads back to München and to a prominent businessman. He seems to have made a reputable living for himself; pity his son didn't follow his example!" Wenzel said with a jibe.

"His bail was set at a million Deutsche Marks. He's still incarcerated though, as his father won't post bail for some reason. Apparently, he blew a gasket when he found out what was going on. I don't blame the man, having worked so hard to build the business to what it is now."

"I can understand his sense of frustration. Herr Köhler senior is

112

from a bygone age, brought up to believe that honest toil brings rewards. His son, on the other hand, having enjoyed a life full of rich trappings, seems to have succumbed to greed and corruption. It can ensnare the best of us, Detlef," remarked Wenzel.

She left Schmitt in the corridor and headed for her office.

The detective strode on alone and, reaching his own office, unlocked the door. He found it frustrating that Angela always saw the glass as being half empty whenever there was some progress made with a case. Schmitt thought that identifying the bureau's original owner was a positive step forward in his investigation.

****

The counter surveillance unit had been monitoring Kaolin Gütertransport's milk tankers as they made their daily journeys. Twice a month, two of them left their normal routes, travelling to two remote properties; one, in a forested area of Waldkirchen and the other located near the town of Hauzenberg. The drivers parked up for a few hours at night before continuing on to a dairy processing plant in Passau. Both the vehicles' movements and the outbuildings had been kept under observation for several weeks. Officers also eavesdropped on the crime syndicate's business and home phone conversations. When sufficient information had been gathered, Wenzel ordered the most frequently used site to be taken down, with those found at the scene arrested and any contraband seized.

It was a damp, somewhat foggy night and intermittent rain had left the ground slippery underfoot. The task force had lain up for some time in the surrounding woodland and fields. They watched as the two lorries made their way up the lane and entered the disused barn. The main doors were then secured.

Detlef had earlier briefed all personnel taking part in the sting, ensuring that they understood their roles. He had already begun receiving feedback from the various vantage points by radio. When satisfied, he gave the signal for the ordnance team to silently edge their way forward, their mission being to provide access to the building. Once everyone was in place, Schmitt gave the codeword for the attack to commence, using the microphone strapped to his throat.

"All units, fir tree, I repeat, fir tree, move in!"

Having checked two steel side doors and finding them locked, explosive charges were positioned on them. These were then ignited, blowing the doors off their hinges and allowing the lead assault group to storm the building. Flash-bang grenades were lobbed in, taking immediate effect and disorientating the suspects. Through the haze of the gas, officers began barking instructions, which were slightly muffled by their respirators. As they came across the gang members, they were ordered to lie, face down, on the floor, their hands being secured behind their backs with cable ties.

One individual attempted to discharge his Kalashnikov but was quickly subdued with a few rounds from a Heckler & Koch MP3 machine-gun. The impact threw the man against the wall of the barn, before he slid to the ground, motionless.

"I want this area locked down!" yelled Schmitt over the noise and commotion, as those inside frantically tried to escape.

Police tactical support units began a mopping up operation, checking that the prisoners were secure before placing hoods over their heads. Word came over the radio from the surveillance helicopter above. Using thermal imaging cameras, they had observed two figures running from a small outbuilding in the direction of the nearby forest.

"All Oskar units, take down the Tangos. Over," said Schmitt, as he listened to the commentary coming through his earpiece.

Using night vision goggles, the police units began to close in on the fugitives, ordering them to lie on the ground with their hands behind their backs. The command was ignored and, within minutes, a running gun battle had erupted, yellow muzzle flashes piercing the night as shots were exchanged. The fleeing men sprinted through the forest, jumping over piles of deadwood. Stopping occasionally, they let off a salvo of bullets at their pursuers before loading fresh magazines and continuing their escape. Officers pressed themselves tightly behind large pine trees - which afforded them limited protection - and returned fire. Some of the rounds missed their intended targets, splintering tree trunks and branches. The helicopter shadowed the pair, using a powerful floodlight fixed under the fuselage, which lit up patches of the woodland below.

Schmitt hit the send button on his radio.

"Oskar 1, situation update. Over."

"Receiving high calibre, sporadic fire from hostiles. Over," replied the unit commander.

"Where are they? Are they still in the forest? Over."

"Yes, yes. They are about a hundred metres away from the meadow. Over," said the man as the cacophony of gunfire threatened to drown out their conversation.

"Oskar 1, contain them. They must not leave the operational area, I repeat, they must not leave the operational area. Do you copy? Over."

"Understood. Over and out."

After a period of cat and mouse evasion, the fugitives came to a clearing on the edge of Waldkirchen Forest. Turning in mid-flight, they, once again, opened fire on the advancing law enforcement units before being cut down by a concentrated hail of bullets. When the area was safely quarantined, Schmitt arrived to examine the scene of the shooting for himself and was briefed by the commander whose unit had engaged the two individuals. They walked over to where the corpses lay, the officer illuminating their bloodied faces with his flashlight as Schmitt took a folder from under his bulletproof vest. He began looking through a montage of police photos but none matched the deceased.

Detlef made his way back to the barn, ordering the main doors to be unlocked, which dispelled the gas created by the grenades. The detective watched as the loading hatches of the tankers were swung open. Inside, they found ropes tied to a hook which had been welded within each vessel's loading access points. Attached to the ropes were large packets, treble-wrapped in dense plastic. Once removed, a small sample of the substance contained within them was chemically tested and found to be pure cocaine. The scene was photographed, and all the evidence labelled and shipped off to a secure storage facility to be used later, during the trial. Schmitt left other officers busily processing the site and returned to Pullach, where he typed up a preliminary report of the night's events, before heading home.

CHAPTER TEN

Wenzel was studying the crime case photo montage on the wall as Schmitt entered the room.

"Good work on your drugs bust, Detlef; there were no casualties on our side. The planning obviously paid off."

"Thanks. The firefight was intense, to say the least."

"Still no word on the shooter of the customs officials?" she asked.

"No, nothing," replied Schmitt. "Any fingerprints or DNA was destroyed when the BMW was torched. A car fire was reported to the police by a member of the public who had been sleeping over at his allotment off BrudermühlStraße, in the west of München. The witness was woken by a small explosion and looked out to find a vehicle burning at the main entrance. Passing motorists saw a male crossing the carriageway, making his way to the adjacent apartments on GaißacherStraße. Unfortunately, the trail ends there. We have four lots of CCTV imagery of the route the assassin travelled but, when the lab people tried for a close-up of the suspect, the image pixelated. There is nothing concrete to identify the perpetrator."

"I know you don't like some of his methods but we need von Harz out there on the street, persuading someone to talk. A month has now passed and the relatives want to bury their dead. Furthermore, Bonn wants answers, both to these murders and to the whole Serb racketeering business."

"I think there is still a bit of mileage in Eugen Köhler."

"Well, you know where to find him, Detlef. No one's bothered to make bail for him yet."

"I think he would sooner see his skinny little ass out of Stadelheim than spend any more time locked in a cell. Given the hardened criminals in there, someone will surely make him their pillow for the night before too long."

"Just get von Harz's arse into gear and see what he can uncover. That man seems to need a cattle prod to spur him into action!"

"Okay, I take your point. I will put him on to it while I pay the little prince a visit and see how co-operative he wants to be now."

"Let's get something concrete for the suits in Bonn, Detlef. I don't need them ringing me every two minutes, moaning about what the red-tops are writing in their morning editions."

Red-tops were the local morning newspapers. They had printed exaggerated headlines, stating that Germany's law and order was out of control. Highlighting the recent murders of the customs officers and the way they were carried out, the papers were laying a challenge at the Federal government's door, in Bonn.

****

Frieda Köhler had held her counsel for long enough regarding the imprisonment of Eugen and the failure of her husband to help him. Walking into the kitchen of the family villa, she screamed, "What sort of animal are you, Curt, that lets your son rot in a common jail? Answer me, you pig! Don't think you can ignore me this time; I want Eugen out of there!" she cried as she stared into her husband's vacant gaze.

"He is not my son," replied her husband, "he is a poor excuse for a man who has besmirched the good name of the bank and all it stands for. Let those he has lain with get him out of trouble. It's of his own making after all, is it not?"

"Now, you listen to me for once; what's yours is mine. I own half of that bank and I will get my son out of that hellhole, do you hear me?"

Curt nonchalantly ate some pistachios from a bowl on the countertop.

"You're such a silly woman, always have been. You own only the clothes on your back. You don't think I would let you anywhere near the fortune I have amassed? You signed that away years ago, my dear, or have you forgotten that? The day you locked me from our marital bed…. well, you know the rest," laughed her husband as he washed his hands before putting on his overcoat.

Frieda froze, trying to comprehend what her husband had just said. She made a lunge for Curt, in an attempt to hit him. It was a futile gesture. Her husband towered above her, holding her wrist whilst mocking her feeble effort at retaliation.

"You're a beast!" shouted his wife. "An absolute beast, Curt," she repeated, backing away.

"Yes, dear, you're probably right. As you say, I'm a real beast! Anyway, the point is that you signed over to me any shares or interest you had within the group in return for the gesture of two thousand marks paid into your personal account for the rest of your natural life. So, you see, there's not much you can really do for your little runt, is there? Come, Krista, walkies!" said Curt as he sauntered out of the house towards the canal for his leisurely evening stroll with the family's Golden Retriever.

As the front door of the house closed, there was silence.

"Who have I have married?" whispered Frieda as the reality of the situation sunk in. It all started to fall into place. When she needed something, Curt would either buy it or deposit enough funds into her account; he refused her nothing. She ran upstairs to her study and unlocked the top drawer of the bureau before pulling out a series of folders. Frieda opened the one marked *Title and Deeds*.

As she studied the faded document, nausea began to rise within her. She ran to the bathroom and let it pass down the bowl. Standing at the washbasin, Frieda splashed cold water on her face. It was all true. Her husband had always looked after their correspondence and, as such, she never questioned what she was authorizing. It was there in black and white. She had signed her life's inheritance away for two thousand Deutsche Marks a month. All legal and above board. All witnessed by the family solicitor, now deceased. That night, Frieda took the sleeping pills that her doctor had prescribed for depression and went to bed early.

****

Resigned, Ralph stubbed out his cigarette and headed into the prison. Huzjak had spelled it out for him, in no uncertain terms, that he was to find a way of releasing their money from the frozen bank accounts. He had finally agreed to visit Köhler following his threats to have him evicted from the penthouse apartment. The ex-soldier was getting too old for grunt work and that billion Deutsche Mark inheritance would keep him comfortable for the rest of his life, if he could just get the son of a bitch out of jail.

Eugen was already seated behind a visitor screen.

"What's happened, Ralph?" he asked, shocked by his lover's injuries.

Lutemeyer, his face badly bruised, was wearing a heavy plaster to help correct the position of his nose, following the assault in the bar.

"Someone tried to mug me. Don't worry, it looks worse than it is; you should see the other guy! I'm sorry I haven't been to see you sooner. How are you?"

Eugen lost his composure as the tears rolled slowly down his face.

"Oh, Ralph, it's just awful! These people are animals! I've had urine thrown at me from the upper floor and some of the inmates have even groped me, making propositions of a sexual nature when we're queuing in the canteen. You must get me out before something terrible happens. I can't…. take…. much more of this!" he cried.

"Have you reported it to the warders? You need to make a complaint."

"What's the point? The guards are just as bad, turning a blind eye to all the sordid comments and behaviour."

"Has your family been in contact with you?"

"Just my mother. Father still refuses to provide the surety to the courts and those I used to call friends fail to return my calls now. Ralph, you created this damned mess; I'm begging you, please get me out of here!"

The one-time bank manager began to weep uncontrollably.

"Listen to me, Eugen," soothed Lutemeyer, panicking to keep him quiet. "Just hold tight; I have people working on this. The cops have got it all wrong. In the eyes of the law, you were just doing your job. Okay, so some paperwork was misplaced but, all in all, you're in the clear."

"Do you think so?"

"No sweat. Your father will eventually calm down. He's just old school, with his principles and all that. Leave him for a few days and he will speak with the judge," said Ralph, in a convincing manner.

Eugen's partner started to talk about what was happening in everyday life, to keep off the main subject. He said his goodbyes at the earliest opportunity and Köhler returned to his cell. Eugen gathered all his strength to face another night in prison. The wailing, shouting, and other sounds that he could make no sense of, frightened him like nothing he had ever known before in his privileged life on the outside.

Handing in his visitor pass, Lutemeyer left the prison and walked to the car park. He pulled a Camel cigarette from the packet and lit it, taking an extra-long draw to settle his nerves. Exhaling slowly, he reflected upon what it had been like inside the prison when he had served his time there. It wasn't the visiting area where the trouble lay. Oh, no, the prison cells after lights out, that's where depravity met innocence. The guards ignored, no, they simply blocked out the strange noises throughout the night. The screams and the crying were the sounds of some poor unfortunate becoming somebody's plaything or perhaps an inmate who hadn't paid his dues to those in control of a wing. One thing was crystal clear to him; Lutemeyer did remember the person who put him there and that person's days were numbered.

He came out of his daydream with a jolt. From what he had heard, Eugen's father had been so incensed that he had disowned him and, if he was left in there any longer, someone would almost certainly take a shine to him. Ralph knew that he was running out of options. The crime bosses wanted their money back and the likelihood of sharing the Köhler family fortune was gradually disappearing. It had all gone horribly wrong. No one was happy and he had been given the task of sorting it out. But how?

****

Amélie had gone into town with Erhard to do some shopping and Schmitt was at home alone, having taken a day's leave. With time on his hands, he decided to call the Bundes archives war office. Detlef asked the researcher to examine the records of anyone with the surname Gotthard, the signatory of the documents uncovered at Schorfheide. Two people with that name had enlisted in the Wehrmacht in 1939. They had both been killed during action in Russia but neither had the Christian name of Frank. At Schmitt's request, the young man also reviewed Curt Köhler's war record, given that his fingerprints were present on the Reichsbank paperwork.

Köhler's army report stated that he was born in Dresden. He left school and became a trainee bank teller in the Dresdner Bank at the age of fifteen. He joined the Wehrmacht in 1939 and was made a corporal in the 4th Panzer division a year later. Köhler spent six months in Russia during the Wehrmacht's operation Fall Blau, the taking of the industrial area of Donets Basin. His unit came under a sustained Russian counterattack and an enemy shell tore the turret off a nearby tank as he was directing operations, resulting in a deep wound to his left thigh and severe concussion. Köhler spent two months in a military hospital in Berlin. Following his discharge, he was reassigned to the Reichsfinanzministerium Wilhelmstraße, where he worked as a chauffeur.

Records showed that the corporal's entire family was among the three quarters of a million-people killed during the horrendous allied bombing of Dresden. During the last months of the war, he was sent as part of a ragtag unit to bolster existing detachments on the Western Front, in a last-ditch effort by Hitler to suppress the allied invasion.

The American 3rd Division had endured fierce fighting during their push north, finally reaching the deserted town of Neustadt. General Obstfelder's 7th army, whilst launching attacks on the advancing enemy, had started a tactical retreat eastwards. His men spent the night in Coburg before moving out at first light, as advancing US infantry entered the town centre. Köhler was badly injured during the closing stages of the battle. His medical records stated that he had suffered shrapnel wounds to his left arm during the allied assault. With his arm disabled, he had used his right hand to help feed the ammunition belt into an MG-42 machine gun. It provided its distinctive burping sound as his colleague, in long bursts, strafed the advancing enemy. Köhler's unit eventually surrendered, having been overwhelmingly surrounded by the Americans.

He was processed by the US Army war crimes investigation unit at the former concentration camp of Dachau before being sent to the Fort Regent prisoner of war camp on the island of Jersey, in the Channel Islands. The camp had opened in May 1945 to house the thousands of captured German prisoners of war. Schmitt noted, with interest, the addendum in Köhler's file: '...the subject is of low self-esteem and poses no threat due to his limited intelligence. Recommended duties: hard labour.' Köhler was imprisoned at Fort Regent for two years before being included in the denazification programme, eventually returning home to Germany.

Detlef looked at his notes in bewilderment. How did a lowly driver in the army motor pool become a billionaire? It didn't make sense.

On contacting the Bavarian state archives, Schmitt established that the lists of people found in the Reich Chancellery file had been killed in München, during the allied carpet bombing of the city in November 1943. That's that document ruled out, he thought. No point in chasing ghosts. But what was the list there for in the first place?

It was already half past three in the afternoon. Detlef decided to head downtown and meet up with Amélie and Erhard, having spent enough time researching dusty files. As he arrived in the city centre, he looked at his watch. He had ten minutes to kill.

Schmitt walked across to München's main railway station and stepped out onto the platform, just before the Nuremberg express arrived. Looking out onto the empty line, he placed himself in the turmoil of 1945. Trains were arriving from all over Europe, laden with stolen property. The station reverberated with the continual screaming of their whistles and the screeching of brakes as they reached their destination. Throughout the chaos, army officers were barking orders, trying to keep things moving. People were trying to escape the scorched earth apocalypse in which they now found themselves. It was only a matter of time before the Red Army, approaching from both the east and the south, cut their exit routes off completely. The ordinary German citizens were now hedging their bets on the Allies showing them greater mercy than the Russians ever would.

As the passengers shuffled around the detective, impatient to get home to their loved ones, Schmitt asked himself one question. *One tonne of Reich Chancellery gold and assorted currencies had sat on this platform but where did it go to?*

****

Schmitt was enjoying a chauffeur-driven ride in Herr Janzyke's limousine. The judge had requested a meeting with Herr Köhler senior at his home on Thomas-Mann-Allee in the Bogenhausen district of München and the pair would shortly be interviewing the owner of the bank at the centre of their investigation.

Janzyke had been saddened to read the newspaper report of the attack on Schmitt in the multistorey car park.

"How are you feeling, Detlef?" he enquired as the car travelled through the heavy München traffic.

"A lot better, thank you, sir. At least internal affairs have cleared me of any wrongdoing. The witness statements determined that I had acted in self-defence."

"I am glad everything has worked out for you, Detlef, and that you are now in good health."

The car made its way along the Max-Joseph Bridge and onto MauerkircherStraße, finally arriving at an imposing residence bordered by an almond-coloured wall. The driver pressed the intercom button which was recessed into the wall below a polished brass plate with the name *Sandweg* etched into it. They waited for the gates to be opened. The property was very secluded, set in mature woodland with a nearby land canal providing complete privacy. It was a nineteen thirties period house that seemed to have undergone a sympathetic restoration. The gates silently glided open and the car swept along the paved driveway up to the house. When the vehicle had stopped, the driver got out and opened the doors for Schmitt and the judge. They were greeted by a butler who led them through the house to the banker's study. Köhler was seated at his desk, dressed in casual clothes and displaying a fine tan from a recent foreign holiday.

"Gentlemen, welcome!"

Rising from his chair, he greeted the men warmly, shaking their hands.

"Please, please, take a seat. Walther, some coffee for our guests!" demanded the host as his visitors settled themselves on an Ercol studio couch.

CHAPTER ELEVEN

"Before we begin, gentlemen," declared Köhler, in an effort to take control of the meeting, "I would like to introduce Herr Kleber, my lawyer. He will address any legal issues you may have."

Using his Pfeilring cigar cutter, the banker laboured meticulously as he trimmed the end of his Upmann cigar. Having completed the task, Köhler lit it, taking a long draw before softly exhaling the smoke and allowing it to rise gently to the ceiling.

"Oh.... I do hope you don't mind me smoking? It helps me relax," he explained as he settled into a high back armchair, studying the two officials intently.

Judge Janzyke overlooked the banker's melodramatics and made the introductions. Köhler eyed the detective with disdain. Here was the specimen who had the audacity to tell him what he could and could not do in his own bank! This damn meeting should not be even be happening, he thought. The procedures that had been put in place many years ago seemed to have failed, largely due to the incompetence of that idiot, Kampfle. He had always known the man was incompetent but he was so easy to manipulate! Köhler mentally prepared himself for whatever questions the pair had for him. He was resolved to humour these people and send them on their way.

The banker was jolted out of his daydream by the judge who, having waited long enough, had decided to get the interview underway.

"Herr Köhler, please let us begin as I have other places to be today. You are not under caution and, as such, you are free to stop these proceedings at any time. Should I find your replies obstructive to the questions put before you, I will proceed in a more formal manner, placing you under an official caution. Do we understand one another?"

Both Köhler and his legal advisor nodded in acknowledgement. The CEO was now intrigued as to what these people wanted with him.

In addition to his paperwork, Janzyke had brought with him a small, silver and black, C100L Grundig tape recorder which he proceeded to place on the antique writing desk that served as Curt's place of work. He intended to record, verbatim, the entirety of the interview. This manoeuvre took both the banker and his lawyer by surprise.

"Why do you find the need to record the meeting if it is an informal interview, Herr Janzyke?" asked Kleber as his client touched his arm.

"Kleber, just go along with it, please. Let them do their job; we don't want to be accused of obstruction of due process."

The judge took out a series of papers - including a set of prepared questions - from a manila folder on the desk. Janzyke had refused Köhler's solicitor an earlier request for a copy of the questions which were to be put to his client.

"Herr Köhler, I would like your help with a few queries. You are a German National, by birth?"

"Yes."

"The date and place of birth?"

"I was born in 1922, in the city of Dresden."

"Your blood type?"

"I am blood group B."

"Could you also provide me with your national insurance number?"

The banker supplied the information requested, which - along with the other details he had given –confirmed what the judge already knew.

"Have you ever had a criminal conviction, Herr Köhler?"

The banker let out an exasperated sigh.

"Let's not beat about the bush, gentlemen," he said, beginning to lose patience with this little game. "You both know full well that I have a criminal conviction; driving whilst under the influence of alcohol, isn't that the legal definition? I was foolish enough to drive home after a dinner function. The police stopped and breathalysed me in Hannover. As a result, I lost my licence and I now have a minor criminal record. I fail to see where this questioning is going, Herr Janzyke!"

The judge disregarded the retort and pressed on while Schmitt stayed quiet, observing Köhler as a person and seeing how he reacted to the questions being put to him.

"How long have you been the primary shareholder of the Munchener Assistance Banking Group?"

Köhler's verbal jousting stopped abruptly. He quickly looked to his lawyer, who whispered that he should only provide information that was stored at Companies House records office, which anyone could have access to.

Composing himself, the banker slowly began to explain both his past and current position within the banking group.

"I was employed as deputy manager of the bank in 1947, by the owners, Helmut and Sophia Schröder, having answered a job advert when I returned to Germany after the war. As part of the terms of my employment, I was given a five per cent shareholding of the company. In return, I was required to generate a fifteen per cent growth in business each year. If I achieved this target over the next six years, I would receive an additional ten per cent shareholding. I indeed managed to do so, under very difficult trading conditions. This provided me with a total of fifteen per cent holdings in the group."

Having taken a little time to complete his notes and cross reference them with the information he had at hand, the judge continued to probe further.

"How did you come by the additional fifty per cent of shares, Herr Köhler?"

"An opportunity arose to purchase them in 1976; they belonged to Frau Schröder. The sale followed protracted, but successful, negotiations between her agent and my solicitor at the time, Herr Bräun. The purchase of these additional shares brought my overall holdings to sixty-five per cent," answered Köhler smugly as he slowly drew on his cigar before blowing the smoke into the air.

"Could you tell me who holds the remaining thirty-five per cent shareholding of your group, Herr Köhler?" asked the judge, removing his glasses and placing them on the desk.

Seeing that his client was a little uncomfortable with this last request, Köhler's lawyer decided to answer on his behalf.

"To the best of our knowledge, twenty per cent of the holdings are owned by a Swiss investment group. The rest of the shares are held by a UK registered company. However, I am not in a position to apprise you of the management makeup of the company or of its interests. Of course, all this information is readily available from Companies House but I am sure you are aware of that, Herr Janzyke!" said the lawyer arrogantly as his client nonchalantly looked on.

"You are quite correct, Herr Kleber. I can have a member of my staff investigate further, if need be," replied Janzyke, putting his glasses back on and looking directly at both Köhler and his lawyer. "One more question, Herr Köhler. Have you.... or your bank.... either wittingly.... or unwittingly.... ever been involved in any unlawful activity against the state of Germany that such an action has resulted in a financial crime being perpetrated, either in the state of Germany or in a foreign land?"

Kleber attempted to deflect the question.

"My client could not possibly answer that with any reasonable degree of accuracy. The banking group's customers are aware of the bank's code of conduct and their transactions are regularly monitored internally, as required by law. They know they are to conduct their activities in a fit and proper manner. Herr Köhler prides himself on operating a fine and upstanding institution and I must state, for the record, that he is respected throughout the industry," he argued.

"Herr Köhler, come, come," interrupted the judge, tired of the filibustering and the long drawn out answers by the solicitor, "I merely require a simple yes or no. I'll repeat the question, just for the record: have you, your group or any of your customers ever been involved in unlawful activity against the State of Germany that has resulted in a financial crime being perpetrated against it?"

"You have my son in custody," replied Köhler, in a frustrated tone, as his lawyer prepared to call the meeting to a close. "Go, speak with him. My group is clear of any involvement in the fraud he unwisely committed. The answer to your ridiculous question is a definitive no!"

"I will ask you one last time; have you, Herr Köhler, ever been involved in any unlawful activity against the State of Germany that has resulted in a financial crime being perpetrated against it?"

"Categorically, no, Herr Janzyke, I have never been involved in a financial crime against the State of Germany. I refute the very thought of the allegation!" answered Köhler as his anger reached boiling point.

Janzyke, having satisfied himself with the answers he had received, gathered up his papers and rose from his seat. Schmitt also stood up. As if on cue, the butler entered the room and swiftly escorted them out of the house and into their waiting car, without so much as a goodbye from either party.

****

"What did your guests want, Curt? Has there been news of Eugen's release?" asked Frieda anxiously as her husband came into the kitchen.

"They were two civil servants with nothing better to do with their time than come here and interfere in other people's lives," he replied.

Köhler calmly took a glass from the cupboard and poured himself some fruit juice that had been chilling in the fridge.

Frau Köhler had been observing an unspoken truce, in the hope that her husband would relent and pay the bail that would facilitate the release of their son from prison. Frieda had listened attentively to the judge's questions whilst standing silently outside the study door. Why were they interested in Curt's nationality? What crime had he committed? Was it not their son who was at the heart of this whole infernal mess?

"Why did they need to speak with you, Curt?"

"They sought reassurance that there had been no other acts of fraud perpetrated by my group."

"Had there?"

"Don't be so stupid, woman. The bank did enjoy a good reputation until Eugen decided to play banker."

"Please don't talk about him in such a disparaging manner, Curt. We must help him. Please do something, I beg of you!"

"I can't. Let the legal system take its course; it might teach him a thing or two regarding his actions."

"Don't do this, Curt," Frieda pleaded in vain as her husband ignored her pleas and returned to his study, closing the door.

Sometime later, she watched her husband leave in their chauffeur-driven Mercedes; he had taken Herr Kleber with him. Alone, once more, in the large house, she felt powerless to help her son.

****

Following a meeting, Judge Janzyke called into the Pullach office to be updated on the Serbian Mafia fraud inquiry and the case relating to the documents confiscated from the hotel near Berlin. Seated at her desk, Wenzel gave the latest information to the judge who, having put down his coffee, began toying with a piece of Battenberg cake on his plate. Pausing for a sip from her own cup gave Janzyke an opportunity to provide her with some news.

"Angela, the solicitors for the logistics company have made an application to the High Court for their funds to be returned which, given their criminal activities, will be laughed out the front door."

"And so, it should, Paweł. On another note, I've recently been informed that the Swiss authorities intercepted a non-liveried, Bacutrans-registered vehicle, heading for the Balkans with a consignment of Glocks, Heckler & Koch MP3s, ammunition and grenades with launchers. They were concealed in an assortment of used lorry parts."

"What?" Janzyke set the now disintegrating cake on the plate. "How many loads are getting through? Do you actually know?"

"The answer to your question is no, we don't. All traffic heading to the Balkans is experiencing four kilometre tailbacks. German customs' authorities are pushed to their limits with people trying to flee the area. We are monitoring the situation as best we can."

"Okay, I understand, but if there are a lot of weapons transiting our country that won't sit well with our allies in NATO!"

"Calm down, Paweł, we aren't on our own. There is a European-wide alert to inspect traffic suspected of heading for the Balkans. Our neighbouring states have also been put on full alert as reports indicate that they are making similar seizures of illegal armaments en-route to Bosnia. These thugs are trying to muscle into other countries besides ours."

Schmitt, who had remained silent throughout the exchange, spoke up.

"If I may interrupt, sir, our team has been able to bust a major drug smuggling operation, following the fitment of electronic tracking aids to Kaolin Gütertransport's dairy delivery vehicles. We seized over one tonne of cocaine which had been placed in two dairy tankers that were transporting milk to several processing plants."

"What if the drugs had contaminated the milk? Countless people could have been killed! Do we know what the total value was?" asked Janzyke.

"We estimate the street value to be in the millions. Here are some stills taken after the raid," explained Schmitt as they viewed the colour images that were displayed on the projector screen. "The target premises were being used to break the bulk cocaine consignments into manageable units for sale on the streets. We managed to net a significant number of major criminal players; some of them have been long-suspected of illegal activities and some are new to us."

Wenzel took control of the briefing once more.

"Having carried out follow up searches, we have netted a further one point three million Deutsche Marks, in cash. This is in conjunction with counterfeit cigarettes, perfume and clothing. It has been a major blow to the Serbian crime bosses."

"This has been a positive outcome for the department; well done!" exclaimed Janzyke. "Don't let up; work on those people you have arrested. I can assure you that I will not be lenient when I have the culprits before me in my chambers."

Wenzel thanked the judge for his words of encouragement and began winding up the briefing.

"We are still sifting through the evidence gathered in the subsequent raids, Paweł. We do expect to make further seizures and arrests in the coming days. However, time is against us. We need to act quickly on the leads we have secured, to catch those who orchestrated the whole operation."

The judge rose from his seat and went out to the crime room, where he thanked the team for their efforts. He also thanked Schmitt personally, for his instinctive approach to cracking the drug smuggling ring.

"Angela, could you arrange a press conference, say.... two o'clock, tomorrow? I feel we must send out a clear message to these people that Germany is not and will not become a safe-haven for them. Good work, everyone," added the judge.

As Schmitt was clearing his desk to go home, he received a phone call from Frau Köhler, requesting a meeting at the Hotel Vier Jahreszeiten, on MaximillianStraße, the following week. She would not reveal the nature of the invitation, only saying that she felt it important that they should meet up. Detlef decided to bring Claudia Reinhold with him to provide female support. If the case was extremely delicate, he did not want to cause undue stress to the elderly lady.

****

It was a calm, still morning. Just after 7.35 a.m., a blast shook the neighbourhood of Nymphenberg, on the outskirts of München, where the residents of MenzingerStraße had been busy preparing for work or to take their children to school. The rear windows of the large, white mansion were blown out of the building, allowing the flames from the fire that erupted to extend from their voids. The pagers of Wenzel and her team sounded, minutes after the blast occurred; the state-linked security alarm had been triggered, sending a message to the local police station. The emergency services, along with the gas and electricity companies, arrived quickly. The fire authority secured the blast site and assessed the condition of the damaged structure before allowing the investigation to begin. Wenzel, Schmitt and von Harz walked up to the cordon as the details of what had taken place at Judge Janzyke's home were becoming clearer.

"What's happened? Has anyone been injured?" asked Wenzel, showing her warrant card as a senior fire officer rushed by.

"We don't know yet," he replied. "At present, the gas is being shut off so that the fire can be thoroughly extinguished. Once we deem the building is safe, you can go in."

Thinking that the judge was inside the house, Wenzel frantically called his mobile phone. He eventually answered it; he and his wife had been having breakfast in a Nuremberg hotel. The couple had gone to the theatre the previous evening to see a performance of Swan Lake. They were scheduled to return the same night but, having met some friends, they decided to make it an overnight stop.

"Angela, the gas system was checked and certified only two months ago. How could it have been faulty?"

"That's not important, Paweł. The fact that you and your wife are safe is the main thing. We will be able to make a full report once we are given access to the building."

"What time was the blast?"

"It happened shortly after 7.35 this morning; why do you ask, Paweł?"

"Has our cleaner been accounted for?"

Twenty minutes later, the chief fire officer allowed the various teams to enter the house, having put their Hazchem clothing on to avoid contamination of the site. They found the twisted body, resting against the remains of the rear French window. She still wore the Marigold gloves that she had always used when cleaning. That morning, Herr Janzyke's cleaner of twenty years had arrived at seven twenty precisely. Having found no one at home, she got on with her day-to-day routine.

The detectives walked past the corpse as it was being photographed by forensic officers. The scene in the living room was like a battle zone, with debris strewn everywhere. It was becoming clear that the seat of the blast had occurred in the downstairs bathroom. One wall was completely torn away, the blast projectiles scattered across an open plan dining and living area. Shards of wood and masonry had embedded themselves into walls, pictures, and even the large, walnut-coloured grand piano that stood majestically in the centre of the room.

Wenzel came across Stefan Weber, the police forensic officer, who was examining a small piece of plastic. He removed his mask and informed her that his team were no closer to finding out what had caused the blast. The debris would be collected as evidence and taken back to the lab for analysis. Weber had ordered that the processing of the cleaner's body take priority. Having been photographed in situ, the deceased was gently placed in a body bag and removed, without delay, for autopsy.

Schmitt left his colleagues to sift through the devastation. Zipping up his jacket under the protective clothing, he joined the forensic technicians as they combed the rear of the property for clues. The three-storey mansion, with its slate roof and inset dormer windows, sat in an acre of woodland, close to Nymphenburger Castle. It was a quiet, affluent suburb, inhabited mainly by professional people. The judge and his family had lived there, undisturbed, for twenty-two years. The detective stood in the garden and looked back towards the house. Debris littered the beautifully manicured lawn and the walls to the rear were scorched and blackened from the fire.

In his own mind, Schmitt knew that this was retaliation for the speech the judge had made a few days ago, regarding the large seizure of cocaine and criminal assets. Janzyke had vowed to rid Germany from the menace of organised crime and to take all drugs off the streets. He had promised the perpetrators that there would be no sanctuary for them, saying, *"Those involved in the sale of drugs are a scourge on society and it is my mission to drive them out of our country."*

****

Early the next morning, when Schmitt walked into the canteen, he was surprised to find Wenzel already there. She was in the middle of making toast before generously spreading thick-cut marmalade on it.

"Did you sleep here last night?" asked Schmitt, jokingly.

"I may as well have done, for all the rest I got; the neighbours' car alarm kept going off."

"I've got a confession to make, Angela."

"About?"

"The case relating to Curt Köhler's bank has been dragging a little."

"If it has, that's down to your management, is it not? What have you done now?" asked the chief, taking a seat at the table and clasping her mug of coffee tightly, the toast forgotten; suddenly she didn't feel hungry anymore.

Schmitt sat down opposite her and explained that, having failed to determine if the man was who he claimed to be, he had placed a small advert in two of Dresden's local papers. Using an anonymous box number for potential replies, he had given limited personal details regarding Curt Köhler and invited any family members to get in touch. There had been four responses. Of these, one seemed promising.

"Yet again, Detlef, you have chosen to bypass me! Don't think for a moment that our friendship allows you to skip protocol every time."

"I realise an apology won't suffice but I didn't know what else to do."

"You could have come to me first. I would probably have sanctioned the move as it was a sensible direction to take. Have you got a name for this person?" Wenzel enquired.

"Alfred Köhler. He's the Mayor of Eberswalde, a small town, north of Berlin."

"Did you call him?"

"No.... that's what I wanted to discuss with you."

"I'm pleased that you finally remembered I have some authority here."

"May I ask a member of the team to contact Herr Köhler?"

"You may, but don't allow it to obstruct the main investigation.... Now, what about the son? Has he been granted bail?"

"No. I was considering going to Stadelheim to pay him a visit. By all accounts, he's not coping too well. Missing the penthouse and his freedom, I suppose."

"Daddy mustn't want him sprung just yet," remarked Wenzel, putting on a fresh batch of coffee.

CHAPTER TWELVE

"Detectives, thank you for coming," said Frau Köhler as she needlessly smoothed out the cream linen tablecloth before getting up from her seat to shake the officers' hands. She summoned the waiter with the air of a duchess, ordering coffee and Danish pastries.

"Herr Schmitt, how is the judge and his family? I watched the incident at his house on the local news."

There was a total news blackout regarding details of the blast. Frau Wenzel had decided - for the safety of the judge and his family - not to release any information in connection with the incident.

"I can't comment on the case," replied Schmitt. "I hope you understand my reasons. How may I help you, Frau Köhler?"

"I need to get my son out of prison," she replied softly.

"That, I'm afraid, is out of my control. The courts are dealing with the matter now. Your family has not provided a surety for him so I am not able to assist you."

"What if I persuade Eugen to co-operate with you, make him see sense and tell you what he knows…. would that secure his release? I can't raise the sum the court wants. I am begging you, please….it is very distressing for me to be here. My husband controls our finances and refuses to help my child. You must help me; I am at your mercy!" implored Frau Köhler, tears streaming down her face.

Slightly embarrassed, Schmitt and Reinhold looked first at one another and then over to Frau Köhler as she sobbed into her silk handkerchief. Schmitt attempted to calm her down.

"I can't promise you anything as this will have to go through our superiors for their approval but, if your son does provide substantial assistance to the case, I'm sure an arrangement can be made."

"How soon can that be?" queried the mother impatiently, seeing a small ray of light appearing.

"Again, we are promising you nothing, Frau Köhler," echoed Reinhold. "Please, don't get your hopes up. You look worn out. Why don't you go home and try to rest? We will do all we can to resolve this issue. But, as Detective Chief Inspector Schmitt has already indicated, it is up to our commander and the courts as to what can be accomplished."

After a few moments of contemplation, Frau Köhler got up quietly from the table, thanked the detectives for agreeing to meet with her and settled the account for the table service. She left the hotel, walking out into the warm, autumn afternoon, to hail a taxi.

****

"Hi, all," said Chief Wenzel as she arrived to open the crime room briefing, with her notes under her arm. "I hope you have all had a good weekend and are well rested and ready to go after these thugs! Where do these people think they are, in the Wild West? Do they really believe that they can shoot and bomb at will, in our cities? Who wants to start?"

Muller rose from his chair and went over to the information board.

"Ma'am, I have analysed the specific building access code history on our central computer server, in relation to the recent incident. Someone from inside the government accessed Judge Janzyke's computer six days ago, installing a ghost program that would have allowed the perpetrator to monitor the cases being worked on by him. It also could have provided progress reports and the direction in which our inquiries were taking us. Judge Janzyke's personal files, as are all government files, are encrypted and protected using our bespoke BIRGER program. The security encryption is second to none and, normally, safeguards our many systems from cyber-attack."

"It damn well didn't safeguard this system, Heinz! Have you and your team made any progress at all which would enable the culprit to be traced?" bellowed the chief, having received an irate phone call from the justice minister in Bonn.

"We are working on it, ma'am."

Muller consulted his notes, not wanting to get his situation update wrong, given the mood in the room.

"A Government laptop was reportedly stolen from a member of staff at Koln railway station, two weeks ago. We thought it had been used to enter our system but this was not the case. The true point of insertion has been narrowed down to the office of the Ministry of Economic Development."

"Why was the laptop's security clearance not withdrawn?" Wenzel demanded to know.

"It was withdrawn, as a matter of security protocol, although it was expected that it might turn up in the Deutsche Bahn lost property office."

"What else?" asked the chief, tersely; the report was becoming more and more depressing.

"The main target of the attack was the Government estates' department," explained Muller. "At six forty-five, someone accessed a computer in the admin office and hacked into the system. The files covering our security contractors' clearances provide code settings for all Government buildings and their alarm systems."

"Heinz, do you mean to say that they could have got the code for Judge Janzyke's residence?"

"I don't know for certain at this point in time, but it's a possibility. The team are still working on it."

"Right, Heinz, thanks for your input. Claudia."

"Sorry, ma'am," said Reinhold, skimming hastily through her notes. "My team has been studying CCTV footage of the entrances and corridors of the Ministry of Economic Development. An unidentified female, posing as a cleaner, arrived with the normal shift at six in the morning. At six fifty, she went into the admin office; this is the breach that Heinz mentioned. By seven a.m. she was out, just before the guard made his rounds again. The incursion was timed to the minute. The cleaners on duty have all been questioned. They thought the individual was a new start, as they were a person down on the cleaning crew. The suspect is eastern European; when she did speak, it was in broken English. She was wearing a padded, hooded jacket, gloves and a scarf," explained Reinhold, winding up her report as quickly as possible considering the frame of mind Wenzel seemed to be in.

"I take it the cleaning company is German? Who's next? Can someone let me have some good news, please?"

Konigsberg spoke first.

"If I may, ma'am?"

The chief indicated for her to continue.

"The judge's house showed no signs of forced entry, regardless of the damage the building sustained because of the blast. None of the doors or windows had been tampered with."

Muller cut in.

"On the night before the blast occurred, the software for the alarm and CCTV was, inexplicably, accessed. The program was altered to switch the house security monitoring system off between the hours of seven and nine a.m."

"So, the whole thing was set up to murder Janzyke and his family?"

"It seems so," answered Muller.

"It's not only the attempted murder of the judge now, given that a defenceless cleaner was caught up in the blast!" exclaimed the chief.

"We have the actual explosion on film, if you would like to see it, ma'am," interjected Konigsberg.

Overtly annoyed that her friend and his family had nearly been assassinated, Wenzel nodded her approval as she took a mouthful of coffee. Konigsberg dimmed the lights. The images presented the blast from two different angles. The concealed hall camera showed the cleaner entering the house to begin her day's work and provided the forensic team with irrefutable evidence of the actual base of the explosion. Further images, taken from a camera to the rear of the property, demonstrated the severity of the bomb blast as debris was deposited over the extensive lawns.

"Whoever is behind this breach has also accessed the judge's appointments for the next two months," added Muller as the team viewed the images.

"Herr Janzyke's complete itinerary has already been rescheduled, as a security measure," replied Wenzel.

"Ma'am," said Konigsberg as the film ended and she put on the lights, "the explosive charge was Czech Semtex; the size of the device is estimated to be around forty grams. The bomb maker used a disinfectant dispenser to house the components and it was placed in the downstairs bathroom. The dispenser is of the type you would buy in any supermarket. The explosive was fitted with a very small, commercial detonator, wired to four AA batteries. The detonation switch wire was connected to a mercury tilt switch. It was attached to the toilet seat, a very crude setup indeed. When the cleaner lifted the seat, detonation of the bomb was instant. A lesser quantity of explosives would have been sufficient. The device was intended to kill and maim as many people as possible. I have been able to identify the mercury switch as being made in the former Czech Republic, the batteries were sourced in Nuremberg and the detonator was made in Italy but had been modified; it is typically used in the quarry industry. There were no prints, I'm afraid."

"Have any of you got any new information that might point us in the right direction of the bomber?"

Wenzel crossed her arms and sat back in frustration as yet another murder had taken place which - she suspected - had all the hallmarks of the Serbian Mafia.

The still image of the blast-damaged mansion remained on the screen whilst the members of the team sat, staring into space, lost in their own thoughts. Schmitt was the first to speak, as he recounted the conversation with Eugen Köhler's mother at the Hotel Vier Jahreszeiten.

"Get straight onto it, Detlef," ordered Wenzel as she stood up to leave. Go to Stadelheim and try to turn him; he's the key to all this.

String the little shit along and see if he can deliver the information we require. If what he gives us is grade A, then we will spring him into a protection programme, if necessary. We need anything that can lead us to the killers. One more thing, everyone, be vigilant. Keep your personal issue Glocks with you, always, including when off duty. These individuals seem to be taking no prisoners, as far as those involved in putting an end to their criminal operation are concerned. There will be no more press briefings until significant arrests have been made. All of you, please, take no chances; ensure that you always have backup. Let's get this scum off our streets!" she declared before bringing the meeting to a close.

Wenzel had clearly been shaken by the recent events. She was an excellent manager but had not been working in the field for quite a while. The closest she had got to regular active service was when attending live ammunition training exercises with other European police forces. Schmitt, seeing the effect the case was having on the chief, hoped the pressure would not upset her sense of focus.

****

Reinhold and Schmitt left the office as soon as the briefing was over. They travelled along SoyerhofsStraße on their way to interview Eugen Köhler at Stadelheim, hoping that a few weeks in a cell surrounded by hardened criminals had made him more co-operative. Upon their arrival, they made their way to the guard room where they handed in their weapons and collected visitor passes. Schmitt greeted the prisoner as he was escorted into the interview room.

"Good day, Herr Köhler."

"I find nothing in the least good about being held in this place, Detective," answered Kohler as he shuffled over to the desk where the two officers were seated, his hands and feet in shackles.

"How have you been treated?" continued Schmitt as he arranged the paperwork he had brought with him.

"Where should I begin?" sighed Köhler. "For a start, I am under constant threat of being beaten and raped, even though I am supposed to be afforded protection in here! Do you realise the kind of people that I am surrounded by? You have got the wrong person, Detective; what I did was merely a clerical error. I demand protection or, better still, an immediate release!" he cried, before breaking down and weeping uncontrollably.

As he searched for a handkerchief in his prison uniform, Reinhold passed him a packet of tissues. With the handcuffs restricting his movements, he eventually retrieved one from the pack and dabbed his eyes with it.

Eugen Köhler was a shadow of his former self, with his sunken eyes and sallow skin. Schmitt studied the prisoner. Perhaps his mother had been telling the truth and there was now a possibility that the person in front of them might, just might, be prepared to cut a deal.

"Welcome to our world, Herr Köhler! You know, you can help yourself; just give us the information that will lead to the prosecution of those involved in the money laundering operation," Schmitt suggested.

"I told you before, I can't do that. You people don't…. you just…. don't…. understand," sobbed Köhler as he broke down once again.

Schmitt looked at Reinhold, somewhat perplexed as to what their next move should be.

"Eugen," said Reinhold, taking the prisoner's hands in her own,

"I've been around these institutions. I know what the people in them are like and what they are capable of. Won't you at least try to co-operate and make it easy on yourself?"

Köhler looked up from the table to which he was shackled.

"How can I? I've just about lost everything."

"Perhaps all is not lost, Eugen, but the longer you leave it, the harder it will be to go back to your former life."

"You want me to turn in my partner, the man I love? That's something I'm not prepared to do!" replied Köhler.

"What has he got to do with all this?" questioned Schmitt.

The prisoner looked at the detective, considering his question. What had Ralph got to do with all this? Everything and nothing! Ralph had got him into this bloody mess and yet he had not done anything to secure his release. It had been a week since he had even heard from him. It started to dawn on Köhler that he had been a blind fool, doing whatever it took just to please his lover. Now, look where he had ended up. His father, ogre that he was, had been hard to work for but at least he had provided him with security throughout his life. Now he was reduced to the level of a common criminal.

Reinhold tried to get him to see reason.

"Do yourself a favour, Eugen, and co-operate with us. The people you are protecting aren't exactly queuing up to get you out of here, are they?"

"No, it's out of the question.... I.... can't. I've got nothing more to say to you. Let me go; you know you can't keep me here!" argued Köhler in a faltering voice.

Schmitt got up from the table and began to make his way out of the room, followed closely by Reinhold. The detective stopped unexpectedly, causing Reinhold to collide with him.

"Herr Köhler, you've had your chance. I won't be wasting any more time with you. Our next meeting will be in court!"

Schmitt stormed down the prison corridor, frustrated that he hadn't got the answers he would have liked.

Disappointed, the two detectives handed in their visitors' passes and went to retrieve their firearms from the guard house armoury. As they were about to leave, a member of staff approached them, informing them that the prisoner they had just visited urgently wished to speak with them.

"Herr Schmitt, as I was escorting Herr Köhler back to his cell, he appeared to experience a panic attack and he then collapsed," explained the prison warden. "I did my best to revive him and calm him down."

"Well, how is he now? Is he alright?"

"He is somewhat settled but wants to speak with you and the good lady, once more."

Schmitt and Reinhold returned to the interview suite where the prisoner was already waiting for them. They both sat down at the table, facing the ex-banker.

"I wish to make it clear, Herr Köhler," warned Schmitt, "that, if you're messing us around, you'll go straight back to your cell. There will be no second chances!"

"Please, Herr Schmitt, I am willing to assist you in any way I can."

"You can start by giving me the name of the person who made the cash lodgements to your father's bank."

"His name is Ralph Lutemeyer. We are in a relationship and he currently lives with me."

"We will continue this conversation when we get back to Pullach. Herr Köhler, move!"

"Thank you, Detective. As I've stated, I genuinely want to help your department with their inquiries."

Schmitt frogmarched Köhler out of the prison gates, much to his relief. He would not have to endure another night of torment in Stadelheim. In the rear of the patrol car, Reinhold secured Köhler's hands behind his back, using handcuffs. Sitting beside him, she fastened both of their seat belts for the journey. Schmitt, checking his mirrors, exited the prison car park and drove down several side streets to ensure they weren't being followed. Köhler was either an asset or a liability, Schmitt couldn't decide which, but the detective urgently needed fresh intelligence, regardless of how insignificant it was. Whilst leaving in a report some days earlier, the detective had spotted a Government communiqué on Wenzel's desk; it did not make for pleasant reading. In it, the Minister of Defence had offered to provide additional technical assistance for Wenzel. It was polite ministerial language, indicating that if she was not up to the task of fighting organised crime and terrorism, he would find someone else to take on the challenge.

CHAPTER THIRTEEN

Schmitt immediately called one of the team back at the office. Using the national police computer, an identity check was carried out on Ralph Lutemeyer. The name drew a blank; no such person existed. Detlef was now all but losing his patience as he glared at Köhler, who sat forlorn in the back of the car on hearing the news.

"Herr Schmitt, I'm telling you the truth; your information is wrong. Ralph is a real person, please, believe me!"

"You really are a pathological liar. Not only have you wasted our time but you have let your mother down, yet again. I am going to return you to your snug little prison cell, without delay," said Schmitt menacingly as he looked over his shoulder and reversed the vehicle into a side street, ready to head back to Stadelheim.

"Please, Detectives, don't do this! Fräulein Reinhold, speak to your colleague. You must take me home, where I can provide you with photographs of Ralph, on vacation with me."

After some debate, they made their way to Köhler's penthouse on FrauenStraße. The threesome entered the complex and took the elevator to the fifth floor. Köhler tentatively opened the door of his residence, appearing relieved to find that his partner was not at home. He led them straight into the bedroom, where he lifted a platinum silver picture frame from the bedside cabinet. In it, was a photo of Lutemeyer and himself, on a recent short break in South Tyrol.

"Herr Köhler, what did you say your partner's name was?" asked Schmitt, studying the image in the frame before passing it to Reinhold.

"Ralph Lutemeyer," replied Köhler, wondering where the confusion lay.

"The person in this photograph is an individual by the name of Claus Stein."

"No, that's impossible! Do you take me for a complete numbskull, Detective? I think I should know my partner's name, having lived with him for the past six months. You must be mistaken!"

"Herr Köhler," said Schmitt as he walked into the lounge with Eugen in tow before sitting down on the Italian-made, leather sofa, "I personally assisted in putting this man behind bars. He spent four years in the institution from which you have just been released. That's Claus Stein, alright. So…. he is the elusive cash courier who's been making deposits into the Munchener Assistance Bank!"

Köhler felt faint. He sank down into a small armchair and began to explain to the detectives how the laundering scam had started. Affection had turned to recklessness as he fell in love with Stein. Schmitt and Reinhold began to look over the rest of the apartment. They examined Stein's belongings for an additional address.

"Are these all of his personal effects?" queried Schmitt, having exhausted their search.

"No," answered Köhler. "There are more of his belongings in the basement. Please, let me show you."

He mustered his last ounce of strength and stood up. Sourcing a key, they all made their way down to the cellar.

"That's strange!" he exclaimed, finding it impossible to insert the key. "This seems to be a new lock!"

Schmitt turned and put his face close to Köhler's.

"Don't try that shit with me or you're going back to your

girlfriends in Stadelheim!"

"I swear, I'm not playing games, Detective! My key doesn't fit; Stein must have changed the lock!"

Reinhold walked over to an adjacent cellar and borrowed an old weighing scale counterweight that was being used as a doorstop by another tenant. After a couple of blows from Schmitt, the lock fell to the ground. Reinhold handcuffed Köhler to a nearby drainage pipe and the detectives began their search of the cellar. After a few minutes spent inspecting two grubby suitcases full of Stein's clothes, they had found nothing of importance. Schmitt's attention was suddenly captured by an antique chest of drawers.

"Why is this cabinet sitting on these expensive rugs?" he asked, studying the odd arrangement.

"I really don't know," replied Köhler, trying to peer around the door, hindered by the handcuffs attached to the drainpipe. "They shouldn't be like that. The last time I saw them, they were placed upright. I stored them here after a water leak that nearly flooded the apartment. My goodness, the weight will damage them! Herr Schmitt, would you and your colleague be so kind as to remove the unit from them. It's been some months since I was last down here; Stein must have moved things around."

As the two detectives struggled to lift the heavy unit off the floor coverings, Schmitt decided to pull out the rolled-up mat that was closest to him. It was unusually heavy; something wasn't right, he thought. When the antique rug was fully unrolled, it revealed a camouflage-patterned, canvas rifle case.

Reinhold passed a tissue to her partner as he knelt and slowly unzipped the case, which contained a military-issue Heckler & Koch

PSG1 7.62 sniper's rifle with two full clips, a Hensoldt ZF 6x4 PSG1 telescopic sight and a Brügger & Thome silencer. The hairs on the back of Detlef's neck rose. Was it possible that this was the gun used to murder the customs official? The silencer would explain why no one reported shots having been fired so close to the apartments. As he looked up at Reinhold, he saw that the expression on her face seemed to confirm a similar train of thought.

"Claudia, this may be the murder weapon," he whispered.

He then pointed the barrel of the gun at the two suitcases - ensuring there would be no ricochet - and gently drew back the breech bolt, examining the chamber to see if there was a round present. Satisfied that it was in a decommissioned state, he laid the firearm on its case, ready for the forensics team.

Schmitt went out to the hallway and removed Köhler's handcuffs. Once inside the cellar, the banker grabbed onto some wooden racking to support himself, as he saw the rifle and its ammunition laid out on the open rug.

"Before you start, Detective," he stuttered, "I…. I have never set eyes on that weapon…. never! It's not mine! Please, you must believe me. I don't even possess an air rifle; I have no interest in blood sports!"

Schmitt studied Köhler's face. At this moment in time, he looked at his most vulnerable, more so now than when they had collected him from Stadelheim. Even though the detective knew the gun did not belong to Eugen, he planned to use it to apply more pressure, thus ensuring his complete co-operation.

"It's in your cellar. How do you explain that?"

Wild-eyed, Köhler appealed to Reinhold.

"You know I'm not capable of using such a weapon. It's…. it's not mine! I've never seen it before today! It must be Stein's, yes, that would explain everything. He used to be in the Bundeswehr, you know."

Reinhold played along with her colleague's ruse.

"In view of your previous activities, I would put nothing past you! Using your partner as a scapegoat to save your own neck; have you no self-respect? This find is beyond coincidence, Herr Köhler, given the recent company you have been keeping."

"No, Fräulein, you are wrong."

Schmitt grabbed Köhler and pinned him, face first, against the wall, handcuffing his hands behind his back once again.

"Herr Köhler, you do not have to say anything but it may harm your defence if you do not mention, when questioned, something which you later rely on in court. Anything you do say may be given in evidence. I'm charging you with being in possession of a firearm, without a licence, in suspicious circumstances."

Schmitt called Wenzel and reported what had been found in Köhler's home; the dwelling was pronounced a crime scene. Members of the local police force - along with the team from Pullach - were dispatched to go over the entire apartment and cellar area. When the officers arrived, they began to close off the street. Schmitt and Reinhold identified themselves before walking Köhler up from the cellar and out of the building.

"Where to now, Detlef?" asked Reinhold as she fastened first Köhler's and then her own seat belt.

"Pullach. Our friend here has a lot of additional issues to address," answered Schmitt, belting himself into the bucket seat.

****

As the drama unfolded, Stein looked on cautiously from behind the graphics-covered window of a convenience store a hundred metres away, just off ZwingerStraße. He watched, mystified, as his partner was secured in the rear of the car, wondering what could have happened now. After all these years, his nemesis was once again interfering in his life. Stein had just found a parking bay and was about to go home for a shower and a change of clothes. He had almost reached his destination when two police patrol vehicles drove past him at speed. They had their blue lights and sirens on as they pulled up sharply outside the apartment block, forcing him to swiftly change direction.

Stein left the shelter of the store, where he had been pretending to look for something to buy. He glanced up the street at the police activity before walking briskly down ZwingerStraße and over some waste ground.

****

Schmitt drove off, in the direction of Gärtnerplatz. He knew it was now imperative to get Köhler off the streets and back to Pullach as soon as possible. Detlef firmly believed that the rifle was connected to the shooting of the customs officer, which made the banker a more valuable resource to the case.

Whilst navigating the S2 through the heavy München traffic, Schmitt had been exchanging glances with Reinhold as she sat in the rear seat, guarding Köhler. The detective had noticed the grey Opel Ascona some distance back. At first, he thought it was his imagination but then its erratic behaviour caught his attention in the exterior mirrors as it attempted to blend into the evening traffic.

The car had been weaving around other vehicles but trying to stay far enough away so as not to arouse suspicion. Schmitt turned nonchalantly, at the last minute, onto CorneliusStraße, with Reinhold watching his every move. Looking into the rearview mirror, Detlef observed a post office van being cut up as the Opel made a last-minute turn across its lane, causing the driver to break abruptly. Schmitt thought that this was somewhat strange behaviour as no one knew they had taken custody of the prisoner. Were they being followed? He throttled the five-cylinder engine to discover if somebody was, in fact, shadowing them.

The unmarked police car powered down CorneliusStraße, at times on the wrong side of the road, overtaking numerous road users and narrowly avoiding pedestrians. The shabby Opel seemed to increase it speed; it was currently some five vehicles behind Schmitt. Stein continued to redline the worn 1.8 litre fuel injected engine in every gear as he tried to keep up.

"We have a hostile in pursuit of us," Detlef informed his colleague as his speed intensified. "Call for back up!"

Reinhold leaned over into the front passenger seat and identified herself on the police radio, putting out a call for any available unit to provide assistance. She continued to deliver a running commentary of their current coordinates before withdrawing a Glock pistol from her holster and removing the safety catch.

As he approached Corneliusbrücke, Schmitt - with absolute precision - veered left onto EhardStraße, at speed. Their seat belts tightening, Reinhold and Köhler hung on to the interior grab handles to avoid being thrown around in their seats. The tyres fought violently for grip as the power from the four-wheel drive system sent the vehicle into a sideways drift.

"Detective, what's wrong?" shouted Eugen, beginning to panic as he attempted to look out of the rear window. "Why are you driving so fast? Are we being followed?"

"An incident has occurred and we have been asked to return to base. Just sit tight, Eugen; we will be there shortly," Reinhold said reassuringly.

Schmitt, trying to concentrate on his driving, gave a slight correction to the steering and the car righted itself from another small drift around a waste bin as the chase continued along EhardStraße. They came to a road crossing that took them onto AuenStraße; he was using his entire advanced driver training to try and shake off their pursuer.

The detective made a challenging right turn onto ArndtStraße. Again, the vehicle's four wheels snatched at the loose road surface for some semblance of grip, only just avoiding a collision with a large skip that was being used to store debris from nearby road repairs.

Regaining his composure, Schmitt continued to put some distance between him and the person pursuing them. The engine delivered a deep, burbling note as the revs remained close to the red line in the lower gears. As Schmitt sped through the narrow, built up area, they came to a progressive right hand bend. The S2 began to slide and lurch somewhat as it left the damp tarmac - the tyres now meeting the greasy, cobblestone surface - before regaining grip and continuing their exodus to Pullach.

A few minutes later, Stein came upon the same surface, with the Opel at full momentum. The understeer was upon him before he could right it, the car resisting all attempts at correction. It ploughed across the road, colliding with a meals-on-wheels delivery van which had been waiting to merge at the junction of ArndtStraße and HolzStraße. Schmitt and his passengers were unaware of the accident as they eventually emerged onto a main highway that would get them safely back to Pullach.

At the crash scene, Stein was slouched back in his seat, semi-conscious, having hit his head off the A pillar due to not wearing a seat belt. He had pressed violently on his brakes to stop the Opel before ploughing into the driver's side of the Mercedes van. The impact was severe, forcing the engine and gearbox backwards into the bulkhead. Stein fell out onto the road as builders from a nearby construction site forced open the door to release him. When he became aware of his surroundings, Stein pushed his rescuers back. They tried to restrain him but he finally managed to break free, upon which he ran off into the maze of streets. A mobile police patrol, which had responded to the call made by Reinhold earlier, arrived at the scene and began questioning the witnesses, while an air support helicopter searched the immediate area.

Dazed, Stein paused briefly in an alleyway to catch his breath whilst mopping the blood coming from the cut on his forehead with his sleeve. It was then he realised that he had left his Makarov pistol in the boot of the car. Stein looked up at the sky. Blood and sweat momentarily stung his eyes before he saw the helicopter hovering a short distance away. It was quite near to the crash scene and was beginning to move in his direction.

****

"Frau Köhler," said Schmitt, welcoming her into his office, "please, sit down. How is Eugen?"

"Thank you for seeing me, Herr Schmitt," she replied as she

seated herself in front of the detective, dressed in a smart, beige trouser suit. "Eugen is a lot better psychologically, thank God, now that he is out of that awful place."

"He has only himself and some common sense to thank for that. The safe house may not be perfect but at least those who seek to harm your son won't find him."

Detlef poured some water for both Frau Köhler and himself.

"Eugen is able to supply the answers that will enable us to put a lot of people away. As you are aware, Frau Köhler, his world is in turmoil now but we can help him to get his life back together."

"Herr Schmitt, I sat down and had a long talk with my son, probably one of the longest conversations we have ever had. I have persuaded him that it is in his best interests to help you with your inquiries. His father has disowned him but, if I'm honest, that happened a long time ago. I am all Eugen has and I have a little set aside that will help us both."

"What do you mean, help you both?" asked Schmitt, somewhat puzzled by the statement.

Eugen Köhler's mother seemed different somehow. He couldn't put his finger on it, but she was stronger, more resolute in her thinking.

"Herr Schmitt, please take this," she replied, handing him a mauve-coloured envelope.

Thinking it was her way of thanking him, the detective pleaded, "Frau Köhler, if there is money in here, I must insist that you take it back."

"Granted, my son made a grave mistake in processing the illegal money lodgements but he did not inherit that repugnant trait from me, Herr Schmitt! No, the envelope contains a letter, addressed to me, along with a safe deposit key that will unlock what appears to be a very important document. I am completely in the dark as to its contents, but my friend deemed it noteworthy."

"Please, continue," urged Schmitt, his interest now aroused.

"I believe the document may right a wrong that occurred many years ago."

She took a sip of water from the plastic cup on the table.

"Who was this friend?" Schmitt enquired, fingering the brass key he had removed from the envelope.

"Helmut Schröder. He was commandant of the Wehrmacht training camp in Waggum, where my husband was stationed."

"Helmut Schröder? The former owner of the Munchener Assistance Bank?" asked Schmitt, making a note.

His query went unheard as Frau Köhler sat there, motionless and unspeaking; then, looking down, she blessed herself and joined her hands in prayer. Schmitt sensed there was something that had pained this lady for a very long time, of which she was now preparing to unburden herself.

After a few minutes of silence, she raised her head.

"Detective Schmitt, what I am about to say rekindles very painful memories for me, you must understand that. I beg of you not to interrupt. I cannot relive this moment ever again as I have blocked it from my mind for a long time. Shortly before he passed away, Helmut gave me the envelope you now hold, telling me to hand it over to the police if my husband ever maltreated me, or any member of my family. I feel that time has now arrived. Whatever may be in the safe deposit box, please do with it as you wish."

Detlef was only half listening, his thoughts focused sharply on the contents of the box. Frau Köhler's voice, now becoming stronger, concentrated his attention on her again.

"My husband is an autocratic person. It is his way, his standards, irrespective of who he is dealing with. I have managed to live with his mood swings and tantrums for quite some time, since we were married, I suppose. When Christoph, our firstborn, arrived, in nineteen forty-eight...." Frau Köhler paused, her thoughts somewhere else. "I thought, perhaps.... for the first time, in several years, Curt was becoming more compassionate in his manner, a little more caring. I put it down to the growing relationship between him and our son. As the years wore on though, and the business grew, the old Curt returned once again. I thank God that Christoph shared none of his father's loathsome qualities."

By now, Frau Köhler seemed to be in real physical pain as she explained to Schmitt how her son had immersed himself in his father's world.

"Christoph tried to please his father, who was the light of his life, at every given opportunity, to earn his affection, but the man had neither the capacity nor the inclination to satisfy his son's desire for a little warmth or tenderness."

The detective was about to interrupt the woman as she paused once more but thought the better of it, taking a drink of water instead.

"Christoph and I were as close as can be," she continued, tears now falling in slow trickles down her face. "Having carried him inside me for nine months, I shared his heartache. Curt's disinterest left his mind in disarray and he didn't know which way to turn to gain his father's approval. Christoph worked hard at university, where he achieved outstanding grades in business management. After graduating, he tried to put forward fresh ideas that would have brought about corporate growth but Curt immediately dismissed them, identifying their weaknesses in a cruel, condescending manner. My….my poor child was ridiculed, time after time, and I could only watch from the sidelines as there was no reasoning with my husband."

Frau Köhler stopped for a moment. Schmitt thought she was going to faint; her naturally pale complexion was now a deathly white.

"Are you okay, Frau Köhler? Do you want a break?"

"No….no…. I'm fine…. really, I'm fine," she replied, reaching into her handbag for a fresh tissue. "As I said, this is very painful for me…. My husband had his own personal gymnasium in the cellar of our second home, where we lived before moving to our current address. Christoph would use it a lot, mainly, I think, to impress his father. Not that he would have noticed; he often told the boy that he was wasting his time there. Our son had never been selected for the school hockey team, although that never bothered me…. I loved him with all my heart. The morning it happened…. yes, it was a cold, October morning," remarked Frau Köhler as if it were yesterday. "As I looked out of Christoph's window, I could see that the grass was covered in a heavy frost."

She smiled briefly.

"Christoph had not come down for breakfast and I had gone to his bedroom to fetch him but the room was empty. Sometimes, he would get up early for a workout before going to the bank so I went to the gym. There…. There he was." She broke down, choking on her words. "My….my little boy was…. I found him hanging from a rafter. Why? Why did his monster of a father drive him to do that?"

Schmitt looked on helplessly. He felt as if Frau Köhler was

enduring a thousand lashes of a whip, so palpable was her pain.

"My son hanged himself because he could not live up to his father's expectations. His neatly written note explained it all. It is something no parent should have to experience, least of all a mother, the last words of one's firstborn, delivered in such a way. His father didn't even have the decency to take his own flesh and blood down off the cheap, ten-mark rope! No, that unpleasant task was left to our poor gardener who brought the step ladders and lifted Christoph's body down, laying him on the cold, hard floor. Could you do that to your own child, Detective?"

Schmitt thought of Erhard at home, asleep in his little blue Babygro.

"I am so sorry for your loss. I have a young son of my own and I cannot begin to understand your grief."

Frau Köhler turned on the detective, speaking in a hushed, but harsh, tone.

"No, Herr Schmitt, you could never understand the pain of giving birth to a child only to have him taken away at such a young age. I wish you long years with your son but I'm not here for your sympathy, Detective. My husband has never taken responsibility for our son's death. Like the evil masters he served under, he believed Christoph to be a weak person, not a true German. Only a fiend could think that way. What I've given you is a key to something my friend thought important, so use it wisely. May my husband be damned to hell for what he has done to my family over the years!"

With this, Frau Köhler got up and grasped Schmitt's hand.

"Herr Schmitt, please look after my only son; let no further harm come to him. Someday, he will be released, having paid for his mistakes and, together, we will rebuild our lives. Good day and, once again, thank you, both for your time and your assistance."

Frau Köhler left the office and was escorted out of the building to a waiting taxi for her journey back to München.

CHAPTER FOURTEEN

A few days later, Wenzel listened as the team brought her up to date on their inquiries. Dr Heidi Konigsberg was first up. She had a lot of information regarding further results of tests carried out on debris from the explosion at Judge Janzyke's residence. Having finished the briefing, she opened another file.

"I now have the results of the forensic tests carried out on the Opel Ascona car that was involved in the high-speed pursuit of one of our own vehicles. First, I wish to begin with the Russian-made PB 6P9 Makarov pistol, found in the luggage compartment. I can confirm that it was used in the murder of two individuals. One was a known drug dealer from the outskirts of Denning, the other was Ernst Einhard, the Customs and Excise border guard. Ballistic tests have matched the bullet removed from the victim in the WinterStraße apartment to that fired from the Makarov during a lab test. The fingerprints found on the weapon were those of the convicted criminal, Claus Stein. His DNA was also present on the Makarov pistol and in the car."

Schmitt spoke up.

"Claus Stein was my drill sergeant at Heuberg. He served four years of a five-year sentence for the sexual assault of several trainees at the base. I helped to convict him by testifying at his trial."

Other members of the team stared in disbelief at the revelation.

"Really? I wasn't aware of that, Detlef," declared Konigsberg.

She continued.

"Strands of a black, synthetic fibre were retrieved from the apartment on WinterStraße. They had been snagged on a loose splinter of the damaged doorframe in the living room, probably left there as the killer made his escape. Having eliminated the victim's clothing, we were able to make a positive match to a black fleece found in the crashed Opel car which, again, had Stein's DNA all over it."

Wenzel was writing feverishly throughout the forensic officer's synopsis of the evidence to date. She was about to interrupt Konigsberg but decided against it as she had another meeting later in the day and had yet to prepare her notes for it.

"The Heckler & Koch sniper's rifle, found in the cellar of Herr Köhler junior's apartment, was used in the killing of the Customs officer, Manfred Friedel, who was found, shot dead, in the supermarket car park. It was reported stolen from Heuberg military base, in 1992. At this point, I must make it clear that, to date, it has not been linked to any other crimes. Claus Stein's fingerprints and DNA were all over the firearms, ammunition and accessories. Eugen Köhler has never handled the weapons. The results point to Stein as the sole person responsible for at least three murders."

"Let's not tell Köhler that for the time being," suggested Schmitt.

Wenzel shoved her glasses into her hair and stretched out her numb arms to improve her circulation as she asked the obvious question, "Have there been any sightings of Stein or any new leads?"

There were low mumbles around the table. Heads moved from side to side, indicating they were no further to locating the whereabouts of the hitman.

"What else?" asked the station chief in frustration.

Claudia Reinhold meekly put her hand up.

"Yes, Claudia? Please, give me something positive!" joked

Wenzel, trying to lift the mood in the room.

"About the pursuit that Detlef and I were involved in, an unregistered pay as you go phone was found in the crashed vehicle."

"And?" quizzed the chief, worried that more disjointed evidence had now been uncovered; the case was labouring at such a slow pace.

"My team has analysed the mobile phone company's records. Of the calls made and received, one number of significance came up. It belonged to the phone found on the person who attacked Detlef in the multi-storey car park: Ivan Zivkovic. There was a call made to the assailant's mobile, fifteen minutes before the assault and another, fifteen minutes after."

"It was a co-ordinated attack, then?"

"It would appear so. The incident was obviously well planned. I recovered a deleted text message from Stein's phone to Zivkovic's. It confirmed the make and registration number of Detlef's car, as well as the address of the car park he was in at that time."

Schmitt looked on in consternation as the facts became clear.

"So, Stein has been stalking me, for God knows how long! I'm supposed to be an intelligence officer and I was completely unaware of it. I'm slipping!"

"I take it there is definitive proof that the mobile in the crashed Opel belonged to Stein?" queried Wenzel.

Konigsberg was first to interject.

"His fingerprints are all over the device. He, or someone using it, made a call to Dubravko Huzjak, a loan shark and bar owner from the Moosach area of München, only ten minutes before the incident. At least Ivan Zivkovic had the sense to delete any messages he had sent or received!"

"Thanks, Heidi. Please don't beat yourself up, Detlef," said Wenzel as she tried to reassure Schmitt that he had taken all necessary measures regarding his own security. "Stein was the one to have tripped up this time. If he was as clever as the rest of the lowlifes, he would have disposed of the SIM card once the job was carried out. Currently, there is a nationwide alert for his immediate arrest. Law enforcement officers, in the first instance, have been ordered to take him into custody. Should he resist, they are to stop him, using deadly force," she announced.

As the meeting ended, the chief asked Schmitt to step into her office.

"Please sit down, Detlef. I think, perhaps, you should take some leave. What has been revealed in the meeting today may compromise your involvement in the investigation and…."

"No way! You are not doing this to me, Angela!" said Schmitt, interrupting his boss. "I have given my all to lead this team and I haven't put a foot wrong. Just look at the drugs bust!"

The detective was enraged at the accusation being levelled against him by his boss.

"Detlef, I'm not saying…."

Schmitt cut his boss off in mid-sentence for the second time.

"Angela, forgive me, but you are way out of line. Stein is just another cog in the Serbian Mafia puzzle; it just so happens that I have had some previous involvement with him. He's the criminal, not me. I feel you're creating a problem that, until now, did not exist!"

"Detlef, you're the one who's out of line," countered Wenzel. "I'm running the show here and I make the decisions, not you!"

"I understand, but I still think your judgement is clouded."

"You need to apologise for that comment. I won't put up with this continual insubordination!"

"I'm sorry, Angela, that was uncalled for."

"You may carry on with the investigation but, if I feel you are crossing the line at any point, you're off the case. Is that understood?"

"Yes, ma'am."

"Close the door on your way out."

The detective left Wenzel's office and went up to the roof to cool off. He hadn't realised just how tense he was. Holding onto the protective guard rails, his knuckles were turning white, betraying the anger he was feeling. He was more than disappointed with Wenzel. How could she have suggested such a thing, that he step down from the investigation? He had never, ever, given Stein another thought until now and he was as shocked as anyone to learn of his involvement in the case.

Suddenly, it all made sense. The ex-convict had always lived the high life. Upon his release from Stadelheim prison, Stein would readily have found some form of illegal employment to provide an income in keeping with his rich lifestyle. Schmitt had harboured no ill will against his former drill sergeant but his endeavour to have the detective killed had changed everything.

On returning to his office, Schmitt sat, motionless, for some time, brooding over Wenzel's words. Seeing Frau Köhler's letter on his desk, he decided to read it.

Commandant Helmut Schröder
Promenade Platz
80333 München

27 April 1975

Dear Frieda

If you are reading this letter, then I know things have become utterly unbearable between you and Curt. I myself have been diagnosed with throat cancer. It's too late now; there is no cure and Dr Büchner has given me four months to live. I feel it is my duty, as an old Prussian officer, to do something that I should have done many, many years ago.

When Curt first walked into our lives, he was a fine, upstanding young man. Alas, he is no longer that person and these papers will prove it. I have always done my best for my family. As you know, a moment of weakness lost me the only woman I ever really loved: my beautiful Sophia. Curt could have overlooked my indiscretion, as I had done for him over the years, but instead he elected to inform my wife of the affair I was having with my secretary. In her anguish and, to a large degree, to get back at me, she sold her shares, giving overall control of the Munchener Assistance Bank to him. He need only have asked and we would have gladly sold our interests and walked away as old age came to meet us. Curt chose to ruin two lives; the only consolation is that I have my son, Tomas. I am so proud that he has decided to go into politics, like his father.

As godfather to Christoph, it broke my heart, as it did yours, when he took his own life due to his father's indifference. It was then that I knew the man had no conscience. It is with heavy heart that I must ask you to take this information to the police. Please, Frieda, I beg of you, don't seek to discover its contents, you have suffered enough. I hope that you will be able to, one day, forgive me for my part in all of this.

Yours,

Helmut

****

Feeling hungry, Detlef decided to grab a late lunch in the canteen but, after leaving his office, changed his mind, opting instead to drive over to the München address supplied by Frau Köhler. At the bank on Karlstraße, the manager - although taken aback by the detective's arrival - co-operated fully, leading him down to the vault room. Together, using both of their keys, they opened one of the many, small compartments in the wall. After being shown to a private booth, Schmitt was left alone to view the contents of the safe deposit box.

Pulling on a pair of surgical gloves, he removed a sealed, manila envelope, along with a Reichsbank compliments slip. Detlef was astounded to see that the slip of paper had been signed by the same Captain Frank Gotthard whose name was on the documents found at Schorfheide. His curiosity getting the better of him, he took a deep breath and tentatively opened the envelope. It contained an affidavit, in which Schröder had made several allegations against Curt Köhler, including murder, identity theft and extensive financial impropriety. Unable to make sense of it all for the moment, Schmitt put the

174

document back in its envelope and, placing both items into sterile, plastic bags, he returned to Pullach with his find.

****

The next day, Schmitt - now on a roll - drove to MarsStraße with von Harz. Wenzel had ordered them to visit Dubravko Huzjak to see what information could be gleaned from the suspect. Schmitt parked outside a small, boutique hotel, where the two officers got out and crossed the road to a tawdry-looking building. At three in the afternoon, the streets were busy with shoppers but, inside the Bon-Bon Club, business was slack. One or two pensioners were quietly sipping their drinks, trying to make them last. The lap dancers lethargically moved around at the back of the building, a little bored, having too few punters and making no money.

As the officers approached the bar, Schmitt addressed the bartender.

"Tell Huzjak I want to speak with him," he demanded.

Upstairs, the club owner was counting a large sum of cash. He had briefly stopped what he was doing, casually observing the two strangers on the CCTV monitor as they entered the club. Huzjak could see they were trouble and was already descending the staircase as the barman met him, mid-flight, on the stairs.

"Can I help you people?" asked the owner as he entered the bar, before going behind the counter and coming to a halt beside an aluminium baseball bat which was sitting on the shelf below.

"I'm Detective Inspector Schmitt and this is my colleague, Detective von Harz. Where can I find Claus Stein?"

"Never heard of him. Now, either you two gents are here to buy a drink or a dance; anything else and you're leaving," replied Huzjak, setting the baseball bat down on the counter in an intimidating manner.

Moving like a cobra, von Harz grabbed the owner, forcing his arm up his back before slamming his face into the bar.

"Threatening an officer is not a very clever move, Huzjak. Answer the question," whispered von Harz into the man's ear as the suspect tried to wrestle himself out of the detective's fierce grip.

Instinctively, with his free hand, von Harz frisked him down before recovering the TT pistol concealed behind the Serb's back in his belt.

"Tut-tut, do I really need to ask if you have a permit for this?" he enquired, holding up the firearm for Schmitt to see before placing it on the bar.

Huzjak suddenly lunged backwards and attempted to headbutt von Harz. At lightning speed, the detective stepped aside and, dropping him with a punch to the kidney, the man fell to the floor, where he was handcuffed.

"Please, don't be unreasonable, Huzjak. Let's start again, shall we? My colleague is going to allow you to stand up, as long as there is no more drama," declared Schmitt.

Von Harz heaved the bar owner off the floor, twisting his handcuffs uncomfortably and pressing his face down onto the countertop. Huzjak shook his head in submission and von Harz released his grip on the cuffs, allowing him to stand up. Blood was now seeping and congealing from Huzjak's broken nose. Von Harz took a few steps back, helping himself to a glass of lemonade from the drinks optic as the disgruntled owner looked on.

"I don't know who you're talking about, Detective. I've never heard of this person."

The Serb's broken nose gave an impression of him having a cold as he glanced over his shoulder at von Harz, who had been looking around the bar for contraband.

Schmitt studied the prisoner. He was around two metres tall, stockily built, with a dark complexion and shaven head. There had been scant intelligence data on him. The Serb had been born in the northern municipality of Prijedor, close to the border of Croatia. He had been a transient person during his teenage years, living in several orphanages, both in Yugoslavia and Romania. The most up to date information was from the authorities in Slovenia, who had arrested him for extortion before he jumped bail.

"You do know him. As a matter of fact, you were in contact with him quite recently."

"You have the wrong guy, my friend. I'm just trying to earn a living! You and that thug come into my bar, assault me and plant a weapon on me!" said Huzjak indignantly.

Von Harz reached over and slapped the Serb on the head at the very suggestion.

"Don't get smart, Huzjak! We don't do fit ups. You were stupid enough to have the weapon on your person," stated von Harz.

Schmitt had seen and heard enough. The barman had sloped off during the commotion and the conversation with Huzjak was getting them nowhere.

"Jürgen, make sure the cuffs are locked. I'll look around upstairs, see if Herr Huzjak has anything else he shouldn't have," said Schmitt as he called the local police station, requesting that their detectives come and search the club. He instructed them to seize all CCTV videos, phone records and items for which there was no receipt.

"Please don't do that, Huzjak, you're still a good-looking man," said Schmitt, sarcastically as the prisoner continued to resist arrest before von Harz once again subdued him.

When the local officers arrived, Schmitt briefed them of the charges and what they were to look for on the premises. After reading Huzjak his rights, the two detectives loaded the prisoner into their car, bringing him to Maillingerstraße police station where they questioned him for over four hours. The Serb yielded very little information that they didn't already know. He had chosen to remain silent, having called his solicitor on arrival at the station.

"Herr Huzjak, I will ask you again, where is Claus Stein? We already know he has been working for you. CCTV records show him entering your bar and an altercation taking place between you both," stated Schmitt, having received a call from the detective leading the search of the Bon-Bon club; video cassettes found in Huzjak's office had been looked over before being bagged as evidence.

"Herr Schmitt, my client has nothing further to add. If you have no other evidence to produce, I would respectfully call for his release."

Schmitt viewed the solicitor before responding.

"Herr Bösen, I find your request surprising. Not only is your client guilty of assaulting Claus Stein, he was in possession of an illegal firearm and tried to resist his arrest. Herr Huzjak, can you explain the two carrier bags that were found in your office, containing two hundred thousand Deutsche Marks?" questioned Schmitt as he rubbed his temple to stem a migraine that was coming on.

"No comment, Detective, other than it is my client's hard earned money, which I expect to be returned to him," replied the solicitor.

"Herr Bösen, unless your client has receipts for the monies, it will be confiscated under the proceeds of crime."

"That's total crap; it's my money!" snapped the prisoner.

"Detective, what you and your colleague did to my client amounts to entrapment."

"Herr Bösen, your client can be seen on the video footage. He is brandishing the said weapon at Herr Stein, having just physically assaulted him. I hardly find our handling of his arrest a fit up, if that's what you're implying," countered Schmitt.

The solicitor conferred, in a whispered tone, with his client.

"Irrespective of your allegations, I once again request that my client be released on bail," argued the solicitor.

"In my view, Herr Bösen, your client is a definite flight risk. Take the issue of bail up with the judge when you come before him. Your client will remain in a cell here until then, before being transferred to Stadelheim," stated Schmitt as he and von Harz got up to leave the room.

One way or the other, Schmitt would find Stein. The money launderer and chief suspect in the murder of the two customs' officials was now on the loose and a danger to everyone.

CHAPTER FIFTEEN

"Angela, I need a word."

"About?"

"Frau Köhler came to see me. She provided us with an affidavit, written by the former owner of the Munchener Assistance Bank, Helmut Schröder, and witnessed by his, now deceased, solicitor. The document contains a series of allegations against her husband. I thought you should look at it."

"Is it of any importance to our investigations?"

"Indirectly."

"How?"

"Herr Schröder alludes to the homicide of a pensioner in 1972, citing Köhler as the killer."

"That's a pretty serious accusation from a dead man. Let me see it," ordered the chief tersely.

She began to read the letter.

"I know it could just be a case of sour grapes but there is a possibility that it might actually have happened."

"It appears to be a lot of hearsay, since both the author and his witness are no longer here to substantiate any of it. Schröder is claiming that not only is Köhler a murderer but he has robbed the Reichsbank and, what's more, he's taken on a false identity along the way! Really, Detlef, we don't have time for fairy tales. I suggest you hand this one over to the cold case section."

"At least let me see if there is a case file relating to the alleged murder of this man, Emil HaffenFuß. I'll do the legwork in my own time."

"Fine, that much I will allow. I've enough problems without you stirring up another hornet's nest!"

"Thanks, Angela."

Schmitt proceeded to gather his team's recent reports, to get an overview of the Serbian Mafia case to date. Afterwards, he phoned Amélie to let her know he would be late home and was relieved when, on this occasion, she didn't argue with him. Recently, he had been working more nights from the office than he would have liked to.

Sometime after seven that evening, Schmitt placed the call.

"Hello, is that Neuhausen police station?"

"Yes, that is correct. Officer Breidenbach speaking. How can I assist you?" said the voice on the other end of the line.

It was the constable's turn to be on the late shift that night and Schmitt detected a hint of weariness in the man's voice.

"Please excuse me for calling at this hour. I am Detective Chief Inspector Schmitt from the counter intelligence office at Pullach. I have a reference number for an old case file here. Would you check if the evidence and subsequent case report are still in your archives?"

"I'm afraid I can't leave the desk, Detective. We're short staffed, and the others have finished their shifts and gone home."

"I appreciate that, but I am investigating a very important case. I need to know if you still have the complete dossier."

There was a moment's silence before the officer reluctantly answered.

"What is the number, sir?" he enquired, resigned to assist a fellow law enforcement colleague.

"MNP2230072M."

"I'll just go and check the evidence log."

The officer left his post, returning a few minutes later.

"Detective, you will be pleased to know that everything connected to the enquiry is here, from what I can tell."

"May I call in and collect the file tomorrow? We are currently working on another case and the evidence you have could be related in some way."

"If it can help to bring closure to the investigation, be my guest."

"Many thanks for your assistance," said Schmitt, ending the call.

****

Schmitt went to the forensic lab to see Heidi Konigsberg. He had given her the cold case file for re-examination in Pullach's modern forensic centre.

"Hi, Detlef, come in," said the technician as she removed her lab coat and hung it up.

She sat down at her desk, her mini skirt exposing long, tanned legs.

"You look exhausted! You really need to slow down, but I suppose you're here to discover what I've got on the cold case?"

"Indeed, I am, Heidi. The intrigue of this man Köhler captivates me. Come on then, what has your room of applied chemistry uncovered?"

"You seem to want to keep it in the family. What is it with the Köhler household?" smirked Konigsberg, handing Schmitt her report.

"Was I right?" he asked, opening the file.

"Very much so. It must be where his son gets his criminal streak from!"

Schmitt gave her a mischievous look before studying the report.

"This is great, Heidi. I'm going to see Angela later to try and arrange an arrest warrant."

He gave her a winning smile and turned to leave.

"By the way, Detlef, before you go…."

"Is there something else?"

"Helmut Schröder."

"Yes, what about him?"

"His prints were also on the documents found in Berlin. I cross-referenced them with those on the affidavit. It raises the possibility that he may have been in contact with Köhler in the 1940s, long before they went into business together in München."

"Interesting…. the plot thickens, Heidi. Catch you later."

Schmitt exited the lab, taking both the affidavit and Konigsberg's report with him. Back at his desk, he sat deep in thought, idly thumbing the evidence bag which contained the faded compliments slip. Then, snapping out of his private musings, he rose and strode purposefully down the corridor, quickly reaching his destination.

"Angela, have you got a moment?" queried Schmitt.

"You have two minutes and no more! What's up?"

"I got the results back from the lab."

"What results?" asked the chief, rolling her eyes at yet another distraction.

"I collected the original file regarding the cold case I spoke to you about. Curt Köhler's DNA is on the murder weapon as well as on HaffenFuß's clothing."

"Is the lab one hundred per cent sure? I'm not going on a wild-goose chase, on half-baked evidence."

"Heidi ran the test twice; once, on a single hair obtained from the victim's clothing and again, on the partial DNA sample found on the knife used in the murder. There was enough of Köhler's genetic material present to identify him as being the main suspect."

Wenzel scanned Konigsberg's report.

"I hope you've dotted the i's and crossed the t's on this one!"

"I've covered every avenue, Angela. While going over the case file, I noted that a white sports car had been seen in the BaaderStrasse area around the time of the murder. Bearing in mind how many high-performance cars there would have been in the country at that time, I examined the Köhler family's own vehicle records. There was, and still is, a white VW Karmann Ghia, registered in Frau Köhler's name."

"What does that prove?"

"On a hunch, I had it checked out in the lab. Frau Köhler was most obliging, in telling her husband that the car was being serviced. The vehicle had not been cleaned properly after the stabbing and our technicians found blood residue, absorbed into the carpet in the scuff panel under the dashboard. It provided a positive match with the victim's blood found on the assailant's knife."

"How would Köhler have been able to get in and out of the apartment without being heard? Surely someone must have noticed something?"

"The police report states that the residents heard no disturbance on the night of the homicide. One of his neighbours heard HaffenFuß playing tracks by Puccini on the evening of the murder, as he often did, commenting that it helped her sleep. Around eleven thirty, she was awoken from a deep slumber by the aria, *O Mio Babbino Caro*. It was being played unusually loudly for the duration of the track. Then, as it ended, the building fell silent. Before falling asleep again, she made a mental note to speak with Emil regarding his lack of consideration for others. The old lady thought no more of it until the police arrived at her door the following morning."

Schmitt stopped to drink from the cup of water he had brought with him before continuing his report into the murder, as pieced together from Commander Schröder's affidavit and the police evidence file.

"The crime was only uncovered the next day, after the tenant failed to answer the door to gas engineers who had turned up to install a new cooker. When the police arrived, they found the victim lying on his back, in a pool of blood, with a knife in his chest. He had died of multiple puncture wounds to the upper body area. The Dual brand record player was still running. There were no fingerprints found, either at the flat or on the weapon and, with no witnesses, the investigating officers had nothing further to go on. This all coincided with the accidental release of Thomas Schwarzkopf from the Breitkopf Institute nearby. He had been sectioned for the heinous murder of a young girl in the town of Hochstadt, many years before, and became the main suspect as it was his modus operandi that Köhler used. Two days later, Schwarzkopf's body was discovered floating in the land canal, a suspected suicide. The case was then closed."

"So, let me get this straight, Detlef; the poor wretch took the fall for Köhler?"

"Unquestionably. If the technology we have now had been around then, Köhler would have been behind bars sooner. He manipulated the whole situation from the start. Who would have suspected a fine, upstanding citizen like him of committing murder?"

"Well then, the only thing that's left for me to do is to raise an arrest warrant from Judge Janzyke, hopefully by this afternoon. I must say, that was a long two minutes!" added Wenzel light-heartedly as Detlef gathered his files and returned to his office.

****

It was seven thirty the next morning when Schmitt pressed the button to summon the lift which would take him to his office. It had been a number of weeks since he had spoken with Frau Köhler. Her son was now co-operating fully, identifying other Serbian Mafia accounts that the team had mistaken for legitimate businesses. The elevator doors opened; Frau Wenzel stepped out into the corridor and greeted him.

"Hi, Detlef, can you have everyone in the case room for eleven? Please ensure they have any up to date information with them as there is a helicopter waiting to take me to Bonn for another damn security briefing!"

Just before eleven, Schmitt and his team filed into the crime case room. Wenzel opened the meeting.

"Morning, everyone, I've just come back from a code red security meeting in Bonn. Don't look so glum; our masters are very pleased with the seizures and arrests we are making. Our Italian counterparts have detained several suspects who were found to be connected to the cocaine smuggling route we busted. The street price has rocketed in Europe, which leads them to think there may yet be an attempt to open a new supply route. Peter, what new evidence has Herr Köhler revealed, to date?"

Lang had been interviewing the banker over the last five days, auditing suspect accounts and having the assets frozen. He described how Stein had exerted pressure on Köhler – through emotional blackmail – to launder money via bogus accounts. Köhler had not wanted to lose Stein and felt that he had no option other than to comply with his partner's demands.

On one of those lonely nights, when they had rowed over the money and his lover had stormed out of the apartment, an idea came to him. He decided to manipulate the bank's own business accounts when the other members of staff had gone home for the evening. He executed his plan on the days when his father had been working in the bank. Köhler senior always examined the balances before signing them off. His son then simply transferred the Serbian Mafia capital later, after his father had left. It was Curt Köhler's arrogance which ensured the operation worked seamlessly. He had never given Eugen an ounce of credit for the way he had transformed the group's financial systems. The legitimate methods he suggested for hiding share transactions or schemes designed to avoid paying income tax were rubbished, and Köhler junior was laughed out of the office.

During these covert evenings, he had electronically moved large sums of money from the Munchener Assistance Bank into other financial institutions. Eugen had created cloned, internal banking accounts, which were normally reserved for bank finances only. He stored the assets to be laundered there, in preparation for future transfers. They were then used to purchase shares on the Frankfurt, Paris and London stock exchanges, the bonds being retained for roughly two weeks before being sold. The monies were deposited into an account in the Luden Privatbank AG, Zurich, before ending up in an account in Liechtenstein.

"There the trail ends," explained Lang. "We are awaiting an

international warrant to secure the records from the financial institutions in Liechtenstein and Zurich and for the companies listed by Köhler. All joking aside, we should have this guy working for us. He sets up financial tracks that even a Native American couldn't follow."

Wenzel sat in silence for a while before responding.

"Well done, everybody. Keep up the pressure on these people. Cripple them both of their finances and their structure and, most importantly, put them out of business!" she added as the team left the room.

****

Frau Wenzel was unable to reach Judge Janzyke until the following afternoon. She was in his chambers as he read the evidence placed before him.

"Right, Angela, there is more than overwhelming evidence before me to issue an arrest warrant."

"Thank you, Paweł, I'll get my guys onto it immediately," replied Wenzel as she lifted the authorisation and quickly headed back to Pullach.

****

Schmitt and von Harz walked through the revolving doors of the München Continental Hotel and into the lobby. Frau Köhler had phoned earlier, informing him of her husband's schedule.

"Good evening. Is Herr Köhler here?" Schmitt asked the young female receptionist.

"Yes, he is in the restaurant, with guests. Whom shall I say is calling?"

"My name is Detective Chief Inspector Schmitt but don't worry,

I will find him myself. Thank you for your assistance."

"How do you think this will go down, Detlef?" asked von Harz as they hurried through the reception area.

"I don't care, one way or the other but, for him, probably not good. If he's here, we are bringing him in."

"Good evening, gentlemen, do you have a reservation?" the maître d' enquired as the pair entered the restaurant. "Excuse me, gentlemen, have you booked a table?" he repeated as they strode past him. "Gentlemen, please…. you can't just arrive unannounced…. please…. stop!" protested the maître d' in vain, whilst trying to keep up with them.

Von Harz gently restrained the man, bringing him to an abrupt halt as he presented his warrant card. The maître d' quickly backed off and the detective continued to follow his boss through the restaurant.

Staff and guests alike had already noticed the disturbance. Upon hearing the raised voices, Köhler looked over as the two men approached.

"Herr Köhler, please stand up," Schmitt requested.

"What is the meaning of this, Detective?" the banker demanded to know.

He had been entertaining two American industrialists. The investors had come to München as part of an overseas trade mission. They were interested in leasing a new, large industrial estate that Köhler's group of companies had recently developed.

Schmitt totally ignored his protest.

"Stand up, Köhler. You're under arrest for the murder of Emil HaffenFuß, in 1972. You do not have to say anything. However, it may harm your defence if you do not mention, when questioned, something which you later rely on in court. Anything you do say may be given in evidence against you. Do you understand?"

Köhler and his guests stared in disbelief.

"Do you understand the charge I have put before you?" repeated Schmitt. "Stand up!"

Köhler remained in his seat.

"Yes, I do, Herr Schmitt, and your accusation is totally absurd. You can't just barge your way in here like this; it's police harassment! Please leave immediately. Speak with my solicitor and he will arrange a time and place of convenience to answer this groundless allegation," argued Köhler, now somewhat uncomfortable.

Mindful of the other diners watching, Schmitt knew that he needed to end this charade.

"Herr Köhler, I won't ask you again; on your feet…. get up!"

"I've never heard such nonsense! Now, if you will excuse us, Detectives," replied Köhler dismissively as he resumed eating his Dover sole, which had been pleasingly arranged on fine, Dresden porcelain and placed on a table dressed in Irish linen.

The two Americans looked on in astonishment as the brinkmanship was played out.

"Gentlemen, please carry on eating. These officers are just leaving," Köhler assured his guests.

Schmitt signalled to von Harz, who walked around the table and dragged Köhler up from his seat. The rapid action sent a full bottle of Romanée-Conti wine crashing to the floor.

"Herr Köhler, place your hands behind your back," demanded von Harz, brusquely handcuffing him.

"Please continue to enjoy your meal, gentlemen. I am sorry for the interruption, everyone," apologized Schmitt as the banker was unceremoniously led through the crowded restaurant and out to the detectives' car.

On their arrival at Bayerstraße courthouse, they found Judge Janzyke waiting patiently. Schmitt and von Harz, along with Detective Bäcker who had handled the original murder inquiry, stood behind Köhler and his lawyer during the proceedings.

"How does the defendant plead?" asked the judge, who was dressed in an evening suit. He was to accompany his wife to an opera after he completed the hearing.

"Your Honour, the way my client has been treated is totally outrageous. These men have publicly humiliated him front of the good people of München. I wish to make a formal complaint regarding the behaviour of the arresting officers," replied Kleber, having had just ten minutes with his client to brief him.

"Save me the amateur dramatics, Herr Kleber! Guilty or not guilty?" said the judge, savouring every moment of the arraignment.

"Not guilty, Your Honour. Counsel requests that my client be granted bail."

"Bail denied."

"But.... Your Honour!"

"Herr Kleber, this case is not as straightforward as you may think. I have been reliably informed by the prosecution that your client is a considerable flight risk."

"Nonsense! My client...."

"On the strength of the information provided," interrupted the judge, "the prosecution and I have no faith in your client ever appearing for trial."

"Your Honour, if I may add that my client is a well-respected member of the community, with many business interests here. He is not a flight risk."

"Be that as it may, Herr Kleber, your client will be safely tucked up in our fine institution at Stadelheim, where we can keep an eye on him until his next appearance."

"You can't do this!" argued Köhler as his lawyer tried to shut him up.

In a quiet and measured voice, the judge reaffirmed his authority.

"Oh, believe me, I can, Herr Köhler! I am doing just that. Take him away."

"You're a disgrace…. bloody immigrant! Coming to our great country and trying to deprive me of my freedom! Who gave you the right, you piece of Polack trash?" yelled the banker, his temper getting the better of him.

"Herr Köhler, let me refresh your memory. Your, I mean, our, great constitution, which the people of Germany voted for in 1947, gives me the right to deliver justice throughout the state of Germany. You are now in contempt of court, but I will deal with that later. Now, if you don't mind, I have an opera to attend and you have delayed me for long enough. Guards, take the accused away," ordered the judge.

Janzyke put on his overcoat and scarf before leaving to join his wife, who was waiting outside in their chauffeur-driven limousine.

As Köhler was being bundled out of the courthouse and into a prison van to be driven to Stadelheim, von Harz couldn't resist some black humour.

"You'll be in good company where you're going, Köhler. The Perlacher Forst Cemetery is just behind you so you'll sleep like a log!"

The banker sat, with his head in his hands, as the doors of the prison transport vehicle were slammed shut. Schmitt gave von Harz an exasperated look and made his way to the car.

****

Detlef wearily closed the apartment door and hung up his jacket.

"You're late, honey; rough day?" enquired Amélie.

"Nothing a cup of Jacobs' won't fix…. How's Erhard?"

Amélie switched the kettle on.

"He's been a real sweetie today. He had his bath an hour ago and is out like a light. Nina rang; she said she hasn't heard from you for a while."

"I've been meaning to call her."

"You'd better, before she sends over a search party!" she joked, setting down their coffees and toastbrot spread with Nutella.

"I'll make a note in my diary," said Schmitt, biting into his toast. "Anything exciting across the pond?"

"They're starting a fertility programme soon; Nina's feeling very broody."

Detlef's only sister lived in Pennsylvania, where she worked as a circuit judge. She was married to John McLean, an FBI case officer. The two women had never met but they frequently chatted on the phone. Still excited about her partner's uncovering of the Riesener, Amélie had passed on the news.

"I told Nina about your big find and the secret compartment with the war documents concealed inside."

"Those are state secrets you're divulging!" gasped Detlef, trying to look stern. "What did she say?"

"That you always did have a knack of finding rare things. I also let her know that you've been calling out Gotthard's name in your sleep every night!" teased Amélie as she began to wash their cups and plates.

"I haven't been talking in my sleep, have I?" he asked, a little unsure, having had a few restless nights of late.

"No, but I've heard that name so often now that I feel I know him personally," she giggled, curling up beside Detlef on the sofa. Amélie was right, thought Schmitt; the man was beginning to occupy his every waking moment. He would be glad when this case was finally closed.

CHAPTER SIXTEEN

Schmitt and Reinhold had arrived at Stadelheim prison to interview Curt Köhler.

"Well, Herr Köhler, how are things with you today? You seem a little pale," remarked Schmitt.

"Oh, I'm fine, Detective, just counting the days until I am out of here, which I believe won't be too long when the trumped-up charges you have fabricated are dismissed! By the way, the prison guards tell me that one of our famous cowards was executed in this very institution."

"What are you talking about, Herr Köhler?" asked Schmitt.

"Willi Graf! Don't tell me you have never heard of him? He and his sister, Anneliese, were arrested here in München, charged with anti-Nazi propaganda and inciting our brave young combatants to surrender during the Second World War. Graf was sentenced to death by the courts for high treason and furthering the enemy's cause. Six months later, they beheaded him, right here in Stadelheim. Can you believe it? That's German efficiency for you! They say the Gestapo leaned on Graf as they tried to glean information leading to the arrest of other White Rose members," explained Köhler in a fevered manner.

Schmitt stared at him in disgust before disengaging from the conversation.

"Can I assume you're not going to do the honourable thing and confess to the murder of Emil HaffenFuß?" questioned Schmitt, choosing to stay with the topic of the visit.

Köhler, now seeming deflated, looked at the officer with loathing as he sat, with his arms folded, in the prison interview room.

Schmitt, having put two blank cassettes into the recording machine, began the cross-examination.

"Interview taking place of Herr Curt Köhler, in relation to the 1972 murder of Emil HaffenFuß. Present are Herr Köhler, Detective Chief Inspector Schmitt, Detective Reinhold, and Herr Kleber, the defendant's solicitor."

"May I call you Curt?"

"It's irrelevant what you call me, Detective; I never harmed the fellow," he replied, looking up at the ceiling uninterestedly.

"What motivated you to carry out the murder of Emil HaffenFuß?"

"I didn't lay a hand on the man."

"Your DNA was found on both the murder weapon and the victim's body, along with one of your hairs. Can you explain that?"

"Detective, this DNA tomfoolery is in its infancy and can't really be relied upon. As for Emil HaffenFuß, I met him in my bank on a couple of occasions. A hair could have come into contact with his clothing as we shook hands."

"When, precisely, did you meet him?"

"That was a long time ago, Detective!"

"It's not that long ago, Curt. Come on, dates and times."

"He came to the bank to make money lodgements. I bumped into him two or three times before his brutal murder."

"So, you agree that it was a brutal murder for someone who gave his all during the war, suffering those horrendous burns to his entire body. It was a sad end for a guy who had recently lost his wife and just wanted to see out the rest of his own life in peace."

Köhler remained silent as the detective re-engaged.

"Believe me, Curt, as for the DNA samples we have from you, you can bring all the experts you want to the table but it won't make the slightest difference. We have sent the evidence to the people in England who developed the technique. They achieved the same results that we did. You killed Emil and you will do time for his murder. The waiting game is over; we need answers. Why are you steadfastly refusing to assist us with our inquiries?"

He paused for a moment to drink some water from the cup he had brought with him before continuing the interview.

"Herr Köhler, what is your nationality?"

"I've explained all this before, to both Judge Janzyke and yourself. I am a German citizen, born and raised in this country. Don't try and bring up that old chestnut again."

The banker turned and whispered to his solicitor.

"Herr Schmitt, my client has nothing further to add at this juncture; the interview is terminated."

"Herr Kleber, may I speak with you a moment?" asked Schmitt as the solicitor started to pack away his papers.

Kleber stopped what he was doing and remained seated as Köhler was taken back to his cell.

"Only if you have something helpful to add, Herr Schmitt. As it stands, you're trying to build a prima facie case against my client. It won't wash! If you continue in your course of action, I will speak with the justice minister personally."

"Herr Kleber, let's cut to the chase. The game is over; it's HaffenFuß's corpse that is doing the talking now. Curt murdered the poor man and there's not a shred of doubt that he did it. A jury wouldn't get a lunchtime meal out of their deliberations. Five minutes of consideration and they will convict him."

Kleber remained silent, gathering his thoughts before replying.

"Detective, you show great dedication to your job but, what you must understand is, my client has yet to be convicted of the murder of Emil HaffenFuß. We have employed the best experts in the field of DNA and the weak charges against him will be dismissed. About my client's nationality, which is not in question, can you please explain your interest?"

"No, Herr Kleber, I'd prefer to keep that for another time."

"Then you are clutching at straws. As previously stated, my client is a German citizen and a well-respected pillar of the community. Good day, Detective."

****

Back in his cell, Köhler lay on the bed, recounting the interview in every detail. His photographic memory had not diminished with the passing of time. He remembered that day as clearly as if it were yesterday. It had been grey, dreary weather, a rather off day, when the solution to the problem of Emil HaffenFuß had come to him.

It had given for light rain that morning as Bachmann drove the gleaming S-Class Mercedes out through the gates of the family home, heading for Nuremberg. Köhler had been working on a deal for months, going over the final calculations until the early hours. It was always the finer details to look out for, he thought. His group was about to make their biggest takeover yet – a large engineering company – and he was on his way to conclude the transaction.

The back seat of the car was littered with papers as Köhler

checked for any inaccuracies in the final contract. He had been partially listening to Haydn's Symphony No. 68, which was being broadcast on Bayerischer Rundfunk as the Mercedes glided along the autobahn. Approaching the Manching-Nueberg junction, the ten o'clock news came on.

"A Government minister has stepped down in a sex scandal involving a prostitute, after photographs were sent to his wife," said the anchorman.

"The prick should have been more careful, Bachmann, though I can't really pass judgement, having been found in similar company when the police charged me with driving under the influence!" Köhler chuckled.

"Yes, sir," agreed the driver.

"Ministers are pleased with progress on the accommodation being provided for the athletes attending the München Olympics," continued the newsreader.

The banker smiled. The city council had leased land from him for temporary accommodation for the competitors. He carried on reading the contract prepared by his solicitor.

"Earlier today, a patient was mistakenly discharged from the Breitkopf Institute of Psychiatry in München," announced the reporter.

"Bachmann, Bachmann, turn it up!" barked Köhler.

The driver quickly obeyed and increased the volume on the radio. As he looked in the rearview mirror, he noticed that his boss had removed his glasses and set down his papers. For some reason, he seemed to be taking a great interest in this particular news article.

"The patient had been sectioned indefinitely, ten years ago, for the murder of a teenage girl in the town of Hochstadt. The public is warned not to approach the man as he is considered extremely dangerous. Any sightings must be reported to the police. And now, the sports news...."

Köhler requested the driver to lower the volume as he mulled over the story of the escaped patient.

****

The office was quiet. Most of the team were out, following up leads trying to locate the whereabouts of Dubravko Huzjak, Dragomir Dragovic and Goran Knezevic. A short time after his arrest, Huzjak had – somehow - managed to escape from police custody. It had been reported that he assaulted a duty sergeant in Maillingerstraße police station, seizing his Glock pistol before making off. In the case of Dragovic, a warrant had been issued for his arrest after he shot a delivery driver who had been loading a cash dispenser at a motorway service station. He fled the scene with a substantial sum of money, leaving the driver fighting for his life. As for Knezevic, he was being sought by police about the killing of an off-licence owner during a failed robbery in the town of Straubing.

After much deliberation, Wenzel and Schmitt had decided to assign von Harz as part of the diplomatic team to the German Embassy in Hungary. Being posted as a diplomat was a Government method of placing undercover agents in a foreign jurisdiction to carry out clandestine activities. Wenzel was widening the search to try to close the net around the Serbian Mafia.

Schmitt read Schröder's affidavit once more as he prepared to visit Köhler senior, for a second time. The banker continued to be kept on remand at Stadelheim, awaiting trial for the murder of Emil

HaffenFuß. Had Schröder, in the presence of his solicitor, dictated the letter as a means of mischief or was it really an accurate account of the darker side of Köhler?

****

"Herr Köhler, who are you?" questioned Schmitt.

"Detective, you know who I am, you put me here…. Hello…. Handcuffs!" taunted the prisoner, jangling the chains that secured him to the table; he had lost none of his arrogance from being locked up in a cell.

"In your previous statement, you indicated that you were born in Dresden, where you worked as a bank teller. You also stated that your entire family were decimated during the allied bombings of Dresden, in 1945," said Schmitt as he turned to the next page in the file.

"Please, Detective, let's not waste any more of my time. You have all this information on record," answered a surefooted Köhler as he blew cigar smoke across the table, mocking Reinhold and Schmitt. "Is this why you are here….to go over old coals whose embers have since died with the passing of time? The past is just that. If you have nothing constructive to offer, then this little chat is at an end. Guard, please…. I wish to leave; I've better things to be doing than listening to this drivel," snapped Köhler as he waited to have the restraining chains removed from the prison table.

Schmitt put his hand up, indicating that the warder should remain outside.

"We have recently spoken to a gentleman from Dresden. He was most helpful and was able to provide us with a photograph of a rather young, Corporal Curt Köhler."

The banker stopped fidgeting with his chains but remained silent.

"What's wrong, Curt, lost for words?" taunted the detective. "That's not like you! We took the liberty of having the picture reproduced by one of our forensic artists. He employed an age progression process which was most productive. I thought you might like to see the results."

Schmitt laid the portrait on the desk.

Köhler turned his head slightly, looking down at the artist's impression that had been placed in front of him. The image was a small, charcoal drawing, an interpretation of how the person in the old photograph might have aged since the picture was taken. The banker studied the sketch for a few minutes before contemptuously pushing it back across the table.

"What do you want me to say, Herr Schmitt? You found an old picture, a family snap of someone with the same name as me! So, what? You've had an arty person touch it up. Should I be impressed?"

Köhler took another long draw of his cigar before sitting back in the chair and folding his arms. After a few moments of silence, he decided to expand the conversation.

"Really, what do you want me say, Herr Schmitt? I should have kept in touch more with the family?"

"Detective, you're on a fishing trip!" interjected the accused's solicitor, also becoming irritated with the line of questioning, which appeared to be rather pointless. "Where are we going with this?"

"Bear with me, Herr Kleber. You might want to take off your coat and make yourself comfortable as this may take a while. You know, Curt, you look nothing like the artist's impression and…. after all this time…. you really ought to if you are who you claim to be. Sign your name here, please," said Schmitt pushing forward an A4 sheet of paper.

At a loss, Köhler stared blankly at the detective.

"My client won't be putting his name to a blank page, Detective," stated the solicitor.

"I want to compare your client's normal signature with one we have obtained. It's not a trick."

"You can have the signature for appraisal purposes only. I will take charge of the document, following this meeting."

"Thank you for your assistance, Herr Kleber. Curt, if you would do the honours. Now, Claudia, would you check this signature with that contained in the file?"

Reinhold compared the banker's signature with the one supplied by the great nephew of the person in the photograph. The week before, she had taken a flight to Berlin. From there, she drove to the town of Eberswalde, where she interviewed the recently elected Lord Mayor, Alfred Köhler. He was able to provide her with a lock of his great-uncle Curt's hair, which had been kept in a silver christening locket. He also gave her documentation - including old photographs - belonging to his extended family. One of those snapshots was of Curt Köhler.

"Herr Kleber, I will now present your client with an original specimen of Curt Köhler's signature, in addition to the one he has just given."

The prisoner briefly examined the documents in their transparent folders. He studied his own signature against that of the sample provided.

"As you can see, they are totally dissimilar. Can you provide an explanation of why that is?"

The banker quietly conferred with his lawyer before answering.

"I see no relevance in your questioning; it is merely a difference in one's handwriting. Do you know how many Dresdeners share that name, Detective?"

"As luck would have it, Curt, I am able to answer your query. Having examined the records in City Hall, Dresden, we found that, out of thirty male children registered on your birthdate, only four had the name Curt Köhler. One died at birth, another passed away at the age of six, after contracting diphtheria, and the third child's name was spelt K-u-r-t. So, as you see, that really does narrow our line of enquiry quite significantly. But, I digress. Going back to the question of your signature, I don't see it as just a simple difference in handwriting, not when, as I suspect, you have been building a financial empire using someone else's identity."

"Could you be more specific, Detective? That is very serious allegation you have just made against my client, on top of this frivolous charge of murder," replied Kleber, mopping his brow whilst frantically taking notes.

"Herr Kleber, your client's DNA is stored on the police national computer. We took the sample of hair from a Curt Köhler, formerly of Dresden, and ran it through our DNA system. The results bear no similarity to you, Curt, or whoever you are," stated the detective, pointing his finger at the prisoner.

"Now, Herr Kleber, your client has failed on two counts so far…. It's looking bad for him. But, maybe, he has a slim chance of recovery. Let us continue…. Perhaps he can he redeem himself, eh?"

Schmitt turned to yet another page in the file before slamming the palm of his hand on the table, startling everyone present.

"Oh, no, strike three, and I feel this is the most significant issue to date. Your fingerprints don't match those found on Curt Köhler's 1935 Dresdner bank lodgement book.

"How could you possibly have taken a print from an old lodgement book? God knows, how many people have handled it!" countered Kleber.

"I agree, Herr Kleber, but not everyone would handle the pages inside the book."

The solicitor and his client looked shocked that the laboratory had been so thorough in its test procedures.

"That means you're out, sit on the bench time, Herr whatever your name is. While we're on the subject, what is your name? I.... we, in all sincerity, would really like to know. After the time we have spent together, have we not formed some sort of bond, some form of trust, Curt?" teased Schmitt.

"I don't like your tone, Detective," replied the prisoner, now becoming very annoyed.

"Herr Köhler, I'm not particularly interested in your likes and dislikes," replied Schmitt, leaning over the table. "From where I'm sitting, you're in a lot of trouble. The more we dig, the murkier your past life seems to become."

"Herr Schmitt, I am who I claim to be, a German national. As such, I am entitled to the same rights and respect as any other landsman should have, until proven guilty. I feel you are not affording me those rights. I don't need to prove anything to you; this meeting is over," said the banker, attempting to leave, once again.

"Herr Köhler, remove your shirt," ordered the detective, acting on a hunch, as the prisoner, having had his chains undone, rose from his chair. The man stood immobilised, like a rabbit caught in the headlamps of a vehicle, trying to collect himself.

"I said remove it or, by God, I will have the guards remove it for you!" bellowed Schmitt.

Reluctantly, he took off his shirt. On doing so, an ugly, fifteen-centimetre scar was revealed, under his left arm.

"Nasty scar, Curt; care to enlighten us as to how you got it?"

Schmitt already knew that many SS officers and top party officials involved in war crimes had tried to hide their tattooed blood group and serial numbers. This information had been etched on the inside of the person's left arm to identify their service unit. Using various methods, the officers had assumed new identities and attempted to erase these details. In many cases, this deception was made to avoid being caught by allied war crimes units or Nazi hunters, such as Simon Wiesenthal.

"Herr Schmitt, I'm sure you've read my war records and, if so, you must know that I was wounded during the last days of the conflict. The American Browning automatic rifle is a great locksmith; nothing much stops it. I suppose I should be grateful that the dry-stone wall the round passed through lessened its impact on me."

Schmitt put the file he had been reading from to one side and opened another that Reinhold had handed to him.

"Let me refresh your memory, Curt," he said, leafing through the pages. "Corporal Curt Köhler, if that is your name, was hospitalised in the early summer of forty-two, following a shell injury sustained in the Kerch Peninsula, Crimea. You convalesced at a military hospital, south of Berlin, before being reassigned to the Reich Chancellery motor pool as one of their many drivers. In January 1945, you were transferred to serve with Brandenberger's 7th Army. Once there, you were assigned to other units as reinforcement, to bolster the Western Front, in an attempt to repel the allied invasion that was underway."

The detective looked to the prisoner for a lead.

"Go on, if you must, Detective," he said, relighting his cigar.

"Your unit was later forced to retreat from the district of Landau, driven back to the town of Neustadt, and then to Coburg, by the 101st Calvary of Patton's United States' 3rd Army. There, you and your colleagues acted as rear guards before eventually surrendering. By all accounts, the Wehrmacht put up a faultless defence of the town. Upon your capture, you received medical treatment during a short stint in a field hospital. You were processed at Dachau US military prison camp and subsequently transported to Fort Regent, Jersey, in the Channel Islands."

"Herr Schmitt...." began the solicitor before the detective put his hand up to dismiss his protest.

"During your incarceration, you worked as a farm labourer. In 1947, having denounced all things Nazi, you received a full pardon and returned to München. There, you appear to have found employment at the bank you now own."

The detective paused to take a drink from the disposable beaker. He deliberately sipped his water slowly, waiting for some form of reaction from the prisoner. Returning the cup to the table he asked sarcastically, "Have I left anything out, Curt?"

Schmitt closed the file. Köhler glowered at the detective, eyes locked in a state of venomous hatred towards this man who continued to harass him, trying to destroy his life's work.

CHAPTER SEVENTEEN

"Thank you, Max," said Reinhold as she and Schmitt handed in their security passes at Stadelheim and retrieved their Glock automatics.

"A gentleman was here earlier, requesting a visit with Herr Köhler," the guard informed them, holding out their firearms.

"We've just finished interviewing him. Where is this person now?" asked Schmitt as he holstered his gun.

"Sorry about the mix-up, Detective; he enquired about Eugen Köhler. I told him we had no one of that name here."

"Show me your CCTV records," demanded Schmitt.

"I took the liberty of printing an image of him, as he seemed dishevelled and rather out of place," explained the guard, giving Detlef a copy of the print.

"When was this?"

Schmitt studied the picture before turning to the bank of monitors on the wall.

"About ten minutes ago. There….in the white Mercedes G-wagon…. I watched him as he left the building and went over to the car park."

"Max, put out a call for support. Link into the city's traffic cameras to monitor his movements and keep us updated. Claudia, let's get going; I want to nail this bastard, once and for all!"

The detectives sprinted to their car before they lost Stein completely. The Quattro drifted sideways as Schmitt pressed hard on the throttle whilst exiting the car park. With the blues and twos on, he raced along StadelheimerStraße, overtaking anything in his path as oncoming drivers swerved, flashing their lights in annoyance. The detective ran a red light as he turned left onto Tegernseer LandStraße, only just missing a large beer truck which veered onto the central reservation to avoid him. Detlef kept the pressure on the S2 as it powered along the dual carriageway, heading south of town. He narrowly avoided a collision with a bus, at the junction of BruckenfischerStraße, as it attempted to merge onto the main street. The pace slowed as the traffic grew denser. Just after the junction of Münchener-Kindl-Weg, Schmitt was forced to stop behind other vehicles at a set of temporary, contraflow traffic lights. Reinhold turned off the siren while they waited, impatient to get motoring again.

"There he is!" she shouted, catching a glimpse of the Mercedes ahead of them, waiting in the queue.

"Call it in. I'll try to move up through the traffic and corner him," whispered Schmitt as he got out and Reinhold slid into the driver's seat.

Withdrawing the Glock from its holster, he released the safety catch. Schmitt was within two car lengths when the rear window of the G-wagon shattered. Having spotted the detective in his side mirror, Stein had opened fire. Schmitt, along with shocked motorists, dived for cover.

Suddenly, the jeep reversed into the car behind, ramming it into other vehicles before driving forward, through road cones and onto the carriageway that was under repair. Witnessing the unfolding scene, Reinhold skilfully manoeuvred into the work lane and pulled up, just as Schmitt was about to turn back. He jumped into the passenger seat and they sped off, construction workers leaping out of harm's way as the pursuit tore through the building site.

"Will I hold back a bit?" asked Reinhold.

"No, just drive…. Don't lose him!" replied Schmitt aggressively as he updated the control room on the situation.

Reinhold tried to avoid obstacles along the road, her vision partially obscured by the dust kicked up from the fleeing Mercedes.

"Shouldn't we wait for backup, Detlef?"

"He won't be getting away this time; stay with him, Claudia!"

Schmitt pressed the button on the door's armrest to lower the window.

Stein weaved around construction materials and plant in an effort to escape, intermittently firing off more rounds at the detectives. Reinhold pushed the S2 harder, dropping down into third gear, the four-wheel drive digging into the poor road surface as she struggled to keep control of the vehicle. After what seemed like a lifetime, Schmitt discharged three rounds, one of them puncturing the rear door of the jeep as it smashed through the site barriers and proceeded, at speed, along Tegernseer LandStraße.

Stein returned fire, impacting both the Audi's front wing and windscreen. Reinhold swerved and carried on with the pursuit. Back on a level road surface, Schmitt, leaning out of the window, steadied his hands on the door mirror and fired once more, causing the nearside rear tyre of the Mercedes to explode. The chase seemed to enter a phase of slow motion as Stein's vehicle began to swerve from left to right prior to leaving the road. It somersaulted down the embankment on the left, ending up on its roof, on the southbound carriageway of the E54. Schmitt and Reinhold got out of their vehicle and hurried down the embankment, as Stein was still trapped in the jeep. They stopped midway, hearing the violent screech of tyres. An articulated fuel tanker had begun to jackknife and the driver, fighting to regain control of his vehicle, was unable to avoid the collision which propelled the Mercedes into the central reservation.

The ignition of the tanker's contents was instant. Both drivers were engulfed in a fireball as the 42000 litres of fuel exploded. The detectives bolted up the embankment, chased by the searing wall of heat. Emergency services were on the scene within minutes, with traffic police closing the motorway in both directions so that they could begin to deal with the carnage. Officials from the internal affairs department arrived and took Reinhold and Schmitt's Glocks for forensic analysis, to determine how many firearms had been discharged. Their vehicle was also removed for forensic examination. A copy of video footage from an air surveillance helicopter was given to the IAD team to examine as the two detectives made formal statements regarding the incident.

"Are you alright, Claudia?" Detlef asked gently as he drove back to Pullach.

Reinhold had said very little after the incident. Schmitt had tried to comfort her but she was trembling uncontrollably as he led her back to the car. She had been looking straight ahead, lost in her thoughts, before turning to him.

"It doesn't matter what crimes Stein may have committed; I can't help but feel pity for him as well as the others, and the horrific circumstances in which they were killed.... Such senseless death and injury! That picture will stay in my head for the rest of my life, Detlef."

Schmitt looked across at his colleague, taken aback by how much the incident seemed to have affected her. She was clearly in shock. Her face was wan and her hands, clasped together, were shaking. Nevertheless, Detlef wanted to have his point of view heard.

"I understand how you must feel, Claudia. It was a scene no one should have to witness but I don't entirely agree with you. Yes, granted, it was a gruesome end to the man's life. However, those people who have been killed or injured are the result of his actions. The coward had no future, don't lose sight of that. My only regret is that we have been cheated out of a day in court."

"That doesn't change the fact that he and other human beings have lost their lives today, regardless of who was at fault," contended Reinhold.

She returned to staring blankly out of the car window, abruptly ending the discussion.

Schmitt changed their replacement vehicle up a gear and continued along WolfratshauserStraße. On the way, back to Pullach, there was no further conversation as the officers tried to come to terms with the day's events. The mood in the office was sombre; reports filtered in of innocent people having been killed because of Stein's recklessness. The two detectives appreciated that they would have to live with the consequences of their actions.

Detlef collected his belongings and returned home shortly after four that afternoon. In the flat on Stuntzstraße, the atmosphere was tense. Amélie had seen the report of the motorway accident on the lunchtime news. Later that evening, Detlef sat her down and described what had happened. She was both angry with him and frightened that, once again, he could have been killed. She had just about got over the stabbing incident in the car park, putting it to the back of her mind.

The couple argued for most of the night, Amélie demanding that he resign and join the regular police. Detlef reminded her that it was the job she agreed he should take and it was what he loved doing. He explained that he had no choice as to the situations that arose.

Amélie could not see that both Schmitt and Reinhold had gone out that day to stop and arrest someone; they had not set out to have people killed and many more injured in the process. The couple went to bed, neither of them speaking.

****

Early next morning, the team arrived for work. Frau Wenzel and Gottlieb Holzmann, München's Chief of Police, were already in the crime room. Detlef went over and introduced himself; both Wenzel and Holzmann were very terse with him.

"Good morning, everyone, please welcome Chief Holzmann; he has been brought up to date about the Serbian Mafia investigation. Just to let you know, Eugen Köhler has been given eight years for laundering monies which we have determined are the proceeds of crime. Using his position at the Munchener Assistance Bank, he had been facilitating these people and their activities. For his continued co-operation, the sentence has been reduced to four years and he has been put on the witness protection programme indefinitely. His father, Curt Köhler, continues to be kept on remand in Stadelheim prison for the murder of Emil HaffenFuß as he is considered a flight risk. As you are already aware, during an attempted stop and arrest yesterday, the fugitive, Claus Stein, repeatedly opened fire on two of our officers on a public highway. During the ensuing chase, more shots were exchanged, resulting in the…. well, you know the rest."

Wenzel stopped and took a sip of water. Reinhold and Schmitt avoided eye contact, choosing instead to look at the papers in front of them as the briefing continued.

"International arrest warrants have been issued for the following people: Dubravko Huzjak, Dragomir Dragovic and Goran Knezevic, who are all currently at large somewhere in Europe. Traffic management CCTV evidence suggests that Huzjak and Dragovic are responsible for gunning down a motorway patrol officer who had attempted to stop the car that they were travelling in, during a routine traffic inspection on the outskirts of the city of Győr, in Hungary. The imagery is of good enough quality for the Hungarian authorities to class them as persons of interest. These three men are highly dangerous and should not be approached, unless armed and with adequate backup. Perhaps you would like to add something at this point, Herr Holzmann?"

"Thank you, Frau Wenzel. I won't hide my annoyance at the fact that this department has, for some time, been running an operation that I should have been informed of! However, I have received a briefing from Frau Wenzel who has assured me that I will be kept in the loop from here on in. Yesterday's tragic events bring home what we are faced with every day: the unexpected. A total of fifty-two vehicles were involved in the resulting accident, which left four people dead, ten critically injured and sixteen with minor injuries. I won't discuss the individuals involved as there is an ongoing investigation but what I will say is that there is no room in München for maverick police officers. Thank you for your time."

With the briefing over, Wenzel summoned Schmitt and Reinhold to her office.

"Close the door and sit down," ordered the chief. "I want you to ignore what Chief Holzmann has just said. If we were to explain every last thing to him, nothing would get done. The justice minister knows, that's enough. I have read your statements and watched the video tapes of the pursuit. The audio commentary from your radio communication indicates that you both followed procedures correctly and I wouldn't have expected you to do anything differently. The resulting accident was just that, an accident. It is wholly unfortunate that those innocent people died. Like it or not, Stein's death has saved us a lot of time and money by not having to go through the courts. Nonetheless, given the outcry in the press at the minute, I think it wise that you both take time off until all this dies down. Unofficially, internal affairs are not pressing any charges but we must be seen to be abiding by the rules. That will be all."

As Wenzel was about to start reviewing the reports on her desk which required her immediate attention, Schmitt spoke.

"Is this really necessary, Angela? After all, as you just said, we followed procedure."

"Detlef, I'll explain this only once. You must appreciate that ordinary people were caught up in yesterday's events and now the press are out for blood. Some may view your actions as irresponsible," she countered. "I'm ordering you to stand down; two weeks is all I ask. This does not go outside these four walls but you are to keep your personal firearms and warrant cards. There are too many individuals connected to this case who have not yet been accounted for. Is that understood?"

"Yes, ma'am," said the detective meekly as he got up and left the room.

Reinhold had remained silent during the meeting. The dark

hollows beneath her eyes betrayed a lack of sleep, due to the previous day's car chase and the ensuing accident. It was the first time she had been fired upon whilst on active service and it had caused her to question her position as a counter intelligence officer. In a way, she was glad of the free time being offered to her.

"Claudia, are you okay?" Wenzel enquired softly.

"I'm fine, ma'am, just a little tired."

"Good. I will be instructing your unit to continue monitoring anything that flags up Huzjak, Dragovic or Knezevic, until your return."

Schmitt resigned himself to taking a break. Too much had happened recently and, with the immense pressure at work, things weren't good between Amélie and himself. He had given her suggestion some thought overnight but could not see himself back as a regular police detective again.

****

Detlef made the best of his enforced leave. Travelling by train, he took Amélie and Erhard to stay at his uncle's cottage in the Harz Mountains, where his entire family circle had holidayed for as long as he could remember. He had decided, for the good of his own little family unit, to use the break wisely and spend some quality time with them.

"You can switch that off for a start!" Amélie demanded as she unpacked Erhard's clothes, putting them in the old, carved tallboy.

Schmitt sheepishly turned his mobile phone off, placing it in one of the many pockets of their suitcase. When they had finished unpacking, Detlef opened a bottle of Riesling and poured them both a glass. He then began to prepare the trout his Uncle Horst had caught, garnishing the fish with herbs before grilling and serving it with an accompaniment of baby potatoes and spinach. After the meal, little Erhard, tired from the long journey, was bathed and changed. He fell into a deep sleep as soon as his head hit the pillow.

The couple went out to the porch and sat on the loveseat, watching, spellbound, as the sun slowly drifted behind Brocken peak.

"What are you going to do, Detlef?" asked Amélie as she looked into his eyes.

"Do? I don't follow you?"

"Will you resign? If not for my sake, at least think of Erhard."

"That's a low blow, Amélie. The holiday has only begun; can't we just enjoy our time together for now? I promise to think it over."

She made no reply, burying her head deep into his chest as the last rays of the sun disappeared, creating a beautiful, orange glow in the sky.

****

The warm, dry weather enabled them to explore some of the many mountain paths and rivers, riding old bicycles that Amélie had found in the nearby barn. There were days when Schmitt left Amélie reading a book by the fire while Erhard played in his travel cot, spending his free time fishing, either with Uncle Horst, or alone. On one occasion, he managed to steal away, taking his mobile phone with him. The mast at Brocken peak afforded a good signal which enabled him to make a call to Muller, who updated him on the progress of their investigations.

On the final day of the vacation, Detlef cast his line into the slow-running brook, the float bobbing in the water as it meandered its way downstream. During this rare interlude of total peace and seclusion, he contemplated his life. He loved Amélie deeply; she had brought an end to his downward spiral of misery after losing his parents in an alcohol-fuelled hit and run incident some years earlier, in the town of Wolfsburg. Both she and Erhard meant the world to him but he had no answer to her plea that he leave his job. Was Amélie being unfair to use their son as a means to force his hand? After all, it was just as likely that he could be hit by a tram on a night out as the chance of being injured again or, indeed, killed in the line of duty.

Two glorious weeks came to an abrupt end, and the couple began to pack up their belongings. Uncle Horst would be arriving shortly to take them to the train station.

"Well, have you come to a decision?" asked his partner.

Detlef had wrongly assumed that Amélie had dropped the subject of his occupation. He had given the matter much thought, running all sorts of scenarios through his mind in an attempt to try and please everyone.

"I'm staying on at Pullach for now," he replied, "but if another incident should occur then I will consider a career change. I think I'm being more than fair, Amélie."

She looked at him for a moment, unsure if what he was offering was something she could agree to.

"I don't want to fight but if you renege on this, Detlef, we are over."

"I won't; you have my word on it."

Seated in their railway carriage, the couple smiled at one another while Erhard slept opposite them. Detlef felt that they had reached a turning point in their relationship and that things would be better from now on. Amélie, too, was soon lulled into a deep sleep, her head resting on her partner's shoulder as the intercity express silently sped through the rolling countryside, on its way back to München.

CHAPTER EIGHTEEN

"You look well rested, Detlef; I see you've managed to catch some sun!" exclaimed Wenzel as Schmitt entered her office the following Monday.

"Thanks, Angela. I needed that break. This job can really get to you, sometimes."

"I agree; we haven't been making much progress with the Serbian case. How can I help you?"

"If you remember, one of the allegations made in Helmut Schröder's affidavit was that Köhler had assumed a false identity, his real name being Frank Gotthard. I thought I would carry out a preliminary investigation before confronting him with the claim."

"The state will confiscate his group in its entirety if this assertion proves to be true. What did you find out?"

"After looking through the electoral register, Reinhold discovered a widow with the same surname, who lives in the Miesbach district of Tegernsee. Most of the Gotthard family were killed during the war and she is one of the last remaining relatives. There is a chance that Frau Gotthard may be able to remove the shroud of mystery from the Köhler case. I still have my own doubts about the man's true identity."

"When are you leaving?"

"As soon as possible. Claudia is yet to make the arrangements as I wanted to clear it with you first."

"Very well then. Let Reinhold manage things here. I feel she could do with a bit more responsibility at present."

Since the incident involving Stein, Reinhold had lost her motivation and had become very withdrawn. She had been content to let others take the lead during recent inquiries. Wenzel hoped that managing the team might bring out the old Claudia again.

****

Two days later, Schmitt drove through the town of Miesbach and along the rural MiesbachStraße, until he came upon a small village. There, he followed the road left, onto Panoramaweg, finally turning right, into the driveway of a small, two-storey house.

"Frau Gotthard, how kind of you to speak with me," he said, getting out of the car and shaking the hand of the elderly lady, who had come outside to greet him.

"It is my pleasure, Herr Schmitt. You've travelled a long way, so it is the least I can do. Besides, Fraulein Reinhold was most persuasive. Please, come in, or the neighbours will start to gossip!" she laughed, showing him into her home.

Frau Gotthard was of slight build and had obviously looked after herself over the years. Her house was plain but immaculately kept, furnished in the typical, old Bavarian, farmhouse style of dark oak. During a light lunch prepared by the householder, she recounted her own life story.

"This is my Rudi," said the old lady, holding up a framed photo of a Wehrmacht officer. "He died, saving his comrades in Russia, during the Second World War."

"I'm sorry for your loss."

"Don't be, Detective. I was only one of Germany's many war widows."

When Frau Gotthard was comfortable, Schmitt set up the tape recorder and, with pen and paper at the ready, he began the interview.

"What can you tell me about your husband's aunt and uncle?"

"I can only relate what his mother, Dorothea, told him; you do understand?" replied the woman.

Schmitt turned the tape recorder off for a moment.

"I understand, Frau Gotthard; it has been some time. Please, at your own pace."

The detective once more activated the recorder.

"Gorch was born around 1900 and was a wayward child from an early age. You know the type?"

"Yes, I deal with them every day, ma'am."

Frau Gotthard rose and opened the window of the hot, airless room. As she returned to her seat, a large, marmalade cat entered through the opening and jumped off the sill, giving her a fright before wandering off into the kitchen.

"That's Panzer, he'll be the death of me! He's probably been out in the fields, killing mice. Now…. what was I saying? Gorch's life of crime began on a petty scale. Partially driven by hunger, he would thieve eggs or chickens from local farms. He also stole crops from neighbouring properties under cover of darkness, selling them in nearby towns the next day to help support his family. The police received numerous complaints and often came looking for him. He did his best to avoid being caught as the constables would issue summary justice when they found him."

"In what way, Frau Gotthard?"

"There and then, behind a barn or an outbuilding. They didn't spare their batons and boots in those days, no, they didn't hold back at all! When he was eighteen, Gorch met his future wife, Fieke Erkenbald. She came from the town of Weyarn, some distance from his home. She was the eldest of three sisters who worked their mother's ancestral farm; their father had been killed in the Great War. As time wore on, Fieke became more and more smitten with Gorch and tried to involve him in helping around the farm. In the beginning, it was a novelty, milking the cattle and taking part in the harvest. But his interest soon waned and he went back to thieving. Gorch and Fieke decided to get married in 1920, against the wishes of Frau Erkenbald who was aware of Gorch's background. She was quite incensed, forbidding her daughter to marry him. Forgive me, but the young man was a total reprobate."

"Seems like a piece of work, alright."

"Oh, he was. Eventually, the couple, with the permission of their parents and the local pastor, were married, in a civil ceremony at the local Rathaus, in Miesbach."

"I don't think I would be too keen to allow a daughter of mine to marry a man like that either, Frau Gotthard."

"Please, call me Constanze. Yes, that's why I wasn't surprised when I was told you wanted to speak with me about the family. May I ask what this is in relation to, Detective? Fraulein Reinhold was rather tight-lipped on the phone."

"I can't go into details, Constanze, but it is connected to a case we are investigating at this present time. Did they have a son named Frank?"

"I'm not sure. They moved away very suddenly."

"Forgive me for interrupting; do carry on," said Schmitt, silently giving up hope of obtaining any meaningful information from the lady.

"Well, they set up home on the outskirts of Miesbach. At a time when other people were suffering hardships following the Great War, Fieke was enjoying the money and food her husband brought home from his robberies. Gorch's crimes got more brazen with every burglary. What was the name of that town now.... Tratberg? Ah, yes, that's it.... the young scoundrel robbed a house in Tratberg. It was the home of a retired doctor, I believe...."

As Schmitt stood in the kitchen, waiting for the kettle to boil, he was certain he had the wrong family but decided to continue with the interview as a courtesy to the old lady. Given her age, she probably didn't get many visitors, he reasoned, as he carried in the tray of freshly made coffee and home-baked cakes.

The woman, taking a slice of apfelkuchen, picked up where she had left off.

"During the robbery, there was a struggle with the homeowner; as a result, he suffered a stroke. Gorch ran off, leaving that poor, old gentleman to be found the next morning, cold and unconscious! The couple absconded, as the hangman's noose would be waiting for Gorch in Landsberg prison if the police ever caught up with him."

"Have you any idea where Gorch and Fieke went?" queried Schmitt.

"Somehow avoiding detection, they made it to the town of Schwerte, on the outskirts of Dortmund, where they stayed with a relative for about six months. We know this for sure because Fieke sent her mother a postcard from there, sometime later. That's the last anyone ever heard of them."

"So, there were no further postcards, or anything else to indicate where they went?"

"I'm sorry, no. On the one hand, his family were glad to see the back of him, God knows, he caused so much trouble. But they loved him all the same. They assumed that the couple had been killed during the war. Gorch would probably have been conscripted into the Wehrmacht and Fieke may have died during an air raid."

"I've checked with the war records department. They have details of his brothers being called up but there is no record of Gorch ever being enlisted."

Frau Gotthard sat for a moment, nursing her coffee, whilst dabbing at her eyes with a silk handkerchief. She glanced out of the window as a local farm tractor drove by.

"Herr Bochum likes to keep himself busy, doesn't he?" the widow casually remarked as if Schmitt knew the farmer personally. "It would have been nice to know what became of them. Perhaps they were killed during the Blitz?"

Schmitt decided to bring the interview to a close.

"Alas, that's a question we'll never be able to answer. Thank you for your time, Constanze. If nothing else, I've had a day out of the office, in a beautiful part of the country."

"It's one of those mysteries, isn't it? Like so many families during the war, relatives went missing and were never found. Well, goodbye, it's been lovely meeting you," said Frau Gotthard as she walked the detective out to his car.

"Thank you for all your assistance, Constanze. If I find out any more information as to what happened to the couple, I'll let you know."

With this, Schmitt got into the S2 and headed back to München.

Reinhold's research had clearly been wide of the mark. As he travelled over the quiet, Bavarian back roads, he made up his mind to have words with her on his return.

****

Back in his office at Pullach, Schmitt typed up his report. All in all, he felt the trip to Miesbach had been disappointing, to say the least. He had fully expected to find a connection to Frank Gotthard. That damn name kept appearing at every turn but, like a mirage, it vanished in the haze.

****

"Good morning, everyone," said Wenzel as she brought order to the case conference. "Detlef, how did your visit to Frau Gotthard go?"

"Not very well; there was no trace of anyone by the name of Frank Gotthard, military or otherwise."

"It was a long shot."

"It was more than that, Angela! Well, I'll just have to turn another stone and see what new leads are under it."

"People, listen up. In the Serbian conflict, General Jakov Tuvić has ratcheted things up in Bosnia. His Republika Srpska forces have now taken over the UN "safe area" of Srebrenica, in the east of the province. Early reports suggest that up to 8000 people, mostly men and boys, have been executed."

Muller was about to speak when the chief put her hand up, silencing him.

"The women were segregated and sent to Bosnian-held territory. Unconfirmed reports are coming in of them being raped and killed. We are currently waiting on verification from the UN of these reports. Heinz, you were going to say something?"

"Who the hell had charge of the area? Surely there were enough peacekeepers to ensure the refugees' safety?"

Wenzel read from her report.

"I quote, *'hundreds of Dutch military peacekeepers representing the United Nations Protection Force were guarding these people at the time'.* For whatever reason, they allowed the town to fall to the Serb militia. The Bosnian Serbs' commanders are demanding the closure of all civil and commercial traffic to Sarajevo."

"Surely the UN isn't going to give into these people's demands?" queried Schmitt.

"All I know, at the moment, is that the UN is considering closing the only route into Sarajevo. The road is a vital lifeline, both for civilian and commercial traffic. This action would leave the city totally dependent on relief aid. This will undoubtedly create a humanitarian crisis for those unfortunate people who are unable to escape the area."

"Has the UN got no balls, Angela?" Schmitt asked.

"Their hands are tied by protocol," replied Wenzel, shrugging her shoulders.

She turned to Reinhold.

"Claudia, have you anything to add?"

"We have seized two additional consignments of weapons coming across the French border. The find included assorted handguns and submachine guns; forensic teams are currently working on the serial numbers."

"What about the two Serbian fugitives? Has von Harz had any sightings of them?"

"No. He reported that they have either gone to ground or fled to another jurisdiction."

The station chief was increasingly of the belief that von Harz was on a junket. He had been having much too good a time in Hungary, with nothing to show for it.

"Get him back here where he will be of more use. People, I want results on my desk. These guys have been given too much slack to date. Go out there and find them!" snapped Wenzel, obviously under continued pressure from Bonn.

****

Schmitt had just sat down at his desk when the phone rang.

"Hi, Detlef, sorry for ringing you at work."

"That's not a problem, John. What's up?"

"Nina was chatting with Amélie a while back."

"John, please give Nina my apologies. I promised Amélie I'd call her but it completely slipped my mind!"

"It's okay, buddy, she knows the pressure you're under. Listen, that's not what I'm ringing about. Your little lady just happened to mention the papers you found during the G8 summit with the name Gotthard on them. Am I correct?"

"That's right; I've got a gut feeling about them. I think they may be linked to a much larger case I'm currently working on."

"Well, I don't know if this is connected in any way, but Nina was looking through the local rag for garage sales that we could go to at the weekend. She's still hoping that, one day, she'll turn up a genuine piece of Chippendale! Third page in, there was a report about an elderly homeowner who had been shot during a botched robbery."

"John, I don't want to seem ungrateful but where does this figure in my investigation?"

Sitting in his office at home, McLean laughed out loud at the impatience of his wife's brother.

"You never change, Detlef, always looking to grasp the nettle! The victim was a high school teacher, by the name of Eva Gotthard, a spinster from Boalsburg, here, in Pennsylvania."

Schmitt straightened himself up in his seat.

"Did you say Gotthard?"

"Now I have your attention!"

McLean relayed the little he knew about the attempted burglary. The woman was currently hospitalised with life-threatening injuries.

"I thought I'd take a little mosey over and talk to the local law enforcement officers, see what I can find out about the family," he concluded.

"John, it would be a complete waste of time driving across country and maybe finding nothing of significance."

"No worries, buddy. Nina and I could both do with some downtime and, if I find something of use, I'll call you. Give my love to Amélie and Erhard. Bye."

With that, Schmitt's brother-in-law hung up. Whilst John meant well, Detlef felt that it was a stretch of the imagination to believe that the newspaper article could possibly have any bearing on the case involving Köhler. Placing the phone back in its cradle, he put the topic to the back of his mind and opened an envelope he had been handed by a member of staff. It contained a letter from internal affairs, exonerating both him and Claudia of any wrongdoing in relation to the deaths of Claus Stein and the other victims of the motorway accident. It did, however, provide some recommendations should a similar scenario occur in the future. Schmitt returned the brief to the envelope and thrust it in a drawer, wanting nothing more than to forget the whole episode.

CHAPTER NINETEEN

Running late, Schmitt knocked on the door and hurried into the interview room at the finance courts, where Judge Janzyke was already questioning Tomas Kampfle in relation to his evasion of tax and being a shareholder in a company that was in breach of the NATO ban on supplying weapons in support of the Bosnian conflict.

"Detective Inspector Schmitt has entered the room," noted Wenzel as Janzyke continued with his cross-examination of the suspended finance minister.

"Yes…. Upon the advice of my accountant, I decided to create a charitable trust…."

Janzyke cut in.

"My dear Kampfle, we have been over this a dozen times. It's an offshore shell company, based in the Channel Islands but registered in Yorkshire. Is that correct?"

"Yes, that is right."

"Well then, it's a tax haven; stop splitting hairs."

"I disagree."

"Just as a matter of interest, how did you acquire a fifteen percent shareholding with the Munchener Assistance Bank?" Janzyke asked.

"That's none of your damn business!"

"Can we leave my client's personal life out of this?" requested Herr Bötel, the minister's solicitor.

"Fine, fine, I will respect your client's wishes."

"It's alright, Bötel, I've got nothing to hide. Perhaps I should clear up this matter, once and for all," said Kampfle, having had a sudden change of heart. "My father was Helmut Schröder, the former foreign minister. He had an affair with my mother, who was his secretary at that time. When their liaison became public knowledge, she decided to move back to her hometown of Würzburg. However, she neglected to inform Herr Schröder of my existence and, as a result, I was estranged from him for the first ten years of my life. It was an accidental encounter during an election rally that brought us together. My mother had taken me into town to buy new clothes for my return to school. As we exited a local store, we came face to face with Father, on a walkabout with his election team. It didn't take him long to spot the resemblance."

"Was Herr Schröder named as your father on your birth certificate?" queried Schmitt.

"No, Detective. Initially, after our chance meeting, Mother wanted nothing to do with him, but she finally agreed to let him see me if the status quo was preserved. I'm not in favour of double-barrelled surnames; I like to keep things simple."

So, Schröder's absence from the birth documentation was the reason the team had not connected Kampfle to the overall investigation. This went some way to explain his earlier phone call to Wenzel, thought Schmitt.

"Can we get back to the main topic, everyone?" requested Janzyke, a little irritated by the unwarranted interference.

"Upon the death of my father, I was summoned to a firm of solicitors to hear the reading of his last will and testament. I was very shocked to discover that he had gifted fifteen percent of the bank to me. At first, I was reticent to accept the inheritance, given the hurt he had caused my mother, but I now believe that my father was trying to make good his long absence from my life. The only proviso he made was that I assist Herr Köhler in upholding the integrity of the bank."

"Did your father ever discuss his past?"

"In what respect?"

"His years in the Wehrmacht and his career following Germany's surrender?"

"We never really talked about it as the past holds no appeal for me. What I did learn from my father was how to be a leader of people and the qualities one needs to be a good politician."

"You didn't pay enough attention to him, given your current predicament. Greed seems to have won over your moral values, Herr Kampfle. This is what I find hard to understand. You have led a comfortable life, inheriting a large shareholding in a major German bank, yet you chose to defraud the working man of much needed revenue that could have been invested either into healthcare or to create jobs."

"Herr Janzyke, if I may?" interrupted the minister's solicitor.

"Go on, if you must."

"My client has paid any tax due on his earnings to the relevant tax authority where the parent company is registered."

"Don't play clever with me, Herr Bötel. Not even on your best day would you be able to pull the wool over my eyes. Your client has a shareholding in a German financial institution, based here, in München, for which he received dividends and was liable for tax. Germany is his domicile address. Is this not correct?"

"With the greatest of respect, Your Honour, I am not, as you put it, trying to pull the wool over your eyes. Yes, my client does live in

Germany but, if I might add, given his travel schedule, it could be argued that Herr Kampfle resides in many other countries also."

"Herr Bötel, dress it up as you like but your client's archaic attempt to evade tax has come unstuck. The UK and Channel Island banks have been most co-operative," said the judge, patting the numerous files he had placed on the table.

Both the minster and his lawyer appeared shaken by this bombshell.

"My client has paid his tax to the relevant authorities!" repeated Bötel.

"The monies were earned in Germany, Bötel. Your client is guilty of tax evasion, to the tune of ten million Deutsche Marks, which he will most certainly pay back, believe me."

"Can we make a deal?"

"No deals. A custodial sentence will follow the repayment of the monies, with interest."

"I find that totally unreasonable, Herr Janzyke. Surely there is no need for a custodial sentence?"

"Spare me the drama, Herr Bötel! Your client has enjoyed the good life for long enough. He has abused his position of trust. I daresay the good burghers of Germany might find such behaviour unreasonable. He expects them to pay their taxes while he seems to have tried every trick in the book to avoid paying his own! Your client will have his day in court, for both tax evasion and illegal arms dealing."

"I knew nothing about that; I'm just a shareholder!" protested Kampfle.

"Ignorance is no defence, in the eyes of the law. As a non-executive director and shareholder, you have a duty of care to ensure due diligence is applied at all times, Herr Kampfle."

Janzyke began to put away his papers.

"Judge, surely some sort of arrangement can be made?" pleaded the solicitor.

"Herr Bötel, let me make it clear. Your client should get comfortable with the idea of living a little closer to his friend, Herr Köhler. I think we can all agree that Stadelheim prison will be your home too, for at least the next six years, Herr Kampfle," said the judge as he signalled for Schmitt to read him his rights.

The finance minister was taken to a nearby courtroom where there was a short hearing and the charges were read out. Bail was set at two hundred thousand marks, with the accused ordered to surrender his passport and report to a police station once a week. After the proceedings, Kampfle - head bowed - left the building, with the ever-faithful Herr Bötel in tow.

****

"May I speak with Mr Schmitt, please?"

"Speaking."

"Hi, Detlef, John here. I just wanted to bring you up to date on the case involving the Gotthard lady."

"Ever the professional, John; I should have known you'd chase it up!"

McLean chuckled and began to read from the file on his desk.

"Eva Gotthard's father, Gorch, was a German immigrant who sailed, with his wife, Fieke, from the port of Hamburg to New York, in 1921. Gotthard found work at a local timber company in Boalsburg. The couple settled there and raised four sons and a daughter. By all accounts, he was an ignorant son of a bitch who got himself into a few barroom brawls but, other than that, he had a clean sheet. Eva's parents passed away six and seven years ago, respectively."

"Where are the sons now?"

"Pass."

"What do you mean?"

"Just that; very little is known about them. The children were your everyday, neighbourhood kids, very bright and academic. Some of the boys went on to further education, where they majored in chemistry and finance. The daughter was a home bird who, after her graduation, taught at the local elementary school until her retirement. The brothers went clean off the radar in mid-1939, the father being suspected of their murder for a while. They have neither been seen nor heard of since then."

"So, your data systems have no pertinent information on the four men?"

"No, Detlef; believe me, I've looked high and low for these dudes!"

"I don't doubt you."

"Anyway, I decided to visit Miss Gotthard in hospital after her operation to recover the slug. She had suffered considerable trauma and was very evasive during the little time I had to question her. She claimed she didn't know anything regarding the whereabouts of her brothers but she did give me permission to look round her apartment."

"Did you find anything of importance?"

"Not one thing. I took the place apart; there were some letters from her mother and greetings cards from her father but nothing relating to her siblings. I've sent you a hard copy of the school's yearbook photo of 1936, with all the brothers' images highlighted."

"I don't know what to say, John. I really appreciate the trouble you've gone to."

"Listen, Detlef, all this may be unrelated. I don't want to get your hopes up, buddy. It's probably just a coincidence."

Schmitt weighed up the facts. He had no desire to antagonise Wenzel any further, but his brother-in-law had gone out of his way just to speak with this woman on his behalf. He felt obliged to give the matter some consideration.

"John, thanks for taking the time to look into this possible lead."

"Well, that's not the end of the story, Detlef."

"Why?"

"Miss Gotthard died of septicaemia three days after my visit, because of embedded lead fragments. The surgeons had tried, unsuccessfully, to remove all of them."

"I'm sorry to hear that."

"So was I, Detlef."

"Once again, John, thank you. Give my love to Nina. Bye for now."

"Will do. Goodbye."

Schmitt was cautiously optimistic. The odds of a married couple called Gorch and Fieke Gotthard fleeing Germany and emigrating to America seemed fair. The brothers' yearbook photo would provide him with even more answers, the detective was convinced of that. He now had to figure out how best to use the information his brother-in-law had given him. Detlef opted to say nothing to Wenzel about it for the time being, choosing instead to carry out separate, covert lines of inquiry, with Reinhold's help. He would owe Claudia a big apology if the trip to see Constanze hadn't been in vain.

****

"Ah, Herr Schmitt, so good of you to call. A fresh face breaks the monotony in here. I see you've brought your beautiful assistant, Claudia; I hope your boss isn't working you too hard!" exclaimed Köhler as the detectives walked into the room, prepared for another long interview.

"Herr Köhler, let's stop wasting each other's time. What is your true nationality?"

"Why, Detective, I thought you were clear on that one. I'm a German national and proud of it!"

"I don't believe you are. I suspect you of being, at best, a non-native national!" argued Schmitt, in a disparaging tone.

The banker looked up, mystified. No one had ever dared speak to him in that manner. Recovering his composure, he countered the statement.

"That is a very broad assertion to make."

"I don't think so. You're in denial, deluding yourself; you're no German!" said the detective, trying to get a reaction from the prisoner.

"Herr Schmitt, I am terminating this interview right now. Once again, we are merely going around in circles," complained the solicitor.

Schmitt cast a sideways glance at the man before placing blank tapes into the recorder.

"Interviewing Prisoner Curt Köhler in the interview suite at Stadelheim prison. Present are Herr Köhler, Detectives Schmitt and Reinhold, and the prisoner's solicitor, Herr Kleber," stated Schmitt, placing his coat on the back of the chair.

"What was your relationship with Helmut Schröder, Curt?"

The prisoner appeared momentarily taken aback before answering, "He was a lifelong friend."

"Where did you first meet him?"

Again, there was some hesitation before he replied.

"He gave me my first job, after I returned home from the war."

"Is it not also the case that he was your commanding officer at the Wehrmacht training camp in Waggum, near Braunschweig?"

"Well, yes, that is correct."

"And before the war, you had worked as a trainee bank teller in Dresden?"

"Yes."

"What do you know of Frank Gotthard?"

For the first time, the blood drained from Köhler's face. Schmitt glanced at Reinhold. She, too, had noticed a change in Köhler's composure.

"Okay, let's forget about him for the time being. Why did you tell your best friend's wife that her husband was having an affair with his secretary? Was your motivation to break up their marriage?"

Köhler was silent for a moment before responding.

"Sophia was a dear friend and I couldn't bear to see her deceived in such a way. The affair, though discreet, had continued for quite some time. As German foreign minister, Helmut had an extensive and busy schedule, covering all four corners of the globe. His personal secretary was expected to travel everywhere with him; an act of intimacy was inevitable."

"Why was such an act inevitable, Herr Köhler?"

"Fräulein Kampfle was an incredibly good-looking woman. It

would have been hard to resist temptation."

"I think you told tales to create a favourable situation for yourself."

"I don't quite follow your train of thought, Detective."

"You wanted to take full control of the bank, did you not?"

"That's a slanderous remark! I didn't need the damn shares. I held enough stocks to control how the bank was to be managed. Yes, I admit, I did take up Frau Schröder's offer but that was before they went on the open market."

"Who was Frank Gotthard, Herr Köhler?"

"I believe he worked in the Reichsbank though I can't be sure, as so much time has passed. I think he was in one of the departments that handled the confiscation of overseas Jewish assets. I don't know the specifics. I held a position in the motor pool, as a driver."

"When did you first meet Gotthard?"

"I was appointed as his driver, around November 1943."

"What were your duties?"

"Mainly just driving, taking him and others to where they needed to be. I fetched things or ran errands. I was, in effect, what some might call a gofer."

"Fetching what, exactly? Contraband goods? Prostitutes?"

"I'm afraid it was nothing as exciting as what you're implying, Detective. If a member of the higher ranks ran out of an item, such as boot polish or shaving soap, I would see that it was replenished. I was also called upon to hand deliver important documents from time to time. For the record, Herr Gotthard never used prostitutes."

"How can you be so sure that he never paid for sex? Did you socialise with him?"

"Military doctrine forbade mingling with the lower ranks. Gotthard had no need to pay for sexual services as women seemed to flock to him. He was an attractive man."

"Were you attracted to him?"

"Don't be absurd!"

"You never know, Curt, those sorts of things did happen, although they were definitely kept in the closet for fear of Himmler's suppression of homosexuality directive. It would only have taken one loose tongue to receive a visit from the long coats of Prinz Albrecht Straße. Perhaps you were afraid to express your feelings openly?"

"Really, Detective, you've got a sick mind! I am not gay, nor have I ever suffered from homosexual tendencies. You haven't got a clue what life was like during those dark days. The economic situation was dire. Rationing became oppressive; a child would have been sent to a concentration camp for the simple act of stealing a handful of sugar. More so, one never knew if they would be alive the next day, given the escalation in allied air raids. Why all the questions about my past? Where is this leading to?"

"I might ask the same question, Detective Schmitt. What has any of this has got to do with the charges laid before my client?" added Herr Kleber.

"I'm just trying to tie up a couple of loose ends, that's all. So, you never met Helmut Schröder when you worked in Berlin; is that what you're saying, Herr Köhler?"

"Yes…. wait…. ah…. yes, we did meet once. On that occasion, I had collected a party of Wehrmacht officers from Rangsdorf airport. They were driven out to Hermann Göring's Carinhall estate, at Großen Döllnsee, for a hunting weekend."

"When was that? Who was present?"

"I'm not sure."

"Not sure of the year? Or not sure who was present?"

"Detective, let's stop this, it's all about nothing," said Köhler as he began to light his cigar.

"Answer the damn question," bellowed Schmitt, taking the cigar from Köhler and throwing it across the room.

"There was no need for that Herr Schmitt," retorted Kleber, retrieving the cigar.

"Your client should continue to answer my questions then."

Köhler looked at Schmitt coldly for a few minutes before resuming.

"It was in the spring of 1942. Commanders Krebs and Schröder, Captain Henschel and Corporal Gotthard were present at the hunt. There were other officers too, whose names escape me. Do you realise how long ago this all was, Detective?"

"You said you never met Gotthard until November 1943?"

"Herr Schmitt, how can my client be expected to remember where he was fifty years ago? You probably can't remember what you did last month!" argued the solicitor.

"I arrested your client, that's memorable enough, Herr Kleber."

"When did you first meet Gotthard and, more so, what was your involvement with him, Herr Köhler?"

"As I said previously, I was just his driver. I've nothing more to add, Detective."

Schmitt was exasperated but chose not to show his annoyance as the prisoner steadfastly remained silent.

"That's fine, have it as you wish. Herr Kleber, I'm going back to speak with Judge Janzyke. I will await his instructions as to how he wants me to proceed. We know your client is an imposter and it is only a matter of time until we uncover his real identity."

"Do what you will, Detective; waste the taxpayer's money," replied the solicitor picking at his fingernails.

"And when that happens, everything will be gone, including his group of companies," interjected Reinhold. "Every cheque and contract your client has ever signed will be a deemed a forgery. You should urge him to come clean and save everyone a lot of work."

"Curt, where is the bunker…. the Eichhörnchen Nest?" asked Schmitt as he leaned over the table, trying to goad the banker.

The faint glimmer left as quickly as it had arrived in Köhler's eyes when the question of the structure was put to him but he did not respond.

Detlef began to pack away the files he had brought with him.

"Well, good day, Herr Schmitt. I'm sorry for bringing you all the way here for nothing!" grinned Köhler.

Schmitt quickly glanced at Reinhold as he drummed his fingers on the table. He had given what he was about to say a lot of consideration, unsure of how the prisoner would react.

"Curt…."

"Yes?"

"I, too, am sorry."

"Why is that, Detective? Sorry that you've wasted my valuable time?"

"No, not at all; it concerns your family."

"Is Frieda unwell? My son? Please, tell me!"

"It doesn't concern your immediate family. It's your younger sister, in America."

Köhler took a quick look over at Schmitt, as he continued his habit of quietly fidgeting with his handcuffs.

"A recent robbery went disastrously wrong in your hometown of Boalsburg. As a result, Eva is dead."

The room was at once filled with an uneasy silence as the prisoner's gaze fell to the floor.

"Kleber, please get me out of here.... now," murmured Köhler, his voice failing.

The solicitor called for the warden, who came into the room and led the prisoner back to his cell.

The two detectives sat quietly, unable to gauge Köhler's true reaction to the information.

"Herr Schmitt, your use of mind games is totally unwarranted. Herr Köhler lost not only his sister but his entire family during the war. I will be making an official complaint as my client's unjustifiable detention here is having a detrimental impact on his mental wellbeing. Do you actually have any new evidence to hold him with?"

"I take offence to your allegation of mind games, Herr Kleber. I believe your client's faculties are very much intact and he is leading you a merry dance but you, for whatever reason, are unable to see it. However, good luck with your complaint, should you wish to make it official."

Kleber made no reply and departed, leaving Schmitt and Reinhold alone.

"What was all that about?" asked Reinhold.

Schmitt explained the details of the case, as recounted by his brother-in-law.

"How can you be certain that Köhler is related to this lady, Detlef?"

"The simple answer is I can't."

Claudia was shocked at Schmitt's blasé attitude as he packed away the files.

"I have a bad feeling about this, Detlef. I think it would have been better to have approached the subject of his alleged sister's death in a more sensitive manner. Perhaps you ought to have discussed it with the prison doctor first."

"It's done now," replied Schmitt icily.

CHAPTER TWENTY

Three weeks later, the two detectives returned to Stadelheim. Schmitt had been focusing his attention on recent findings related to the Serbian Mafia and had had limited time to study Köhler's medical report, to try and gain a little understanding of his current mental health.

"Do you believe that he really is Frank Gotthard?" queried Reinhold.

"I just don't know, Claudia; Köhler is so deep and resolute that he appears to be unbreakable."

"Perhaps you should tread more cautiously, Detlef. I just can't put my finger on it, but something's not right with him. He acts as if he is staying in a five-star hotel rather than a correctional facility."

Having handed in their Glocks and collected their visitors' passes, they walked down the drab, linoleum-lined, corridor. Following Schmitt's announcement to Köhler that his sister had been killed, Wenzel had been advised by the prison's chief medical officer that his patient was in no condition to be interviewed at present. She had put Detlef on notice that he was to proceed with sensitivity during any future interview sessions.

"What are the chances that we'll be able to speak with him at all today?" Reinhold enquired, pressing the intercom button on the security door leading to the medical wing.

The electrically-assisted door swung open for them to pass through.

"The infirmary won't discuss inmates' details over the phone. We'll have to wait until we've spoken with the head shrink to find out when Herr Köhler will be in a position to talk."

They continued down another long corridor until they reached the office of Doctor Lömann, the chief psychiatrist at Stadelheim. On entering, Schmitt made the introductions and they shook hands.

"Please, take a seat, Detectives; make yourselves comfortable. Coffee?"

The doctor went over to the machine that was quietly percolating in the corner of the room.

"Yes, black for both of us, thanks," answered Reinhold.

Lömann passed them their drinks and studied Schmitt for a few minutes before speaking.

"So, it was you, Detective Schmitt, who set Herr Köhler off into his regressive state?"

"Set him off?" asked Schmitt, slightly perplexed.

"Please correct me if I am mistaken but I have been advised that you callously notified the patient that his only sister had died, even though it was clear from his war records that she had been killed during the bombing of Dresden, along with the rest of his family."

"With all due respect, I was unsure if we had the right person. I...."

"If you'll excuse me, Herr Schmitt, your behaviour is typical of law enforcement. Your goal is to solve crime, lowering the odds until you have concrete proof that the person or persons you suspect are guilty. I find what you have done to be grossly irresponsible."

"Now, hold on a minute, Doctor...."

"No, Detective, you must understand that a shock like that can scar the psyche. Your outburst may have left him, in the long term, mentally unstable."

Schmitt considered the facts. Yes, he had heard all this before, during the many lectures he attended at Police College in Munster, having studied there for two years before becoming Detective Chief Inspector. While there was a lot of truth in what the doctor had said, Detlef privately refused to allow Köhler the benefit of the doubt with regard to his mental wellbeing. Given that his DNA was all over the weapon used in the killing and a hair sample belonging to him had been found on the victim's clothing, there was now indisputable evidence to make the charge of premeditated murder stick.

"Please, Doctor, don't try that one with me," argued Schmitt. "This guy's mental state is as secure as a Doettling safe. We've been on his case for quite some time now and he hasn't broken. I couldn't begin to describe the sheer arrogance of the man!"

"Herr Schmitt, after your last interview, Herr Köhler returned to his cell where he broke down and cried like a child, for four hours. I was informed about his fragile state by the warden on night watch," explained the doctor as he scraped hardened tobacco from the pipe he had taken from the drawer in his desk.

"I find that hard to believe," argued Schmitt.

"Believe it, Detective. It is known as post-traumatic stress disorder, a condition brought on by a very harrowing event that has occurred in the patient's past, often during active service. "

"I was wondering when the war might raise its head, Doctor."

"There's no need for that facetious attitude, Herr Schmitt. The inhumane way in which you revealed the news to the man seems to have triggered a memory that he had managed to suppress in his subconscious."

"Perhaps it was a little tactless of me, but I find it hard to grasp that he would have been affected in such a way."

"Detective, you are presently working with someone whom you genuinely believe to be a murderer?"

"That is correct."

"Anyone who is involved in such levels of depravity as murder is deemed to be somewhat unbalanced in the first place, would you not agree?"

"Okay, I accede."

"And you have found Herr Köhler to be rather unstable at times?"

"Well, yes, but…"

"Exactly, Herr Schmitt. You didn't really know who you were dealing with, yet you proceeded to inform that person in a cold, matter of fact way, that his sister had just died! As I said earlier, this information may have inadvertently unlocked a disturbing incident that he had chosen not to face up to. Yes, sometimes such episodes are unavoidable. Nonetheless, they can be triggered with a reappearance of a past event that has damaged their emotional stability."

"This is all well and good but his sister only died recently!" countered Reinhold.

Herr Lömann appeared a little confused by the remark.

"But I thought that…. she wasn't killed during the war?" he enquired.

"We are awaiting DNA evidence from the FBI, in order to confirm that she is a sibling," Reinhold replied.

"This only serves to justify my argument that your behaviour was irresponsible, Herr Schmitt. Talk to me again, when you are in a position to corroborate the victim of the shooting is, indeed, Herr Köhler's sister, Detectives."

"When can we interview Köhler?" enquired Schmitt after a few minutes.

"I can't give you an answer at this point in time. I am sorry to say he is not in good shape. In his mind, the charges against him are a simple misunderstanding. His conversations are quite erratic. One minute he is animated, saying that he longs to travel back to the *'old country'*, wherever that may be, to see his family once more, then he becomes totally uncommunicative. He has also spoken of the need to secure Jewish assets to build a better Germany; this may relate to his past but I'm not yet sure where the connection lies. At one point during a therapy session, he even insisted that it was someone called Frank who had caused him to be incarcerated."

"Did he actually mention the name Frank?"

"Yes, he did. Why should you doubt me, Herr Schmitt?"

"Doctor Lömann, I don't doubt you for a moment but I believe that Herr Köhler may not be the person he claims to be. I can't go into too much detail, right now."

"You may be right, Detective. The man is most definitely displaying positive psychopathic traits."

"In what manner, Herr Lömann?"

"Psychopaths are incapable of experiencing normal human emotions, such as love and compassion. Therefore, they generally react without considering the consequences of their actions. As with the prisoner, they show extreme narcissistic behaviour. By building up his corporate empire, Herr Köhler may have fulfilled his own egotistical needs, regardless of the needs of his family or those around him."

"Well, he has committed murder to cover his tracks."

"To cut to the chase, Herr Köhler seems to have led a somewhat reckless life, oblivious to the pain and suffering inflicted upon those with whom he came into contact. His type can be extremely charismatic, taking advantage of people and situations through sheer manipulation. Having spoken at length with the prisoner, I found him to be highly articulate and persuasive. Theoretically, he could easily have charmed his way into Herr HaffenFuß's apartment to carry out the murder. On the other hand, you could have the wrong man?"

"The evidence is irrefutable. Herr Köhler did, indeed, kill the old gentleman."

"I believe you, Detective."

"How do you intend to treat his condition, Doctor?"

"In this instance, I would advocate past life regression. It is a hypnotic technique that enables the retrieval of the patient's subconscious memory."

"Will that help to stabilise him?"

"Hopefully, yes. There are many well-documented cases where information gained from the patient during a past life regression has been used as a stepping stone in paving the way for their psychological recovery."

"Could you explain further, Doctor?"

"Herr Köhler will take part in a number of therapy sessions, with a specialist in past life regression. During these sessions, they will focus on a specific time or event in their life which may have led to the crisis. The episode will then be dissected, examined with an imaginary microscope, so to speak. This will provide us with a clearer understanding of the patient's mental wellbeing as we try to mend those psychological building blocks within his mind."

"So, you're saying that the information obtained during one of these meetings will ultimately relate to the prisoner's past life?"

"Don't be getting your hopes up, Herr Schmitt. The therapy is only to try and pinpoint the moment in time when things went awry for the patient."

"I understand, Doctor, but what you uncover may be useful in our investigation."

"Doctor-patient confidentiality, I'm afraid. Our discussion today is merely to provide you with a brief outline of his condition and the treatment plan I have put in place. I will not be at liberty to divulge what is discussed during the sessions. What I will say is that it may make Herr Köhler more co-operative when he is ready to speak with you again. Regrettably, I can only treat his condition, Herr Schmitt; there is no long-term cure for psychopathic behaviour. On the contrary, our conventional methods of treatment can enable a patient to become even more skilful at disguising their true character and many learned people have been outsmarted by their duplicity. If only I had invented a remedy, I could have retired by now!"

"Then the best-case scenario would be to improve Herr Köhler's condition so that we may continue to question him?"

"Yes, nothing more. I hope I have been of some help. Oh, Herr Schmitt….by the way…. Herr Köhler asked me to give you this."

Schmitt took a crumpled piece of ruled paper from the doctor. On opening it out, he saw a series of random drawings, illegible notes and calculations of some kind.

****

"This is all that he gave me, Angela," said Schmitt, showing her the page full of seemingly meaningless scribbles when they met in the corridor at Pullach.

"How is he?" enquired Wenzel.

"We never got to see him. I spoke with Doctor Lömann at length and he is of the opinion that Köhler has suffered some sort of mental breakdown."

They looked at one another, with more than a little scepticism regarding the psychiatrist's diagnosis.

"Lömann considers Köhler to be a psychopath. He readily believes that his own feelings and behaviour are that of a normal person. He is a chameleon who will show emotion, if need be, to achieve a purpose. Lömann went on to say that Köhler may talk about remorse but his behaviour will, in most instances, undermine his real intentions."

"Can he safely be interviewed yet? We need to be careful that any evidence gathered is watertight and, more importantly, admissible in court."

"I will bear that in mind, Angela. Lömann phoned me earlier today. Köhler has been suffering from a severe chest infection and is to be examined by the hospital doctor shortly but he has requested that Claudia and I meet with him as soon as his health improves. If he is happy for us to proceed with the formal interview, we'll head back to Stadelheim at the first opportunity."

Schmitt followed Wenzel into the case conference room, where the team had already assembled.

"Okay, let me bring all of you up to date on the latest

developments," she said. "Herr Kampfle has been charged with tax evasion and failing to inform Parliament of his interest in the various companies that he has invested in. He may also be charged with contravening the UN embargo on arms that is currently in force in relation to the Bosnian conflict. He has resigned his ministerial post forthwith, while a parliamentary inquiry is conducted. We have yet to determine who ordered the breach of the alarm system that resulted in the explosion at Judge Janzyke's home."

Angela began to read from a report she had just received. The body of a female had been discovered in a commercial waste bin, in the town of Manching; cause of death was strangulation. CCTV images showed a woman being dropped off by a cleaning company, at the heart of the security incursion in Bonn. She was then observed walking in the direction of an apartment complex, some distance from the city centre. Close-ups confirmed the deceased and the 'cleaner' to be the same person.

"This murder was clearly internal housekeeping by those involved in accessing the computer network at Government offices, to ensure that there were no loose ends. Please, everyone, redouble your efforts. Consider every possible lead, regardless of how trivial it may seem. We aren't making enough progress in finding these people. That will be all."

CHAPTER TWENTY-ONE

Schmitt and a few of his team had arrived at a branch of the Munchener Assistance Bank in Regensburg, north of München, following a suspected cyber-attack on its IT infrastructure. Von Harz, Muller and Bachmeier were there to assist him in the investigation of what the manager, Gerhard Schwarz, believed was an attempted electronic assault on the bank. Given their current case and the freezing of Serbian-controlled assets, Schmitt was taking no chances.

"Herr Schwarz, can you provide me with details of the incident, please?" asked Schmitt, shaking hands with the manager.

"About two weeks ago, we started to get more than our usual flow of spam mail. Our firewall and antivirus system is frequently updated to deal with this kind of occurrence under normal circumstances."

"What changed?"

"I don't know for certain. We had checked our internal traffic usage. This measure ensured that members of staff weren't browsing sites they shouldn't be."

"What about new programs, data from customers and the like?"

"Any floppy discs or external traffic are quarantined and checked before they enter into the main system."

"Anything else?"

Schmitt looked around the manager's wood clad office with its sleek, ultra-modern furniture.

"There was a fire at the telephone junction box, just up the street, on Friday night, three weeks ago. The blaze started at around half past eleven but was quickly extinguished after a call to the fire department. The fire authority believes that a flammable liquid may have been poured into the casing, following a forced entry of the door."

"Were the police called?"

"Yes, of course! They put it down to vandalism caused by local youths with nothing better to do."

"Did it affect the bank in any way?"

"I would say so! We were offline to the rest of the group for most of the weekend."

"How did that affect you, operationally?"

"In one word, badly, Herr Schmitt; everything was at a standstill. Our customers could not transfer or withdraw funds and all overseas transactions stopped. Our domestic transactions had to be temporarily reassigned to München."

"But you got up and running again?"

"Yes, we did, but not without considerable inconvenience both to ourselves and our clients, not to mention the loss of trade. They say trouble comes in threes; I thought my troubles were at an end."

"What do you mean three? Have there been other incidents?"

"Well, I didn't want bring this up, Detective."

"Please, Herr Schwarz, I need all the information you have, however irrelevant it may seem."

"Six weeks ago, my home was broken into. The intruders ransacked the place. They tore out the small safe that both my wife and I kept personal items in, clean out of the wall!"

"Were there any documents relating to the bank stored in it?"

"Most definitely not. The thieves stole a lot of our family heirlooms, along with my wife's jewellery and some cash.

"Have the police any leads or suspects?"

"No. Their inquiries are continuing but they seem to have put it down as a random house burglary, nothing more."

"Herr Schwarz, you mentioned a third incident."

"Yes. Four weeks ago, in the early hours, police officers were out on patrol. They came upon a Volkswagen Caddy van, parked on waste ground off Bahnhofstraße, close to the bank, an area which would normally have been devoid of vehicles at that time of night. When they went to investigate, they heard the muffled sound of ladders being placed quietly against a wall. On closer inspection, two males were spotted attempting to enter the rear of our building. Regrettably, they managed to give the police the slip and fled the scene."

"There was definitely no correspondence of any kind, relating to the bank, in your house safe?"

"None; I leave my work here. I made that agreement with my wife when I took up the position."

"When did you accept the post?"

"Six years ago, …. why do you ask, Detective?" questioned the banker.

"I'm merely trying to form a picture of events, Herr Schwarz. Don't you find it strange that your home has been broken into, two individuals have tried to gain entry to the bank, a fire is started in the phone junction box, and now the business comes under cyber-attack? Have the detectives been fully apprised of all these incidents?"

"I can't say for certain."

"You can't say? I would have imagined that, as a pillar of the community, it was your duty to inform them and to keep track of their investigations!"

"I see where you're coming from but is it not the police's responsibility to keep me informed?"

"I apologise, Herr Schwarz. Perhaps I was being a little overbearing but it is imperative that I establish the facts. We all have a shared responsibility. Don't you think it is possible that there is a connection between these recent occurrences?"

"Forgive me, Detective, I hadn't really given it any thought. Do you think there is a link?"

"It's too early to say but I wouldn't rule it out. I will have to study the completed police reports on all the incidents before making any judgement. Now, tell me more about this cyber-attack, Herr Schwarz."

"According to our IT engineer, someone tried to gain access externally to our IT infrastructure. To be specific, a total of nine attempts were made within a three-hour period, to access the frozen assets of Serbian-held accounts. I am glad to say the success rate was zero, bar one instance, which we think was a genuine error. The hacker or hackers were, on that occasion, one digit out in the sort code for the Serbian account. The deposit account they almost gained access to belonged to a small dog charity, which held minimal funds."

"And the bank's security systems were able to thwart those involved?"

"Thirty seconds into the breach, our firewall detected something was wrong and overrode the program, effectively shutting the intruders out. Our IT guy described it as being a granule fall type of software, which had been placed in our servers."

"What's a granule fall?"

"It's comparable to the contents of an hourglass. Once one part of the rogue coding moves through a fissure of an IT system, the process of penetration is virtually unstoppable."

"Where are your engineers at now in resolving the problem?"

"Our program removed the virus and the engineers have rewritten part of our mainframe software to prevent anyone from gaining access again."

"Well, thank you for your assistance, Herr Schwarz. If we may, I would like my staff to continue their investigation here."

"Please do, Detective, you are most welcome. If there is anything we can help you with, just ask."

"Thanks, I will," replied Schmitt.

As his phone began to ring, he stepped out into the corridor to take the call from Wenzel. When the conversation ended, he beckoned von Harz over.

"Jürgen, speak with the security staff; see if they have noticed any suspicious activity recently. When you're done, ask Muller for a hard copy of all files that were accessed during the incident. I also want all written and read files created in the last eight weeks. We need to establish a motive as to why the bank was targeted."

"Okay, boss."

The detective suspected that the Serbs were somehow involved in hacking the bank's computer system and, if they were, they had just upped the stakes to try and have their assets illegally returned. Schmitt vowed to himself that the evidence his team gathered would be incontrovertible for the courts. With the help of Detective Bachmeier, the data would be systematized and compiled in a format that would allow them to create an accurate profile of the offenders. In doing so, the information would, hopefully, enable the team to target the intruders, whoever they might be.

Detective Muller, Pullach's chief computer analyst, was busy examining the bank's mainframe network to identify the point of entry. The chamber contained rows of processors acting as central servers for the branch's customers to carry out their many transactions. If the bank's systems had been genuinely hacked, he sought to confirm if it had been accomplished from outside the bank, or by someone working from within.

"Well, Renate," said Schmitt, walking up to the female officer while she watched Muller scrutinize the endless columns of numbers appearing on his computer screen.

Renate Bachmeier was a criminal profiler who had recently joined the team at Pullach. She had trained as a lawyer before serving as a barrister, later returning to university to study criminal psychology. Her task was to investigate the bank staff and their everyday activities, singling out those who could pose a threat to the bank's security. She would study the behaviour of the staff for any hint of criminality or moral weakness. During police interviews, the average person would be uncomfortable with relentless questioning whereas a hardened lawbreaker would have more resolve. Renate would also pay particular attention to their social backgrounds.

"I'm good to go, Detlef."

"Have a chat with the members of staff, Renate. See if they have been aware of any suspicious activity, either in or around the bank. With a little luck, one of them may be able to offer us some useful information on the attempted breach. If you have doubts regarding any of the workers, contact Pullach and get someone to check the national crime computer. One of the employees may have a spent criminal record, or be associated with an ex-con. Try some female bonding; enquire if there have been any sudden, new romances or relationships."

"It may take some time, Detlef."

"We have a few days."

"Okay. I'll head down to human resources now and take a look at the personnel files before I bring in the employees."

"One other thing, Renate. When you're finished with each member of staff, caution them under the Official Secrets Act not to discuss the matter with their colleagues. We need to keep the place sterile. I don't want any contamination of evidence," Schmitt warned.

Schmitt needed to make some urgent calls and, after a little searching, found an office which was unoccupied, thereby offering guaranteed privacy. Having been on the phone for some time, he rose and walked down the corridor to check on von Harz's progress. Entering a storeroom, he discovered his colleague hanging out of the window. He was examining the main junction box, where a series of communication cables entered.

"What have you found, Jürgen?"

"Not a lot. It's a pretty antiquated communication system. I spoke with the manager, who informed me that the current infrastructure is to be removed, after which the cables will be concealed in the wall and surrounded by an armoured casing. Work begins next week as part of a major systems' upgrade."

"I am convinced that this is the work of the Serbs, Jürgen. They can't access their assets due to the intervention of the courts. Given what has taken place here, they are now intent on recovering them by electronic means. They aren't going to back down."

"It was only a matter of time before they tried a different approach."

"Muller's sophisticated programs should be able to probe the bank's IT systems, to ascertain whether it was an external or internal breach. Hopefully, the attackers have left enough of an electronic signature for him to follow the trail. Heinz will be looking for possible, undetected past intrusions and their original entry location. The challenge will be to find those responsible for providing the technical facilities and to figure out where the suspects are operating from, now that we know their motivation for the access. With Bachmeier's help, we should be able to confirm if the hackers had inside assistance."

"What shall I do now, Detlef?" asked von Harz, lighting a Camel cigarette; although the detective very rarely smoked, he found it a hard habit to break.

"Speak with the local phone company and get contact details for the engineers who repaired a damaged telephone junction box three weeks ago; it's just up the street from the bank. Ask if they noticed anything that shouldn't have been there. Piece together all of the information, including the time of the attack on the bank. When you get back to Pullach, try and find out if the culprits were based in Germany or in another jurisdiction," added Schmitt.

****

The detectives spent three days poring over electronic and CCTV records, along with interviewing the staff, as they tried to identify who it was that had launched the cyber-attack and from where it had originated. Bachmeier eventually ruled out any internal involvement of the bank's employees in the crime.

As the team were close to completing their inquiries, Schmitt decided to go for a walk in the direction of Bahnhofstraße. He stopped at a sweet shop to buy some mints, taking one from the packet before strolling casually along the road. He arrived at the now-repaired junction box where an old man stood, reading a newspaper, his little Cairn terrier asleep on the pavement at his feet. The detective began to examine the structure, noting that the phone company had made good the repair.

"Can I help you, sir?" asked the stranger, looking at Schmitt inquisitively.

"Oh, I'm so sorry to have disturbed you. My name is Detective Chief Inspector Schmitt. Please, excuse me, I'm just inspecting this junction box."

"Josef Brönn," replied the man in a rasping voice, evidence of years of heavy smoking. "The phone company did a great job on it, don't you think?"

"They did, though I'm not really here to judge their workmanship, Herr Brönn. The repairs should have been unnecessary. It's a shame that the young people who caused the damage cannot find a better way to occupy their time than resorting to vandalism."

"What are you saying, Detective?" asked the man as he folded up the paper, his curiosity aroused.

"Apparently, the unit was set on fire by several juveniles from the area."

"But the kids didn't start the fire!"

"What do you mean?"

"Don't believe what they say around here, Detective; the kids didn't set the junction box on fire. Yes, they did kick in the door that night but only to try and put out the blaze with their cans of beer! Listen, I know these young guys. They're a bit rowdy and they smoke a little weed but they're generally good kids. You need to look for the two guys who were messing around with it earlier on."

"Can you elaborate a little, Herr Brönn?"

"A Volkswagen van arrived here.... let me see if I can remember.... yes, around half eleven one night, about three weeks ago. They opened the junction box and worked at something inside for thirty minutes or so, then they left."

"Did you report it to the police?"

"No, why would I? They're useless!"

"Where were you when the incident occurred?"

Herr Brönn raised his blackthorn stick and pointed to a large clump of trees a short distance away.

"I had taken Bernhard for his walk before bedtime, as I do every evening. We had just reached the big spruce tree over there when the van pulled up and two men got out. I thought it was odd that repairs were being carried out at night so I stopped to keep an eye on the pair of them, staying in the shadows where I wouldn't be seen. One individual carried out the job whilst the other seemed to be keeping watch. Now I come to think of it, they were obviously up to no good. I don't know what they did but I'm certain it caused the fire."

"I'm sure the phones being down caused some inconvenience to the neighbourhood?"

"You're telling me! We had no bloody phones for almost two

days! My Aunt Ruby couldn't contact the missus and was in a right strop until the line was eventually fixed. Ruby doesn't get out much and relies on the phone for keeping in touch with the outside world."

"Thank you, Herr Brönn, you have been most helpful."

Schmitt shook the old man's hand and turned back towards the bank.

"Not at all, Detective, but remember: don't always blame the kids!"

As Schmitt made his way further along the street, he mulled over what he had heard. Having reached his destination, he entered Bahnhofstraße police station where he introduced himself to the officer in charge of the case.

"Herr Mönke, what do you make of the overall situation?" asked Schmitt as he sat down and studied the middle-aged man.

Mönke was of medium build, with fair hair, thinning on top, which revealed a flaking scalp. He sported a denim shirt, jeans and a tan leather jacket, reminiscent of a washed-out detective from a 1980s' German crime series. Mönke seemed to look at everything else but Schmitt when he addressed him.

"Well, Herr Schmitt, first of all, let me just say that I'm a little surprised to be speaking with a member of counter intelligence about what really is a local matter! That being said, I have looked at the events in their entirety. Yes, there has been some interest shown in the bank, what with the break-in at the manager's home and the unknown individuals seen loitering at the back of the bank. In my view, however, these two incidents appear to be unrelated. The fire at the phone box was simply a case of local vandals, high on alcohol and drugs."

"Forgive me, Herr Mönke, but that's not the view of a local resident."

Schmitt related the old man's account of events on the night of the fire.

"Damn it, I can't carry out a proper investigation if people won't come forward with information!" countered the officer, feeling somewhat chastened.

"Please understand I am not here to interfere, in any way, with your enquiries. I have been brought in to investigate an attempted breach of the bank's IT system. It is my firm belief that the cyber-crime and the other recent happenings in Regensburg are linked."

"Herr Schmitt, I wasn't suggesting that you were trying to get in the way of my work here; indeed, I would appreciate your input. Take a look at this."

Schmitt read the document he had been given. It was an intelligence report relating to information received from a local grass, suggesting that there may be an attempt to rob the bank. The date and time had not been confirmed, nor the identity of those involved.

"Herr Mönke, have you and your team put in place the necessary measures, should the raid go ahead?"

"We are currently trying to track down those involved and have increased our patrols in the area."

"That is to be commended but what steps have you taken in respect of the Schwarz family's personal security?"

"None, why?"

"Come on, Herr Mönke! Their house has been turned upside down and the safe removed, in addition to the other incidents in the town. Don't you think there may be a connection?"

The officer gave a sigh.

"Herr Schmitt, be assured that I will review their situation immediately."

"It's a pity you didn't do it sooner! Can you provide me with copies of all the crime reports?"

The officer slammed the door as he left the room, soon returning with a file full of papers.

"I have made copies, as requested, Herr Schmitt. I see the gravity of the situation and, without further delay, I will be putting in place measures to increase the security of both the Schwarz family and the bank. Could you keep me informed of your progress in order that I can update my case files?"

"Of course, I will. Thank you for your co-operation, Herr Mönke."

Schmitt took the sheaf of papers and left. He felt that Mönke had been a little sloppy in his approach; as a detective, he should have spotted the link in the crimes earlier. At this moment, he was missing Amélie and Erhard and he longed for a soak in a hot bath, with a cold beer in his hand. His team would, no doubt, be packing up their equipment by now, ready to head back to München. They had all been away from home for long enough.

The detective strode back into the bank, the chill of the air conditioning meeting him like a wall of ice, cancelling the balmy weather outdoors. He surveyed the busy scene, with customers coming and going. It seemed to be back to business as usual. He made his way to the manager's office, knocking on the door before being invited in.

"Please, take a seat, Herr Schmitt. Would you like a coffee?"

asked the manager.

"No, thank you, I'm fine."

"Have you any news?"

"No, nothing of importance. I would like to ask you a few more questions, Herr Schwarz, if I may. I need to know if there has been anything out of the ordinary, apart from the events that have already taken place."

"I don't follow you, Detective?"

"What I mean is, have any strangers been seen recently, either around your home or at the bank?"

"No, things have been pretty much as normal. Why do you ask? Is there something I should be aware of?"

"How much money are your tellers allowed to have with them in the kiosks?" continued Schmitt, ignoring the banker's questions.

"Ten thousand Deutsche Mark floats. Larger amounts can be given over the counter, provided the customer places an order in advance. We require at least two days' notice, to ensure that it is a genuine request. We have several safeguards in place to prevent attempted robbery, including bullet-proof, tellers' windows. There are always at least ten employees present on the floor during opening hours."

"What about time-delay safes; when can the cash or monies be withdrawn?" asked Schmitt as he rose from his seat and went over to the window.

"The system we have in place is designed to prevent the opening of the vault until it reaches the pre-set time of our opening hours, Detective."

"What if you or one of the employees is forced to open it during, say, an armed heist?"

"Herr Schmitt, even if the correct combination is entered, the system will not allow an unauthorised override. This can only happen when two of the bank group managers and the company secretary permit such an action."

"What is the vault's security rating?"

"It is one of excellence. The vault is fabricated in such a way that the time locks are deployed inside the door. They are designed with a sophisticated, time-delay release system. The company secretary and I must be present to open the vault for everyday business. It would take someone, using extreme force, over thirty hours to penetrate the structure, never mind accessing it! Why all the questions, Herr Schmitt? You are beginning to give me cause for alarm."

Detlef was observing the city skyline from the large office window.

"Herr Schwarz, where is the staff car park?"

"We have underground parking for our senior members of staff."

Schmitt thought for a moment. Something puzzled him but what was it? Too late, he had lost his thread and turned his attention back to the current query again.

"What form of security is in place for the parking area?"

"We have a CCTV system and a guard patrols the area regularly. Staff members have swipe cards that record their arrival and departure."

"Herr Schwarz, bearing in mind what has occurred recently, I would be inclined to step up my personal security, if I were you. I feel that, given the failed cyber-attack on your bank, there may well be an attempt to kidnap you or members of your family."

"What have you based this assumption on, Detective?"

"The series of events you have experienced of late. The phone exchange was definitely tampered with, not by local children but by the same men who attempted to break into the bank."

"How do you know that?"

"I'm afraid I'm not at liberty to disclose that, Herr Schwarz. I believe those involved may have tried to place a crude form of electronic interceptor into the phone box. It was intended to piggyback your IT system using the exchange as a mule, but the lines became overloaded and caught fire."

"What you are saying is extremely worrying, Detective."

"I have spoken with the local police. They are aware of your circumstances and are making the necessary arrangements to protect both you and your family."

"It is an immense relief to know that my family will be safe. What should I do as to my own personal security?"

"I would advise you to change your routine immediately. Alter your working hours and your route to and from the bank. Create a code word with your wife that assures you she is fine. Detective Mönke will advise you on how best to safeguard both yourself and your family."

"I appreciate your assistance, Detective. You have been most helpful."

"I wouldn't be doing my job if I didn't present the facts as I see them. Do you have children?"

"Yes, a boy and a girl. They are both currently studying at the University of Edinburgh."

"Please, keep in touch with them; remind them that they are in a foreign land and that they need to be on their guard. Ask them to be cautious of anyone new to their group of friends, anyone who is trying to befriend them. Of course, nothing may come of what we have discussed but I feel it's better to be safe than sorry, Herr Schwarz."

"I understand your concerns and I will keep them in mind, Herr Schmitt," said the banker as he walked him to the door, where they shook hands and said their goodbyes.

Detlef made his way out of the building to the waiting car and climbed into the passenger side. With von Harz in the driving seat, the foursome wearily embarked on the hour-long road trip back to München.

CHAPTER TWENTY-TWO

The case conference was well underway. Muller was giving details of the electronic evidence his unit had uncovered, which showed that the hackers were technically well organised.

"The gang used a sophisticated, multi-frame system to launch the attack via separate computers. By reverse engineering, I have started to unravel their trail. The first lead showed that it began with someone accessing the local phone exchange in the town of Kiel, using an unregistered phone connection. With the aid of rogue dial tone software, they were able to acquire an international phone number through which the perpetrator linked into a slave computer in the town of Plzen, in the Czech Republic. The remote software program then made consecutive connections to a similar set up, in the town of Pécs, in Hungary, before eventually linking up to a command system in an empty office in the city of Budapest," explained Muller.

"The properties used for the cyber-attack are owned by a large property concern. The parent company CEO is believed to be the ex-Stasi sergeant, Erich Niemeyer," added Lang. "He also owns assorted properties in Bulgaria and, furthermore, he is an expert in IT, having a company that specialises in IT management solutions. He disappeared, under suspicious circumstances, just before the fall of the Berlin Wall. One point five million marks, in American and French currencies, were stolen from an Interflug freight depot at Schönefeld Airport, East Berlin. Niemeyer, along with other accomplices, was suspected of it but the case was suddenly dropped, as unification gathered momentum."

"So, he may be behind the attack?" asked Wenzel.

"Anything's possible, Angela."

"Heinz, please continue," said Wenzel.

"The second, partially successful, operating platform was based in Northern Romania, in the town of Carei, near the Hungarian border. They were using specialist software which created a domino effect. Each computer followed the relayed instructions, without error. I am reasonably certain that the operating program may have been of military grade software. The coding enabled the culprits to anonymously attempt entry of the bank's IT systems from the various sites I have mentioned. The package was able to create bogus internet users, regular web surfers to the untrained eye. It was designed to be autonomous in its endeavour to gain access to the bank's network. To date, I have been unable to identify the accounts into which the transfers were to be deposited."

"Who are these people, Detlef?" questioned Wenzel.

"Landline and mobile phone traffic interception indicated, through voice recognition, that the former Bosnian Serb sergeant, Goran Knezevic, may have had a hand in organising the sting. Knezevic was injured during sustained infantry shelling but, after a long convalescence, reports suggest that he is now in reasonably good health. He is also suspected to be active in raising funds for the war campaign."

"Is the bank's security system fit for purpose, at this point in time?" she asked.

"Very much so," replied Muller. "Their IT people have informed me that the entire group's online security has been fully upgraded. A large, engineering works in Nuremberg, which is owned by the bank, was the last of the group to get the software improvements, removing any chance of further electronic attacks."

Wenzel called an end to the meeting.

"Okay, that's a lot to take in, for now; please complete your reports and pass them on to Detlef. Thank you all, once again, for the efforts you have made in the investigation of this case. Would you step into my office for a moment, Detlef?"

Wenzel closed the door to her office and turned to Schmitt.

"Do you think we stand a chance of getting these guys?"

"This Knezevic is a real nasty piece of work, Angela. The information we have leads me to believe that he will stop at nothing to ensure victory for Serbia. As for Niemeyer, he's an enigma. He and his wife seem to spend most of their time in either Hungary or Russia, coupled with periodic visits to north Africa and Asia. I am reliably informed that the CIA are keeping tabs on him. Several individuals have prospered in the Hungarian town of Győr since Niemeyer moved there and Soviet diehards treat him as a godfather. I imagine he will be hard to get at if it's proven that he was involved in the online hacking of the Munchener Assistance Bank computer systems."

"What do you suggest, Detlef?"

"Do you want the honest truth?"

"Yes, warts and all."

"If we could get Niemeyer and his henchmen in one place for long enough, we could fly in covertly and make a forced rendition. If they resist arrest, we finish them, there and then."

"What are the chances of that happening?"

"It's just a question of being in the right place at the right time.

If the local intel is correct, we can be inserted close to the targets, lie up for a while and observe who is coming and going. When the operators are in place, we go in, secure the area and neutralise them, before calling in an air evacuation."

"It might work. The countries that the bank hacking scam passed through aren't out of reach of our forces."

"We'll deal with them later, Angela. In the meantime, we will need Special Forces' helicopters on standby, close to the extraction point, until we are ready for pick up. By the time the alarm has been raised, we'll be long gone."

"Thanks for this, Detlef. I'll give it some thought before presenting it to the justice minister."

****

Schmitt left the Finanz court in München, having given evidence with other members of his team in relation to the Kaolin Gütertransport AG prosecution. The transport manager had received ten years for evasion of customs' revenue, income tax fraud and employing illegal, foreign nationals. The two Bacutrans company directors were, in their absence, also given ten year sentences for aiding and abetting the crimes.

In an effort to clear his head, Detlef invited Reinhold to a local coffee house, parking near the taxi stand at Rindermarkt.

"How are you feeling, Claudia?" he asked as he bought a parking ticket. "You've hardly spoken about the incident involving Stein."

"What is there to say, Detlef? We were both simply doing our duty. If you really want to know do I blame you for what went down that day, then the answer is no, I don't. Perhaps you and Stein did have history together but we did what we are paid to do, as partners. After all, I chose to continue driving the car. I could have stopped the pursuit at any time but I decided to run with it. So, as far as I am concerned, the matter is closed. I am fine…. truly, I am. What happened will not impede me in carrying out my duties," said Reinhold, with a sense of resolve.

"Trust me, Claudia, I wasn't in the least suggesting anything of the kind. I'm just concerned for you, that's all."

"How are things with Amélie?" she asked, to change the subject.

Schmitt had talked less and less about his home life recently. The crash involving Stein had caused a rift in his relationship with his partner.

"Same old, same old. We're just going through the motions at present. Amélie knew what I was getting into when I applied for the post. She was aware of the risks involved. Whatever happens, I won't be changing jobs for her!" said Schmitt, trying to justify his decision.

"Have you sat down with her and been open about what happened?"

"As best I can but, each time I try to talk about it, Amélie changes the subject."

"She'll come round, Detlef. You must remember that it was a frightening experience for our loved ones as well as for us. Just give her time to adjust."

"Believe me, I have. Frankly, it is nearly impossible to explain such an event to someone not involved in the complexities of our jobs," replied Schmitt as their coffees arrived.

They sipped their scalding drinks in silence, as the traffic passed by and taxis shuttled their fares back and forth at the nearby rank. Schmitt contemplated how to move the Munchener Assistance Bank case forward to a speedy resolve. The owner, Köhler senior, was still mentally unfit to be interviewed and, though Eugen was helping enquiries to the best of his ability, only his father held the answers that Schmitt required. The photographs, promised by his brother-in-law, John McLean, had not yet arrived. Detlef had phoned John who assured him that he had put them in the post, suggesting that he give it a few more days. If they had not arrived by then, he would either send fresh copies or fax the photos, although the images would not be as sharp.

One of the last pieces of the puzzle was the old blueprint, which still made no sense. However, other elements of the case were slowly coming together. At the very least, Köhler would certainly do time for the murder of Emil HaffenFuß.

Schmitt had been quietly looking at his colleague as she played with the frothy top of her coffee. She was exceptionally pretty, with a stunning figure, and those dark brown eyes emanated tranquillity, unquestionably complimenting her personality. Detlef had recently started to take Reinhold with him on his inquiries. He found her to be an excellent detective, intuitive and highly intelligent, with no rash tendencies, unlike von Harz. Schmitt could always rely on Reinhold to conduct herself with the utmost integrity in any given situation.

"Are you ready to go, Claudia?" he asked.

"Surely there's no need to rush back just yet, is there, Detlef?"

"Normally, I would agree, but I need to speak with Angela. Something's been bugging me."

"Care to share it with me, seeing as it is truth and coffee time?" she jested.

"It's nothing more than an educated guess, at the moment."

"Please, tell me; you know I don't like to be kept in the dark," pleaded Reinhold, having set down her cup.

"I think I may have figured out where the bunker is."

"Where? In Berlin?"

"It's best that I run it past Wenzel first. I don't want to be left with egg on my face."

Schmitt paid the bill and the pair crossed the road to their vehicle, the car merging into the afternoon traffic as they made their way back to Pullach.

****

"Angela, do you have a minute?" asked Schmitt, spotting his boss in the corridor.

"Let's go in here," she replied, finding an empty office. "Anything of importance?"

"I have reason to believe that the Eichhörnchen Nest bunker was constructed at the bank on Marian Platz."

"What makes you so certain?"

Schmitt explained how, during his visit to Regensburg, he learned that the banking group had built on every single piece of property they owned, the one exception being the Japanese garden on Marian Platz. Eugen Köhler had often suggested that the land could be used to extend their place of business but his father always rejected such a proposal. Detlef contended that there was merit in at least having an electronic ground survey carried out, to either prove or disprove his theory.

"This is pure conjecture, Detlef. What can you hope to gain, if you do find it?"

"Evidence of Köhler's past dealings and, with a bit of luck, discover who he really is."

"I'll need two quotes for the survey and I want to know how long the process will take. If it's too costly, or time-consuming, then forget it; you have enough of a workload to keep you occupied."

With that, Wenzel turned on her heel and strode out of the room.

****

Schmitt had just sat down to prepare the staff overtime budget for Wenzel, who had gone to a conference, when there was a knock on his office door and Peter Lang, head of Pullach's financial crime department, entered.

"Yes, Peter, how may I help you?" he enquired.

"I have just had a meeting with the acting CEO of the Munchener Assistance Bank and the operations manager of the Karl Credit Bank, in Braunschweig. It seems that the Serbian godfathers are still intent on recovering their capital."

"Go on."

"On the tenth of June, Karl Credit Bank wrote to the Munchener Assistance Bank, informing them that they had received a purchase offer from a Gustav Brünn, in relation to the sale of a large block of flats at Richard Strauss Place in Wolfsburg, north Germany. The purchase price was DM 900,000 and the lot included limited car parking space, together with an additional area of scrubland. Handel and Company of Leipzig were the solicitors engaged to carry out the transaction on behalf of Herr Brünn, who was to forward a deposit of DM 200,000. Some three weeks later, on the second of July, a Hungarian firm of estate agents wrote to Handel and Company; they were handling the sale for the owner, a Frau Ingmar Röhmann-Niemeyer. Meanwhile, Köhler's bank had carried out a credit check on the applicant which confirmed that his finances were in good health and, as a result, the bank agreed to provide Herr Brünn with a mortgage loan of DM 700,000."

"So, get to the point, Peter, what's the issue?" asked Schmitt, as he tried to concentrate on the task before him.

"A secretary by the name of Fräulein Berger, of Handel and Company, was appointed to deal with the mortgage for the purchase of the flats. She duly processed and signed a certificate of title, forging her employer's name, as she had done on other occasions when Herr Handel was out on business. The contract, consisting of a fixed sale price of DM 900,000 and an agreed mortgage advance of DM 700,000, the sum being borrowed, was posted to the Munchener Assistance Bank. The mortgage loan of DM 700,000 was paid into Handel and Company's own account, but Herr Brünn's deposit never materialised. Sometime later, the DM 700,000 advancement was electronically transferred to the Hungarian firm of estate agents, the payment authorised by Fräulein Berger."

Schmitt had forgotten the staff overtime budget for the moment and began to take a closer interest in what Lang was trying to explain.

"What have they done, Peter?" asked Schmitt, holding his hands up in defeat.

"A land valuation agent carried out a survey of the property, including the surrounding land, before appraising it at around DM 1,100,000. Having received a positive report, the bank asked Fräulein Berger to prepare the paperwork for the sale. However, Frau Röhmann-Niemeyer had earlier instructed Berger to register the neighbouring scrubland and car parking space as a separate holding. Consequently, the wasteland and parking area was registered with the land registry office as Brucknerweg 57. We are unclear as to whether or not it was an oversight, but the secretary inserted only the registry number relating to Brucknerweg 57 on the loan contract."

"Are you telling me that the Munchener Assistance Bank paid DM 700,000 for a piece of waste ground and a small car park, instead of an apartment block?"

"Correct. What's more, it seems that this is not the first time Fräulein Berger has been involved in such property scams. On other occasions, she just failed to put any reference number on the contracts for mortgages or home improvement loans' applications. If challenged, Berger promised the lenders that the contracts would be amended but they never were. This is her biggest scam to date. Handel and Co.'s insurance company is to pay the Munchener Assistance Bank back their monies."

"Who's behind this, Peter?"

"The Hungarian estate agent is a front company, just one of many, controlled by our friend Erich Niemeyer and his wife, Ingmar."

"Who originally applied for the loan?" asked Schmitt as he stretched his legs under the desk.

"We don't know yet. The company, which was set up a few years ago by Frau Niemeyer, has mainly been involved in smaller, rentable, property purchases in Germany, as well as holiday homes in Italy and Yugoslavia. Handel and Company have been most co-operative in assisting us with the inquiry. They are reviewing all the property contracts with which Fräulein Berger has been involved. The scam could not have worked without her collusion and, consequently, she has been suspended, pending an internal inquiry by her employer. A keen-eyed clerk at the lending bank spotted the incorrect land registry numbers on the title deeds as she was filing them away. The official cross-referenced the deeds before contacting land registry who confirmed that it was, indeed, a car park that the bank had purchased," explained Lang.

Schmitt considered the facts for a moment. Was this someone merely taking advantage of the banking system or was it something more sinister?

"Have the regular police spoken with Fräulein Berger?"

"Yes. They have also taken away her passport, releasing her on a surety of DM 100,000."

"Peter, we need to pull out all the stops. Examine the Niemeyers' bank accounts and any related business interests, however removed they may be. If you find anything of significance, pluck it like an old jumper until it unravels. See if you can connect other companies with the Niemeyer family. One more thing; speak with our attaché in Hungary and ask him to call in a few favours, to find out if there have been amounts similar to those taken in the land scam that have been lodged with the banks there. I'll inform Reinhold to put tabs on the phones of the Niemeyers' and their associates."

CHAPTER TWENTY-THREE

It was Saturday afternoon and the temperature was in the high teens. Detlef and Amélie had taken their son to the English park for a picnic. The city's recreational area was full of people enjoying their weekend break; some had lit barbecues, and small groups of teenagers were dancing to the music of guitars played by their friends. Detlef, casually dressed in a sweatshirt and knee-length chinos, took Erhard down to a shallow pool where other children were splashing around with their parents. While they were away, Amélie removed a tartan blanket from the baby buggy, laying it out on the grass, close to the Isar River, and placing the food they had brought with them on it.

After their light repast, Erhard, now exhausted, was put into his stroller for a doze. The couple packed up their belongings and went for a leisurely walk, arriving at the large, wooden, Chinese pagoda. Having found a table free, Detlef went over to the bar where he ordered a small glass of rosé for Amélie and a beer for himself. A local radio station was playing 70s' pop music in the background. While waiting for their drinks, the local news came on.

"In the past few minutes," said the presenter, "it has been announced that the former German finance minister, Tomas Kampfle, has died. It is believed that he suffered a fatal heart attack at his home in Bonn, yesterday afternoon. The minister had recently been linked to tax evasion and was also suspected of having interests in an arms company that is alleged to have been involved in the exportation of weapons to Bosnia, in contravention of the United Nations embargo…. A man has been arrested and charged with stealing a truck. The….."

Detlef didn't wait for the presenter to finish. He quickly paid for the drinks and returned to the table where Amélie and Erhard were waiting for him. He began to talk about the news bulletin but, on hearing it was a work-related topic, Amélie switched off. Detlef hurriedly changed the subject to everyday trivia about their friends and family for the rest of the afternoon.

They rode the tube train back to their apartment in silence, Schmitt reflecting upon the unexpected death of the minister. Kampfle had been released on bail after surrendering his passport. Until his sudden demise, he had been awaiting trial for his tax evasion. The inquiry into the alleged breaking of the arms embargo was still ongoing. Following international pressure, the Swiss authorities had taken a greater interest in the case and had been investigating the arms company at the centre of the scandal. Its owner had yet to return from a business trip to the African continent. Detlef resolved to put it all to the back of his mind for now and just enjoy the rare, weekend break with his family. Monday's problems would come soon enough, he thought.

****

"Are you having any success, Herr Lehmann?" asked Schmitt as the engineer and his team continued to drag the ground radar scanner across the marked-out area.

"It's starting to form some kind of shape, Detective."

"Give me a call if you find anything of importance."

Schmitt and von Harz sipped from their disposable coffee cups as they waited patiently by the Japanese maple tree. It was Schmitt's hope that the search would identify any anomalies under the surface of Köhler senior's beautifully manicured garden at the rear of the bank. Wenzel had taken some convincing before allowing a team of engineers to be brought in to search the grounds. There had been a very heated debate in her office the previous week, over the release of funding to secure the services of an outside contractor who could assist them in the search for the Eichhörnchen Nest.

The bunker blueprint, which had been found at Schorfheide, had bugged Schmitt since he had first laid eyes on it. What had really ignited his curiosity, however, was his visit to the Münchener Assistance Bank in Regensburg, the scene of the attempted cyber-attack. He had observed the marked difference in the group's property development strategy there, compared to that of the München branch. Two days before the scanning was due to start, Schmitt had visited the bank on Marian Platz and had paced out the garden. Its measurements were very similar to those found in the blueprint produced by Albert Speer's office in Berlin. The detective had a fascination, bordering on an obsession, regarding the significance of the plot of land known as the Japanese Garden. Why had Köhler never developed the site? Even at the request of his son, he had refused.

"Herr Schmitt, do you have a moment?" enquired the chief engineer, his team having just completed their scan of the garden.

"What have you found, Herr Lehmann?" asked Schmitt anxiously, afraid that he had just wasted some of Wenzel's limited budget.

"There is definitely something down there."

"Yes!" cried Schmitt, punching the air. "What can you see?"

"For a start, the monitor clearly shows a perimeter wall. There is a clay fill between the wall and the adjacent building."

"How do you know that?"

"The presence of clay gives a lower spike on the graph. The boundary wall is constructed of concrete; those faint lines are the outlines of reinforcing bar, both in the walls and the roof structure. That black band is the complete perimeter wall."

Schmitt observed a small anomaly to the left of the screen.

"What is that break there?" he asked.

"Perhaps if you tell me what I'm looking for, I could identify the images on the screen more precisely?" Lehmann replied.

"I was hoping to find some kind of bunker or underground extension."

"Well then, Herr Schmitt, congratulations are in order as that's exactly what we appear to have here. I would say that the irregularity you asked about is a door or passageway, right there, where the main building ends," explained the man, pointing to the screen.

"The imaging is amazing, Herr Lehmann! Are you able to tell me what the black shapes scattered around the room might be?"

"At this moment, your guess is as good as mine. They could be anything, perhaps old packing cases, furniture or munitions; you won't know for certain until you get in there. Whoever built the room may have closed off the entrance."

Schmitt studied the images with interest. How were they going to get into the bunker?

"Is the bank aware of the existence of the room, Detective?"

"That's a good question, Herr Lehmann."

"It's quite a find in the centre of München!"

Schmitt, preoccupied, was looking out over the garden.

"Indeed…. Roughly what depth is the structure?"

"Approximately three metres."

The engineer's curiosity finally got the better of him.

"What do you intend to do next, Detective?" he enquired, bringing Detlef out of his musings as to what might lie under their feet.

"I don't know just yet but, in the interim, this discovery must remain confidential as it now falls under the Official Secrets Act. We are currently involved in a major investigation and the structure below us may be linked to the case. I would therefore request that you and your staff do not divulge what you have seen here," warned Schmitt, who didn't want anyone, least of all the press, to know of the existence of the construction until he figured out a way of gaining access to it.

"That won't be an issue, Herr Schmitt; we pride ourselves on our discretion. I will send you a full report, with copies of the scans carried out today," he said, shaking hands with the two detectives before leaving to assist his colleagues in packing away their equipment.

"So, there is something down there after all!" exclaimed von Harz, lighting a cigarette. "You have had a bee in your bonnet ever since you found that old blueprint."

"For all we know, it could be full of Zyklon B gas or enough munitions to blow up half of München!" replied Schmitt pessimistically.

Schmitt and von Harz left the garden and made their way to the acting CEO's office.

"Herr Markel, is it possible that we could take another look at the safe deposit vault?" asked Schmitt, wanting to go over the layout of the vault room once more.

"Of course! I would be pleased to assist. Follow me, gentlemen," replied the manager, leading the detectives to the lift.

On reaching the ground floor, they were met by a security guard who, on instruction from Herr Markel, opened the large, grey, highly polished door. Behind it could be seen row upon row of small, uniform, stainless steel containers with two chrome locks on each of them.

"Here we are," said the manager, dismissing the guard.

From his jacket pocket, Detlef pulled out the crumpled piece of paper that Doctor Lömann had given to him on Curt Köhler's behalf. Among the innocuous scribbles were little sketches of a forest, a lake and various sized boxes. There were also images of two, upturned, wooden chairs beside what appeared to be a comma. The final drawing resembled two springs and another comma, side by side.

"What's that, Detlef?" asked von Harz, peering over Schmitt's shoulder at the doodles on the sheet.

Schmitt disregarded the detective's question, his mind elsewhere as he surveyed the neat little deposit boxes adorning three quarters of the cellar walls. In an alcove to the left, stood the entrance to the bank's main vault. Its large, stainless steel door bore the inscription, *Fabrik Julius Schuler, Hamburg & Ottensen*.

"Herr Markel, how much money is your main vault capable of holding?"

The manager was taken aback by the forthright question.

"I couldn't possibly….!"

"It's alright," said Schmitt, putting his hands up to reassure the manager, "I just want a rough idea of its capacity."

"Generally, around ten million Deutsche Marks, give or take the odd thousand. Why do you ask, Detective?"

"Forgive me, Herr Markel, I'm just trying to work out a square metre problem I have been left with," he explained as both the manager and von Harz stared at him in bewilderment.

Detlef walked away from the Julius Schuler vault and over to the far wall, where he studied the various deposit boxes. Some of them were sure to be concealing someone's dark little secret, he thought. No doubt, some contained admissions of murder, adultery or tax fraud. Several, perhaps, held a little life insurance policy, in the form of damning blackmail evidence that a very public figure would rather have seen destroyed.

Schmitt pored over the images on Köhler's scrap of paper. Suddenly, it came to him that the upturned chairs, springs and commas represented two numbers: 339 and 449.

"Herr Markel, may I ask who owns the two deposit boxes numbered 339 and 449?"

After consulting the file held by the security guard, the manager replied, "No one, Herr Schmitt; they seem to have remained empty, for some unexplained reason. You would need to discuss it with Herr Köhler. Why do you ask? Is there an issue?"

"No, not really…. Would you be so kind as to open those two units for me, please?"

"Under normal circumstances, Detective, I would have asked for a warrant before granting access to an account holder's deposit box. However, as they are empty, I see no harm in meeting your request but there is a slight problem."

"Which is…...?"

"Unfortunately, I do not hold the partner keys for the boxes.

Again, you would have to speak with Herr Köhler, who may be able to assist you."

"I could, as you mentioned, go and get a warrant, Herr Markel, but, as you are here, perhaps you would oblige us and open the units," insisted Schmitt.

"Detective, I assure you I am not in possession of the keys!"

Schmitt looked at the manager sternly. Knowing he was beaten, he reluctantly went and collected the 'missing' master key, inserting it into the first unit. Within a matter of minutes, the deposit boxes were open.

"Give me a flashlight, Jürgen," said Schmitt as he removed the cases from their compartments.

Setting the boxes on a table, he opened them, one at a time, finding them both empty except for an old rag in one of them. Using the torch, Detlef peered into the void left by their removal. At the far end, there appeared to be some sort of metal lever. The detective inserted his arm, using it to measure the length of the now empty space; the security box was some three centimetres shorter than the vault in which it had sat. Schmitt looked at the other safes around the walls. They all seemed to be in uniform lots of five units wide by fifteen units deep, fixed to the surrounding walls.

"What exactly are you looking for, Detective? As I said, the boxes are clearly empty; Herr Köhler is going to be very displeased that I allowed them to be opened. I'm sorry, but I feel there's not much more I can do for you," added the manager, looking on helplessly as Schmitt disregarded his comments and continued to rummage about in the open safes.

"Köhler, you crafty old devil!" exclaimed Detlef suddenly,

taking two steps back. "Jürgen, come here and put your brawn to some use. Get your hand right to the back of each safe and try to move those bars."

Schmitt passed his colleague the old rag.

"Which way?"

"I don't know; take your pick."

Von Harz duly obeyed the order and, with some toing and froing, released the mechanism in the bottom safe, pulling the metal bar towards him. The upper unit provided some opposition before it, too, moved. Jürgen pulled out his arm and the two detectives managed to swing a section of the safe deposit units away from the wall.

"My God!" exclaimed Herr Markel, just as the guard came in, hoping to find out what was taking place.

"Get out!" barked von Harz, sending the man scurrying back to his post.

"Yes, it is a quite an interesting sight," replied Detlef as those in the room viewed a grey painted, reinforced door. It was covered in cobwebs, having remained concealed for an indeterminate amount of time.

"Detlef, I presume that this is your Holy Grail, land of the Eichhörnchen Nest," teased von Harz, shaking Schmitt's hand. He intended it not merely as a joke but also as a compliment to the sheer doggedness of his boss in finally bringing the old blueprint to life.

"Thanks, Jürgen."

"No, I mean it; you're the most determined person I know!"

"What is this all about, Herr Schmitt?" enquired Markel.

"You will find out soon enough, Herr Markel, but not today. I, myself, am unsure of what is behind the door and, I must admit, I am as intrigued as you are. However, I am afraid you will just have to show some patience, as I have done."

"But how did you know the room existed in the first place, Detective?"

"I will admit I've had my suspicions for quite a while now but the ground survey confirmed that there is some form of construction behind this door and it is my belief that your CEO is well aware of it."

Schmitt went to phone Wenzel, to give her the good news that the funding provided had not been misspent.

"Please, no more games, Herr Markel. Do you have a key for this door?" questioned Schmitt on his return.

"Detective, really, just look at the age of the door! It was put in place long before I was born; the manufacturer's plate is dated 1944. No, this time there is definitely no key. The existence of the door is a complete surprise to me!"

"I take your point. I could make a call and get our lock guy up here straight away?"

The manager nodded his head forlornly, in agreement.

"Jürgen, I want that door opened today! Tell Hans to bring plenty of releasing agent in case the hinges and locks are seized," ordered Schmitt, studying the door as von Harz made for the elevator.

Hans Grüber, Pullach's locksmith, arrived some twenty minutes later and began working on the door to try and gain access to the bunker. Grüber was one of Pullach's veteran agents, having served there for a total of twenty-four years. One area Hans excelled in was manipulating anything resembling a locking mechanism. He was driven by the challenge of outwitting his opponents, more so than complying with a given order. He had also honed his skills in covert breaking and entry operations, making copies of classified files or planting sensitive material. His department was not hesitant about inserting compromising evidence against high profile people, regardless of their standing in life. Grüber had, on many occasions, been called in to assist with the installation of counter surveillance equipment in all types of property. If there was enough space, Hans could make a device fit any item it was to be placed in.

"Any luck, Hans?" asked Schmitt.

Grüber was sweating profusely as he struggled with the mechanism.

"They're Tresore locks, Detlef! Köhler spared no expense when he ordered this door. But, don't worry, I've brought a little bit of plastic should it get messy!" explained the engineer.

"Plastic explosives?" asked von Harz, looking at both the manager and Schmitt

"You won't be letting any explosives off in this bank, Detectives!" the manager stated firmly.

"Sorry, sir, just having a laugh," said Hans contritely as one of the lock mechanisms made a loud click; the tradesman had skilfully manoeuvred the tumblers using delicate, manipulative probes, tailor-made from hardened steel.

"You're finished here, Herr Markel," said Schmitt.

The acting CEO was led out of the room.

Detlef walked forward and gently pulled the handle downwards. The door remained stubbornly in place as he tried pulling it outwards. After another good tug, the ten-centimetre-thick steel panel gave way, revealing a large, dark, room. He used the flashlight as he grappled around the inside wall just past the door frame. Having brushed away the cobwebs, he located the light switch and flicked it down. The bunker walls transformed into a faded, yellow hue as the light dimly reflected off them before one of the bulbs popped and failed. The air was thick with the smell of mildew. Schmitt removed a pair of surgical gloves and a face mask from the crime scene kit that Grüber had brought with him.

"Jürgen, make sure your mouth is covered if you're going in as the air in there will be carcinogenic," he warned. "Hans, see to it that no one else comes in."

"Right," he replied, assuming his position by the bunker door.

Schmitt and von Harz walked gingerly inside. To their right, there were several shelves filled with old bank documents. Schmitt decided to examine a few of them; they were regular savings accounts records, dating back to 1947. Further along, there were locked filing cabinets; Schmitt nodded to von Harz to get Hans in to deal with them. Detlef moved quickly through the bunker, the beam of the torch cutting through the dust that had been disturbed. The lamp momentarily shone on an old, faded, swastika emblem before Schmitt focused it directly on a bizarre looking structure.

"What is that eyesore?" asked von Harz, upon entering the room with the locksmith.

"It would seem, gentlemen, that someone has been busy making pedestals from the remains of wooden casings that may have been used to transport Reichsbank gold."

Hans went straight to work on the filing cabinets. Once opened, they were found to contain customer accounts' records, up to 1969. The file directory identified stock exchange share transactions and overseas currency trading accounts. In other documents, there were name indexes showing records of large cash deposits having been made into individual accounts.

"Hans, do the needful, please," Schmitt requested, when they reached a large, steel cupboard, situated against the far wall. After a few seconds, the lock's internal mechanism surrendered and the doors opened. On the top shelf, wrapped in plastic, were numerous black and white photographs which Grüber handed to Schmitt. The detective immediately began sifting through them.

"Detlef, who are these four, fine-looking, young Wehrmacht soldiers posing in front of the Brandenburg Gate?" queried Hans as he caught sight of one of the snaps.

"That guy, second from the left, looks just like a younger version of Curt Köhler," remarked von Harz as he took the flashlight and shone it directly on the image.

"Look at the cheekbones, and his jawline," added Schmitt.

"There he is again! Is he actually posing while counting money?" interjected von Harz as he began sifting through the photo treasure trove.

"It would seem so, and on this very pedestal, if I'm not mistaken," noted Schmitt, glimpsing the faded swastikas stencilled on the wood.

His eye was suddenly drawn back to the steel cupboard where a wooden box, marked *Nuremberg Ball Bearing GmbH*, rested on the floor. It was nailed shut.

"This is heavy, guys!" observed Schmitt, straining to lift the box up onto a nearby shelf before looking around for something with which to prise it open. Hans passed Schmitt an old claw hammer that had been sitting on one of the shelves. Once open, the detective pulled out the uniform of a Wehrmacht Captain, complete with calfskin boots. Turning back to the case, he next extracted a remnant of black linen cloth, underneath which a sizeable object lay, wrapped in the same type of material. With some effort, Schmitt carefully removed the item, placing it onto the pedestal to avoid evidence contamination. He gently peeled back the outer covering.

The team looked on in shock. The flashlight's beam reflected off a bright, 1936 stamped, Reichsbank gold ingot which bore the serial number 3246; its weight imprint indicated 12.5 kg. The ingot had the typical Nazi symbols emblazoned on it, an eagle holding a laurel wreath in its claws, and a swastika insignia within the wreath.

"I think you've got your man, Detlef!" exclaimed von Harz.

"Correction, Jürgen, we've got our man! Call in the forensic team straight away; this is now a crime scene, guys," said Schmitt, leading the way out of the bunker.

CHAPTER TWENTY-FOUR

The party streamers came out of nowhere when Schmitt walked in to the crime room a few days later. Opening a bottle of champagne, von Harz filled plastic cups as Wenzel and the team toasted Detlef's success in uncovering the elusive Eichhörnchen Nest. When the festivities were at an end, Wenzel handed him a brown, A4 envelope.

"This has just come from our Berlin office, Detlef; it was sent there by mistake," she said.

Detlef went over to the desk, nodding at his boss to follow him. Inside the package was the school yearbook photograph that Schmitt's brother-in-law, John McLean, had promised. He placed the image alongside the one of the four, young Wehrmacht soldiers that had been found in the bunker. Wenzel leaned over to study both prints more closely.

"Angela, do you see that guy?"

"Which one?"

"The taller one, second from the left in both photos…. just there."

Schmitt pointed at the figure in the snapshot.

"Who is he?"

"That is a ghost from the past. In those days, he was Corporal Frank Gotthard, the person who went on to kill Emil HaffenFuß. He is our Reichsbank employee, the man we have all known for so long as Curt Köhler!"

Wenzel carefully examined the image.

"Yes, I can see the similarity now, Detlef. Where did you get the yearbook photo from?"

Somewhat embarrassed, Schmitt looked up from the prints lying on the table and explained how his brother-in-law had assisted him. Detlef could see by the expression on her face that Angela was none too pleased with him.

"When were you planning to share your findings with the rest of us?" she asked, after an awkward silence.

"I thought it best to wait until I had enough evidence. There was no point in bringing you information unless it was accurate. The other three individuals in the photos are his younger brothers."

"And where are they, at this moment in time?"

"No one knows. The military records department has no paperwork to say they even enlisted and nothing to help us ascertain if they are alive or dead. As soon as Herr Gotthard is well enough, I intend to pay him another visit. As it stands, Helmut Schröder's affidavit has provided an accurate account of Gotthard's criminal past but it remains to be seen if his biggest escapade, to date, is true."

"And what would that be?"

"That he robbed the Reichsbank. I'm certain that he did carry out the theft but proving it is another matter."

"Detlef, you know I have the utmost confidence in your abilities but don't spend too much time on it. I fully appreciate that Gotthard seems to have led a very deceitful life. If he has a case to answer, the state will have no choice but to relieve him of his financial empire. The finance courts will take possession of the group's assets, regardless of the jurisdiction in which they are registered."

"At least his poor wife should stand a good chance of having her property returned after being swindled out of it by her unscrupulous husband. I was shocked to hear the news about Tomas Kampfle, though. Who would have thought it, a heart attack at his age? He never even got the chance to clear his name."

"I need to talk to you about that, Detlef," said Wenzel as she took Schmitt's arm, steered him into her office and closed the door.

"Why all the cloak and dagger, Angela? Is there something I should know?"

Wenzel grabbed a file from the stack of paperwork on her desk and sat down on a burgundy leather sofa, motioning Schmitt to take the seat facing her.

"The public has been led to believe that the shock of Kampfle having to tender his resignation following the tax avoidance scandal probably brought on a heart attack, which resulted in his untimely death."

"Well, didn't it?" questioned Schmitt, his curiosity now aroused.

"The family doctor examined him at home and pronounced him dead, stating the cause to be a heart attack. But, the toxicology report from the autopsy revealed high levels of scopolamine in his system."

"He was poisoned?"

Wenzel nodded her head as Detlef stared at the ceiling, having been told the disturbing news.

"As you are aware, Kampfle had been given enforced gardening leave, Government speak for being officially suspended. Ironically, he was in his garden on the day he died. His housekeeper had been working in the kitchen all morning and had called out to him, at around 12.30p.m., to let him know that lunch was ready. Some fifteen minutes later, when he had failed to arrive for his meal, she went outside to look for him. The poor woman found him lying, face down, in the greenhouse, having impaled himself on a small garden rake as he collapsed. The implement had pierced a major artery supplying blood to his heart, inducing a fatal heart attack."

"How long has the housekeeper worked there?" enquired Schmitt.

"She's clean, Detlef. She has been with the couple for over fifteen years and is considered one of the family. Tomas was known to have had a sweet tooth; it's on his parliamentary register of interests that he received gifts of expensive chocolates from his associates on a pretty regular basis. Following the outcome of the toxicology report, detectives went back to the property and removed the remains of a box of Swiss-made liqueurs, found in his greenhouse. Tests confirmed they contained highly dangerous levels of scopolamine."

"That stuff is lethal! It's used as a, so-called, twilight sleep. Taken in small doses, it gives the user a buzz, makes them more active. In a larger dose, it's bloody deadly!"

"Correct. Irrespective of falling on the rake, the antidote would not have saved Kampfle's life, given the large quantity he consumed."

"Have you any idea who was behind this?"

"Erich Niemeyer."

"He's moved on from racketeering then…. How did you link him to the killing?"

"Quite by accident, really. An unmarked police vehicle, patrolling the E50 motorway in the direction of the Czech border, stopped to assist the driver of a Mercedes estate car to change a flat tyre. As the officer approached the motorist, he immediately recognised him to be Čedomir Adrijana, one of the main crime godfathers in Serbia who was being sought by Interpol. The officer drew his weapon and forced the fugitive to the ground before his colleague placed both the man and his female passenger in handcuffs."

"So, we have one of the biggest fish in custody now?"

"Yes, along with his mistress. Adrijana had DM 272,760 in cash with him, concealed in the rear quarter panels and doors of the vehicle, along with two kilos of hash in the spare wheel."

"Those traffic officers hit pay dirt, Angela; it was a good result for everyone. What I don't understand is why he allowed himself to be so exposed; you'd think he would have used one of his mules to transport such a risky consignment."

"Greed, or arrogance maybe but, you're right, it was a good day indeed. Adrijana's tart also had four unregistered mobile phones, together with a further six unregistered, clean, SIM cards in her handbag. What's more, the prat had a Colt 45 automatic, which had been used to kill a Dutch diplomat, in the door pocket of the car. Muller's team forensically examined the phones and the SIM cards; it was established that one of Adrijana's mobiles had repeatedly been used to contact Erich Niemeyer. In addition, whilst unofficially trawling through numerous international bank accounts, Peter Lang came across DM 700,000 that had recently been lodged into a Belgian account which was registered to one of Niemeyer's shell companies. The money was later transferred to the bank account of one of Adrijana's companies, in Hungary."

"You've been very busy, Angela."

"No more than usual."

"Do you think the money transfers are the proceeds from the Wolfsburg apartment mortgage scam?"

"It's feasible. What's more alarming is that when the forensics team were processing Kampfle's home, an unregistered mobile phone began ringing in his office. It was concealed in a drinks cabinet. One of the officers attempted to answer it but the battery failed."

"What was a man in his position doing with an unregistered phone? Did he have a lady friend hidden somewhere?"

"None that we know of. Muller managed to trace the last call to yet another unregistered phone. By using the mobile phone masts in the country, close to where the call originated, he was able to identify that the call had been made by someone in Niemeyer's private residence in Hungary."

"So Kampfle may have been in contact with Niemeyer, or vice versa?"

"It seems a distinct possibility; the man was definitely up to no good. Niemeyer also has shares in the same Swiss armaments company as Kampfle, the same concern who are thought to be breaching the UN arms embargo on Serbia. The minister was also illegally processing export certificates for unnamed third party users."

"He was allowing goods to leave the country without first identifying who would actually have final ownership of them?"

"Precisely, Detlef. The items could be shipped to virtually anywhere in the world. There were also deleted text messages, from both Adrijana's and Niemeyer's phones, to Kampfle, ordering him to have our inquiry into the München bank stonewalled. Furthermore, he received a demand for the injunction that had been placed on their assets to be lifted immediately and a request for continuous updates on where the least intrusive Government border searches were taking place."

"Our minister was a real dark horse, wasn't he? …. What's the status with Adrijana?"

"He was warming to the idea of making a deal with us but only if he could keep the money we confiscated and disappear."

Schmitt broke into a fit of laughter at the thought.

"That's a big ask, given that Interpol were after him for murder. As you said, Angela, the fool had the Colt 45 cannon used in the killing of a prominent individual in his car. He would need to be selling some very hot potatoes to get away with that one."

"Unfortunately, he now has very little in the way of bargaining chips to get off the charge."

"Why?"

"His girlfriend has already made a deal. She has a recording of Niemeyer ordering the hit on Kampfle. The one-time prostitute made the tape during a car key swap party, keeping it as an insurance policy against Adrijana, in case he decided he no longer needed her. Dubravko Huzjak was given the job of carrying out the meticulous lacing of the chocolates and organising their delivery to Kampfle's residence."

"He was actually recorded demanding the hit?"

"Yes. He stipulated that the sweets had to be dark mint liqueurs, nothing else. It was known that Kampfle's wife hated that type of chocolate and so it eliminated her from becoming a casualty. The maid told detectives that the confectionery had been delivered by Deutsche Post on the morning of the killing. The accompanying card purportedly stated that the gift was from a business associate. Kampfle had eaten three of the chocolates right away before potting plants in his greenhouse. Copies of both the autopsy report and the audio recording are on your desk. Adrijana's partner has been most co-operative in assisting us with our inquiries. She has been put into our witness protection programme until we get these people to trial. I'll decide later where to place her in the long term."

"Will she hold up? Criminals turned witnesses have a habit of retracting their statement at the last minute."

"It's a chance we'll have to take, I'm afraid. The most damning bit of evidence we have recovered, to date, is the code that was used to gain access to Judge Janzyke's alarm system. If you remember, the breach was made via the office computer at the Ministry of Economic Development."

"Also on Kampfle's phone?" asked Schmitt.

"Yes. There is no doubt about his involvement in the incident at the judge's house. The deleted code was on his ghost phone; although erased, the information can still be accessed by using the appropriate software," explained Wenzel, rubbing her brow in a futile effort to relieve the throbbing migraine that had plagued her for the last two days.

"We will need to present the tape to Judge Janzyke and let him decide what action to take, Angela. Granted, our ex-minister was a crook but he should have been allowed to live out his days in peace."

"I know, Detlef, he was just a human being like the rest of us," replied a now very tired Wenzel. "I haven't yet notified Bonn about his shady dealings. I thought I'd wait until the funeral had taken place, to allow the man some dignity before all hell breaks loose at the Ministry of Justice."

She had worked the previous night till late, preparing a state of affairs report on organised crime in Germany. The American

Secretary of Defence was scheduled to arrive for an unofficial visit in the coming days and his counterpart in Bonn was looking for as much information as possible, to brief him on Germany's efforts to strangle Serbian funding.

"Leave it with me, Angela. I can promise you that someone is going to pay for Kampfle's death."

Once back in his office, Detlef began to review the case files relating to the arms' shipments seized at the German-Swiss border. The accompanying third party export certificates, originating from the Ministry of Economic Development in Bonn, had been falsified. The interest of the customs' authorities had been stirred by the final destination address marked on the transport documents: Yugoslavia. Schmitt set down the files and placed a call to Reinhold.

"Claudia, I need you to speak with the local police crime unit in Bonn. Find out where a box of chocolates that had been sent to Herr Kampfle was purchased, and which Deutsche Post sorting office processed the delivery."

"Is there something wrong?"

"It seems that the minister was poisoned; I'll have a copy of the report ready for you later today. In the meantime, Claudia, pull out all the stops."

"I'm on it, Detlef."

****

Wenzel and Schmitt had called in to the finance courts on IsmaningerStraße to bring Judge Janzyke up to speed. The judge had been listening to the voice on the audio cassette; it was clear and precise as the order was given for Tomas Kampfle to be assassinated. When the recording ended, Janzyke spoke.

"You're certain that the person giving the order is Erich Niemeyer?"

"We've run voice recognition software on it a dozen times; it's definitely him."

"I have already made some discreet calls to my associates in the Hungarian Ministry of Justice. Given Niemeyer's political contacts, there is no chance of him ever being extradited to face trial in Germany; he has too many irons in the political fire. Now, don't get me wrong, this man will be brought to justice. I'm simply not prepared to wait forever on a regime change in Hungary that would facilitate his return to Germany for any legal proceedings."

"Paweł, if I might interrupt?"

"Please, go ahead, Angela," murmured Janzyke, looking at his watch; he was running late for another meeting.

"Detlef and I have been giving the matter some consideration."

"Continue," said Janzyke as he took a sip of orange juice from a glass sitting on the Bau table.

"Thanks to the triangulation of transmitter masts close to Niemeyer's home address in Hungary, we have been able to monitor his phones, twenty-four-seven. Moreover, we have been able to intercept further calls that were made using other, unregistered mobile phones. The handsets and SIM cards seem to be changed every month, undoubtedly to avoid being compromised. He is taking a trip to Morocco in four weeks' time, to meet up with Middle Eastern arms dealers whom we suspect of also being involved in drug running and people trafficking."

Wenzel passed Janzyke a file containing material collated by the IT engineers at Pullach.

"Niemeyer and his wife will be travelling on false passports, under the name of Urdrovsky," continued Schmitt. "The IT department was able to gain online access to the travel agent's computer system; he frequently uses the same company when making bookings. In the file, you will find the airline's passenger manifest; I have highlighted the two individuals. We believe some of his heavies may be taking the flight with them."

"Are you proposing to seize the couple in Morocco, Angela?"

"It's doable, with assistance from local officials, although seeking forgiveness later is always more expedient than requesting co-operation. However, with insurrection mounting, the Moroccan authorities seem to have enough to deal with, at this point in time. Ideally, it would be better to try and apprehend the couple a little closer to home, for a number of reasons."

"Right, I understand. Total denial then, perhaps a covert operation on European soil?"

"Yes, Paweł," replied Wenzel in a nonchalant manner as she began to put the papers she had brought with her back into her attaché case.

"Then I'll take my leave of this conversation. If I do see Niemeyer's face spread over the morning edition of the German red-tops, I can only speculate as to how his capture was achieved," said Janzyke, tapping his nose.

****

Wenzel lowered the vehicle's sun visor to counteract the harsh glare of the crisp, winter afternoon as Schmitt steered the S2 out through the grandiose, wrought-iron gates of the finance courts.

"The idea of taking the Niemeyers out on their own turf is

starting to appeal to me, Detlef," she said. "I need a comprehensive intelligence update on both their properties and their movements, without delay, along with an operational strike plan. For the greater part, you and your team will be on your own in this so choose only your best operatives, those who will blend into the landscape. The embassy will provide any resources or logistics that you may require."

"I'll get right onto it."

"Good. By the way, where are we concerning the bureau? I'm nearly out of excuses. You can tell someone you're out of the office just so many times! The hotel owners are angling on using the purchase of the hotel from the Government as justification to claim ownership of the piece. After all, the terms and conditions in the sale contract stipulate that the building, lands and contents are included," Wenzel pointed out.

"I'll have an answer for you by next week, Angela," Schmitt assured her as he brought the vehicle to a stop at a set of traffic lights.

Detlef knew the issue of the bureau would have to be resolved at some stage. He had been working on it with the assistance of a friend from New Scotland Yard in London. His inquiries had been going well and Schmitt was confident that he would soon have some positive news that would hopefully get the hotel owners off Angela's back. When the lights changed, he steered the car onto Fraunbergstraße and continued their journey back to the office

CHAPTER TWENTY-FIVE

Schmitt and Reinhold had just arrived at Stadelheim to interview Frank Gotthard. Detlef grabbed his padded jacket, along with files from the back seat of the Audi, and the pair shared a silent look of apprehension before entering the building. Having checked in their firearms at the prison's armoury, the detectives collected their visitors' passes and made their way to Herr Lömann's office. The psychiatrist had requested a meeting before he would allow any further access to the prisoner.

"Herr Lömann, so good to see you again," said Schmitt as Reinhold and he shook hands with the doctor.

"Please, sit down and make yourselves comfortable," said Lömann, gesturing to them as he poured coffee for his guests.

"How is the patient?" Schmitt enquired, stirring brown sugar into his cup.

Lömann didn't respond immediately to the question, electing to work some more with his pipe as he coaxed the tobacco to begin drawing a little more co-operatively. Eventually, he conceded defeat and, setting the pipe down on an ashtray, replied.

"Herr Gotthard is in pretty good shape, considering."

"Is he fit to be interviewed?" queried Schmitt, who was straining at the leash and hoped to be told that the prisoner was legally capable of being questioned.

"I am of the opinion that Herr Gotthard will be most accommodating."

"Are you saying that his condition has been stabilised, Doctor?"

asked Reinhold.

"Not in the least, Fräulein. Put simply, the treatment we have used focuses mainly on a person's perception of how their life is playing out. This encompasses their thought processes, images, beliefs, and how these things impact on the way they behave and deal with their emotional problems."

"A form of guilt trip?" suggested Schmitt as he idly looked up at the ceiling, having heard enough of this apologist's view of Gotthard.

"That, Detective, if I may say, is not only a crude appraisal but also a misleading one. To elaborate further, once we have explored a patient's underlying problems, we then come to a decision on how best to eradicate or, at the very least, alter any negative thinking or behavioural patterns that may be leading to other difficulties."

"Herr Lömann, how long does the treatment last?" queried Reinhold, in an attempt to ease the tension in the room.

"Cognitive behavioural therapy sessions can take anything from six weeks up to six months to make any real progress. In much of the cases though, the changes in a patient's behaviour are clearly noticeable. As a result of the treatment, Herr Gotthard will, hopefully, be able to come to terms with why he has lived his life in such a manner," explained Lömann, taking the pipe from the ashtray in a futile attempt to resuscitate it once more.

"So, we can, with care, question him?" asked Schmitt, frustrated by the doctor's long-winded explanation.

"Yes, you may interview Herr Gotthard," Lömann confirmed, picking miniscule strands of tobacco from his white coat. "However, before you leave, I must inform you that he had to be admitted to the prison hospital with the chest infection I told you about. On x-raying him, doctors found a large, cancerous growth in his right lung. The prognosis, I'm afraid, is terminal."

"Are you sure, Doctor?" queried Schmitt, trying to take in the unexpected news.

"Quite sure. Herr Gotthard has no more than six months to live, so I would advise you to make good use of the remaining time you have with him, Herr Schmitt."

The two detectives rose from their seats.

"Thank you, Herr Lömann; good day," said Schmitt, closing the office door behind them.

As the pair approached the interview suite, they found Herr Kleber waiting outside.

"Herr Schmitt, could I possibly have a word with you and Fräulein Reinhold before we commence with the interview?"

"Why, of course, Herr Kleber, though I am surprised to see you here. I thought Gotthard would have put new counsel in place by now. How can we help you?"

"First, I must apologise for the way I spoke to you the last time we met. You were right; I had been blinded by Herr Gotthard as he had been my client for many years. Funny how you think you know someone, Detectives! He has requested that I continue to represent him and says that he is willing to co-operate with your enquiries in any way he can."

"Well then, let's start with a clean slate, though I must notify you that I will have to re-arrest your client today, given that he has been living under an assumed identity. I intend to reintroduce the charges of murder, gross fraud and falsification of state documents."

"I don't quite follow you.... gross fraud and falsification of state documents?" quizzed Kleber.

"Let's leave that subject parked until I have put the charges before your client. Is that not what he pays you for, Herr Kleber, explaining why he is not guilty?"

"As you wish, Detective."

The party walked into the interview suite where Gotthard sat, reading a copy of *Hobby* magazine.

"Herr Gotthard, how are you feeling? It's been a while since we last spoke," said Schmitt as he and Reinhold placed their files on the interview table and sat down.

Schmitt studied the prisoner. He had aged tremendously. His eyes were sunken and he had lost a significant amount of weight, although the prison had supplied him with a uniform that seemed to fit well.

"Herr Schmitt, Fräulein; I'm good. A lot has happened since we last met."

"Yes, it has," replied Schmitt.

"I am conscious of the fact that when your inquiries are concluded, it would be safe to say I won't be leaving this place," stated Gotthard dispassionately.

Unprepared for such a forthright statement, the faces of the two detectives betrayed their shock.

Pleased with himself, he added, "Oh, don't look so surprised, you two! After all, I am a criminal!"

"Frank...."

"Kleber, don't speak; you're wasting your breath."

"I thought we had discussed this?" argued the solicitor.

"It's over. I've only got a few months left, in any event, so let the detectives get on with their job."

"Herr Gotthard, for the record, can you please formally identify yourself and your country of birth?"

"Frank Christoph Gotthard, Boalsburg, Pennsylvania, United States of America."

"Do you acknowledge that to be your real name?"

The man leaned a little closer to the microphone for everyone's benefit.

"The name I have provided was given to me by my parents, at birth, Herr Schmitt."

"Can you please stand up, Herr Gotthard?"

The prisoner followed the now familiar procedure and slowly rose to his feet, pushing back the chair on which he had been sitting. He looked so small, thought Reinhold as she passed some papers to Schmitt.

"Frank Christoph Gotthard, you are hereby charged with the murder of Emil HaffenFuß in München, in 1972. You do not have to say anything. However, it may harm your defence if you do not mention, when questioned, something which you later rely on in court. Anything you do say may be given in evidence. How do you plead?"

"Guilty, as charged," replied Gotthard.

Kleber shook his head in exasperation at his client's candid response.

"You are also charged with fraudulently carrying out financial transactions for profit against the state of Germany. From 1945 to 1994, you wilfully committed wide-ranging acts of property fraud. You also, with the collusion of the late, former finance minister, Herr Kampfle, used unfair means to secure lucrative Government contracts, namely the management of the civil service salary administration. How do you plead?"

"I wish to defer my plea until I have a clearer understanding of the charges, Detective," replied Gotthard as he looked over at the file the officer had read the charges from.

"Are you happy to continue, Herr Gotthard?"

"I've no objections, Herr Schmitt."

"Herr Kleber, have you any concerns?"

"No, but if, at any time, I feel that my client is not up to this, I will have no hesitation in calling a halt to the proceedings," replied the solicitor.

"I fully understand, Herr Kleber. Then let us begin. Herr Gotthard, why did you murder Emil HaffenFuß?"

Gotthard looked around the room for a few moments before answering.

"To put it bluntly, Herr Schmitt, he was in the wrong place at the wrong time."

"Can you clarify that statement?"

"Things were going well at the bank, with many areas of the business thriving. At that time, the Olympics were being staged in München and a lot of my properties had been rented out to the International Olympic Committee, to provide accommodation for the athletes. As a group, we could do no wrong, financially."

Just then, Gotthard paused. The detectives and the lawyer waited patiently until the prisoner came out of his reverie.

"I had just been out, for coffee and a Danish with a business associate, at a nearby café. As I was entering the bank on my return, I heard a male voice calling me by my real name. I froze with the shock of hearing it after so many years. The person continued to address me, his voice getting louder as he approached from behind."

"What did you do, Herr Gotthard?" asked Reinhold, who was busily taking notes.

"I just couldn't ignore the man, not with so many customers and staff present, so I eventually turned around and came face to face with Emil HaffenFuß. It was as if I'd seen a ghost. He was a strange creature!"

"Why would you call him that?"

"HaffenFuß had been a fine-looking man before the war, dashing, some might say. The horrendous burns he suffered when a phosphorous shell accidently went off in his tank had left the wretch.... I don't know.... how would one......? How would you describe the man kindly, Herr Schmitt?"

"As an unfortunate victim of an unjust war, Herr Gotthard. That's how anyone with an ounce of compassion would describe him."

Ignoring the retort, the prisoner continued.

"With the passing of time, Emil had become just another casualty of the conflict, blending into society as best he could, despite his grotesque appearance."

Schmitt noted Gotthard's demeanour; therapy had clearly done little for this man's sensitivity. He was as callous as ever in his description of HaffenFuß who was so pitilessly murdered, simply because he had recognised his old friend.

"How could you be so calculating as to murder such a frail, old man? He had barely laid his wife to rest!" argued Reinhold.

Gotthard looked down at his hands. Reinhold instantly regretted the aggressive way she had presented the question.

"I can fully appreciate your outrage, Fräulein," said the prisoner. "When Emil HaffenFuß walked back into my life, I was another person altogether. No one, and I mean no one, was going to undo what I had built up! I couldn't take the chance of him finding out that I was not the person he thought I was."

"Who did he think you were? What exactly did you say to Emil when you came face to face with him that day?" probed Schmitt.

"It was just idle chitchat, the kind of small talk that old friends make when they meet again after many years of separation. I fobbed him off with a sob story, telling him that I had an appointment with the manager as I was trying to secure a business loan to keep my company afloat. The poor sod bought it, hook, line and sinker!"

Gotthard chortled loudly as he recalled how HaffenFuß had offered to help him with his supposed financial difficulties.

"After that, I took care to avoid the man when he visited the bank. I would observe the fool scanning the main foyer in the hope of seeing me. Following that first encounter, I personally made a point of finding out where HaffenFuß lived; I got the necessary information from the accounts department records. I began following him, just to see who he socialised with. I watched him as he made his weekly shop, and even visited his local Kneipe, where he was a member of the pub's darts team. All this enabled me to understand who, if anyone, would be concerned for Emil should he break with his normal routine, or meet with....."

He paused, rubbing his index finger over his brow as if reflecting on the fateful night in 1972.... "an untimely accident."

"That sounds so cold-hearted, Herr Gotthard."

"I didn't mean it to be."

"Premeditated murder is a cold-hearted act, whatever way you look at it."

"Maybe."

"What ultimately prompted you to take action?" queried Schmitt.

Gotthard chuckled quietly, seeming to have remembered something humorous.

"I wasn't prepared to go on looking over my shoulder every day, just waiting for that particular knock of the police at my door. The incident at the Breitkopf Institute really sealed HaffenFuß's fate; I had to move as quickly as possible. *Carpe diem*, isn't that what they say, Fräulein?"

Reinhold made no reply, taking the question as rhetorical.

"It's not often that an institution like that inadvertently frees such a disturbed person! You know the rest, Detectives. You have my DNA on the murder weapon, along with the other evidence which has kept me here," said Gotthard.

The prisoner fell silent.

Content with the cast iron confession and the material evidence he already had, Schmitt turned to Gotthard's solicitor.

"Can we proceed with the next charge, Herr Kleber?" asked Schmitt, opening another file.

Kleber nodded.

"Herr Gotthard, can you identify the three individuals with you in the two photographs, marked as exhibits 1A and 1B?" quizzed the detective, placing the images on the table.

Gotthard showed no emotion as he studied both the copy of his school yearbook photo and that of the young men posing in front of the Brandenburg Gate.

"Let me make one thing very clear, Detective. I have not seen those people for some considerable time. I will assist you with your enquiries into the crimes I have committed but the individuals in the pictures are out of bounds," he declared resolutely.

"They are your brothers, are they not?"

"I will not answer any questions pertaining to these men, Detective, but you have certainly been very diligent, I'll say that much. Where on earth did you find the Berlin photo?"

"Come, come, Herr Gotthard, I think you are aware from whence it came!"

"I haven't the faintest idea! You seem to have me at a disadvantage."

"The picture, as well as several other items, was found in a room adjacent to your bank. I believe you call it the Eichhörnchen Nest."

Gotthard was slow to reply.

"To what room are you referring, Detective?"

"The one Albert Speer's office drew up the plans for, Herr Gotthard."

Schmitt placed a copy of the bunker blueprint on the desk but the prisoner disregarded it. The detective briefly deliberated before deferring the query. Detlef was now opting to play the long game, preferring, at this stage, not to push Gotthard too hard for answers.

"Herr Gotthard."

"Yes, Detective?" replied the prisoner as he momentarily stopped fiddling with his handcuff chains and looked up.

"Whilst you were busy lining your own pockets at the expense of the downtrodden and demoralised German population, my grandfather was fighting a real battle in the Ardennes; it was called survival. He wasn't someone who simply played at soldiers until it all got too serious. He stood shoulder to shoulder with his comrades to the end, unlike you."

"Where are we going with this, Herr Schmitt?" Kleber interjected.

"Okay, let's talk about a different matter then. Having lived the life of another man for so many years, both Herr Köhler's family and my team would like to know what became of him."

"I don't follow you, Herr Schmitt?"

"What happened to Curt Köhler? Where is he?"

Gotthard resumed playing with his chains. Waiting for a reply, the detective removed a fresh piece of gum from its foil wrapping and began to chew. At last, the prisoner spoke.

"Curt…. Curt…. Ah, poor Curt, I knew you wouldn't remain quiet forever, you spirit of the past! Herr Schmitt, where did this all start?"

"Start? Now I don't follow you, Herr Gotthard!"

"For one thing, where did you get the notion that I was not who I claimed to be and how the hell did you find out about Emil HaffenFuß?"

"That was quite simple; the man you betrayed told us everything."

The banker appeared mystified by the detective's cryptic answer.

"I am afraid you will have to enlighten me, Herr Schmitt. There were several - sorry, that's an understatement - countless people whom I may have offended over the years. I was in the business of making money, not friends."

He gestured, in a passive manner, with the open palms of his hands.

"It appears that you shouldn't have double-crossed the person who had set you up for life. Helmut Schröder sold you out."

"But how? He can't talk; he is long dead!"

"The dead seem to find a way of getting their point across where you are concerned, Herr Gotthard."

"He was in no position to know of my dealings," countered the prisoner, disconcerted by the new line of questioning.

"Herr Kleber, we have in our possession a sworn affidavit made by the late Herr Schröder, your client's one time business partner. In that document, one of the allegations is that Herr Gotthard killed Emil HaffenFuß. Our investigations have substantiated his claim, that being one of the reasons why we are all here today."

"Schröder must have guessed that I had taken HaffenFuß out of the picture. I mentioned to him in passing that I had run into Emil at the bank."

"So, you told him of the encounter?"

"Unfortunately for me, Detective, yes."

"That makes things a little clearer. Now, back to Curt Köhler. Did you really know the man, Herr Gotthard, or was it a name you randomly picked out of thin air?"

Gotthard paused for an instant and then whispered into his solicitor's ear.

"Herr Schmitt, my client has tired somewhat and wishes to return to his cell; I do hope you understand."

"Of course, Herr Kleber; we can come back another time. I feel that we have made good progress today. I would like to expand on the last theme we covered during our next meeting, if your client is agreeable?"

"I think we can carry on with your line of questioning. Frank, do you wish to continue with this topic?"

The prisoner nodded and got up to leave the room, walking unsteadily down the corridor, a result of the high dosage of pain medication he had been given.

CHAPTER TWENTY-SIX

Schmitt and Reinhold were seated across the table from Gotthard and Kleber in the prison's interview room.

"Why did you use Curt Köhler's identity?" asked Schmitt.

"It was convenient, I suppose."

"Convenient?"

"He was an extremely troubled man. Once, when driving to a meeting, Curt confided in me about ending his own life. He remarked that all his loved ones had been wiped out in the Dresden bombings and he had nothing left to live for. On hearing this, I was quite sure that no-one would miss him if he were gone."

"So, you took advantage of someone who, in all probability, was suffering from post-traumatic stress?"

"Not at all, Detective; I'm no shrink. I didn't know if he would really carry out his threat. He was a very private person and kept much to himself. All I knew was the unfortunate soul had lost his entire family."

"That is the first time I have heard you speak with any form of compassion for another human being, Herr Gotthard."

"Perhaps the therapy is working after all!" teased the prisoner. "Curt was similar in facial features and stature to myself; we could have been mistaken for brothers. I could not have wished for a better likeness."

"Apart from the fact that Köhler was your appointed driver, did you ever socialise with him?"

"In what way?"

"You know, go for a meal or a drink in the evening, when you were off duty?"

"I assume you carried out your national service in the Bundeswehr?"

"Yes."

"Then you don't seem to understand military protocol, Herr Schmitt. I was a captain by the time he had been assigned to my office. As a rule, officers didn't mix with the lower ranks. Good God, how would that look when one is trying to improve one's standing in the Wehrmacht? Köhler knew his place and carried out his duties as a good soldier would. I had a very hectic schedule during the war, attending meetings throughout Europe, so any interaction with him was purely professional."

The prisoner fell silent, resting his hands on the table whilst fixing his gaze upon Kleber's briefcase that lay against the wall. Schmitt used the break to write a few notes.

"Helmut Schröder.... who would have thought it?" Gotthard suddenly exclaimed, taking those in the room by surprise. "Is it really true that he had been keeping a record of my activities?"

"That is correct, Herr Gotthard. Was he not your camp commandant at Waggum?"

"Yes, he was; I take it someone has begun filling in the blanks?"

"I am not at liberty to say, but be assured that we are examining each allegation thoroughly," confirmed Schmitt. "Where was Curt posted; is it possible that he was sent to the east?"

The prisoner leaned across and whispered something to his solicitor in relation to the information Schmitt had provided. Kleber brusquely told his client to proceed as he wished.

"Köhler had voiced his fears that, as with all Wehrmacht staff fit for combat, he might be sent eastwards. I advised him to do what any proud soldier would; go and support his colleagues on the Russian Front. Of course, this was of no concern to me as I would be taking no part in the last forlorn attempt at defeating the Red Army. I had much left to do in Berlin."

"That we are aware of. You didn't go east. On the contrary, it seems a unit of Patton's Third Army took you prisoner at Coburg."

"Yes, Herr Schmitt, that very much sums it up."

"What became of Herr Köhler? I suspect you had some involvement in his disappearance, given that you assumed his identity."

Gotthard made no reply. He laid his head on the table before covering it with both hands, almost toppling the IV stand to which he was attached. He began rocking himself gently, from side to side.

"I think this would be a good time to take a break," said Kleber, sensing that his client was going into one of his mood swings. In recent days, Gotthard had veered from being a pleasant and charming person one minute to expressing near violent tendencies the next.

"Yes; I think now would be a good time," agreed Schmitt.

"Shut up, Kleber, you annoying man!" cried Gotthard. "The lying has gone on long enough. Herr Schmitt, if it pleases you, I am willing to tell you where to locate Köhler's remains…. that is, if they are still interred where I left them."

"That would be very helpful, most of all for the sake of his family. Where are they to be found?"

Gotthard sat back and folded his arms in submission.

"I buried him, in a shallow grave, at the side of the northbound carriageway, near the village of Ketzin. If my memory serves me well, it was at the embankment below the motorway flyover crossing the S76."

Kleber hurriedly murmured a warning to his client.

"If you don't like the arrangement, Claus, there's the door!" declared Gotthard.

"This is utter madness, Frank. Do you realise what you're doing?"

"Emil HaffenFuß has sealed my fate already. Your views have been taken on board, Claus, but I'm doing it my way," insisted the prisoner, his voice barely audible.

"Herr Gotthard, let us be clear about this. Are you confessing to the murder of Curt Köhler?"

"Yes, Detective, I am. In March 1945, I killed and buried Curt Köhler. Hopefully, they have not altered the area; his remains should still be below the flyover," replied Gotthard, with a look of expectation on his face.

"Herr Gotthard, please stand up."

"I know the drill, Detective."

"Frank Christoph Gotthard, you are hereby charged with the murder of Curt Köhler, in or around March 1945, in the district of Berlin. You do not have to say anything; however, it may harm your defence if you do not mention, when questioned, something which you later rely on in court. Anything you do say may be given in evidence. How do you wish to plead?" asked Schmitt.

"I won't drag this out, Detective. Köhler is dead; that you can all be assured of. I am guilty of the charge," replied Gotthard quietly, feeling a little light-headed as he looked at the medication flowing into his body from the drip. The doctors had added morphine to the cocktail, to make him more comfortable during the interviews.

"Detectives, you have heard my client's admission of guilt, which I feel is quite reckless, but he has chosen to ignore my counsel," said Kleber.

"Herr Kleber, I think we should adjourn this interview until we have substantiated your client's allegation that he has murdered yet another person."

"As you wish, Herr Schmitt, although I seem to be serving little purpose in being here as most of the advice I have offered my client has gone unheeded."

"That is your client's prerogative, Herr Kleber. I will let you know when our next meeting is due to take place."

****

Following a court order, the roads service had created four hundred metres of single lane traffic in both directions of the motorway bridge, north-east of Berlin, near the alleged crime scene. Local police, using specially trained dogs, had carried out a systematic search of the area described by Gotthard. There had been a few false leads as the dogs had mistaken the scent of decomposing roadkill for human remains. Three days of clearing undergrowth on both sides of the flyover and making various test holes eventually led forensic officers to the right location. The victim was found, wrapped in the roots of a large beech tree that had grown at the site sometime after the crime had taken place. Whoever the killer was, he had gone to the trouble of placing rocks over the deceased to prevent animals from gnawing at the corpse. This had allowed the tree's roots to propagate in the shape of a basket, which cradled the skeletal remains.

Wenzel had instructed Schmitt to go to Berlin and liaise with the regional police there. Given Gotthard's violent past, he needed to substantiate the prisoner's claim that, almost fifty years ago, he had murdered Köhler. If validated, it would hopefully bring closure to the dead man's family at long last.

Arriving early Sunday morning, Schmitt was driven to the site by a police officer. A collapsible canopy had been erected to protect the crime scene from the elements as a winter storm made its way in from the east. Recovering the evidence was a protracted affair. The forensic officer used a small trowel to expose the victim, taking copious photographs of the remains before gently cutting away the tree roots to remove them, trying not to contaminate the site in the process.

Schmitt walked over and introduced himself to the veteran doctor of forensics as she came out of a tent. Removing her gloves, she shook his hand. Dr Limffert was a tall, elegant woman in her late fifties, with long, greying hair; she had resisted the urge to keep her original colour and wore it twisted into a neat bun while she went about her duties. She worked part-time with the Berlin police department and delivered lectures at colleges throughout the country. Limffert had been at a loose end. Her husband had gone deep-sea fishing near Kiel with his friends and she was about to hit the town with her chums. Having received a call from Pullach, the duty officer at Charlottenburger Chaussee police station had called her from the list of forensic officers available for weekend work, just as she was on her way to meet them.

"Excuse the mess, Detective. I was looking forward to a

weekend clubbing with my girlfriends, in my stilettos, rather than traipsing through the countryside," said the forensic officer in a jovial manner as she raised her muddied, white Wellington boot.

"No need to apologise, Frau Limffert. I've seen much worse in my time; victims found in water or swamps are the most unpleasant. May I ask how the dig is going?"

"Well, Herr Schmitt, could I perhaps begin by asking how you found out that human remains had lain here, undiscovered, for nearly fifty years?"

"Purely by chance, to be honest," he replied, delivering a condensed version of the evidence he had chanced upon in the hotel at Schorfheide.

"And I thought my job was intriguing! Forgive me, I've been so rude, Herr Schmitt," apologised the doctor as she touched the detective's arm. "You're here for an update on my findings. The victim was definitely male; both the tree roots and the non-acidic soil played a part in preserving the scene."

The officer led Detlef into a small, temporary structure near the dig, where the skeletal remains had been laid out on a collapsible table.

"He may have been a soldier, although there were no dog tags or any other form of I.D. present. This is what's left of his uniform."

Detlef cast an eye over the scraps of dark blue cloth, spotting what appeared to be a tunic collar and a pair of trousers. There were also some grey-blue buttons, a belt with a double hitch aluminium Wehrmacht belt buckle and the remnants of leather boots.

"You say *'the victim'*; I take it he met with a sorry end, Doctor?"

Limffert lifted the remains of the skull, allowing Schmitt a closer view.

"It's evident that the poor wretch had been summarily executed. The cranium was tilted forward and he was shot in the back of the head. A 9mm round from some form of handgun was used."

"Probably.... given the size of the entry hole," commented the detective as he examined the skull, having put on a pair of surgical gloves to avoid contamination of the evidence.

"No probably about it, Herr Schmitt; I don't give up that easily!"

Doctor Limffert turned and pointed to a metal detector that stood in the corner.

"When you're sent out to a job in the sticks, especially on the weekend shift, you come prepared," she added, rummaging in her briefcase.

Limffert produced a plastic evidence bag containing the bullet that she suspected had killed Köhler and handed it to Schmitt.

"It doesn't seem to have deformed too much; the bullet still has some of the original profiling. This was an unexpected bonus, although there won't be much opportunity to try and forensically match it to a weapon," said Schmitt as he examined the slug. He knew that Gotthard would have had any firearms in his possession confiscated by the allies upon his arrest in 1945.

"I thought as much myself although, now we have the victim's remains and someone has allegedly confessed to the killing, we should have enough to achieve a sound conviction," observed Frau Limffert, taking back the bullet.

The pair walked out and over to a makeshift tent that protected the crime scene. Using a lamp powered by a nearby generator, Schmitt was able to look at the carefully excavated site. The depressions in the ground below the large tree outlined where the victim had lain for so long, undetected. In a small area of the excavation closest to the motorway, Schmitt could see the indentation where his head had rested in the soft earth.

"I take it this is where you found the bullet?" he asked, pointing to the small, yellow flag embedded in the bank.

"Yes. If my calculations are correct, the victim was brought to the site and executed. He was more than likely forced to kneel down before being shot, falling face first into his burial place. There was a difference of roughly thirty centimetres between where the body came to rest and where I found the slug. This guy was a real pro."

The forensic officer demonstrated with a calibrated steel ruler.

"His executioner would have stood…. right where you are standing now, Herr Schmitt."

"Just thinking about it gives me the shivers," said the detective as he hastily moved slightly to the left. "You believe he was a serving soldier then?"

"Yes, I do, Herr Schmitt, despite the absence of dog tags. My husband, Erwin, is a keen military enthusiast; over the years, I have accompanied him to many museums and military historical gatherings. The uniform is that of a Wehrmacht field service unit, possibly one of the Panzer regiments. When I get a chance to examine it more thoroughly, the buttons should provide some insight as to which regiment it belonged."

"I may be able to help you a little with that, Doctor. From the information we have gathered, Curt Köhler was formerly a tank driver in the Fourth Panzer regiment. In 1942, he was involved in a military campaign, in or around the Don River near Voronezh, in Russia. His medical records indicate that he was injured during the assault; if the victim is Köhler, you should find damage to the left femur."

Schmitt produced a copy of Köhler's army medical report.

"As you can see, he was then sent back to convalesce in a military hospital in Berlin before being seconded to the Reich Chancellery, where he worked as a driver in the motor pool."

"You've certainly done your homework, haven't you, Detective? Once I have carried out a full analysis of the crime scene and any further evidence uncovered, I will provide you with a copy of my report. I take it the civil police will be handling the case now?" asked Limffert inquisitively.

"No; it will remain part of a much wider, ongoing investigation. I must admit, it has been like peeling back the wallpaper in an old house; each layer we remove exposes another underneath."

"That's the joy of law enforcement, Herr Schmitt. Well, I am going to pack this lot away and go home. My husband will think I'm doing a line with someone if I don't show my face soon!"

Limffert shook Schmitt's hand, promising to get her report to him as soon as possible.

The detective accepted a lift back to his hotel in one of the patrol cars, staying overnight in Berlin before flying out of Tegel Airport the next day.

****

"Good morning, Angela," said Schmitt as he walked into her office following his visit to the Ketzin murder scene.

"Hi, Detlef. How was the trip?"

"Cold, wet and windy."

"Not much different here. And how did the dig go?"

"Better than we could ever have dared to hope for; human

remains were uncovered at the site."

"So, Gotthard was actually telling the truth?"

"It would appear so. Doctor Limffert, the forensic officer, has already carried out a preliminary examination of the victim back at her lab. His teeth had been knocked out to prevent identification; scientific officers had to sift the surrounding soil to recover them."

"The man is depraved, Detlef," Wenzel commented, after the detective had finished describing the crime scene in graphic detail.

"Gotthard's behaviour no longer surprises me, Angela. Look how he has treated his family - if what Frau Köhler has told me is to be believed - it's no wonder the Köhlers are so dysfunctional!"

"What do you mean?"

"His psychopathic personality, coupled with egocentric behaviour, resulted in a total disregard for the welfare of his wife and children. The raison d'être for his actions was to fulfil his own aspirations, oblivious to the impact it was having on the family's mental wellbeing. The suicide of his first son is testimony to this."

"It would be hard to come to terms with the death of any child, never mind a firstborn, Detlef."

"I know, Angela; I cannot imagine my life without Erhard. It's going to take a lot of lawyers and money to sort this sorry mess out. Gotthard's family will undoubtedly lose everything to the state."

"Well, let's leave that to those who are qualified to handle these types of disputes, financial or otherwise. Gotthard's charge of the murder of Curt Köhler stands. I will send the file to the state prosecutor once the reports have been completed."

Wenzel fell silent, gazing out of the window into the nearby forest that surrounded the Pullach complex, in deep contemplation.

After a while, she turned back to face Schmitt.

"That man has treated human beings in the same way one treats a used cigarette. Having served their purpose, Gotthard seems to have simply stubbed out their lives because they did not fit in with his long-term plans. He has no respect for his fellow man. Detlef. Ensure that nothing is overlooked; turn his banking group upside down and unearth any shred of evidence that can be linked to Gotthard. Have the external auditors systematically analyse every file recovered from the bunker, specifically for financial improprieties, either at home or in a foreign jurisdiction."

"They are doing so, as we speak, Angela. Peter Lang has put more people on it, owing to the large amount of paperwork."

"Take Reinhold back to Stadelheim and pay that louse another visit, Detlef. I want to know his damn life story; is that understood?" ordered Wenzel as she slammed the drawer of a filing cabinet closed.

The detective had never seen his boss so incensed. The callous acts perpetrated by Gotthard for the sake of his own selfish goals seemed to have had a noticeable effect on her. Perhaps it was the station chief's turn to take some leave, a spell away from all this, he thought. Detlef left her office, quietly closing the door behind him.

CHAPTER TWENTY-SEVEN

Wenzel had briefed the justice minister in Bonn regarding Erich Niemeyer's activities. Because of the intransigence of the Hungarian Government to extradite the man, she had been given the green light to use whatever means necessary to bring both him and his organisation before the courts.

Schmitt was updating the chief on a recent covert operation.

"Hans and Irena have just returned from Hungary where, without too much difficulty, they gained entry to a building owned by Niemeyer."

Irena Svobodová had joined the Pullach team a few months earlier. She was born in Prešov, Slovakia, her Muslim parents fleeing to Berlin in 1972, when she was eight. Irena was an excellent linguist, speaking French, English, Hungarian and her native Slovak.

"Did they find anything of interest?"

"The complex, which is situated on Bajcsy-Zsilinszky Way, has four floors. There are run-of-the-mill shops and boutiques on the ground floor, the property agency is located on the second floor, and the computer consultancy service occupies the third. The building's security system was laughable, according to Hans, but he would say that!"

"And on the fourth level?"

"It appears to be mainly used for storing old mannequins and boxes."

Wenzel pondered for a moment, lost in thought as she tried to visualise the building.

"Once inside the IT office, Irena managed to access and copy the data from the computer hard drives, although there seemed to be an empty docking station for a MacBook laptop. Some days later, a man was observed leaving the building, carrying a computer bag, so the team tailed him to his place of residence. During a search of the office, Hans had retrieved an old utility bill from the wastepaper basket; it matched up with the IT guy's home address. We are currently running his details through Interpol, to see if he has form."

"Has Muller's team made any sense of the retrieved data yet?"

"The consultancy firm is hacking into its customers' mainframes, using remote access software concealed in the business accounting program provided by Niemeyer's agency. This allows the disabling of the company's firewall system. An identical home page is then created, permitting the hacker to pick and choose which of the protected files to download, all from the office in Győr."

"Industrial espionage?"

Schmitt nodded as he turned to another page in the file.

"I had our people check some of the German multinationals that were using Niemeyer's company to clarify if they had suffered intellectual or financial loss."

"And had they?"

"Yes. Two companies, one in Berlin, the other in Hannover, both had the schematics for their products reproduced by a plastics' moulding manufacturer in Russia. The Russian company made near-perfect copies, with the finished goods on display at an industrial fair in Milan, months ahead of the owners' scheduled launch."

Wenzel shook her head on hearing the news.

"Have there been advances made regarding the property fraud?"

"Again, there were no issues accessing the property company's computers. However, one special point of interest was a journal, concealed behind a storage cabinet. Here are some of the photos that Hans took."

"This is intriguing; it appears to be a record of financial transactions in the UK, Holland and, in one case, Denmark."

"According to an addendum in the book, the Danes have no idea that a crime has taken place. It's a mirror image of the property scam in Wolfsburg, Angela. We have installed electronic surveillance equipment to monitor the landlines, mobile phones, computers and the everyday activity within the offices."

"Does this guy really think he is untouchable?"

"Niemeyer is well-respected in Győr. He has brought much employment to the city and is always contributing to worthy causes, including election campaigns."

"Do you know what security measures have been taken, in and around the family home?"

"It would be fair to say it's well rigged to detect the presence of unwanted visitors, although the absence of blueprints currently has us at a disadvantage. In the meantime, we have placed a tracker in the IT guy's car so that we can monitor both his movements and his conversations. The device's battery life is around three weeks, depending on activity. As for his boss, he won't be the easiest to keep tabs on as his minders accompany him everywhere he goes. Local intelligence has indicated that the district police deal harshly with anyone acting in a suspicious manner near Niemeyer's house."

"Are there any other strategies in place?"

"I am currently preparing another covert operation. Muller will be sending Hans and Irena back to Hungary to carry out a break and entry operation at the town hall in Győr, where they will secure the plans of Niemeyer's new family home, just off the Új-sor Road. Travelling on Austrian passports and posing as a couple enjoying a hiking trip, they will pass through the area and hopefully get a closer look at the layout of the building. Satellite images show that the residence is situated in a dense forest, surrounded by a few smallholdings, with many more isolated houses dotted throughout the area."

"When is this operation likely to happen?"

"There are a few loose ends to take care of; perhaps within the next couple of weeks."

"Detlef, once you are in possession of the plans, I want you to come up with a workable stratagem that will allow a full-scale rendition to take place. Draw up a list of the team's requirements: passports, travel documents, money, and any other resources needed, including weaponry. I will then make the arrangements to have everything shipped to our embassy in Hungary."

"What about lodgings?"

"On their arrival, an embassy liaison officer will take our people to a safe house, where the equipment will already be waiting. I will ensure that the accommodation is within a reasonable distance of the target area. Any changes and I'll call you."

"I'll get on to it as soon as the plans arrive."

Schmitt remained in his office until late, reading through case files in preparation for a meeting in Ingolstadt the following morning. Returning to Stadelheim later in the day, he and Reinhold were due to resume questioning Gotthard.

****

In München, the weather had turned colder, with blustery snow showers. To make matters worse, the detectives came up against heavy traffic as they made their way to Stadelheim. When they eventually reached their destination, Schmitt parked the S2 and, once inside the prison, the pair stepped briskly down the corridor.

"Herr Gotthard, Herr Kleber, how are you both?" Schmitt enquired as he and Reinhold entered the interview room.

"Good day, Herr Schmitt, Fräulein Reinhold," replied the prisoner, while his solicitor nodded in acknowledgement of their presence.

Schmitt noticed Gotthard's sallow complexion, and his eyes were bloodshot, as if he had slept badly.

"Herr Kleber, is your client well enough to proceed with the interview?" he asked.

"My client…."

"I am well enough to answer a few questions, Herr Schmitt," interrupted Gotthard cheerily.

Reinhold inserted two new cassettes into the recording device to chronicle the question and answer session that was about to take place.

"Herr Kleber, following our last conversation, your client stated that he murdered Curt Köhler and buried him at the scene of the killing?"

"That is correct, Herr Schmitt," replied Kleber, skimming through his notes.

"Herr Gotthard, please describe how Herr Köhler met his death."

The prisoner gazed blankly at the detectives for a short while before answering.

"Could you be a little more specific, Herr Schmitt?"

"You admit to killing the man?"

"Yes."

"If you did murder Köhler, as you claim to have done, how did you go about it? Was he garrotted or poisoned; did you beat him to death?"

"It wasn't that straightforward, Herr Schmitt."

"Then tell me, in your own words, how you killed him."

"Sodium amobarbital."

"What?" asked Schmitt, confused by the short answer.

"Sodium amobarbital, Detlef," whispered Reinhold. "It was used as a truth serum during the Second World War."

"Let me explain further, Herr Schmitt; I injected Köhler with sodium amobarbital to find out his life's history."

The others in the room stared at the prisoner, unable to comprehend his detached manner regarding the torture of another human being.

"There's no need for alarm, people; far worse things happened during the war. Just look at the gas chambers!"

Gotthard held up his hands in defence of his statement.

"Life seems so expendable to you, Herr Gotthard, a simple commodity."

"Everything in life is a commodity, Herr Schmitt; that's how the world revolves," answered the prisoner coldly. "I interrogated Köhler for around fifteen hours, until I knew enough about the man to see me through after the war."

"Your outrageous account of torturing Herr Köhler has been noted but you still haven't told us how you actually killed him."

"You may call it torture, Detective; I call it survival of the fittest. Köhler was a weak person who would never have made it to the end of the war anyway. His wealthy uncle secured him the job in the driving pool as an act of charity."

"Most people would disagree with your reasoning, Herr Gotthard," argued Schmitt.

"Fine…. have it as you wish, Detective; you're entitled to your opinion. Given his sorry state, I had to drag Köhler from the mobile works office, where I had been questioning him, to the side of the flyover. I forced him onto his knees at the edge of the pit I had already prepared and I dispatched him, using my Walther P38 9 mm semi-automatic pistol."

"Do you still have the weapon?"

"Alas, no; it became a souvenir for some American general. It's a shame really as it was a gift from my former boss, Captain Otto Henschel. The P38 was a great gun; it very rarely jammed!" Gotthard declared smugly.

Schmitt was more than content with the prisoner's testimony, which totally confirmed Dr Limffert's theory of how Köhler had met his death. Considering both the physical and mental anguish the man had been subjected to, and his subsequent murder, the detective felt a sudden urge to reach across the table and throttle Gotthard for such a vile misdeed.

"Herr Kleber, following your client's admissions today, the charge relating to the murder of Curt Köhler stands. Herr Gotthard's statement concurs with the autopsy results we received."

"You found him then?" said Gotthard, exuding an air of satisfaction, pleased that it had been proven he was telling the truth.

"I understand, Herr Schmitt," said Kleber dryly, ignoring his client. "I will, of course, expect the forensic report to be delivered to my office, without delay. Is there anything else you wish to discuss?"

"There is the matter of the Munchener Assistance Bank using the accounts of people killed during allied air raids, but that will keep for now."

Kleber glanced up from his notes.

"I didn't quite catch that, Detective. What did you say?" queried the solicitor.

"It doesn't matter at this point; we can deal with it at our next meeting, Herr Kleber," said Schmitt as he and Reinhold began to pack away their files.

****

At Pullach, following an audit of the documents uncovered in the bunker on Marian Platz, the financial crime team was starting to create a picture of the bank's transactions after the war. There was so much additional data that they had drafted in extra staff to process it all.

"Well, what did you uncover, Peter?" asked Schmitt as he entered the finance office and took a seat.

"My guys revisited the list of names you found at the Hotel Bergensee," said Lang, leafing through a large file. "We compared them with the old records found in the concrete chamber at Marian Platz. As has been confirmed already, the people named all died in or around October 1943."

"I take it there is some relevance to the case?"

"Gotthard's bank had been using their identities to buy and sell shares. Some of the victims have had accounts as recently as 1976, most with sizeable amounts of capital in them."

"That lowlife has been making money off the dead? Do you have addresses for these people?"

"Post office box numbers only. A good majority of them were Jews."

"Who serviced them?"

"We are unsure, at this moment in time. Documents show that, in 1944, the bank was coming very close to collapse; the Jews were being rounded up and sent to the east. The confiscation of their assets placed a heavy financial burden on the institution. The Munchener Assistance Bank had lent heavily to a few, large, Jewish banks in Regensburg and Mannheim, at a time when no one else would supply them with credit. The banks serviced major industries, including rubber, leather and engineering businesses, as well as smaller enterprises such as corner food stores, haberdasheries, jewellers, tailors and publishers. With the Jewish population in concentration camps, there were no longer communities to provide trade for the businesses."

"So, it was a double-edged sword for everyone?" interjected Schmitt.

"Yes; the Munchener Assistance Bank had inadvertently overstretched itself, big time. More worryingly, Karl Wagner, the elderly owner of the bank, had no choice but to foreclose on the defaulting Jewish businesses as Himmler's cronies were waiting in the wings to buy them at fire-sale prices. Many businesses had taken out bridging loans using their company deeds, buildings, land and personal property as collateral. When they defaulted, the bank was left with no option but to foreclose, taking control of their assets and, thus, enlarging its corporate portfolio."

"The bank burdened itself with almost worthless companies, then?" asked Schmitt, beginning to understand where the conversation was leading to.

"Yes and no. Some became profitable, once in Aryan ownership; Himmler had made it very clear to the German people that they were to purchase their goods from Aryan businesses only. However, we did uncover correspondence which indicated that the Munchener Assistance Bank was having an ongoing cash-flow problem, with other banks and businesses demanding that their outstanding accounts be settled in a timelier fashion. This seems to have been rectified by March 1945; no more threatening letters and all accounts appear to have been paid promptly."

"Remind me, Peter, where was Gotthard at this time?" asked Schmitt, his mind a blank due to the copious amounts of information that he was trying to process.

"According to his war records, he was somewhere in the south of Germany, trying to dodge American bullets, I would imagine. By 1952, Gotthard had become manager of the Munchener Assistance Bank. When he was contacted by the Jewish Restitution Organization and informed that they had been authorized to recover any Jewish business portfolios in the American zone of occupation, including those previously seized by the bank, he engaged a solicitor to preside over exploratory talks. Following lengthy negotiations with the organization, the bank purchased the businesses at a reasonable market value."

"Taking into consideration what we now know, and what was found in the bunker, would you agree that Gotthard did rob the Reichsbank, as Schröder claimed?"

"I believe so, Detlef. From the date the gold left Berlin to its arrival at the Eichhörnchen Nest, the fortunes of the bank had never looked so good. In addition, Heidi has confirmed that the Reichsbank gold bar now in our possession was produced in or around 1943-44."

Schmitt paused to take a sip of the coffee Lang had just made before speaking.

"Peter, let's focus on the names of the deceased for a minute. They served no purpose other than to be used as pawns, thereby allowing the bank to prosper?"

"I agree."

"Why did the social security department or the tax office not pick up on the scam? Someone, somewhere must have made an innocent enquiry between 1943 and 1976?"

"I considered that possibility, Detlef. The Americans oversaw civil administration for Bavaria up until 1949. Someone in the American armed forces civil department may have been involved in a cover-up, discreetly losing any queries at that time. Two years later, Helmut Schröder became München's elected mayor and would have had control over the many local Government departments. That was before he became Minister for Foreign Affairs, of course."

"Going on your findings, Peter, we seem to have overwhelming proof that Gotthard is also guilty of tax evasion."

"That's another nail in his coffin, so to speak. The additional charge won't make much of a difference though; he has already lost everything."

"It's quite a catalogue of crimes for which, under normal circumstances, he would have paid heavily in jail time. Some might argue that a higher authority has already decided upon his punishment," said Detlef, getting up. "Anyway, thanks for your help, Peter."

"All in a day's work, Detlef."

It was true that the justice system would show no mercy to the man for the evils he had perpetrated, thought Schmitt. There again, Kleber, with the support of Dr Lömann, could easily submit a plea of guilt through diminished responsibility, which would assist in reducing the sentence. His worst fear was that Lömann could interrupt a session at any point, telling him that Gotthard was medically unfit to be interviewed and that any evidence would not be admissible in court.

On leaving Peter Lang's office, Schmitt decided it was time he went home. Zipping his coat closed to keep out the winter chill, he hurried to his old Quattro coupé and gently eased the car out of the compound, joining the slow line of Friday night commuters. There was a light drizzle of rain as the traffic made its way out of Pullach, in the direction of München and beyond.

CHAPTER TWENTY-EIGHT

Detlef spent a relaxing weekend at home with his family. Wrapping up well, they managed a visit to the English park, enjoying hot chocolate at the Chinese Pagoda, before the rain became more unrelenting and turned to hail. Then, confined to the flat, he made the most of his time with little Erhard.

Monday came around all too soon. With the assistance of a friend in New Scotland Yard that he had met whilst at Police College in Münster, Schmitt had been able to track down a person of interest to an address in Kent, in the south of England. Seated in his office, he began to dial the number he had been given; in placing this call, he was attempting to close one part of the bank investigation. The phone remained silent for a few seconds before the international dialling tone could be heard in his receiver. It rang for some time, which had happened on three previous occasions. Just as he was about to hang up, someone answered.

"Bradbourne House," said the well-spoken female on the other end of the line.

"Good morning, Madam," said Detlef, in his best English. "Is that Mrs Madeleine Chabrier?"

"Yes, that is correct. You have me at a disadvantage, I'm afraid; to whom am I speaking?"

"Please, excuse me. My name is Detective Chief Inspector Schmitt, of the German police."

"German? Has my husband been involved in an accident? He is

attending a medical conference in Dusseldorf this week."

"Forgive me, Mrs Chabrier, my English is not so good. There is nothing to be worried about; this call has no connection with your husband. I am conducting an investigation here, in Germany, and I believe you may be in a position to help me. If you wish, for your own peace of mind, I could provide you with a contact number for a detective in New Scotland Yard who can vouch for me. Would you be willing to answer a few questions?"

There was a short pause on the line as the householder made up her mind as to whether she should proceed with Schmitt's request or just hang up.

"I'll try, Detective, though I can't guarantee I will be able to further your enquiries."

"I was hoping that you would provide me with some information about your grandfather."

"My grandfather? Did I hear you correctly, Detective?"

"I know it seems a little strange but I need to be sure that you are the person I should be speaking with in relation to our enquiry."

"Are there any legal implications? Perhaps I should call my lawyer?"

"There is no need for concern. My questions relate to a very old case which, with your co-operation, may well be resolved today."

"I will take the call in my husband's study, Detective Schmitt. Would you allow me a few minutes?"

"Of course, Mrs Chabrier; I am in no hurry."

Before long, there was a click and the woman was back on the line.

"What information do you require, Detective?" she asked.

"The name of your grandfather and where he was born."

"My grandfather was Dovid Solomon. He was born in Trappes, a small village to the west of Paris."

"Where did Monsieur Solomon reside, circa 1940?"

"Grandpapa had purchased a magnificent sandstone apartment at 2 Rue Beaujon, in Paris, in the late 1920s, I believe. It was a splendid place, Detective; the Arc de Triomphe was a mere two-minute walk away. After one too many glasses of port, he would often reminisce about his life there. He loved to sit out on the balcony in the evening, absorbing the sights and sounds of the city and watching the swifts darting and diving in the summer heat."

"Did your family retain ownership of the dwelling?"

There was a long pause following Schmitt's query.

"Are you there, Mrs Chabrier?" asked Detlef, unsure if the call had been terminated.

"Yes, I am here. You must forgive me. Grandpapa died suddenly, in 1953, and your questions have brought back many memories. He decided to remain in England after the war, and so the property was sold. My grandfather was subjected to much evil before he decided to make his escape with his wife and my parents. He left behind both a city and a nation polluted by German barbarism…. I do apologise, Mr Schmitt, my last comment was not directed at you."

"There is no offence taken, Mrs Chabrier. I have, with the aid of the French Government, managed to piece together some of Monsieur Solomon's life. My counterpart at New Scotland Yard provided me with your contact details."

"Are you able to share your findings with me?"

"I would be delighted to. Your grandfather was, indeed, Dovid

Solomon, a wealthy draper, who supplied fine fabrics to the top design houses. As a Jew, he was forced to flee from the SS in 1941, together with his wife, son and daughter-in-law. They left behind their home, located on the corner of Rue Beaujon, and sailed to Dover. Following the allied invasion and the freeing of Paris, my understanding is that someone later purchased the fire-damaged property from Monsieur Solomon."

"An accurate account, Detective; my parents never shielded me from what had taken place during those dark days. Having been told the fate of Jews in Poland and other eastern states in Europe, Grandpapa was concerned for his family's wellbeing if they remained on their native soil."

While other Jewish Parisians had buried their heads in the sand, Dovid Solomon had had the foresight to get his loved ones out of France altogether, taking money and most of their valuables with them. Then, leaving them in the relative safety of the English countryside, Dovid had returned to Paris to try and sell their home.

He had been making his way from Rue des Rosiers, in the Jewish quarter, to Rue Beaujon, to meet a prospective purchaser; his intention was to remove the last of his belongings while there. En route, he narrowly avoided running into the Gestapo, who were on the lookout for any Jews they had missed in their Vél d'Hiv roundup. A sympathetic gendarme, recognising Dovid, encouraged him to lose himself in the backstreets and return to England at the first available opportunity. Monsieur Solomon later heard that a high-ranking SS captain had taken the apartment for his own personal residence during the occupation.

"Mrs Chabrier, thank you for your patience. I have just one more question I wish to put to you. Was there a piece of furniture which held particular sentimental value for your grandfather?"

"Every piece was special to him, given the amount of time it took to collect them. Grandpapa had worked very hard to build up his business. As you said, Detective, he was a wealthy man; his apartment reflected that."

"I do understand, Mrs Chabrier. Please don't think me insensitive but I need to know if your grandfather could have taken one piece with him, just one item, what would that have been?"

"I suppose it would have been the Jean-Henri Riesener bureau; Grandpapa adored it, with its beautiful woods and fine inlays. Mother and Father used to describe how he would make up his accounts there, dressed in his Japanese silk kimono and sipping from a glass of the finest cognac. I never abandoned hope of finding the writing desk but the French war ministry was unable to trace it. We even looked through the catalogues of the world's major auction houses but, alas, it never came up for sale."

"Would you have a photograph of the bureau, perhaps one taken in the Rue Beaujon apartment before 1941?"

"Probably. Why do you ask, Detective? Would I be right in saying that you contacted me in relation to the Riesener?"

"Having spoken with you, I am now convinced that your grandfather was the original owner of the Jean-Henri Riesener bureau we currently have in storage here, in München."

The line went quiet. Detlef could hear Mrs Chabrier softly weeping, obviously absorbing the fact that her grandfather's writing bureau had been found after so many years. When the lady had composed herself, Schmitt told her the story of where and how the long-lost piece of furniture had been discovered, adding that it had been in Herman Göring's home at Döllnsee-Schorfheide for a period, during the war.

"Mrs Chabrier, there will be some forms to fill in before I can release the bureau to you."

"I understand, Detective. Might I ask what condition it is in?"

"Being a lover of antiques, I am pleased to say that it is in excellent order; time has been kind to it. You will have to present the photographic proof of ownership we discussed, along with personal identification, before the bureau can be returned."

"Detective Schmitt, I really can't thank you enough for the painstaking work you must have carried out to reunite me with the Riesener. It will mean so much to have it back."

"Believe me, my own life will be somewhat quieter now that I have found its true owner. My boss has given me grief ever since I confiscated the piece. I don't think the hotel owners will be too pleased though."

"I do feel a little sorry for them."

"That's a natural response, but the hotel group will simply have to accept this morning's outcome. Well, it's been a pleasure to speak with you, Mrs Chabrier. I will contact you again to finalise the paperwork; when completed, the bureau will be released into your custody," said Schmitt as he bid farewell to the lady.

"Once again, Detective Schmitt, thank you for all you have done. I look forward to hearing from you soon. Good day."

Elated, Schmitt sank back in his chair; the Riesener enquiry was now finally closed. He felt genuine joy for the family in England, tempered with a trace of sadness for the owners of the hotel at

Schorfheide. After all, their cellar had provided a safe refuge for the bureau during the Cold War. Detlef knew he would not be the hotel's favourite guest, should he ever return there, but the rightful owners would soon have the bureau back in their possession. That was all that mattered.

****

Some days later, Schmitt sat – once again – facing Gotthard in the interview suite at Stadelheim Prison. The now-familiar scene was completed by the presence of Reinhold and Kleber. The detective was weary; he had been planning a covert operation in Hungary, to get Niemeyer back onto German soil. The Hungarian justice department was being intransient, refusing a request to have the Niemeyers extradited.

The extradition warrant alleged that Erich Niemeyer had been involved in the murder of Tomas Kampfle. He was also implicated in the murder of Judge Janzyke's housemaid and in the attempted murder of the judge and his family, following the explosion at their home in Nymphenburg. Frau Niemeyer was charged with mortgage fraud and money laundering in Germany. Both were also indicted for living off the proceeds of crime.

Schmitt spoke with Dr Lömann before entering the interview room.

"How is the patient today?" he enquired.

"His condition remains stable for the moment but, as I said earlier, I would urge you to conclude your investigation as soon as possible," advised Lömann.

"One thing has confounded me since my last visit, Doctor; can you tell me why Herr Gotthard has suddenly become so compliant?"

Taking a Swiss army knife from his pocket, Dr Lömann extracted a pointed tool and began to clean his pipe, as he considered the question for a moment before replying.

"The prisoner is experiencing something quite unfamiliar to him; vulnerability, and an emptiness in his life. The fact that Frau Köhler-Gotthard has started divorce proceedings has had a huge impact on the man; he no longer has any power over her, as he did during their marriage. You have denied Herr Gotthard his freedom but, to some degree, he is still calling the shots, exercising his last vestige of control over your investigation. The interviews allow him to relive his exploits and achievements, if one can describe them as that. To all intents and purposes, Herr Schmitt, you are, yourself, a prisoner until the case is concluded."

"I can't fault your analysis, Herr Lömann; I suppose we are all prisoners, in one way or another. Are you still happy for us to continue questioning him?"

"Yes, you are free to proceed; he is mentally stable and lucid, if that is what you wish to know. Herr Gotthard will tire easily though, so don't be surprised if he begins to doze off."

****

Having settled themselves in the interview suite, Schmitt laid out the documents from Schorfheide on the table. Gotthard looked at them for a few minutes before picking them up.

"So, you found the bureau, Herr Schmitt?"

"Yes, we did, Frank."

"You really don't like to be defeated, do you, Detective?"

"I'll take that as a compliment then?"

"Credit where credit's due; I had an inkling you were on to me but I couldn't be sure. I was convinced the Russians had confiscated the bureau or that it had been destroyed by artillery fire during the Red Army's advance. Where did you find it?"

"Where you last saw it, perhaps, Herr Gotthard."

"At Göring's hunting lodge? Wasn't there a new hotel built on the site a few years ago?"

Detlef sat quietly for a few seconds, taking on board what the prisoner had just said.

"That is correct, but the hunting lodge was preserved. Someone had decided to hide the bureau by bricking it up in the cellar as the Russians were advancing. After that, it was forgotten about until builders uncovered it during the renovation work."

"How did you come across the compartment housing the documents, Detective?"

"My partner has a degree in fine arts and antiquities and I share the same interests. She once demonstrated on a similar bureau where the compartment was to be found."

Gotthard shook his head in submission; everything was beginning to fall into place. He now understood why Schmitt and Janzyke had called at his residence all those months ago, their line of questioning focusing on his personal background as well as his meteoric rise within the bank. Eugen's money laundering debacle had merely been a sideshow; Schmitt and his team would have been calling with him one way or the other.

"I suppose we should get started, Herr Schmitt."

"I agree; time is not on our side, Herr Gotthard."

"That is true, Detective. Time is no longer my friend so I am willing to assist you with your enquiries. I can assure you that there will be no interruption from Herr Kleber, who is receiving an attractive fee just for babysitting me," explained Gotthard as his solicitor absent-mindedly looked up from making some notes. Whilst discourteous, the remark his client had made was true; he would be paid a large retainer simply for being there.

"The prison psychiatrist has informed me that your illness is terminal, Herr Gotthard, but you do understand that I must prosecute this case until its logical conclusion?"

"I understand, Detective; let us dispense with the sympathy and get this over with."

Whilst Schmitt and Reinhold both felt a tinge of sorrow for the man, they had a job to do. The prisoner's health issues held no sway with Judge Janzyke, who had conferred with two of his colleagues regarding Gotthard's physical condition. However, due to the catalogue of offences perpetrated, they had decided to show no leniency and to continue with the prosecution of the seventy-two-year-old. The investigation was to carry on until there was enough evidence for all the cases to be brought to court.

"Let's start with these names of deceased people, Herr Gotthard. Most of them are German-Jewish citizens. Have you anything to say regarding them?"

Gotthard surveyed the list, running his finger down the page before stopping at a random name.

"They were just customers."

"We are aware that they were customers of your bank; can you expand on your explanation?"

Gotthard shrugged his shoulders and sat back in his chair.

"You must have known that they had all been killed in October

1943 and yet their accounts remained open," argued Schmitt as the prisoner remained expressionless, in continued silence.

There was an awkward moment before the questioning resumed.

"Herr Gotthard your bank has been using the identities of these dead people to trade in stocks and commodities. Was it a: a tax scam, b: a money laundering exercise, or c: both?"

"I haven't seen the documents you are describing for quite some time."

Some of the victims' bank accounts remained open, right up to 1976, the capital being used to buy shares in foreign companies. Those investments have since provided a handsome return."

The hint of a smile appeared on Gotthard's face. Clearing his throat, he replied.

"Forgive me; I am not myself, Detective Schmitt. I have agreed to co-operate with your investigation and I will honour that arrangement. Yes, I did use the identities of those killed in the allied carpet bombing of München in October 1943. You make it all sound so simple but you're a mere civil servant, unable to understand the finer points of commerce. Helmut Schröder's father-in-law had done his utmost to hold the business together but he paid the ultimate price, suffering a fatal heart attack in the process. The bank was within a year of collapse."

"So, you decided to provide a helping hand?"

"If you say so."

"That's exactly what I'm saying."

"Hitler was shipping the Jews east, which left the Münchener Assistance Bank holding Jewish lending institutions and businesses as securities for the debts they had accrued. Eventually, there would have been no one left to service those liabilities, thanks to Himmler and Heydrich's final solution of mass extermination."

"So, the bank had little to no money, Herr Gotthard. What was using the identities of dead people going to achieve?"

"Have you not figured that out for yourself, Herr Schmitt?"

"Figured out what?"

"Those people enabled the bank to function. They had removed their money and assets from the bank before their deaths, as some of them made plans to flee Germany. I quietly replaced the original balances."

"What with? The ledgers indicate that the bank had no available funds to carry out such an undertaking," Schmitt contended.

Whilst wishing to show some compassion because of the prisoner's current physical condition, his patience was wearing thin. Schmitt was in no mood to play games.

"Detective…. Detective…. Detective….!" sighed Gotthard, a little exasperated that no one seemed to have grasped what he assumed to be obvious. "Either you are not as clever as I thought or you are teasing me!" He held up the evidence bag containing the Reichsbahn transport order. "This slip of paper brought the bank back from oblivion. I was responsible for the movement of one tonne of mixed gold coins and bullion, thirty million Reichsmarks and additional foreign currencies. The order was destined for the Kali und Steinsalz mine near the town of Merkers for onward shipment to Portugal. It was discreetly redirected to the Eichhörnchen Nest and used as required."

Reinhold turned sharply towards Schmitt. Had they heard him correctly? Was Gotthard really admitting to the theft?

"Are you saying that you stole all this from under the noses of your superiors?" asked Reinhold, trying to comprehend the statement.

The documents found in Riesener's bureau had led to more questions than answers. Now there was a glimmer of hope that Gotthard would fill in the blanks, telling them the whole story of how he pulled off the heist. Everything began to make sense; the hidden bunker adjacent to the bank's vault was within walking distance to München's main railway station. The Münchener Assistance Bank's insolvency issues during the turbulent days of World War Two had been smoothed over by the large cash injection it received. Gotthard quietly looked at those seated around the desk, as the smile grew wider on his cracked and receding lips. He would never know how tirelessly the team from Pullach had worked in bringing the evidence together, much less make sense of it.

CHAPTER TWENTY-NINE

Schmitt had waited for over a week to get an appointment at his local health centre. He wanted his doctor to examine a mole that had appeared on his arm; it seemed innocuous but, nevertheless, it was worrying him. The surgery was full that morning, mostly mothers with their newborn babies and the odd pensioner hobbling in. As he sat there, his thoughts turned to the robbery of the Reichsbank. He earnestly hoped that Frank Gotthard was now prepared to give the definitive truth about his involvement in the crime. His co-operation would enable Detlef to go to Wenzel with enough evidence to bring down one of the biggest financial institutions in Germany.

Following the disclosure of the man's double life, the main business magazines were already speculating on what lay ahead for the banking group. The existence of the bunker on Marian Platz had - somehow - been leaked to the press, even though both the manager and the vault security guard at the Münchener Assistance Bank had signed an oath under the Official Secrets Act. Janzyke ordered local detectives to raid the offices of papers who had printed articles, their editors-in-chief having to appear before a magistrate to explain their actions. Bundes Chancellor Herzfeld did not want to open any old wounds; the scandal could ignite all sorts of new claims from the families of holocaust victims.

Later that day, Wenzel and Schmitt met with Judge Janzyke in his chambers.

"Paweł, have you any news?" asked Wenzel.

Janzyke took a quick sip of his coffee before replying.

"As you both aware, the exposure of Herr Gotthard's highly successful and, some might say, ingenious scheme to misappropriate gold and mixed legal tenders has caused great embarrassment to the authorities. I have been trying to put together a workable plan that would benefit the state but not attract any unwanted attention. I've had a chance to run it past both the new finance minister and the justice minister."

"What were their views on the subject?" enquired Schmitt.

"They were somewhat taken aback by the magnitude of the offence, but agreed that if the allegation has substance then, rather than making this known to the public and creating a hornets' nest, we should keep a lid on it. If other countries get wind of this, they may seek to claim ownership of properties or demand financial restitution. That being the case, I have decided to handpick a team of financial experts from my department to carry out a feasibility study of Gotthard's companies, as soon as possible. Their brief is to forensically examine the group both in Europe and, in particular, overseas. They will search for offshore shell companies, examine the share make up of any investments made in other commercial or non-fiscal businesses, in short, identify its net worth. On completion, the inspectors will provide me with various action plans, including its possible dismantling."

"Do you think it will come to that?" queried Wenzel. "It's a very successfully run concern."

"Angela, put yourself in the ordinary German businessman's shoes. This gangster set out to rob the Reichsbank and, to all intents and purposes, he got away with it. He put his opposition at a clear disadvantage by throwing the Münchener Assistance Bank a much-needed lifeline."

Janzyke rose and began to pace the floor.

"Go on, Paweł; sorry for the interruption," said Wenzel, suitably chided.

"That's okay; I'm just trying to do the right thing for everyone concerned. Whatever decision I make should not have any negative financial implications for the country. After all, it was state capital that enabled Gotthard to create his financial empire."

"Does this mean that there is a high probability of the business being put out onto the open market?" quizzed Schmitt.

"It's a definite option, although what I will say is that, if dismantled, the individual portfolios must remain in German ownership."

"If the group is to be broken up, it should be done within a workable timeframe," suggested Wenzel.

"I believe that would be the best way forward. I have appointed one of my junior judges to oversee the investigation; she will report to me and another High Court judge. Given my involvement in the case to date, I wish to put myself at arm's length regarding this sensitive issue, thus refuting any suggestion from either the press or Government ministers of bias, on my part, in the final determination of the group's future."

"Some of the documents found in the Marian Platz bunker point to the fact that the late Tomas Kampfle, our former finance minister, provided much support to the Münchener Assistance Bank. The evidence indicates that he made available to the bank confidential Government documents which were used to secure lucrative contracts, including the civil service salary administration," explained Schmitt.

The judge took off his horn-rimmed glasses and cleaned them with a silk handkerchief. When he was satisfied with the result, he placed the handkerchief back in the breast pocket of his jacket.

"Detlef, let it go," he said, returning to his chair and sitting down. "If we went after Gotthard's every indiscretion you would have time for nothing else. Let's analyse the facts for a moment. He seems to be co-operating with us; am I correct?"

"Yes," answered Schmitt.

"The man has lost everything, his family, his business, his freedom. Now he is terminally ill and it is highly likely that he will die in Stadelheim."

"I take your point, Judge."

"What about Frau Giselbert?" asked Wenzel.

"His ex-wife will be allowed to keep her personal net worth, plus a little interest, for assisting us with our inquiries. This will be in addition to some personal items, including her late father's summer home," declared Janzyke before drawing the meeting to a close.

****

Snow was beginning to fall as Schmitt drove through München's heavy commuter traffic that morning. Both he and Reinhold were in a sombre mood, the only sound coming from the police radio as it chattered endlessly in the background. Gotthard's health was deteriorating and there was always the worry that he would not be medically fit to bring closure to their investigation.

On their arrival at Stadelheim, the pair were relieved to find the prisoner already waiting for them, with Kleber by his side. However, he appeared frail and emaciated. A saline drip stood on a wheeled stand beside him, its tube inserted into his left arm.

"Good morning, gentlemen," said Schmitt. "How are you feeling today, Herr Gotthard?"

"The cancer drugs are, pardon the pun, killing me, Herr Schmitt. They are a drain on my body but, enough about me, your interest lies with the theft I committed."

"Believe it or not, I do have some compassion towards your plight, Frank," replied Detlef, trying to bring a little humanity to the meeting.

"Detective, I'm dying; I don't have time for sentimentalities. Let's just get on with this," he whispered softly.

Reinhold opened one of the folders they had brought with them and presented the documents found in the hotel whilst Schmitt took a back seat.

"Herr Gotthard, do you recognise the papers I have placed before you?" she asked as she began the cross-examination.

He slowly leafed through the assorted, clear plastic evidence bags before answering.

"Yes; they are part of a series of documents used to plan a robbery of the German Reichsbank, which took place in 1945," he replied.

"Are you admitting to larceny, Herr Gotthard?"

"Let's get something clear from the start, Fräulein. What I say here today should be taken as my affidavit; I am too weak to repeat myself. Is that understood?"

Those in the room nodded in agreement, aware that a confession was about to be made.

"I admit it; in January 1945, I stole from the German Reichsbank in Berlin," he said, gradually raising himself up from the chair without being requested to do so.

Schmitt stood up.

"Frank Christoph Gotthard, you are hereby charged with the theft of state gold, money and foreign exchange reserves, the said crime having taken place at the German Reichsbank, in or around January 1945. You do not have to say anything; however, it may harm your defence if you do not mention, when questioned, something which you later rely on in court. Anything you do say may be given in evidence. How do you wish to plead?"

"Guilty, as charged, Herr Schmitt."

With Kleber's assistance, he was once again seated and Reinhold continued the questioning.

"What motivated you to rob the bank? Were your brothers a party to the crime?"

"Fräulein, I won't remind you again. I am fair game; you have apprehended me and that's fine. But don't try to implicate any of my family in this matter. Is that clear?"

"Crystal clear," answered Reinhold. "I will rephrase the question. Why did you decide to carry out such an audacious raid?"

"Were you taught much German history at school, Fräulein Reinhold?"

"Enough to comprehend what Germany and, indeed, other countries suffered through two world wars."

"Then your teachers will have explained that, in 1942, the Ivans were no longer prepared to bend over, with their trousers around their ankles. They began a sustained counterattack against the Wehrmacht and SS units. The peasant boy, Marshal Georgy Zhukov was put in charge of the Eastern Front and began kicking German ass, pushing them all the way back to the river Oder and on to Berlin."

"What has that got to do with lining your own pockets?" queried Reinhold.

"Show a little patience, Fräulein…. Whilst the Russians began inflicting great losses on German forces, Rommel was also getting a bloody nose in North Africa from Montgomery's Desert Rats. Then, in September 1943, the Americans landed on the beaches of Italy. Hitler's plans of world domination had taken a serious knock."

"So, you decided that it was an opportune time to help yourself?" prompted Reinhold.

"Precisely. It was a perfect storm, with Germany sandwiched in the middle of the invading forces. Having listened to Schröder's worrying dilemma of his father-in-law's bank nearing financial meltdown…."

He stopped, catching his breath for a short time before continuing.

"We received a directive from Himmler; all of the nation's paper cash reserves were to be sent to the Reichsbank branch in Erfurt, without delay. Gold reserves were to be transferred to a potassium mine near the village of Merkers; the Reichsbank intended to use the mining complex as their main vault. Unfortunately, the Americans got there first and confiscated the gold and valuable artworks that had been placed in storage there."

"Where did you come into it all?"

"I was initially in charge of the recovery of assets from those filthy Jews."

"What have you got against the Jewish people?"

"They are Jews; they're subhuman. That's enough!"

"How did you go about your duties?"

"I would identify Jewish assets in Europe and beyond and confiscate them. I was also involved in ensuring Jewish account holders did not remove their funds beyond the reach of our administration."

"What happened if they did manage to have them spirited out of the country?"

"I'd do whatever was required to have them reinstated. I was merely following orders."

"Did that include murder?"

Gotthard shrugged his shoulders, his facial expression giving nothing away.

"Okay; we'll revisit that subject later. Do you need a break, Herr Gotthard?"

"No."

"I have an obligation to ensure that you are well enough to be interviewed."

"I'm comfortable. Please, let us continue."

"How did you go about removing the consignment? It would have required a lot of manpower."

"During the last few months of hostilities, the Government was in turmoil. Generals were waiting to see who would blink first and desert their post. It was getting to the stage of every man for himself. I could not be certain that I would even survive to the end of the war so I seized the opportunity to execute the last stage of my plan. I changed the transport order from rail to road; at least it had better odds of reaching its final destination. Hired help was organised in

München."

"You were very sure of yourself," remarked the detective.

"I don't believe I was, Fräulein. If I managed to get out alive, I knew I'd do time in a prisoner of war camp somewhere in Europe; that was a given."

"Who assisted you upon your release?"

Gotthard stared hard at the two detectives. Had they not worked it out yet or were they simply messing him about?

"You really don't know who it was?"

"To whom are you referring? We assumed that it may have been one of your brothers."

"Helmut Schröder, of course!"

"Schröder? So, apart from being your one-time camp commandant, he was also party to the whole operation?"

"Yes, although he was later transferred to the military records office in Stuttgart to be closer to his wife who, by that time, controlled the Munchener Assistance Bank."

"Then there is a possibility that he could have doctored the service records of his Wehrmacht colleagues, yourself included?" suggested Reinhold.

"The man was up to his neck in shady dealings, Detective. He most certainly did redact the military records of several prominent servicemen, in readiness of their capture by the allies. Such notations would have afforded them a more lenient sentence as long as no witnesses to their atrocities came forward."

"Undoubtedly, he put a lot of effort into concealing your past."

"No comment."

"Honour among thieves has held firm until now, but Helmut has finally turned you in," said Reinhold, with some satisfaction.

"Schröder is dead, Fräulein. Who's doing this to me, and why? I have to know."

"Where our information comes from need not concern you," interrupted Schmitt.

"Herr Gotthard, what brought you to Germany in the first place?" asked Reinhold, steering the conversation back again.

"My father."

"Really? That does intrigue me; why send you here?"

"He was a nationalist. Germany for the German people, he used to say."

"Was he a racist?"

"In today's world, I suppose some would call him that. Every evening, he would listen to German broadcasts on an old, long-wave radio in our parlour; the content of the transmissions would undoubtedly fire him up. The speeches made by Hitler, whom my father admired so much, instilled a sense of nationalistic pride in us all. One could argue that we were indoctrinated at an early age."

"Why do you say that?"

"What we heard at home and, consequently, what we believed in, didn't go down well at school. During break times, my brothers and I would often have taken a good beating from the other children after disagreements regarding the fatherland. We always gave the same in return though!" he guffawed.

"That doesn't quite explain why you - and possibly your brothers - came to Germany," argued Reinhold.

The prisoner's breathing became shallower as he showed signs of exhaustion. Claudia knew that they would soon have to end the interview.

"The Versailles Treaty, as created by the Jews, had imposed a heavy, financial burden on the state. I came home to the fatherland to help purify the country, to get rid of the leeches, those parasites that were hell-bent on bleeding Germany dry."

"Do you still hold that view?" asked Schmitt, in disbelief at what he had just heard.

"Where there's money, there'll be a grubby little Jew rubbing his hands together," he retorted.

"I'm sorry to disappoint you, Frank, but it was the world leaders and not the Jewish race who decided that Germany should pay for the carnage it had inflicted, in much the same way as they did following the actions of your cohorts during the Second World War."

"I don't wish to argue with you, Herr Schmitt. That was my reason for coming here and it was with my family's blessing," he replied, the tears beginning to form. "I sacrificed everything I held dear, and for what? I never saw my mother, father or sister again."

Claudia reached over and handed him a tissue.

"Please, do go on, Herr Gotthard. Perhaps you could tell me about your brothers; did you see them again?" asked Reinhold.

"You're not that slick, Fräulein! My brothers, as I have said, are off limits. I took a tramp steamer from New York to Bremen through the Norddeutsche Lloyd Steamship Company. The sailing lasted ten days, during which time we were subjected to the full force of the Atlantic Ocean. The swells were monstrous!"

"Let's assume," said Schmitt, "that you did come alone. Who met you when you reached Germany? There would have been security checks and other procedures to go through to ensure you weren't a spy. An American citizen couldn't become a member of the Wehrmacht so quickly or, for that matter, hold a position in the Reichsbank. You must have had assistance from someone."

"Herr Kleber, I am tired; I wish to return to my cell," said Gotthard as he slowly rose from his seat.

"Herr Schmitt, you heard my client's request. Now would be an appropriate time to terminate the interview," said Kleber.

Schmitt glanced over at Reinhold. They were so close to finding out how a boy from the backwoods town of Boalsburg, Pennsylvania, had risen to the rank of captain in the Reichsbank.

"I agree, Herr Kleber; the session has been long enough. We'll resume next week when your client has had time to rest," said Schmitt, closing the file. "Just one more question, Frank; what became of your brothers?"

"No comment."

"Indulge me. If they were not involved in your wrongdoing, then they have nothing to fear."

Gotthard looked intently at Schmitt for a few seconds.

"The past is best left undisturbed, Detective."

Assisted by a warder, the old man turned his back on Schmitt and shuffled down the corridor to the prison hospital where, nowadays, he was a permanent resident.

"Come on, Claudia; we're out of here," said Schmitt, gathering up his papers.

While the pair walked to the car, his thoughts went to Kampfle and his family. The minister had paid a high price for getting involved with people like Niemeyer, over whom he had no control. The ex-Stasi sergeant's organisation had demonstrated their ability to erase a man's life as if he had never existed.

Drumming his fingers on the steering wheel as they waited in traffic, Detlef remembered a dream he had had some weeks previously. He found himself trapped in a glass box, looking out as the Gotthards stood in front of the Brandenburg Tor, just as in the Eichhörnchen Nest photograph. This time, however, they were laughing and taunting him. He gathered all his strength before running headlong, shattering one of the panes into a thousand pieces. Once outside the box, he made a grab for the men but, on opening his hand, he found only the ashes of the old black and white picture.

Schmitt's head told him that Frank Gotthard's brothers must surely have died in combat and were now lying in some distant war grave, all but forgotten. His heart told him otherwise. More than ever, he was determined to track them down and bring to light the part they had played in the 1945 Reichsbank robbery but, for now, he just wanted to go home.

****

About the Author

Terry Hickland was born and raised in Northern Ireland, and is married, with one son. During the 1980s, he moved to Germany where he immersed himself in the language and culture of the German people. He lived in Braunschweig, Lower Saxony, for a time, finally settling in Wolfsburg.

Returning home, Terry established several successful commercial ventures before joining the education sector. Having graduated from the University of Ulster, he is currently a lecturer at a local college. In his spare time - when he is not writing fiction or screenplays - Terry can be found attending literary and classical music events.

On Marian Place is the first in a trilogy of novels following the progress of Detective Chief Inspector Detlef Schmitt, whose passion for antiques leaves in its wake a trail of murder, robbery and deception that the German Government wants erased at any cost.

As a poet, Terry has also had some of his work published in *The Seasons: A Collection of Poetry and Prose on Spring, Summer, Autumn and Winter*.